Synchronicity Bleue
Le journal d'un Amériquébécois.

Un roman
au sujet
la synchronicité,
l'Âge de Gaia,
et l'avènement de la Nouvelle Terre
dans Nouveau-Québec.

A novel about synchronicity, the Age of Gaia, and the beginning of
the New Earth in New Quebec.

John-Jean

Parlez Bleu New York/Québec

Dedicated to people who speak French, and English-speaking people who Parlez Bleu, ou speak from the heart.
Dédié aux Québécoises et Québécois, et Staffordians wherever they may live.

....

Merci, Francois

...and Dermie, bien sûr.

Chère lectrice, cher lecteur...

Voici une collection d'extraits de mon journal. J'invite anglophones et francophones, également, à lire le journal. L'histoire commence sur la page que vous choisissez.

Dear readers...

What is contained here are excerpts from my diary, which you are invited to read. If you read English, I encourage you to begin at the beginning.

Mario-Jacques
Stafford QC, le 2 décembre 2015.

Les Extraits

Le Prologue, Synchronicity On Rue Principal
Fall 2007

Je suis certain it was no coincidence that I was walking on that part of the highway of synchronicity that runs through Rue Principal in Stafford, Quebec, when I first saw the art work of Gaston Briere.

J'adore everything that is Stafford (my adopted home) so I somehow knew that I would like the art I would find on my first visit to an exposition on Rue Principal, in the fall of 2006. I should tell you, aussi, that I enjoy art de beaucoup de genres, but I especially enjoy art that juxtaposes genres, or juxtaposes the simple and le complexe. J'adore art that looks like la musique du jazz fusion.

La musique du jazz fusion was being played live on Rue Principal, when I arrived at The First Annual Stafford Art Fair, ou L'Expo de Montagne. The skies were playing a fusion also, with a mix of storm clouds that I was not appreciating as much as la musique.

As I strolled the sidewalk, my emotions were stirred again et encore. Les peintures lined up on Rue Principal were très bonnes. Mais, my eyes were constantly being distracted from the canvasses to the skies, as raindrops kept tapping me on the shoulders.

After an hour or so of strolling through the art tents, I was starting to feel rushed, as the intruding rain was touching me more, and starting to show itself. I decided I would look at the work of one more artist on Rue Principal. There was only one more artist whose work I had not yet seen, and his work was set up toward the end of Rue Principal, near the IGA.

At this time, as I was nearing the end of my walk, I began to daydream about what it would look like if a painter used the style of certain comic book illustrators to create serious works of art on canvas. What provoked this daydream? Je ne sais pas. Mais, it is important to mention that my curiousity about what it would look like for an artist to paint seriously with the style of an animator was a curiousity that I had had for years. On this day, I was not visualizing anything like the illustrations one sees in superhero comic books, but something more Disneyesque. I remember that I could not visualize this so clearly in my mind's eye. Je ne suis pas un artiste.

I also remember that my mind flashed to images of work by Frank Frazetta, le Michaelangelo des comic book illustrators. What I was trying to visualize was a Frank Frazetta with far less realism. But I couldn't fill in what, "far less realism," would look like. Encore, je ne suis pas un artiste. I don't recall more than that now, but I remember that I was struggling to put an image in my mind, and I couldn't do it...Et voilà! There was the image that my mind couldn't see, but my eyes could... Wow(!), as the old Americain-Quebecer saying goes: Keep thinking about what your face looked like before you were born, and someday you will see it. I saw, for the first time, the paintings of Gaston Briere. Encore: Wow! C'est ne pas un mot de Victor Hugo, mais c'est le mot which would have come out of my mouth if I did not restrain myself from shouting out loud.

Je vois la peinture of a man and a woman standing before an automobile vers 1955. La peinture reminded me of several photos of my parents, taken in the early days of their marriage, standing in front of my father's vintage car, vers 1955. La peinture, which I later found out was titled *Vers 1955,* also reminded me of *American Gothic*, by Grant Wood. *Vers 1955* et *American Gothic* are both iconic images of times past.

Je vois d'autres peintures par Gaston Briere that reminded me, for some reason, of Frank Frazetta. But it was not apparent to me why I was reminded of Frank Frazetta, because les peintures de Gaston Briere are painted with far less realism than Frazetta's work. Monsieur Briere's work might be poorly described as being like frozen frames from an animated cartoon...if the cartoon was drawn by someone fusing the work of Picasso, Rivera, Modigliani, Lichtenstein, Disney and Frazetta. Using vibrant colors.

As I was looking at Monsieur Briere's work for the first time, I became aware of the presence of a man at my side. It was Gaston Briere, casually studying me, as I was studying his art.

Gaston Briere appeared to me as un jeune 40-ish beau man. He looked like he lifted weights and rode a bike. Mais oui, I later found out that he *does* lift weights and he *does* ride a bike. He also presented his intelligence in a friendly way. This was easily seen dans ses peintures et sa persona.

After exchanging glances and smiles, we introduced ourselves to each other. One of the first things I said to Gaston was that his work somehow reminded me of Frank Frazetta. Gaston arched his eyebrow, then told me that Frank Frazetta was a hero he grew up with, a model of what Gaston once wanted to become: an illustrator of fantastic adventure comic books.

After Gaston told me that, I arched my brow, and said nothing but: "Hmmm."

I tried to figure out just what it was about les peintures that reminded me of Frank Frazetta. The stylistic differences between Frank Frazetta and Gaston Briere are considerable. Gaston projected something from his subconscious that was received by my subconscious, non? That much I believed, the first time I saw les peintures de Gaston Briere.

After we chatted about Frazetta for a while, I turned my attention back to la peinture that first caught my eye: *Vers 1955.* I asked Gaston if there was something that inspired him to do this painting. He told me that he worked from a photo of his mother and father to do la peinture. I responded with a raised eyebrow, and then I told Gaston that I thought of photos of my parents, with my first glance at la peinture. Gaston and I then spent a good fifteen minutes talking about synchronicity, although I don't think either one of us used that word in our conversation. Aussi, I bought *Vers 1955.*

Of all les peintures on display, *Vers 1955* was the first one that Gaston had painted, when he began to get serious about developing his distinctive art on canvas. Bien sur it would be the first one for him to sell to someone. Synchronicity, non?

Though I paid for la peinture, I felt as if Gaston was giving me a gift. I wanted to give Gaston a gift, in return. I thought about giving him a Frank Frazetta calendar, a 1972 Frank Frazetta calendar that I had stored away. I had been waiting for the right time to come, to pass it on to the right person. Gaston Briere had to be the right person for the Frazetta calendar, non? Mais, I learned from his partner, Sandi Schulman, that Gaston was not a collector of things, of any sort. Anyway, c'est bon, mais a few weeks later, after I dug up the calendar in New York, I brought it to Stafford and gave it to Gaston, as a little gift.

Sandi and I both raised our eyebrows when Gaston looked at the Frazetta calendar and told us that there was only one thing that he had a collection of…and that was Frank Frazetta calendars! Gaston also told us that the particular calendar I gave him, the 1972 calendar, was the first in a series, and the missing piece to his collection. Je suis certain that there is a high-brow, raised eyebrow, universal truth punch line that would be fitting here. Mais, I feel compelled to only comment now, as I did then, when Gaston told me how the calendar fit into his collection: *Hmmm.*

Plus Prologue
Fall 2007

Bien sur, there is more. There is always more in Stafford. What I haven't told you yet is what happened when I *began* my walk at the art show on Rue Principal – the first time I met Gaston Briere – that became part of a larger synchronistic experience.

The very first tent that I had visited at the art show contained handmade jewelry, and poetry books, created and written by a Pointe Claire woman named Marie Rozier. As soon as I layed my eyes on Marie for the first time, it struck me that she looked like the iconic rock star Janis Joplin. Right down to the way she was dressed, straight out of *le revolution tranquille kosmic bleus seventies.*

My first words to Marie were: "*Janis Joplin!*"

She laughed and said, "Mais oui! The people, they tell me this."

I took an instant liking to Marie, and her jewelry – which was mostly wooden beads et petite polished stones, attached on leather necklaces and bracelets. Though Marie spoke Anglais only haltingly, and my Francais did not go a heck of a lot more beyond, "bonjour," and, "au revoir," at the time, we were able to communicate assez bien. I found Marie to be sweet and eclectic. Marie told me in broken Anglais that she was the host of a daily programme on a small radio station. The show was devoted to her passions: jewelry-making, poetry, music, meditation, and the art of Canadian native people. It struck me that this was an odd combination of subjects for a daily program, but I said nothing about that.

I bought two bracelets and a small paperback book of poetry that Marie had written. Marie took my e-mail address to add to her mailing list.

In the year that passed after that day, Marie sent me an e-mail maybe once every three months. These were e-mails that announced art shows, jewelry shows, and poetry readings, and they all seemed to be things related to the Abenaki tribe. (I am fairly certain that Marie has an Abenaki heritage.) The three or four e-mails that Marie sent to me, over the course of a year, were written in Francais, and although my reading of Francais was improving, I was never able to understand much of what was written in Marie's e-mails.

This brings me, or almost brings me, to the point of telling you all of this about Marie – which is really to tell you about continued *synchronicity* avec Gaston Briere. Over the course of the year after Gaston and I, and Gaston's girlfriend/partner Sandi first met, we became friends. We began hanging with each other a bit when we were in Stafford at the same time, and when my trips up from New York coincided with Gaston and Sandi's trips to Stafford from Montreal. August 20th, which was around eleven months after the day I first met Marie, et Gaston and Sandi, was Gaston's birthday.

While I was in East End Bay, in New York, I had written a reminder note to myself to wish Gaston a happy birthday, via e-mail. I put the note, which I had written on an index card, next to my computer keyboard, but then I lost it. I probably threw it out while I was clearing a pile of notes that I tend to collect on my desk.

When the 20th of August arrived, I did not remember that it was Gaston's birthday. But my mind was on Gaston, related to thoughts on the subject of synchronicity, meaningful coincidences. I was on the Internet, reading about Carl Jung's theories on the subject of synchronicity, and how Jung was ridiculed by many psychologists for expounding such unscientific views. The thought that I was fabricating synchronicities, out of my imagination, came to mind. I decided to send an e-mail to Gaston, to ask for his thoughts about synchronicity.

When I went on to AOL Mail to write to Gaston, I saw that I had received an e-mail from Marie Rozier. Again, this was on Gaston's birthday (again, which I had forgotten) and it was the first e-mail that I had received from Marie Rozier in at least two or three months. I opened the e-mail and scanned it. Everything was written in Francais. I scanned the e-mail up and down, looking for words and phrases that would stand out, that I would understand... My eyes were drawn to the center of the page, where there was a break in the writing, and within a box it said, in big bold letters, the *only* bold letters on the page: "**Gaston Briere**."

From what I could translate, it appeared to me that Marie was announcing that there was going to be some kind of an event in which Gaston Briere would be speaking. It's a good thing the announcement didn't say that Gaston Briere would be speaking on the subject of synchronicity.

After I studied Marie's e-mail for a few minutes, I sent an e-mail to Gaston. Juste une phrase: "Do you know Marie Rozier?" I thought that perhaps Marie and Gaston knew each other and that the e-mail from Marie was about him.

Within an hour, Gaston sent an e-mail back to me, saying that Marie's name did not sound familiar to him. So, I forwarded a copy of Marie's e-mail to Gaston. Bien sur, Gaston was able to read every word of the announcement from Marie. About two or three hours later I received another e-mail from Gaston, in which he told me that Marie's e-mail had nothing to do with him, and that the Gaston Briere she referred to in her announcement was the manager of the radio station that she worked for. What would you say the odds were that the manager of that radio station would be named Gaston Briere? And that I would discover that fact on *that* day, the day of Gaston's birthday? And that at the moment that I was thinking about sending an email to Gaston, I was instead drawn to the email from Marie? What are the odds?

I sent a quick, final e-mail, to Gaston – to tell him that I noticed some interesting synchronicities between Marie and Gaston, and I would tell him more about it when I saw him at the next art show in Stafford, that would be in September, in another couple of weeks.

When the day for the art show came, I went into town with the hope that I would see Marie there. But when I went to the spot on Rue Principal where Marie had set up her tent on the year before, I did not find her. Instead, I found that Gaston had *his* tent set up at what had been Marie's space! Again, the connection. Again, coincidence. This was just outside the door of The Lie, the restaurant which is my favorite place to hang in Stafford.

I later learned that Marie was not able to come to the art show this time, and by chance, Gaston had been assigned to the location that Marie had on the year before. There were a hundred other spots that Gaston could have been reassigned to, but he was given Marie's spot to set up his tent, in front of The Lie.

Before I went to look for Gaston on Rue Principal, I had a cup of coffee at The Lie, not yet knowing that Gaston's tent was set up near the front door. My thoughts that morning were mainly on some writing that I was doing. One piece I was thinking about writing was about Gaston – a story that would be about his art, and how I originally met him at the Stafford art expo. I planned on submitting the story to an Anglophone magazine or an Anglophone newspaper in the Eastern Townships. My working title for the piece was: *"Gaston Briere Sur La Route De La Synchronicity."* At the time, I foolishly thought that this would be a cute title to use in an English language publication.

At the time, I was also giving a lot of thought to writing a book, perhaps about Stafford, and synchronicity, and other things. I was thinking in terms of writing an outline for the book. I was feeling a compulsion to write this book, and I knew that I needed to have some kind of plan for the book. I couldn't just write a stream of consciousness, reflecting on what I saw on Rue Principal.

On the night before this trip to Stafford, I took a book from my personal library in East End Bay. I had pulled out *Main Street*, the classic book written in the 1930's by one of my favorite writers, Sinclair Lewis. I reread the first few chapters of the book, and the reading did not stimulate a plan for the writing of my own book. But when I put *Main Street* back on the shelf, I noticed the book that stood next to it. It was *On The Road*, by Jack Kerouac. I took the book off the shelf and read random excerpts, from pages I had previously circled. Then I put *On The Road* in my backpack.

I was ruminating about *On The Road*, and the book I wanted to write – perhaps about Stafford, and synchronicity – while I was sipping my coffee, just minutes before I was to discover that Gaston was set up in front of The Lie.

As I said before the sidebar, I found Gaston was installed in the space that Marie Rozier had the year before, when I had bought

12

the bracelets and poetry from her. Gaston's new tent had about ten of his paintings on display. In front of the tent, Gaston had a folding table set up, with a book sitting on the table that contained a portfolio of additional artwork done by Gaston. The only other thing on the folding table was a bracelet, which Sandi had put there a few minutes before I arrived, because the clasp had broken and it had fallen from her wrist.

Gaston, Sandi and I chatted for a few minutes, talking about the weather, talking about my drive up from East End Bay and their drive over from Montreal. Then Sandi excused herself to take a walk down Rue Principal, to see if she might find someone who could fix the clasp on her bracelet. At that point, I thought Marie Rozier might be located elsewhere on Rue Principal. (If Marie had been there, *she* would have been the person to fix Sandi's bracelet, eh?)

When Sandi walked off, Gaston said to me, "Come on, sit down here. I want to talk to you about your book. How is it coming?"

I said to Gaston, "I don't think I have anything yet. No plot, no outline."

Gaston said, "Just start writing and keep writing. Begin the book with the story about how we met. Write about the synchronicity. The story will come out of you." Then Gaston added, as a seemingly unrelated afterthought: "I was thinking, you should read Jack Kerouac's book: *On The Road.*"

Of course, bien sur, bien sur, I told Gaston that I had packed *On The Road* in my backpack, because I thought it might give me some ideas for a book.

That's how I got started on the road to this book, made up of various entries from my diary.

Fall 2007

"Mario-Jacques, The Chronicler"

Do not call me Ishmael, call me Mario-Jacques. My birth certificate says I'm a Mario, but in the language of my people (which is Franglish, ou franglais) I am Mario-Jacques.

I live in East End Bay, out on Long Island, New York, and I live in Stafford, Quebec – which is in the region known as the Eastern Townships. I live in the northernmost and southernmost ends of New England. I am a citizen of the United States of America, but I am a Quebec person. Je suis, I am, un Américain-Quebecer.

I am enamored with Stafford. Je suis enamouré avec Québec. J'adore the environment. J'adore les gens. J'adore la culture.

I consider the culture of Quebec, and the Quebec society, to be superior to that of the United States of America. Pourquoi? I could write a book about that. Let me just say for now that I think the general quality of life is better in Quebec than in the God-shed-his-grace-on-thee United States of America. And, Quebec people have better values, more humanistic values, in general, than American people. No wonder Americans have a penchant for things, and Quebecers have la joie de vivre.

I believe, as do others, that Stafford, Quebec, is now the center of the universe. I used to believe that the center of the universe was located in New York City, and the epicenter was perhaps where the Empire State Building stands, on 34th Street.

People who live in Stafford talk about being "drawn" to Stafford, by a force, by forces. People talk about "energies" in Stafford – energies that people give off, energies that emanate from the mountains, especially from Mount Stafford, and energies that emanate from the many waterfalls, and from the rocks, especially the quartz. (The quartz boulder in front of l'hôtel de ville is there for a reason.) I have been drawn to Stafford. I feel powerfully energized in Stafford – by the people and by the environment. I am told that I bring energy to people, also. C'est bon.

Many people who live in Stafford talk about, "fitting in." People who are drawn to Stafford know what it's like to be a perfect fit with others, with the community. A person who paints fine art and a person who paints houses can fit in, equally so. Francophones, Anglophones, and even this Américain-Quebecer who speaks broken Franglais, fit together nicely, merci.

People talk about Stafford being a place where "healers" come. Bien sur, the healing may be physical, mental, or spiritual.

I feel drawn to Stafford with an intensity that has become progressively stronger, especially within the last year, month by

14

month. If I'm away from Stafford for too long, my batteries start to drain. That's how it is with us Staffordians.

Apparently, all the paths I've taken in my life have led me to Stafford, to chronicle life in Stafford, to put these words before you, dear Diary. Call it my destiny.

Fall 2007, rewind to January 2006

"Live, at The Lie"

One might say that the first chapter of this diary book actually began in January of 2006, even though it is only now that I write anything about it. I think it is important that I enter what happened in January 2006 now, on these beginning pages of my diary, to provide a better context to understand the genesis of my evolution – which has been Darwinian…and biblical…and more.

I had stopped for dinner this one night at my favorite café in Stafford, le café de l'Oeil (which sounds something like, "the café of The Lie," in English). It was on a light snow flake Friday night in the winter of 2006, and I had just finished an eight-hour drive up from New York. It had only been a few months since I bought my little chalet on the mountain, and I was anxious to spend more time in Stafford.

After stopping at the chalet to raise the heat and refresh, I drove down to Rue Principal for dinner. I ate alone at a table in the corner of the room, so I could give studious attention to the environment – both physical and social. I was feeling fatigued when I finished eating, around 20h. I decided to pay the dinner bill and head back to the chalet, to get to sleep early. I was putting my arm into the sleeve of my coat when I accidentally poked my hand in the face of a large man who was sitting alone at the bar. Had this happened in New York, in the greater metropolitan area or where I live on Long Island, it is very possible that this would have become an incident of some kind. But it happened in Stafford, where people are not as guarded as the people who live on Long Island, USA, so this is how my friendship with a Townshipper, Tom Ingalls, began.

Tom responded to my right hand jab with his Canadian instinct for peace and humor. Which is to say, his first reaction was to laugh. Of course, my instincts told me that Tom could not have been born, as I was, in Brooklyn (yeah man, Brooklyn!) New York. As I would soon learn, he was born just a short walk from the café, in the back of a one-room schoolhouse which is now a museum.

There was something about this big teddy bear guy that I liked immediately. How could I not? After I nearly blinded him, he gave me a broad smile and said something like: "I had to duel the last man who did that to me."

I said to Tom, "I'm sorry, and you are more of a gentleman than I am, sir."

Tom responded, "I am someone who likes to give the impression that he is a gentleman. I have begged friends to call me, 'the Abercorn gentleman,' but to no avail. Thank you for your kind words. Please attempt to strike me again." Tom punctuated his words frequently with hearty laughs. I fell in platonic love with this man at first sight. A cool guy.

I could see that Tom was a baby boomer, older vintage, but I could still see his face as a boy, which showed through the surface layer of his face. The gray-white hair on his head was receding and cut short, as short as his closely-trimmed beard. He showed all his teeth when he smiled, and from his Santa Claus blue eyes I could see that he was a jolly soul. Us Brooklyn-born guys tend not to believe in Santa Claus, and we rarely describe someone as, "jolly." But this is what comes to mind as my first impression of Tom.

He guessed that I was not a Stafford person. Actually, Tom told me that he knew for certain that I was, "not from Stafford, not from Quebec, not from Canada, not from Vermont, not from anywhere nearby!" He said that the giveway was, "everything," about me. (I should add, I had already become more than a tourist by this time.) I don't know why he thought this about me, but that's what he said.

Anyway, sitting next to Tom at the bar was another vintage baby boomer, a smaller teddy bear guy wearing a beret, named Henri, known to his friends as, "choo-choo." Henri says he is not sure how he got this nickname, and he can only guess that it was, "perhaps for reasons that are of a sexual nature." I told him that I was not so sure how to interpret those words and I was not going to try. Henri, like Tom, was immediately friendly. He extended his hand and introduced himself as soon as we made eye contact. Henri – whose last name is Richard, like the hockey player – speaks English fluently, and to my ear he has only a slight French accent.

Tom and Henri argued over who would buy me a drink, while I thought to myself: Welcome to Quebec…these people are different.

I accepted a glass of ice wine that they both recommended, which was from a new Stafford vineyard. I had never heard of ice wine before. At this time I had yet to taste poutine, either.

I soon learned that Tom had just retired from a career as a school administrator in Quebec, working mainly in the Eastern Townships. Henri told me that his life is devoted to playing guitar and, "just having fun," after retiring as a carpenter. He had worked as a carpenter on stage sets in film and television studios in Montreal.

When they asked about me, I tried to sound as New Yawk-ish as possible, and I emphasized to them: "I was born in Brooklyn and I am a Sicilian-American – which means I should not be confused with any white bread Americans you may know." The way they laughed in response to this showed me that they were cool, not like so many uptight herd-mentality men that seem to be over-populating the United States these days.

Henri was at The Lie on this night to play the guitar, in a jazz trio. Tom was there to listen to the music. It was close to show time.

Henri took his guitar out of its case and showed it to me. It was a vintage Epiphone, a brand I had never heard of before. Henri was at least slightly impressed that I recognized the guitar as a Gibson clone. He told me that I "must" stay to hear the band. Tom nodded his head in agreement. Then Henri nodded his head toward a woman who looked to me to be a waitress. And she was a waitress, but she was also the piano player in Henri's band.

I asked Tom, "Are you a musician also?"

Tom said, "No, I don't play any instruments."

I said, "You're a jazz fan?"

Tom said, "No. I'm not much of a jazz fan, or a fan of any kind of music. I've never been that interested in music, except for maybe in the sixties. You know, Beatles, Rolling Stones, The Doors.

But I started listening to these guys a couple of months ago, and now I'm hooked. I come to The Lie every weekend to listen to them."

So now my interest was really piqued. Tom Ingalls was never in his life a jazz fan, nor was he ever an avid listener of any kind of music, and he told me that he was hooked on the jazz at The Lie.

I looked at Christine again, standing alone at the far end of the bar, holding a tall glass of dark beer – a Boréale, according to the label on the tap in front of her. (I had never heard of this beer, but I am not a beer drinker, and at this time I had not yet spent so much time in Canada.) Christine wore Johnny Cash black: Black shirt, black pants, black shoes, and a black apron wrapped around her waist. I watched her take off the apron, fold it neatly, and tuck it into a shelf behind the bar. Then I watched her take a thoughtful sip of her Boréale, as if it was a ritual potion that she was taking before her metamorphosis from waitress to jazz pianist.

Christine appeared to me to be an athletically fit, funky-punky, forty-ish woman. Laid back, cool. I looked at her and said to myself: This woman does not belong here. She looked more like an urban woman to me, not a rural woman. And for me, living north(!) of Vermont is living beyond rural territory – it's living in The Great White North, a land of wild moose and bears, not dogs and cats.

Christine walked over to the piano with her beer, and this signaled Henri to join her. I took a seat at the corner of the bar, next to Tom. I looked around the room and saw that most people were finished eating dinner, and most were now drinking glasses of wine, or beer. I saw a couple of people had turned their chairs to face the piano.

To my eye, l'Oeil seemed to be too spacious to be a jazz venue. When I think of jazz clubs, I think of people sitting elbow-to-elbow with other people in the audience, and there is hardly any room to walk between the tables and chairs if you need to go to the bathroom. Vive la difference at l'Oeil. I scanned the room and I could see that the tables and chairs were arranged so that people could sit comfortably, and everyone had plenty of room to walk between the tables. The tables and chairs were not lined up in grids, as they are in Manhattan, to lock as many people as possible into tight spaces. Instead of posters, or framed reproductions, as one would more likely see in a restuaurant on Long Island, or in a restaurant in Ohio, or in a restaurant a half-hour away in Vermont, I saw that The Lie had original oil paintings on the walls. (I later found out that these beautiful oil landscapes were done by a Stafford artist, Marie-Annick Martine.)

My guesstimate is that there were thirty people seated at the tables. The age range was from the twenties to the eighties. Most were chatting in la francais, and many were engaged in bi-lingual conversations, moving in and out of la francais et l'anglais. The sounds made by the conversation in the room was music to my ears, good music for dining.

These Quebecers – mainly from Stafford, or elsewhere in the Eastern Townships, or from Montreal for the weekend – were living la vie en rose, and somehow I had a sense that they realized that. Here they could order *foie de veau à la Victor Hugo*, for 14$ – WITH a near-gourmet soup or salad – and a near-gourmet dessert and coffee. In New York, as in most of McDonaldized America, for the same amount of money they would have had to settle for pizza and Coca-Cola, or the super deluxe cheeseburger and Coca-Cola, with french fries (or "freedom fries" if they were eating in a resto with George W. Bush intelligentsia).

It was not long before my attention was drawn from the diners to the drummer, who was making last-minute adjustments on his seat. The drummer was a twenty-something guy who I would later learn was Jean-Pierre Boulanger, better known as, "J.P." It was easy to see that J.P. liked cymbals. He was using a bass drum, a snare, and five or six cymbals, in addition to his hi-hat cymbals. He sat surrounded with cymbals. The cymbals were all set up unusually low, below the level of his chest. Drummers almost invariably like to set up their cymbals on angles, tilted toward them, with maybe one or two cymbals set low and parallel to the floor. It was noticeable to me that J.P. had all of his cymbals set up parallel to the floor, and low. I soon found out that J.P.'s drumming did the job, but the way he plays the cymbals – the sounds he gets from the cymbals is true artistry.

The first song that I heard from the trio was, "*Caravan*," the Duke Ellington song that is one of my all-time favorites, of any genre. This was a rendition that lasted for about twenty minutes. I have heard dozens of different versions of, "*Caravan*." I have heard the Duke Ellington big band version, the Cozy Cole sleepy jazz version, the Santo and Johnny rock and roll version, and the gypsy mandolin version from the award winning film *Chocolat*. The version I heard on this night of January 2006 at The Lie was unlike any version that I had ever heard before. It was the best performance of, "*Caravan*," that I have ever seen or heard.

Once the trio started to play, it took about thirty seconds for me to become quite absorbed by the music. I turned to Tom and mouthed: "Thank you." He smiled in a way that said, "I told you so!"

This, "*Caravan*," was an enchanting fusion of modern jazz, be-bop, hip-hop, classical music and indeterminate music. There was a measure or two of rock in there, also.

I stayed to hear one set, which lasted for about an hour, and then I chatted for a few minutes with Tom and the band during the break. Cool people. We made quite a connection through the music. I would have stayed longer but I was dog-tired and I needed to get to sleep.

I've heard a lot of great musicians, including some hall of fame musicians, up close and personal, or in standard concerts. The last live jazz performance I had heard, before I saw Henri, Christine and J.P. for the first time in Stafford, was one week before this night, when I had seen Wynton Marsalis and the Lincoln Center Jazz Orchestra, in Manhattan. I loved listening to the Lincoln Center Jazz Orchestra, but Henri, Christine and J.P. topped the LCJO, in terms of stimulating my emotions. By the way, the tickets I bought for the Lincoln Center Jazz Orchestra cost more than $100 a pop. For Henri, Christine and J.P. – "The Cool Nights," as they were called at the time – you were expected to make a contribution into the hat that the Abercorn gentleman Tom Ingalls carried around at the break.

Dear Diary: How do I sum this up? Welcome to la ville de Stafford. Bienvenue au Québec. Vive la difference.

July 7, 2007

"2012"

Treated Francois Desjardins to a late-afternoon dinner at La Cascade today. Je ne sais pas very many of the native French people in la ville de Stafford yet, but I've gotten to know Francois because our paths keep leading us to each other, and I find Francois to be very likeable. Every once in a while I'll chat with him for a few minutes on Rue Principal, or maybe we'll have a cup of coffee together at Café Dumont.

I think it was J.P. Boulanger who first introduced me to Francois, this past winter, while I was having dinner at The Lie. Since then, other mutual friends have *re*-introduced us to each other – at least ten different times, at different places in Stafford. And everyone asks us how we know each other. Now we answer in unison: "Everybody in Stafford keeps introducing us to each other!" It's strange in a very nice kind of way.

Francois is 22-years-old and he has always lived in Stafford, though he has lived out of town for some stretches of time in the last few years. He works a lot in the forests, cutting trees. His absent father died when he was 10-years-old, and his mother raised him and his six older sisters as a single parent, on wages from the IGA and part-time jobs. Francois told me that he did not do well in school, but now he likes to read Plato and books about the ancient Sumerians.

He lives part-time with his mother and some of his sisters, and part-time with different girlfriends. All the women want to mother Francois, because he responds to their nurturing and he has this gentle bad boy personna. He also bears a resemblance to the movie star Paul Newman, when Paul Newman was in his twenties.

He asks me a lot of questions about New York, and about sociology, psychology. He is a little bit impressed that I am a professor at a community college. He asks for advice, about life in general. I respond by paraphrasing Plato, Maslow and W.C. Fields.

Francois says it's good for him to practice his English with me. He has met plenty of people from the states, and from New York, especially from upstate New York, who come to Stafford during ski season. But I'm the first person from the area of New York City who he has gotten to know to any appreciable degree. It's also true that neither one of us know anyone else quite like each other, so we learn from each other.

The last time I had seen Francois was months ago, at le Café de l'Oeil. We sat next to each other at the bar on one of the nights that The Nights were playing. We talked during a break in the musique, and then Francois left with a group of his friends to the open mike night across Rue Principal, at Chez Maurice. The last time I saw Francois, he had paid for my pineau des Charentes and my biscotti at The Lie, without me knowing it. I'm sure he does not have so much extra cash, so I was impressed by his generosity, and that's when I made a mental note to see if I could treat him to a dinner.

When I invited Francois, a few days ago, I told him that I wanted to return his kind gesture of paying for my drink and my biscotti at The Lie, and it would be mon plaisir to treat him to dinner at one of the restos in Stafford, his choice. He picked La Cascade, a good restaurant near the end of Rue Principal that has a modest prix fixe menu, and provides a nice setting for dining. We sat on the terrace, under a vine-covered canopy.

During our meal Francois talked about his hopes for the future. He has a dream, and he has a Plan B. His current dream is to become a rap singer. He would do what he calls: "Quebecois-Appalachian rap," and travel the world. His current Plan B is to raise a family, in a house that he would build himself, somewhere in the mountains near Stafford.

He told me that he hasn't been able to save any money yet, but he's due to get a raise from his boss, and if he can cut down on the money he spends on marijuana, he will finally get a savings account going. He told me that he thought his best shot at accumulating money is to break into the entertainment business, doing his rap thing.

At dinner with Francois I listened with care, digesting my food and his thoughts very slowly. When he gave me his *so-what-do-you-think?* look, just before we looked at the dessert menu, I suggested to Francois that he makes sure he doesn't neglect his Plan B, now or in the future. I offered my thought that the planets have to be lined up just right for even the most talented people to succeed in the entertainment business. Basically, I told him to follow his passions, but take care of basics. And I told him that this was a time in his life to learn as much as possible, and be focused on creating an occupation for himself. Francois thanked me for talking to him with care. With gravity in his voice, Francois said: "Hey Mario, we are members of the same family: The human family."

I had my second glass of wine along with dessert, Francois had his third, and I thought that at least one of us was feeling the affects of the drinks when he asked me: "Why are you here, Mario?"

I replied, "Here? Ici? At La Cascade?"

Francois laughed and said, "No. I don't mean ici, à La Cascade, I mean here in Stafford."

I said, "Well, I really feel like I fit in here. I've never quite had the same feeling about a place before. The only thing I can compare this to is the feeling I had when I was in Sicily, where my parents are from. But I feel far more *drawn* here, to Stafford."

He took a sip from his wine and squinted his eyes, as if an insight was just registered in his mind. He said : "Bien sur, of course…because you are one of: *"The Ones."*

Then he unfolded his napkin on the table, set his wine glass on it, and swirled the wine, as if he was carrying out a ritual of some kind. At the same time, he looked at me with one finger over a small smile.

I said, "Well? It looks like there is more for you to say, but you aren't saying anything."

He said, "This is hard for me, because I do not know how to say it in a good way en *anglais*. I know what I want to say in French, but I do not know the words for what I want to say to you in English. It is so much harder for me to explain certain things en anglais."

The English that Francois speaks is very good, though his French accent and the cadence of his speech are noticeable to my ear. I said to Francois, "If I can ever learn to speak French half as well as you speak English, je pense I will be très happy."

This made Francois laugh. "Hey Mario, I can see that your French is improving! Wow, that is good." Then his face turned serious, as if he had remembered the serious thing that he had to talk to me about. Perhaps because he was thinking in French, he started to talk in French, then went back to English. "Encore, you being one of *The Ones*…I have noticed that there are certain people who come here to Stafford who are special people. You are one of these people. You are not just an ordinary person Mario, I know that."

I interrupted Francois. "Merci beaucoup, Francois. You know, I think you are very special also."

23

Francois said, "Merci beaucoup to you, Mario. It means a lot to me that you show me respect, and that you like me. That makes me think good of myself. What is the right word? Because you treat me the way you do, because you are my friend, and you take me out to this dinner, this helps my, my, my *self-esteem*. Is that the way to say it? *"Self-esteem?"*

I said, "Mais oui. That is correct. Je comprends. You are paying me a high compliment to say I help your self-esteem."

He continued, "Mais oui. You say, *'mais oui,'* like a quebecois, Mario...Encore, what do I want to say? How to say it en anglais? I think there is something happening here in Stafford. That is why I stay here. Sometimes I go away – I go live in Cowansville, I go live in Montreal for a while – but I always feel this magnet that brings me back here, ici à Stafford. I was born here, on Southern Street, the street on the other side of the railroad tracks, behind l'hôtel de ville, the town hall. There are other people like me, who go away but they have to come back. When I am somewhere else, it does not feel right. I start to lose my energy."

I reached across the table and touched his hand lightly with my index finger, to signal that I wanted to interrupt him for a second. I said, "That's the way it is with me. If I'm away from Stafford for more than a month my energy level decreases. It's like I have to get my batteries recharged. But I'm interrupting, Francois. Please go on."

He said, "Oui. I know you know what I am saying. You *have* to know, because you are one of *The Ones*."

I interrupted again. "You still haven't explained what you mean by that."

He said, "D'accord, okay, I am getting to that. I think I need another glass of wine...No, I think that is the problem, I do *not* need another glass of wine. I am not used to drinking wine, I am used to smoking weed. I can hold my weed better...Okay, here is what I am trying to say...I think you are here because you are a healer. I had this feeling about you the first time I meet you. I remember, at the café. Aaah, I did not have the feeling that you were a healer right away...but I had the feeling that there was something about you that was very different. You were not just another touriste from the states, there was something different. *Now* I am in touch with this feeling. I am in touch with this feeling while we have dinner and do

24

our talking. How to say it exactly in English, I do not know, but it is sort of like a *sixth sense* that I have. I can see that you are a healing person. I feel you are here in Stafford because you are a healing person. And there is something else that you have to do here. There is a *reason* why you are here. I do not know what that is, but I know there is a reason, and that it is important. It is a *destiny*."

Francois did not try to hide the fact that he was looking closely at my facial expression, trying to read how I was receiving the thoughts he was sharing with me.

I said to him, "I think I am understanding what you are saying far better than you think I am."

That's when he asked me the question that I could not understand. "You are here for 2012, right?"

"2012?" I answered.

Francois rephrased his mysterious question into a flat statement. "You are here for 2012."

"What's, '*2012*?'" I asked, with some urgency in my voice.

Francois drank the remaining wine in his glass, a mouthful, before he continued. "2012 is when the Mayan calendar comes to an end. A prophecy was made thousands of years ago that the world is going to come to an end in 2012, or something will happen in 2012 to stop the world from coming to an end, and then a new age is going to begin. Some people think 2012 will be the end, some people think it will be a turning point. But the only way it can be a turning point, into a new age, is if people gather together to make a better world. No matter what, a lot of bad things are going to happen. These bad things are happening already. Look at the terrorism. You see what I am saying?"

I said, "I see that we are living in interesting times, that's for sure. But I never heard of 2012."

Francois said, "I am a very spiritual person, Mario. I do not go to a church and I do not practice a religion, but I am a very spiritual person...What is the word? I *rely* on my intuition. My intuition tells me that something is happening now, and is leading up to 2012. My intuition tells me this is why you are here. 2012."

November 10, 2007

"Paddy O'Brien & Zen & The Art Of Motorcycle Maintenance"

My drive from East End Bay to Stafford usually takes between seven and a half   and eight hours. I like to leave East End Bay between four and five in the morning, to beat the traffic on the Long Island Expressway and to beat most of the traffic on Interstate 95, in Connecticut.

On Thursday night, the night before I was leaving, I was ready to go to sleep at about eleven. I shut off my computer, shut off the light over my desk, and went into the bathroom to make one last pit stop before getting into bed. And then, for some reason, I don't remember why, my thoughts turned to a friend of mine, Bob Woodhull, who is now living down in Florida, near Disney. I had been planning for at least a month to send Bob an e-mail, to ask him for his new mailing address. For various reasons, I have long been wanting to mail Bob a copy of one of my favorite books, *Zen and the Art of Motorcycle Maintenance*, as a gift.

While I was in the bathroom the thought occurred to me that I should turn my computer back on and send the e-mail to Bob immediately, without procrastinating any more. But I was sleepy, just about ready to doze off on my feet, so I told myself to procrastinate once again and send the e-mail after I get back from Stafford, in another week. With the remaining energy I had left, I finished laying out my clothes in the bathroom that I would put on at four o'clock in the morning, for my drive up to Stafford. Then I got into bed, shut the lights.

About ten seconds after I pulled the blankets over me, I felt this urge to get out of bed and send the e-mail to Bob. Even though I was tucked away, ready to sleep, and even though I had been procrastinating time after time about sending this e-mail to Bob, I suddenly threw the blankets off, turned on the light on my night table, and jumped out of bed to send the e-mail. It was like I had realized that sending that e-mail was something that I just *had* to do at that point in time, and there was nothing to think about, but to do it. Don't *try* to do it, *do it*. Which I did.

This is not the sort of thing that I am in the habit of doing.

Okay, I get up to Stafford the next day, on Friday, at about noon. I stop for un café au lait at La Cascade, I go over to the bank on rue Principal to change my quickly devaluing Americain monnaie, and I get up to the chalet at about one. As soon as I walk inside, even before I turn the water back on, I phone my good buddy, my Staffordian guru, Paddy O'Brien, to let him know that I'm in town. I catch Paddy at home. He tells me that he's anxious to see me and that he'd like to come right over, to give me something.

Paddy lives higher up on the mountain. In more ways than one. I knew it would take him about ten minutes to get over to my chalet, so I used that time to unpack and to make some chai tea for the both of us.

From the day that Paddy and I first met, this past spring, we've been in sync with each other and we've shared a number of unusual synchronous moments. In fact, it was Paddy who brought my attention to *synchronicity,* at least in terms of giving me the name for this phenomenon – of coincident events connected without cause, but meaningfully. I had been experiencing a lot of coincidences in Stafford even before I met Paddy, but after I met Paddy and we started hanging out a bit, the coincidences I was experiencing in Stafford became more noticeable, if not more frequent. Of course, you're more likely going to find something if you look for it. Mais oui, but that doesn't make what you find any less real. Non?

Anyway, there I was, waiting for Paddy to come over, and I'm thinking about how we keep experiencing synchronicities together. And I'm also thinking that if he wants to take a ride over to Reilly House in Mansonville, which is what he said he wanted to do the next time we got together, we don't have a good vehicle for the drive. I had borrowed a car for the drive to Stafford, because my car was being repaired, and I didn't want to drive the car I had borrowed any more than I had to – especially on the Canadian side of the border, and in the snow. So, while I'm thinking about this and looking out the front window, I see a small gray car that I didn't recognize coming up the road. I didn't think it was Paddy, because he drives an old *Volkswagen Thing*, but when the car pulls up next to mine, I see that it's Paddy who gets out of the car.

I let Paddy in, and while he's taking off his boots I put his cup of chai tea back in the microwave. My delight in seeing Paddy for the first time in three weeks is experienced as a delayed reaction. I go over to him again, and give him a Sicilian-American/Americain-Quebecer hug. I say, "Yo Paddy, wut it be? Ca va?" Once I get to Stafford, I tend to greet people en francais (avec "ca va?") even if they're anglophones, like Paddy.

Though Paddy's been married to a lovely francophone lady for something like fifty years, I never hear him speak French, not even to say, "bonjour." Paddy just smiled at me and said, "Hey, Mario. I thought maybe you weren't here, maybe you went down to the dep because I didn't see your car while I was coming up the road, but then I saw that the car out front has New York plates."

I explained that I had borrowed that car, because my car was being repaired. Paddy laughed and said: "Here we go with the synchronicity again, because my car is being repaired too, and we both borrowed gray cars, eh?"

Okay, so not such a big deal, right? A very minor coincidence that we were both having our cars repaired at the same time, and that we had both borrowed cars that happened to be gray, which is a very common colour for cars. The thing is, as I said, Paddy and I have this very noticeable tendency to experience coincidences together, so this was a bit striking to both of us.

My remark to Paddy was: "C'est vrai, Paddy. It's true. Here we go again with synchronicity." And then I told him that I had been doing a lot of reading about synchronicity. I mentioned that I had been reading references to Carl Jung's theories about synchronicity, and I mentioned that I had just read a particularly interesting book called, *There Are No Accidents,* by a Jungian psychotherapist named Robert Hopcke.

This got Paddy going. He said, "I can't believe what the universities *don't* teach! How did you go to school for all those years and not learn anything about synchronicity? Nothing about synchronicity, nothing about *Unus Mundus.* It's unbelievable." Paddy got himself worked up, fast. Enough so, apparently, that you might say he was pissing mad. As a matter of fact, he suddenly announced, "I got to take a piss," and he headed to the bathroom to do just that.

Aside from the fact that Paddy is a 79-year-old man with prostrate issues, when he gets excited he has a tendency to run off at the mouth, and run to the bathroom. He kept the bathroom door open and he kept talking, as per usual. "Mario, you know I'm a maybe-ist. Maybe those rocks that Crowley found on his property in Mansonville have markings, but maybe not, eh? But I'll tell you something, there's something going on with this synchronicity between you and me. We have to talk about this more," he yelled out. Then he flushed the toilet, adding a Paddy O'Brien exclamation point to his statement.

"It's got my attention," was all I said in response to his comment about coincidences.

Paddy came out from the bathroom zipping up his fly, and he took a seat across from me at the dining room table. He pulled a brown paper bag from the pocket of his ski coat, which he had draped on the back of his chair. He reached into the bag and pulled out a paperback book, which he slid across the table to me. It was a copy of *Zen and the Art of Motorcycle Maintenance*.

November 11, 2007

"I Meet Merlin The Magician"

Dear Diary…As promised, Paddy picked me up bright and early this morning, to introduce me to some people he has wanted me to meet for some time: Merlin The Magician and Merlin's wife, Gwen Beckett. Before today, the only thing I knew about Merlin and Gwen were their names, and that they owned a combination farm/art gallery about 10 kilometers from Rue Principal Stafford.

Paddy has not yet told me what Merlin's real name is, and I haven't asked him. Any time Paddy has referred to Merlin, he has referred to him as if the name, 'Merlin The Magician,' is not a nickname, and as if it is not unusual in any way. So I've been acting as if, 'Merlin The Magician,' is just an ordinary name in Québec for a person to be given at birth.

I soon found out that, 'ordinary,' is not a word that would be associated very often with Merlin The Magician. For that matter, one would not associate, 'ordinary' with Gwen either, for reasons that go beyond being Merlin's partner.

In terms of physical distance, their home is a good kilometer away from their closest neighbor. In their neck of the woods les habs are mainly farmers, artistes, and the wealthy.

Paddy had to go slow and do some zig-zagging around ruts while we were driving on the dirt roads that lead up to the farm. Lately, the changes in temperature – from freezing to fall-like weather and then back to freezing again – have really done a number on the roads. It probably took us twice as long as it normally would to drive out to the farm, and this made it seem all the more isolated – or more accurately, all the more *in solitude*.

I don't know how much land Merlin and Gwen own, but their farm property runs on both sides of the road. Their house, built in 1870, stands fairly close to the road, as many old farmhouses do in the townships. Their barn, a sizeable barn, stands farther back from the road than the house does. They also have a small greenhouse, maybe 10 meters long, which stands on the opposite side of the barn as the house.

We parked in a gravel stone parking area in front of the barn, in a parking area that can accommodate six or eight cars. There was a Range Rover parked in front of the barn, near the entry door. Paddy had it pegged as belonging to someone from Montreal.

Paddy had never given me a physical description of Merlin. I also had no idea whether he was a francophone or an anglophone, or how old he was. But I knew I was looking at Merlin The Magician as soon as I saw him for the first time.

As Paddy and I were walking up to the door, three men came out of the barn. Before he said hello, before he even made eye contact with Paddy or me, I knew that Merlin had to be the man who was cradling in his hands what looked more like a small newborn baby than the large tomato that it actually was. My eyes zoomed in on the tomato, which was more box-like in shape than round, and about 10 inches by 5 inches. By far, this was the largest tomato I have ever seen in my life, and it was a deeper red than the latest

30

chemically engineered tomatoes that are so popular, and so tasteless. The sight of the Merlin tomato stopped me in my tracks, and I did a double-take, which is a response that Merlin is no doubt fond of eliciting from people, on a regular basis.

I focused in on that tomato for a long moment, and then my eyes went to Merlin. He's a 60-ish, tall, thin, pale-skinned man, with thick, almost pure white hair, which extends down to his shoulders. And he has a white moustache and frizzy white beard. I could see, it was obvious, that he was called Merlin The Magician because he looked so much like…himself.

As soon as Merlin saw Paddy, he stopped what he was doing to greet us. The five of us circled and shook hands, with Paddy and Merlin doing the introductions. It turned out that the other two men, Alan and Warren by name, were customers who had just bought two of the giant tomatoes – one tomato to serve at a party that Alan was having tonight, and the second tomato was for Warren to bring back to his other house, in Montreal. These men smelled of expensive cologne, and money.

Before they got in their car, Merlin bowed from the waist, shook their hands gently, and said, "*cheers,*" to wish them off. Then Merlin hustled me and Paddy into his greenhouse.

Earlier, while we were driving over to the farm, Paddy had said to me, "Merlin is a very interesting person – and so is Gwen, in a different way – but Merlin is just   something else." After he said that, Paddy laughed as if he had just told a joke, and added, "he's *different* – and that's something to say, coming from me, eh?"

Again, I began to understand what Paddy was talking about as soon as I saw Merlin with his giant tomato, but when I walked into the greenhouse, and saw what was there, I understood better why Paddy said Merlin was quote-unquote, "something else."

It was double-take time again. The last time I had walked into an environment that looked anything at all like the interior of Merlin's greenhouse was some years ago, at Disney World in Florida, at the *Honey, I shrunk the kids* exhibit – where everything was giant sized. But the illusion in Disney was created by the clever crafting of synthetic materials. What was now here before my eyes was as real as real magic gets. The greenhouse was overgrown with tropical plants. Enormous leaves, fronds, hung down over the walkway, making it look like a path in the jungle.

The first plants I recognized in this jungle, a few feet away from me, were basil plants – which are not to my knowledge indigeneous to tropical climates, but fit the incongruity of a Québec jungle. The basil bushes were bigger-than-life in terms of what I'm used to seeing. I grow basil in pots every summer, in East End Bay, on Long Island, which has a climate comparable to regions in Italy. And I have a friend who is a professional grower of basil plants, in greenhouses. Yet, I have never seen basil plants thrive as these plants were thriving.

When Paddy spoke with Merlin on the phone yesterday, to ask him if it was okay if he and I visited today, Paddy mentioned that I was from Long Island, New York. And that I was an Italian, born in Brooklyn. Merlin was no doubt being mindful of these things when he said to me, in all seriousness, "Mario, what do you think of my basil plants? How would you evaluate them?" He spoke with the tone of a cultured English gentleman.

"These would be blue ribbon basil plants at a country fair in *The Magic Kingdom,*" I intoned with only slight Brooklyn hyperbole.

Merlin's face lit up with a smile. "Funny you should say that, Mario. And it means a lot to me to hear that from you, as you are of Italian heritage, and you probably have substantial knowledge of *basilico.* I don't know if I'll ever get to enter my basil in a contest at The Magic Kingdom, but you might be interested to know that I won a blue ribbon with my *basilico* at the Brome County Fair, this past September."

I said, "Doesn't surprise me," as I began to walk slowly down the walkway, following Merlin.

Next to the basil plant, on the same side of the walkway, was a rosemary bush, perhaps better described as a small rosemary *tree.* The scent from these plants, the rosemary and the basil, was very strong. I swear, the scent stimulated an involuntary hormonal reaction from me, in the same way that real chocolate is said to stir a hormonal reaction, directly from the senses to the pleasure regions of the brain. I come from a long line of Sicilians, so basilico and rosemary are like good chocolate to me.

At this point, Paddy was satisfied that I was in ecstacy, and he decided to excuse himself from the greenhouse to visit with Gwen inside the house, and he needed to use the bathroom. When Paddy went off, Merlin commented, "That Paddy O'Brien is a learned man, in his own inimitable way. I'm sure you are well aware of that, Mario."

I said, "Oh, yes. Paddy's teaching me a lot about meditation, and Eastern philosophies, and tai-chi. He's always recommending books for me to read. We've made a really nice connection with each other."

Merlin said, "I have long felt the same way, Mario. I exchange books with Paddy, as well. You'll have to tell me about your proclivities in reading. They must be similar to Paddy's, so there's a good chance that you and I have something in common, in terms of what we enjoy reading. Interesting."

I was about to tell Merlin about the books stacked up on my night table, when my eyes caught sight of the most unbelievable growth in the greenhouse: a banana tree, plentiful with bunches of nearly-ripe bananas!

Merlin smiled in response to my newest double-take, elicited by the banana tree. With a nod toward the tree, Merlin said, "I believe it is safe to say that the four banana trees I have in this greenhouse are the only four banana trees that are being cultivated right now in Quebec...I would suspect the same is true of the pineapple trees I have over there, on the other side of the greenhouse." I followed his glance to the small pineapple trees, growing next to what I recognized as fig trees.

I said, "Merlin, you're growing tropical plants here! I didn't know one could grow plants like this in Québec, unless you created an artificial environment in an elaborate and costly facility – like a public biosphere, or in a facility within a university, maybe."

Merlin responded, "I questioned whether I could do it, at first. You realize, of course Mario, that the soil, fertilization, the air temperature, the light, have to be just right to provide the necessary conditions for growing these plants. I use a wood burning stove to generate heat for this greenhouse. That alone can be quite tricky sometimes. It is my good fortune to have my 17-year-old son, who is a strong lad, and a willing worker, to help me. In fact, if it wasn't for him, I never would have started playing around with the idea of growing these tropical plants here. You see, his abiding interest is in dahlias, and while we were cultivating his dahlias I decided to branch out to the bananas and the pineapples."

Merlin pointed out the beautiful dahlias that his son is growing, which take up most of the space on one side of the greenhouse. Then Merlin caught sight of Gwen and Paddy walking from the barn to the house. We decided that I could come back on another day to continue the greenhouse tour, so we headed out to the house, to join Paddy and Gwen.

While we were taking off our coats and boots inside the house, I saw on the wall near the entry a bookcase filled with hardcover books, and a collection of mortars and pestles. I noticed right away that a number of books had the word, *"alchemy,"* in the title. I thought to myself: *Of course.*

…Unfortunately dear Diary, this is all I can write about tonight, as I am more than ready to go to sleep.

Late November, 2007

"Paddy O'Brien, a.k.a. Shane Delancey"

Dear Diary…

Though it is questionable as to whether he was ever properly ordained, Paddy O'Brien is a shaman, Irish-Canadian variety. At least to *me,* he is a shaman, Irish-Canadian variety. But Paddy would not call himself a shaman…only a, "Maybeist monk," maybe.

Paddy dowses for water and detects energy fields. He teaches tai-chi, meditation and poker. He used to be a bookie in Montreal, where he went under the name of Shane Delancey. He almost made the Montreal Alouettes football team when he was 19-years-old. He walked onto the Alouettes practice field off the street, with his old high school uniform on, and asked for a tryout, like he was asking if he could sign up in an amateur bowling league.

As Paddy tells it, the Alouettes coaches thought he looked good in his uniform, and he looked slightly less crazy than their craziest player, and he had bigger hands than anyone else on the team, so they gave him a tryout. He proved to them that he knew how to catch a football, no matter how hard the ball was thrown at him, and no matter how hard he was hit after he caught the ball. And if he was a step faster, they might have signed him to a contract on that first day they saw him play. Remarkable enough, they let him practice with the team for a couple of weeks, until an injury to his ankle – from a bar fight, I think – ended his pursuit of a football career. I think he still has friends from that team who are now in the Canadian Football Hall of Fame.

Paddy's also a ski instructor. His skiing style, like his lifestyle, is rather distinctive. To the unpracticed eye, he looks like a muscular and lithe six-foot four-inch First Nations man, skiing effortlessly through the glades, with a long ponytail of silver-gray hair waving behind him, enhancing his balance. A person with a practiced eye will recognize that Paddy can do 108 tai-chi movements while he's skiing down a double black diamond course. Paddy says that when he skies down Mount Stafford he likes, "to flow like water, never resisting, just persisting."

Paddy is drawn to water. Especially flowing water. And rocks. And mountains. Coincidentally, I am also very attracted to flowing waters, to rocks, to mountains. I never realized the extent to which this is true until recently, but I've always lived near waters. I find peace and feel timelessness in flowing waters.

Paddy didn't know any of these things about me, but he sensed that I am a water person. Triple Falls is three magical waterfalls in an enchanted clearing in the woods, on a patch of property in Stafford that Paddy owns. I think he bought this property about thirty years ago, after a big poker win in Montreal. Triple Falls is a place that Paddy goes to on most days, to watch his breath, to meditate.

January 2, 2008

"Carnie Jack et Kerouac"

I drove up to Stafford from East End Bay today. I decided not to take my regular route, from Long Island to Connecticut, then through Massachusetts, and then Vermont to the Canadian border. I don't like traveling up and down the Green Mountains of Vermont when it's snowing, and I don't care how fast they plow the snow off the Interstate. You can't clear the snow as fast as it comes down from the skies. If I'm going to be driving in the snow, I'd rather drive up to the Canadian border through New York State than through Vermont. The New York ride is a flatter ride. I am, I say without shame, what Vermonters call a, "flatlander."

Anyway, it took me 10 ½ hours to get up to Stafford this time. I usually do it in 8 hours or so when I go through Vermont. This time I got lost in New Jersey (which is what usually happens when I drive through New Jersey, and has something to do with the fact that where I drive in Jersey you have to make a right turn before you can go left). And I hit snow in the Albany area of New York. So I was tired, toast, fatigué, when I finally got in to Stafford, at about 2:30 in the afternoon.

But it was good to be back. Back to a community not yet consumed by the corporations. No Wal-Marts. No Big Box stores. No McDonald's. No Americanization, globalization, or capital "B" Bullshitization.

I arrived in Stafford not thinking about the decline of western civilization, but wondering if I was going to experience any noticeable synchronicities. Bien sur, my mind was on the subject of synchronicity, because I have been doing a lot of reading about synchronicity over the last month.

Among the books I've brought up with me is a Jack Kerouac book, *The Dharma Bums*. That book, and *The Tao of Psychology*, were the only two books that I unpacked and put immediately on my night table. The other books I unpacked, about a dozen or so, I piled on a table in the living room.

I went down to The Lie at about 20h and Christine was tending bar. She gave me some Stafford mise à jour avec un verre de vin rouge. Heavy snow has brought a lot of skiers to Stafford from Montreal. The Lie has just had what might have been a record-breaking week, and this was a badly needed shot in the arm for the café. Christine also mentioned that New Year's Eve was a good night at The Lie. She told me that a longtime bon ami, who is a high-end vibraphone player from Montreal, played with her at The Lie on New Year's Eve, as a duet. Christine said they, "smoked."

Christine made a reference to Jack Kerouac, by name, while we were chatting. I forget what she said, but I made a mental note of her reference to Kerouac, even though I didn't think it was so remarkable that she would happen to refer to Jack Kerouac, coincidentally, while I had just began reading another Kerouac book. After all, Christine knew, from some conversations we have had, that I had some interest in Jack Kerouac. But...it was no more than 10 minutes after this conversation with Christine that I got into a conversation with my Staffordian buddy Carnie Jack, and he also made a reference, out of the blue, to Jack Kerouac.

Carnie Jack wasn't so sure I would know who Jack Kerouac was, and I was surprised that Carnie Jack knew who Kerouac was. Carnie is not to my knowledge what one would call a voracious reader, though he is someone who is quite a Jack-of-all-trades, hence the name, "Jack." Bien sur, my surprise may have been the product of my American prejudice, my false belief (intellectual snobbiness?) that this man with calluses on his hands would be so unlikely to have an interest in the writer Jack Kerouac.

Considering that Jack Kerouac's heritage was French-Canadian, I guess there was a reasonable chance that I would encounter people in this little town in the Eastern Townships of Quebec who would reference his name in conversation with me, independently of each other, within minutes of each other, at the same time I had just began reading a Kerouac book. So I didn't dwell on these coincidences at the time, while I was chatting with Christine, and then with Carnie Jack. But hours later, after I got home, I thought back to their references to Kerouac and I thought to myself: *Hmmm, that was synchronicity, a coincidence meaningful to me. Again.*

Janvier 6, 2008

"Meeting le Maire"

Dear Diary...
Had breakfast this morning with the mayor of la ville de Stafford at Café Dumont. Ironically, the name of le maire is Benoit Lamontagne. His home from birth has been in this little town in

Quebec that stands in the shadow of Mount Stafford. "Ben" in Hebrew means, "son of." So the name of the man who is the mayor of la ville de Stafford can be translated to: "Son of the mountain." À-propos and ironic. Synchronistic.

After a wonderful discussion about the past, present and future of la ville de Stafford, et l'Estrie, the Eastern Townships, et Benoit Lamontagne, I came away feeling that Stafford has a man in city hall who is exceptional. He is a class act. He is un tres intelligent man, & he has a deep love for Stafford, the townships, and Quebec.

Ben is a man in his mid-50's, a youthful mid-50's, in attitude and appearance. He has only a little gray in what is mostly red hair. He told me that he has lived in only two houses in his life, both of them in this petite ville de Stafford. His mother was a Francophone with Abenaki blood, his father an Anglophone with Iroquois blood. A lot of Ben's extended family, on both his maternal and paternal sides, live in Vermont, as well as farther north, in Québec. He has traced these family roots back hundreds of years, on both sides of the family. Ben is a man who was given a broad perspective by his family, to say the least.

January 17, 2008

"Kerouac Encore, Synchronicity Encore"

I decided to go skiing this morning and I was hoping to meet Paddy O'Brien on the mountain. Somebody in the locker room who knows Paddy told me that he's 81 years old. I thought he was 79, but I'm not sure if it was Paddy who told me that or if it was someone else. In any case, Paddy is the most athletic eight decades man I have ever met in my life. He's still a double black diamond skier. He skies 4-5 times a week, sometimes more.

It has probably been done already by someone, but one of the books within Paddy could be titled: *"Zen and the Art of Skiing."* When Paddy goes skiing he brings his spirituality with him. This is another thing he shares with others, along with tai-chi, meditation, poker. Bien sur, he occasionally forgets to bring his spirituality with him when he's playing poker.

It was about 9:30 and I was sipping on my morning cup of *Celestial Seasonings* camomille tea, brewed in my microwave, when I noticed Paddy's little Volkswagen Thing zig-zagging through the icy ruts in the road leading up to the cul-de-sac in front of my chalet. I was happy, but surprised to see Paddy, because he is in the habit of phoning me before he comes over. From my front window I watched Paddy park his car, and then walk up to the front steps as if he was in a rush. Bien sur, Paddy doesn't rush, he just gets more energized. His energy level was relatively high today.

Paddy came in and began talking rapid-fire, while he took off his boots and slipped off his ski coat, which he folded lengthwise and placed on the floor, across the threshold of the door. This is where Paddy puts his winter coat when he takes it off at my chalet, or at his chalet. The idea behind doing this is that it's a convenient place for Paddy to leave his coat, and it also serves the purpose of stopping any draft from coming through the bottom of the door. I find myself starting to do this with my own coat. As long as you keep the floor clean, it's a better idea than one might think.

I didn't get a chance to say, "How are you?" I managed to say, "Yo, Paddy…" and then he was off to the races.

"Hey, Mario, I'm going to be with Winston. You know, Winston, the guy I go skiing with just about every day for the past 25 years, the retired accountant from Montreal who's been living at the ashram in India? You met him when you first met me, at the café, The Lie, but like I was telling you, hey, the coincidences, if that's what you want to call them, keep coming, eh, when you're paying attention, and you're building energy fields." Paddy wasn't raising his voice, but his excitement was evident. "Make me a tea, will ya? I can stay a half-hour before I go skiing. Got some things I got to talk to you about. You're going to like this."

While I was putting a cup of water in the microwave for Paddy's tea, he reached into a plastic bag he had, which I could see from the writing on the side of the bag was from Coles bookstore, in Montreal. Instead of pulling out a book, as I expected, he pulled out a yellowed newspaper. He said, "Here's a newspaper I didn't know I still had. It's been buried away somewhere under the pile of books in my chalet for 23 years. Annick found this newspaper and gave it to me. We've got crap all over the place, because Nick is cleaning up the house, because we got family coming over from Ireland. You know all about that. But Annick found this paper, it's called: *Inquiring Mind.*"

I looked at the newspaper, which was a relatively thin tabloid, folded in half. My eyes went to a large photo on the cover page that looked like a head shot of Allen Ginsberg, the Beat Generation poet. I remembered that I had just had an extended talk avec mon ami Harley at his restaurant the other day, about the Beat Generation and about Greenwich Village in the fifties and sixties. Harley and I are talking about putting together a publication here, in Stafford, which would be mainly about the artistic community. We just have rough ideas right now. What I had just said to Harley a few days ago was that there are so many creative and artistic people who have gathered here in Stafford, and the dynamic here is a kin to the dynamic that must have existed in Greenwich Village during the era of Ginsberg, Kerouac, et al.

Then I looked at the headline on the front page, which read: "ROAD NEWS." I thought to myself: "Here's Kerouac again. Could this be a reference to Jack Kerouac's book, *On the Road?* Ginsberg and Kerouac were friends. Hmmm, Kerouac keeps popping up."

I was going to ask Paddy if this thing he wanted to tell me about was about Kerouac again. Paddy and I have been talking a lot lately about the synchronicities I am experiencing in Stafford, including a number of Jack Kerouac synchronicities. But I didn't want to interrupt Paddy while he was talking. I didn't want to throw him off his train of thought, and it was clear that there was a lot that he wanted to say to me.

Basically, what he proceeded to tell me about was his trip to Montreal yesterday, to visit his mother. As is his routine, Paddy stopped at Coles to see if he might find a book. He did not have a specific book in mind, but he went into the store with a feeling of, shall we say, *confident expectations*. He saw a woman working behind the front counter that he knew well from his many visits to the store. She asked how he was doing and Paddy told her that he was doing great, and he was exuding karma from the pores of his skin that said he was doing great. She asked if he was looking for anything special, and Paddy said: "I will find what I am looking for when I see it."

The woman replied: "Well, the way it looks, you'll find what you want right around the corner."

Bien sur, Paddy being a person who follows lighted paths, he decided to walk around the corner of the first row of books. And that's where he found what he wanted, bien sur. In a stack of books on sale, the one book that caught his eye was the one on top of the pile, and on sale from $37 to...$7. It was *The Power of Now*, by Eckhart Tolle. *The Power of Now* is one of about a dozen books I have stacked on a table in my living room, at the chalet. Paddy and I have talked about Eckhart Tolle and *The Power of Now* at least a half-dozen times in the recent past. After he finished telling me how he came to buy the book at Cole's, Paddy said: "When the reader is ready, the book will be there." I didn't say anything about it to Paddy, but I immediately thought back to the episode a few months ago when he just happened, coincidentally, to give me a bag with the book that I was at the time searching for: *Zen and the Art of Motorcycle Maintenance.*

Paddy paused to sip his tea, and that's when I tried to get him back to talking about *Inquiring Mind,* this publication he handed me before he segued into talking about buying *The Power of Now* in Montreal. I asked Paddy, "What about this old newspaper? Why do you want to show this to me? Is this "*Road News*" headline a reference to Kerouac?"

I could see that he did not want to get sidetracked into talking about something else, or thinking about something else, until he finished telling his Coles book store story to me. And it did not look like he quite knew what I was talking about, concerning Kerouac. But he soon segued back to the old newspaper again, anyway. He picked up *Inquiring Mind* from the table and with the excitement of the child within him, he said, "I haven't seen this paper in 23 years! Look at the date there: 'Summer, 1985.' When I got home from Montreal, Annick comes up to me with this paper. She says, 'Here, I found this, and I didn't want to throw it away on you.' And then I look in it, and the first page I come to, right here in these letters to the editor, is a letter that was written about meditation teachers and sex, and this is just what you and I were talking about. Didn't I just talk with you about this on Tuesday? How some of

41

these teachers are sitting in front of the Buddha, and they think they *are* the Buddha. But it can be any kind of teacher. You know what I'm saying? It could be a priest, or someone who teaches children. But you remember, we were talking about this, there's your synchronicity again. You got to read this letter. This letter is why I saved this paper 23 years ago. And that's what we were talking about Tuesday, when we were talking about synchronicity. And didn't I say, hey, 'when the student is ready the teacher will come, and when the reader is ready, the book will come,' when we were talking about these books you are reading – Kerouac's *Dharma Bums,* the Dali Lama book I gave you to read, *Four Noble Truths,* the Progoff synchronicity book…and what else?"

Paddy began rifling through the pages of *Inquiring Mind*, and he pointed out a few articles that he thought I would like reading later on. Then he stopped at a page with book reviews. He said, "Okay, here it is. Take a look at that. See what it says? It's a review of *A Course in Miracles.* That's what we talked about when you came up, what was it, day after New Year's? And we talked about it Tuesday, didn't we? See who wrote that review? It's Roger Walsh. You must read this, okay?"

Then Paddy paused to take a look at his cup of cold tea and to laugh. I asked him if he wanted his tea heated up, but he just continued on. "Roger Walsh is a friend of Winston, the guy I was skiing with this morning."

My reaction was delayed, because I was still computing the number of coincidences here, and I was still wondering if there was a Jack Kerouac connection that Paddy hadn't told me about yet. I questioned Paddy again about this. "What about Kerouac? Is that headline on the front page about Kerouac?"

Paddy refolded the newspaper and laid it down on the table, between us. I looked at the front page. The front page headline read: "*ROAD NEWS: An Interview with Allen Ginsberg about his Journey to China.*" While Paddy scanned the article, I noticed that this was Volume 2 Number 1 that we were looking at, and the *Inquiring Mind* was, "*A Journal of the Vipassana Community.*"

Paddy turned to page 15 of the publication, where the front page story continued. In big bold *italicized* letters on the top left of the page it said, "ROAD NEWS. *All the students want to study English and absorb Western Culture from Gregory Peck to Kerouac.*

Kerouac is considered a big hero. The official American literature textbook, edited in Chinese, with the English text, includes 50 pages of On the Road."

Kerouac, again; Coincidences, again; Synchronicities, encore.

Paddy said, "Jeezus! I didn't see there was anything in there about Kerouac! There it is again, *more* synchronicities! They just keep building on each other. The energy fields just keep building on each another."

To make a long story short, Paddy and I went on talking about these coincidences for a while, and then it was time for him to head out to ski. He picked up his coat from the floor and he was out the door almost as fast as he had decided it was time to go.

March 12, 2008

"I Meet My First Medicine Woman"

Dear Diary...Today I had what some might call, "a miraculous experience." What happened I can only compare to peak experiences in my life. Such as when I looked into the eyes of a newborn baby and saw what some might call, "the universe." What I experienced today was not as intense as that moment, but today I had a spiritual experience of communion, wholeness. Comprenez vous?

Today's little miracle occurred at the home of Gwen Beckett and Merlin The Magician. I took a drive over to their farm in the early afternoon. I wanted to talk to Gwen about the publication I've been thinking about doing – *possibly* doing, if it isn't going to be a time-consuming thing. I know Gwen has had some experience doing layout for newspapers, newsletters, journals. I thought she may have some interest or ideas for this project.

I also wanted to talk to Merlin about quantum physics, having read a book that he lent to me about a month ago, a book called *Quantum Questions*. This book is a collection of essays on mysticism, written by famous 20th century physicists – such as Einstein, and other Nobel Prize winners such as Max Planck, Max

Born, Erwin Shrodinger, and Carl Jung's chum, Wolfgang Pauli, who did some heavy thinking in collaboration with Jung on the subject of synchronicity.

When I got to Merlin and Gwen's I saw Merlin's truck there, but no one answered my knocks on the door of the house, and I could not find anyone in the barn or the greenhouse. Then the family dog, Sylvester, who is Nikola Tesla compared to Rin Tin Tin, came to fetch me and bring me around to the back of the barn, where I finally found Merlin, chain-sawing his way through a huge pile of logs, like a *Marvel Comics* superhuman. There were enough logs in this pile to build a small ski chalet. The logs were between 10 and 20 feet long, and stacked at least a meter over Merlin's head. But I could see that he wasn't going to build a chalet, he was cutting firewood. He has a wood burning stove in the house and he has a wood burning furnace that heats the green house and most of the barn. I didn't want to startle Merlin while the chainsaw was operating, so I purposely stayed out of his peripheral vision until he paused in his cutting, and then I called out to him: "Yo, Merlin! Wut it be?!"

It took a second for it to register with Merlin that Mario-Jacques from Long Island was back in Stafford, standing in front of him. He turned off the chain saw and he had to take off his surgical face mask to give me a big smile, in greeting. He was wearing a brown canvas one-piece coverall, speckled from his shoulders to his ankles with wood cuttings. Actually, he was head-to-foot in wood cuttings. His long white locks of hair, which normally hang down to his shoulders, were tied back in a pony-tail for safety reasons, and he was wearing what I later found out was a coal miners hat.

I said, with an exaggerated Brooklyn-Italian accent: "Hey man, I see you don't fool around when you decide to cut firewood."

Merlin gave me words of welcome and then, in typical Merlinesque fashion, he launched into a very thorough explanation of his log-cutting methodology. He was cutting the logs into lengths for splitting, which he and his son John would take care of in the next phase. Merlin explained that he adhered to a system in which he cut, piled, paused...cut, piled, paused...so that he could keep a steady pace, "without needlessly fatiguing any one muscle group, and without sweating in freezing air." Maybe he looked like The Madman Of Firewood, but there was a method to Merlin's madness, certainement. And I must add, a transcript of Merlin's explanation as to how he was going to cut through the mound of logs could be published in *The Whole New Earth Catalog,* and excerpts from that could be published as poetry in *Kenyon Review.*

Merlin rolled and then lit a cigarette while he was giving me his discourse, and when he finished the cigarette he decided it was time to take a longer break from the woodcutting and have a cup of tea with me. After making a stop at Merlin's wood shop – where I used the hose from Merlin's air compressor to blow wood cuttings off his coveralls and out of his hair – we went inside the house.

We went to Merlin's cozy low-ceilinged den. Merlin sat at his over-sized antique oak desk, the kind with many little drawers and hidden compartments. There is quite a view from Merlin's desk, in front of a large picture window that looks upon a meadow, then forest in the distance. Merlin asked me to stand beside him, to see the light cast by the sun on a large inukshuk in the meadow. He said he would tell me the story about this inukshuk at another time, because he understood that it was a priority for us to address quantum questions at this time.

I have known Merlin long enough to know that his discourse will flow free with his consciousness, but there is always something he is absorbed with that he wants to share with me. I could see that he and I were focused on the same thing tonight: the matter of quantum questions. I was intrigued by the inukshuk in the field – which looked like a work of art, and stood as tall as a human – but I did not want to distract Merlin from the quantum discussion by asking questions about the inukshuk.

I settled into an antique upholstered chair at the side of the desk, and soon had a cup of gentlemanly tea in my hand, made with leaves grown by Merlin.

Merlin turned his body slightly toward me, as a gesture of politeness, while he leaned over his desk and rolled a cigarette. Oddly enough, he was not using his own home grown tobacco, but a blend that he buys from an Abenaki friend. Having removed his coveralls when we entered the house, he was now dressed in his blue thermal long underwear, but still looked the gentleman of the manor in his comportment – dignified, with one leg folded over the other.

In a few minutes Merlin was lightly inhaling, and thinking deeply, and we got into a discussion about the *Quantum Questions* book, and the general subject of metaphysics. If Merlin is absorbed in his thoughts and you ask him, "How are you?" he is liable to bring you *deep* into his thoughts and launch into a dissertation on how the milky way is a remnant of galactic explosions, or start talking about changes in the polar orientations of planet Earth. So it didn't take long for Merlin to warm up in this philosophical discussion and really get going, full-speed, talking about his paradigm for the genesis and evolution of humankind on this planet. I had basically asked him to share his knowledge of quantum physics with me, so I more than welcomed listening to Merlin go on. J'adore écouter Merlin. To say the least, he challenges conventional wisdom. Mais oui, he's more than up to the challenge.

Merlin identifies me not only as a friend, but also as a pilgrim with an open mind. So he doesn't hold back his thoughts when we converse. In our discussion today Merlin did most of the talking and I did most of the listening. The degree to which my mind was stimulated was palpable. Endorphin levels up.

Merlin decided to roll a second cigarette, but switched from his tobacco blend to his cannabis blend. I noticed here another instance of Merlin challenging conventional wisdom. Merlin smokes tobacco without a filter, but makes a filter, or mouthpiece, for his marijuana joints. He rolls up a tiny piece of the cover from a matchbook, and inserts it into the end of his joint. I have not asked him about this yet.

After he finished rolling the joint, and before he could light it up, the house phone rang. It was Gwen, asking if Merlin remembered to put the chicken in the oven, and asking if Merlin could drive to pick up their son John at a friend's house, in 15 minutes. Merlin told Gwen that the chicken was in the pot and he told her that he would be able to fetch John.

While Merlin was talking to Gwen, there was a knock at the door. It was Aileen, a friend of Merlin and Gwen's, stopping by to say hello. She was wearing an ankle-length dark fur coat, suitable for opera or Québec mountain air. My best estimate is that Aileen is somewhere between 40 and 55 years old, it's hard to tell. She has long slick dark hair and a beautiful smile. And she has beautiful aqua blue eyes.

When Merlin introduced us and our eyes met for the first time, she looked at me as if she recognized me, or as if we were meeting as planned. But Aileen had not been invited to the house to meet me. And she had no advance knowledge from Merlin or Gwen that I would be there.

The three of us sat in the den for a few minutes, chatting. Then Merlin stood up to put his coveralls back on, and announced that he had to fetch John, but we were welcome to continue our stay until he returned, which he said would be in about a half-hour or so. By this time, only minutes after she had arrived, Aileen and I were feeling energized by each other as we conversed. So we told Merlin we would stay and wait for him to return.

Aileen soon told me that she was an Abenaki medicine woman! She said this in the same tone of voice that you would expect from someone identifying herself as an accountant. This incongruity was not lost on me, but if I were to have voiced my thoughts out loud, I would have responded: "Ah, of course you are an Abenaki medicine woman. Mais oui. I am surprised only for a quantum moment."

I told Aileen about how I discovered Stafford. Without going into much detail, I told her about feeling like I belonged in Stafford, that I fit in. She told me that she understood what I was feeling, experiencing, and I was quite taken by the depth of her understanding, although I cannot tell you what it was that she said to me that made me feel that way.

We talked for five or ten minutes and then she turned her chair and asked me if I would feel comfortable enough to turn my chair and move it closer to her, which I did. We sat directly face-to-face, an arms length from each other. She leaned forward and placed her hands very gently on top of mine, which were resting on the arms of my chair. Then she closed her eyes, as she removed her hands and leaned back in her chair. I closed my eyes. I stayed quiet, just listening, while she talked. I felt almost hypnotized by her words, but I know what it feels like to be hypnotized and this was different. Within a few minutes, there was a surge of sensations through my body, especially from the waist up, and I might have been frightened by what I was feeling, but the overall experience was as steadying as it was powerful. These sensations were intense psychophysically, as in sex, but this was not a sexual or erotic experience by any means. There was a profound emotional intensity to what I was experiencing, but this was not accompanied by any muscular tension. I can't say that I felt light-headed, but my body felt light. But this was not an out-of-body experience. I was basically in a state *similar* to a hypnotic state. Which would not have been possible had I not felt such trust in Aileen, this medicine woman that I had just met for the first time.

Even though my overall experience of sitting with Aileen is something I will never forget, I can only recreate from my memory a few bits and pieces of what happened, and what she said to me. She told me that I had been drawn to Stafford for a reason, and that I belonged in Stafford. She told me that she knew I was spiritual and that I was here to share myself, my spirit. She said Stafford was a safe place for me, away from a world where more difficult times were ahead, and that Stafford would be a place where my loved ones, my family, would be able to come and be safe. She said I did not have to think very much about what to do, that it was time for me to allow my spirituality to guide me. And she said I should meditate every day.

The most striking of her words came near the end, as is often the case in life. She said to me: "When you are near the end of your meditation, ask the universe what you can do for it, and look for the answer to come to you during the day." Then she softly repeated, in slightly different words: "Ask the universe a question, and the universe will answer you."

I don't remember if Aileen told me that there was no more to say, or if the long silence told me to open my eyes. I remember feeling good tears in my eyes when I opened them, and I said: "Thank you."

I'm not sure how long we sat together from that point until Gwen arrived. It was probably between ten and fifteen minutes. We stayed in *The Now*.

When Gwen walked in she was as excited as a puppy dog to see us. She said, "Well hello to both of you! Merlie's voice kept cutting out when I spoke to him on my cell phone. He modified my cell phone for better reception and I think he made it worse. I heard something about Aileen and Mario being here, and here you are, the both of you! My calls get cut out completely when I get close to where Bailey crosses Hall. I don't know what it is. I am jinxed when it comes to cell phones and the Internet. The only thing I understood was that Merlin was on the way to pick up John. That part was clear enough. But I didn't know whether Mario from New York had left the house, or was coming later. And I wasn't sure if Merlin said *you* would be here Aileen, or if he said you were coming here later, or *not* coming here…oh, forget it. Anyway, the two of you now know each other I presume? I'm sure you both found each other to be interesting?"

Aileen and I both replied "yes" and we both opened our eyes wider, to accentuate the point. I added, "I just had one of the most…intense experiences of my life."

14 Juillet 2008

"On The Road Encore"

Came up from East End Bay to la ville de Stafford aujourd'hui. On the way, a huge strip of a tractor-trailer tire smashed into the windshield of my car. I was about three hours into the trip and driving on I-91, somewhere in Massachusetts, maybe a half-hour south of Springfield. A driver cut in front of me, after passing me on the right, and he immediately drove over this fairly large piece of a truck tire. This piece, which had to be four or five feet long, kicked up on the windshield of my car. I had no time to react or to get scared, because it was over as fast as it happened. The brunt of the impact from the tire was taken by the portion of my car between the windshield, on my side, and the window of my door. But part of the tire also hit near the middle of the windshield. If the tire had hit maybe two feet closer to the passenger side, I believe it would have gone right through the window. I flinched down in my seat, but kept my eyes on the road, and I did not break hard, because I did not want to lose control of the car.

Encore, I didn't have time to be frightened. And I saw no need to pull over to the side of the road right away. I drove for another hour after the windshield got cracked, and then stopped for gas where I normally do, at Robert's, in Greenfield, Mass. I bought a calling card at Robert's and then I spent a good part of an hour on the phone in the parking lot, with my insurance agent in New York, who ultimately advised me to lay out the money to get the windshield fixed in Québec and then present the paid bill to the insurance company when I return to New York. That's what I decided to do.

When I got to White River Junction in Vermont I decided to go the rest of the way on 91, rather than cross over to I-89, as I normally do. I thought I would get to Stafford faster through I-91. Anyway, as I drove, the cracks on the windshield kept spreading. Fortunately, my vision was not impaired enough to prevent me from driving the car for the last six sloooow hours of the trip to Stafford. My greatest concern was getting pulled over by a state trooper. I thought I might get a ticket or be compelled to stop driving the car in this condition.

While I was driving, the experience brought to mind a story from a few years ago, of a woman from Ronkonkoma, Long Island, who suffered injuries – mainly facial injuries, that hospitalized her for months, and I believe required some plastic surgery –after a *frozen supermarket turkey* smashed through the windshield of her car. In Québec you have to be concerned about having an accident with a moose; On Long Island you have to be more concerned about having an accident with a frozen supermarket turkey. The frozen turkey was tossed out the window of a car that was in front of this poor woman, by some pranking kids.

Perhaps the frozen turkey story is about a culture in decline, perhaps it is about forgiving these kids, or perhaps it is about both. It is not a great mythological turkey story, like the story of pilgrims and quote-unquote "Indians" eating turkey together. But the frozen turkey story came to mind after my windshield was smashed by the tractor trailer tire. I hope that truck was not delivering frozen turkeys to a Wal-Mart.

In any case, I had left East End Bay at 9h and I had expected to get to Stafford by 17h. As it turned out, I got in a little after 19h, feeling dog-tired. But I already have it arranged with my insurance company. I just have to get the windshield replaced here in Québec, pay the bill, and bring the receipt back to New York. I'm thinking that the best place to go would be Cowansville Toyota.

15 Juillet 2008

"A Zen Walk To Lac Frog"

Got back from Cowansville and Knowlton in the late morning, after running errands. Then I took a hike with Paddy to Lac Frog. He led, at his pace. The thing is, Paddy does not know what the word, "octogenarian," means.

We hit the trail juste après 12h. I was a little concerned about the path being muddy and slippery in some places. Juste before we entered the woods, Paddy said to me, "It's good that the path is going to be slippery in some spots. It will help us to be more mindful." Juste to make sure that I understood, he added: "You realize which path I'm talking about…"

I replied simply, "Oui, monsieur."

"*'Watch your breath, watch your step.'* That's a sign they should put up here, eh Mario-Jacques? *'Watch your breath, watch your step.'* Hey, that's a pretty good idea," Paddy decided. If Paddy was in charge of the mountain trails, that's the sign you would see next to the ones that tell you how many kilometers are left to get to Lac Frog, or to Tip Top.

I said to Paddy, "I like it. That is *actually* a good idea. C'est une bonne idée, Paddy. They could create a, 'zen walk,' up here."

Before we started on the first leg of the trails, Paddy checked the zippers on his backpack, adjusted some straps, and seemed to make an adjustment to his choppers, his teeth. Then he continued, "Yeah, that *is* a good idea, isn't it, Mario-Jacques? You could take *the path with heart* up to Tip-Top. Every once in a while there would be a sign that says, *'watch your breath, watch your step,'* or, *'be mindful,'* or, *'stay in the present.'* Of course, for the people who come down from Montreal you'd have to have signs that say, *'stay in the present, you stupid ass, or you're going to twist your ankle, or get lost.'*" He laughed at his jokes, as Paddy likes to do.

I just kept repeating, "Bonne idée Paddy, bonne idée."

Not so annoyed, more to offer his wit, Paddy eventually said, "You going to keep speaking to me in French, Mario-Jacques?"

I said, "I need to practice my French, Paddy. Unlike you, a man who has been married to a francophone for 50 years, and does not speak French other than to say, 'pooh-tit,' once in a while, I'm trying to learn."

Paddy replied, a little defensively, "I can speak some French. There isn't much I need to know. But I can get by, if I have to speak in French."

Trying to get a more serious reflection from him, I said, "I'm surprised you don't speak more French than you do, especially since Annick is a francophone. Even if she is bilingual."

He said, "Sais pas, Mario-Jacques." Then Paddy changed the subject. "Okay, we've got to get serious now. In fact, I'm going to get *real* serious now, I'm going to re-do the rubber band in my pony-tail." Encore, his boyish octogenarian giggle.

I watched Paddy let down his hippyish, shamanesque, Abenaki-ish, silver-gray hair. I commented: "You could make some pocket change on week-ends by being a native guide here."

Paddy replied, "A *native* guide? You're trying to be politically correct, professor? If I was going to be a guide on a, 'zen walk,' I would really be an *Indian* guide, wouldn't I? A *real* Indian. If we're talking about Buddha. Right? Or maybe I would be Tibetan. "

I said, "C'est vrai. That's true. Just don't forget that you are very much a, 'spiritual native,' of Mount Stafford."

Paddy thought about that for a second, then gave me his laugh, and said, "Am I a, '*spiritual* native,' of Mount Stafford? That would mean my spirit was born here. No, my spirit wasn't born on Mount Stafford. You got me thinking now, Mario-Jacques. I wonder what my face looked like before I was born."

He put the palms of his hands together, fingers pointed up, and looked toward the sky, as if he was about to begin a prayer. "Maybe it won't rain while we're up here. I don't think it will." Then, looking back to me, he said: "Have you noticed that you've brought the sun with you every time you've come to Stafford this year?"

I replied, "Mais oui. I've noticed that, Paddy. But only for the first day that I'm in town. Then it rains. It's been raining non-stop since April, hasn't it?"

Paddy said, "Yeah, that's right. That's why they've put a lot of rocks on the trails, and more planks. The puddles, you know. Be mindful of slippery rocks. In fact, just be mindful." I made sure that

Paddy saw I was looking at him mindfully, with my eyes opened wider. He ignored my humour and added, "... speaking about being mindful, you said you wanted this to be a meditation walk. You remember the mantra, 'Om Mani Padme Hum?' Just remember, six syllables: *'Ohm – mah – nee – pahd – may – hum.'* Maybe the universe will give us a clear path and we won't slip, or if we slip we won't get hurt too bad, twist an ankle or something."

I tried to stay within three or four strides of Paddy as we made our way up the path. As I walked, I slowly repeated to myself: *"Om mani padme hum, om mani padme hum…"*

Paddy sometimes increased his pace and walked a distance ahead of me, then he'd step off the path to relieve his prostrate, bit by bit I guess. He had it timed so that by the time he had finished peeing, we would be together again on the path. We talked juste un peu, until we got up to Frog Lake, which took us a little over an hour.

When we got to the lake we stopped and stood on the wooden platform, a resting place for hikers. This platform is about 20 feet around, and when you are standing on it you have a great view of the entire lake. The lake is about the size of athletic field – peut-être 400 feet wide, and maybe 600 feet long from the platform to the distant end, where the lake water emerges from streams that flow down from higher up on Mount Stafford. The platform stands about 20 feet above the lake, and about 20 feet away from the water – which is filled with thousands of lily pads this time of year, and je ne sais pas how many frogs, but there are a lot there. And some of them are bigger than any frogs I've ever seen. I would imagine that one of those big frogs could be a meal, though je ne sais pas how edible frogs are, beyond their legs. Anyway, the frogs are part of the beauty of this très belle lake. At certain times, when the blue-green Mount Stafford light is cast on the lake, the setting is une peinture de Monet.

The platform has a roof that covers half of it, to provide some shelter and shade. There is also a simple wooden bench built into the railing. No picnic table. C'est vrai. There is no picnic table! To a quebecer, the fact that there is no picnic table is not, at premiere thought, noteworthy. Mais, to me, an Americain-Quebecer, the fact that there is no picnic table is une omission apparente. I said to Paddy, "No picnic table! I can't believe it!"

Paddy's absent-minded reply was: "No picnic table. No, no picnic table. Yeah, maybe they should put a table up here." I noticed he was looking down at the large rocks near the water, where a few hikers were resting, sunbathing. Rather than focusing on the lack of a picnic table at the lake, his thoughts were there, with the sunbathers. Perhaps most specifically on the 20-something year old woman whose legs looked like they were well-toned from doing a lot of mountain hiking.

I repeated: "No picnic table, Paddy." And added, "This is really *un-American* here, Paddy. There's no picnic table, no concession stand, no Coca-Cola signs."

No response from Paddy. I am learning that people don't talk that much while they're hiking on Mount Stafford, and they don't talk much while they pause at Frog Lake. Noise est une autre omission apparente at Frog Lake. People come up to the lake for a view of pristine nature and because it is tranquille. I was thinking about this when I heard an animal sound that I had never heard before, and which I thought might be the sound of a large animal, perhaps a moose, or a bear. Paddy informed me that the sound I was hearing was the croaking of a bullfrog. And he took the opportunity to rub it in a little bit. "Mario-Jacques, why do you think they call it, 'Frog Lake,' and not, 'Moose Lake,' or, 'Bear Lake?'"

I said, "Mais oui. But I have to tell you Paddy, I've never heard frogs croak like that. How big are the frogs here, 65 pounds?"

Paddy said, "No, they're just regular size frogs. I'll show you. Let's walk down to the beach."

This gave me pause. "The, *'beach?'*" I asked.

"Yeah, the beach. Right there," Paddy said, pointing in the direction of the rocks and marshland. To me, the *'beach'* is where there is salt water, waves, sand. Mais, I didn't say anything about this to Paddy. I couldn't if I wanted to anyway, because he was on his way down the steps to the 'beach' and already in conversation with someone there.

I decided to stay on the platform and take in the view of the lake from there. This is a view of nature with no touch from humans apparent. The lake is surrounded by thick forest, and the only clearing of any size is at the narrow part of the lake, where the platform stands. Aside from the part of the lake nearest the platform, the lake is filled with lily pads, and also fallen trees and tiny islands.

Beneath the platform it is all one large rock slab, and that's where people sunbathe and enter the lake to swim. Two girls, teenagers, were takng a swim there. They spoke Français to each other and to the people who were sitting on the rocks. There were six people spread out on the rocks, and all were speaking Français.

I was surprised to see Paddy begin a conversation with a man by speaking French. Paddy's French accent is worse than mine. J'espere. Though Paddy and the man he was talking to began their conversation en Français, in a few minutes they were both speaking anglais. Which I see as another instance of French accommodating an Anglophone. Which, from my observations, seems to happen a lot in this part of Québec, the Eastern Townships. I suspect the Anglophones of Québec would not agree with me about this, but this is what I see.

I sat myself down cross-legged on the floor of the deck, and just enjoyed the warmth of the sun emanating from the deck to my body, and the feel of the sun on my face. I alternated between meditating and looking out on the lake. I did this for about 15 minutes, until Paddy came back up on the deck, to get a fresh bottle of water out of his backpack.

I said to Paddy, "Okay, I can see there are plenty of frogs here, but I'm surprised the lake does not have a French name."

Paddy replied, "What do you mean? It has a French name: 'Frog Lake.' That's French. You can't get any more French than that, eh?" Encore, Paddy laughed at his joke. Octo giggles.

As dryly as possible, I said: "Very funny."

Paddy took a few more sips from his bottle of water, then went back down to the rocks, to continue his conversation there. I stayed on the platform, stayed in the moment, enjoying the surroundings. I took notice of the fact that there was no litter on the beach. Not on the rocks, where I could see a couple of people eating slices of apple and drinking bottled water. Not anywhere on the beach or in the waters of the lake did I see a single piece of food wrapping, or a Styrofoam cup, or a discarded container of any kind. I looked around for a garbage pail, half-expecting that I would find one brimming over with trash, as is commonplace in the culture I am most familiar with, in New York. Bien sur, there was no garbage pail in sight. Then I remembered, bien sur, the signs at the entry to the trails – where Paddy would like to see a sign that says: "*Watch your breath, watch your step."* There was a sign at the entry that said hikers were expected to bring back with them anything they brought on to the mountain, including trash. Hence, no need for garbage pails on the mountain. Try that in the culture I'm most familiar with, in New York. Et bonne chance.

16 Juillet 2008

"Une Amie À Cowansville Toyota"

I got over to Cowansville Toyota promptly at 8h30m, the appointed time for my car's windshield to be replaced, and I was given a loaner car to use for the day. This was especially helpful because I was able to drive over to Knowlton, where I bought un ordinateur. Aside from that, and a stop at the IGA in Stafford, I kept the loaner car parked at the chalet all day.

I went back to Cowansville environ 15h to pick up my car. Le service femme extraordinaire, Giselle, informed me that she had ordered a new side-view mirror for my car and they could install it first thing Friday morning, if I could get there early. And she told me that it would take peut-être 45 minutes to do the job. I said, "D'accord, merci."

Giselle told me that my French was, "formidable!" I felt formidable that I understood what "formidable" meant.

While Giselle was typing at her ordinateur, I assumed she was preparing my bill for the replaced windshield. But she was working on something else, and she continued to chat with me at the same time. After a few minutes passed and she had not handed me a bill, I said: "How much do I owe you for today?"

Giselle said, "Oh, the cost to replace the windshield was 349$, I think."

I said, "Did you make up a bill? I'll pay it now."

She said, "I have a bill, but you might as well pay me after we replace your mirror, on Friday."

Encore, *Un Moment de Quèbecois.* She was letting me walk out without paying for the work that was *already done!* And she had put in a *special order* for my side view mirror without asking for a deposit! *No* deposit! And I am from another country. Another country!

If I was in New York and I wanted to put five dollars worth of gas in my car without paying in advance, I would have to leave my credit card, or a child who I could prove was closely related to me, avec the cashier. This is a statement of fact, without exaggeration.

Vive la difference à Québec. I looked at the sign on the wall behind Giselle. It said: *"Nous voulons gagner votre confiance...We want to earn your trust."* You see signs like that a lot here in Québec, even in car repair shops. In New York, in the region near New York City, you are more likely to see the familiar sign: *"In God We Trust, all others pay cash."*

18 Juillet 2008

"Noticing Nouvelle Terre In Quebec"

Went back to Cowansville Toyota this morning. Read some of Eckhart Tolle's *A New Earth* in the waiting room. When I was leaving I noticed a woman who was paying her bill who had a copy of *Nouvelle terre* sticking out of her pocket book. Five minutes later, I stopped at Tim Hortons across the road and I saw a man sitting at a table with a copy of *Nouvelle terre* in front of him. Especially since the book was published a few years ago, it strikes me as quite a coincidence that this book would show up like this, on my path in this little corner of the world.

25 Juillet 2008

"Plus Synchronicity Avec Gaston Briere"

Hung avec Gaston Briere à la galerie Bleu. Gaston and environ six other artistes are operating la galerie de l'art on Rue Principal as a cooperative. To keep the costs down, and to boost sales, each of les artistes share la responsabilité to cover the hours of operation. Gaston has a break in his schedule at Vista Films, so he's covering la galerie for three days this week. He will work a lot of days in the summer et probablement the early fall, so that he won't have to cover the hours once he starts directing a new film at Vista.

Gaston drove from Montreal to Abercorn last night in a heavy rain, and he did not get to Sandi's chalet on Scenic Road until close to midnight. Sandi is in Toronto on a business trip, but she is going to join Gaston on the week-end. It's been a while since Gaston and I have been able to talk at any length in-person, so today was an opportunity for us to sit together for a few hours.

I got to la galerie environs 13h. I brought my laptop with me and set it up on Gaston's desk in the back of la galerie. Gaston sat beside me at the desk, and got up when visitors came in, which was fairly infrequent on this rainy day. I never did do any writing while I was there, save for peut-être three ou four sentences, which I later deleted. But Gaston and I were able to talk and catch up with each other.

I talked to Gaston about my writing moving along slowly, parce que I have not been able to seclude myself enough to write, probablement. And we talked about the wonderful evolution in the art Gaston is creating. He is creating a new genre – yet unnamed – and expanding on what he is doing within that genre.

Une peinture en particulaire, a painting that Gaston just finished, caught my eye. This is a painting I might buy. This painting shows a sun-filled bedroom in a mountain country chalet, somewhere in Québec, je pense. It looks like it could be a scene out of an animated film for adults, if every film cell was rendered by a high-quality artist, as Gaston is. The colours in this painting have the striking vibrancy that is trademark Gaston Briere, but what I like most about this painting is the paintings *within* the painting, which are shown on the walls of the bedroom. Each one of those paintings is about a chapter in a larger story, je pense.

A story is being narrated in this painting, and the story is a love story. Mais oui, this painting seems to be part of a romance that Gaston is telling in a series of paintings. I told Gaston that it looked to me like this could be a scene taken from a very different kind of animated movie. He responded that he could understand why I am thinking this and he told me that it all probably came out of his subconscious mind, because he had no intention of telling a story. In any case, I would love to hear what a recognized art critic has to say about Gaston's work. That has not happened yet.

Gaston told me that the owner of une galerie in Toronto saw les peintures à la galerie Bleu and he and Gaston worked out a deal so that he will be showing some of Gaston's nouvelles peintures at the galerie in Toronto.

I was itching to buy one of Gaston's peintures mais I don't have the extra $ now. I decided to settle for buying three postcards that reproduce peintures Gaston has done. Gaston would not let me pay for the postcards, but I told him I would buy him a coffee at le Boni-Soir dep if he would autograph the cards for me. Instead of autographing the cards, he wrote an inscription on each of the cards. On one card he wrote: "Nul n'est prophète en sons pays." On another he wrote out, en français, words of Victor Hugo that Gaston knows I like to paraphrase: « *Il existe une chose plus puissante que toutes les armées du monde, c'est une idée dont l'heure est venue.* » Traduction: "*All the armies in the world are not as strong as an idea whose time has come.*" The two versions are not exactly the same, word for word, but Gaston assures me that he used a valid quote of Victor Hugo.

Here's the punch line – which is a knockout synchronicity punch line. I had a piece of paper in my shirt pocket with that very quotation on it, written en anglais. I was planning to stop at Defpotek later in the afternoon, to ask my friend Lieve if she could make one of her calligraphy creations for me with those words. I was going to ask Lieve to translate those words to French, which Gaston had already done.

After I read what Gaston wrote, I took out the piece of paper from my shirt pocket and showed it to him. He said: "Mario-Jacques, this is amazing. You've really got me thinking about synchronicity. I think I should call you, 'Monsieur Synchronicity.'"

14 Aout 2008

"Different Hikes, Different Mantras"

For the last week I have been hiking on the mountain for two hours every morning and two hours every night. I've been taking Ben Franklin's advice – it has been early to bed and early to rise. I have been waking up before dawn, with much energy.

As per Paddy's advice, I am maintaining the intention of staying in The Now. As per Paddy's advice, while I am hiking I often repeat the mantra: "Om Mani Padme Hum."

I want to keep up the walking when I get back to New York in a couple of weeks. Bien sur, I know I won't be able to walk as much, or as peacefully, when I'm in New York. I will have to be mindful of being menaced by New York drivers on the roads where I hike. Paddy says I may have to change my mantra in New York from, "Om Mani Padme Hum," to: "May my heart be filled with loving kindness."

25 Aout 2008

"Inukshuk Synchronicity"

Took care of loose ends, détails, in preparation for returning to East End Bay demain. Knowing I would be up early, Paddy phoned me at 7h to wish me un bon voyage. He told me that he wouldn't be able to see me today, parce que he had to go to Montreal to look in on his mother. She's going to be 104 this week, and Paddy wants to have une petite birthday party for her, mais now he was squabbling avec her, parce que she did not want any fussing about her birthday.

I was hoping to have a cup of café avec Gaston this morning, mais when I called him on his cell phone environ 8h he was on his way back to Montreal already, and sitting in traffic at the Champlain Bridge. Mais, he was in bons spiriteux, parce que he had sold a painting at l'art show in Waterloo on Sunday. He told me, aussi, that durant his drive to Waterloo he saw an inukshuk in an open field that inspired him to pull over to the side of the road and photograph it. He told me that when he got to Waterloo he set up an easel to paint, which is something he normally does not like to do durant exhibitions, mais he felt so motivated to paint this inukshuk.

It turned out that he literally sold le peinture before the paint was dry on the canvas. The thing is, Gaston said that he woke up this morning avec another thought about un autre inukshuk peinture. Et voila: synchronicity. Parce que he had turned on the radio while he was having his morning café, and he heard a story about inukshuks. Juste a few days ago he didn't know la différence between an inukshuk and a nicely arranged pile of rocks. Stay tuned.

East End Bay, NY
September 4, 2008

"A Hockey Mom For Vice-President?"

Last night I saw Palin speak on television, at the Republican National Convention. This woman has been designated to run for Vice-President of the United States of America, and she is so unknown that even the man who chose her as his running mate – Republican candidate for President, John McCain – had only met her once or twice before selecting her, just ahead of the convention. I assume he can remember her first name. I can't. Bien sûr, my short-time memory isn't the greatest in the world, mais je suis certain most people in the U.S.A do not know her first name, or her last name. Yet.

Many of the delegates were holding up handmade signs that said: "Hockey Mom for V.P." If they had held up signs that said, "I am from La-La Land," I would not have been more surprised by their willingness to participate in such a massively bad joke. A *"hockey mom"* for Vice President of what is probably the most powerful institution in the world? A *"hockey mom"* for Vice-President of a government that alters the fate of humanity by what it chooses to do or not do? If delegates had held up signs that read, "Harvard Grad for V.P." they would have been ridiculed. Alors, what comes to mind is what H.L. Mencken said in the early part of the 20th century – something like: *No one has ever gotten poor by underestimating the intelligence of the people in the United States.* Encore, can so many people be this ignorant? ... What comes to mind is the fact that George W. Bush was elected President two times.

I phoned Henri to find out if he watched the convention last night on the Internet, and what he thought about Palin's performance. Henri's first words on le sujet were: "Do the Republicans have a mandatory dress code for the delegates, Mario? Just about every man there was wearing a suit and tie. I mean, they were dressed for church in the 1950's. I'm surprised the women weren't wearing hats, veils, and gloves. And they all had these smiles pasted on their faces. Talk about not getting it. The Titanic has already hit an iceberg and the Republicans just keep smiling."

I said to Henri, "If McCain wins, I will dedicate myself to learning French, so I can apply for Canadian citizenship. I'll move to Granby for a while. Or I'll move to Charlevoix. I'll move somewhere where I'll have to parle Francais if I want to eat."

East End Bay, NY
October 2, 2008

"Papillon"

Dear Diary...This is one of those days in which I feel an urge to write while I am not in Stafford Qc, but on Long Island, in East End Bay.

J'ai parlé ce soir avec Angela's mother, Lynne, au téléphone. I called parce que I will be going up to Stafford la semaine prochaine

62

et je veux to bring Angela's ashes avec moi, mais I had not yet received them dans le courrier.

The first words out of Lynne's mouth, after she recognized me as the caller, were: "Hi Professor! I was just thinking about you! I was going to call *you*. It must be synchronicity."

She told me that she had already put Angela's ashes in the mail, juste il y a deux jours. We talked briefly environ le sujet de ashes et then we discussed plans for setting up a scholarship in Angela's name. Then we got on to le sujet that Lynne had intended to call me about.

She said, "I've been thinking about you so much, wanting to phone you, but I've been so busy, packing everything up for the move to North Carolina. I was going to phone you tonight, not only to make sure you had my e-mail address, but to tell you about what has happened in the last week. It's all about Angela and synchronicity. It made me think about you. And this is more synchronicity, to get this phone call from you." As she was saying this to me, I could hear la mélancolie in her voice turn to a kind of subdued excitement, the joyless excitement of a mother in mourning.

She added, for emphasis, "I've been wanting to tell you about this since it happened, last week. If you hadn't called me, I would've called *you*...Another synchronicity...Would you like to hear about this? Do you have time for this now, Professor?"

Lynne's voice on the phone sounded so much like the voice of my dear student, her dear daughter, Angela. The similarity struck an emotional chord in me. Quietly, avec a voice that betrayed my intention to speak evenly, I said to Lynne, "I hear Angela in your voice. There is a similar sound and cadence...and I hear the same kindness in your voice. You sound like who you are: the mother of Angela."

Lynne replied, "Ah, you are so kind. Angela talks about you all the time, she thinks so highly of you." I noticed, mais did not comment on Lynne's reference to Angela in the present tense.

She continued, "I'm finding synchronicity in a lot of little things, but I want to tell you about this one thing that happened. I was in Angela's room and I was reading one of her magazines – I think it's called *Soul and Body,* or *Spirit and Body*. It's one of Angela's yoga magazines, you know what I mean? I was reading one of the stories, which I was reading because I wanted to read what

Angela was reading, trying to be closer to her, you know. I won't even go into what the story was about, but it meant a lot to me to read it, and it was helping me to feel close to her, but at the same time I was missing her. Then, at the end of the story, it said, in big, big letters: 'I WILL COME TO YOU AS A BUTTERFLY.' I read that sentence, but didn't think much of it Professor, except that it had something to do with the story – but I won't go into that now. But I was a little weepy, and I said to myself: 'You better get yourself into counseling when you get down to North Carolina.' So I went on the Internet and I looked up counseling centers in North Carolina, near the town I'm going to be moving to in a few days, which is near Wilmington, North Carolina. Two counseling places were listed. Guess what one of them was called? I bet you can guess it."

I said, "I don't know. 'Synchronicity Counseling Center?'"

Lynne said, "No, but that's a very good guess, and you'll see why when I tell you the name...Do you want me to tell you?"

Anxiously but evenly, I replied, "Yes, for sure."

Lynne continued, "The first counseling center listed was the *Butterfly Counseling Center.* Isn't that something? As soon as I saw that, I had this wonderful feeling run through me. I felt like Angela was reaching out to me, coming to me as a butterfly. I felt such a comfort. I thought about you, because we had talked about synchronicity."

I said, "Oh, my gosh. That's certainly a case of synchronicity."

She continued, "Wait Professor, there's more. The next day I was visiting with my daughter, Corrine, at Angela's father's house, that's near here, in the Adirondacks, and I told him about this. I could see that this got Angela's father thinking, but it was more like he was happy for *me*, you know what I mean? He just looked at it like it was a good coincidence that made me feel good. Ron doesn't have...he doesn't have...the feeling inside him...*faithfulness*. You know what I mean? He's very angry, and he's hurting, you know?"

I said, "I know. When I last spoke to him on the phone, to talk about the scholarship for Angela, he couldn't talk too much, because his emotions were weighing him down. We spoke for only a few minutes, but heart-to-heart. His pain was transmitted."

Lynne said, "He likes you. He told me that. He knows Angela thought so highly of you. He knows you gave her something special."

I said, "I feel like *she* is the one who gave to me."

Lynne continued, "I know Angela touched you, as she touched others. That touch is going to be felt by others, as it is passed on by you, and by others. You *know* what I mean. This is what I was talking to her father about, when I was telling him about the butterfly. Then, while I was telling him this, I looked up at this picture that he has on the wall of his living room, that's a picture of Angela and her sister, Corrine. From where I was sitting, the light was shining on the picture so that I could only see Angela and what was on the wall behind her in the picture, you know what I mean? I couldn't see Corrine in the picture, only Angela. There was Angela in the picture, and on the wall behind her, a part of the picture, was a butterfly. I got up and said, 'Look Ron, look at that. While we're talking about this, I'm noticing for the first time that there's a *butterfly* in that picture, right over Angela's shoulder. She's coming to me, and to you, as a butterfly.'"

Lynne paused, to let this sink in and to let me have a chance to say something about it. I wanted her to continue, so I just said, "Another meaningful coincidence. Synchronicity."

She continued. "He saw the coincidence and it had him thinking a little, but I guess he was not ready to receive this yet. But I have to tell you Professor what is maybe the most amazing part of the story. Ron left the next day to go up to New Brunswick. He has a cottage there. This is a house that has been in his family for a long time. I think you know Angela was talking about living there in the future, because she loves Canada so much. We are going to go up there to spread her ashes, next year. We're thinking about January, or maybe April. Some of Angela's friends, and some of your other students, are going to go up there next year, when we do this. We hope you will come too, if you are able to do that. Ron talked about having you go up there the other day, when I saw him. "

"Anyway, he goes to New Brunswick whenever he needs to get away and find peace. After I talked to him about the butterfly synchronicity, a couple of days after that, he decided to drive up to New Brunswick. He phoned and told me that while he was driving up there, going through Maine, he started to think about Angela, and he had to stop driving, he had to pull over on the side of the road, because he was crying. So, he pulled off the road and parked his SUV and took a walk down to this beach. He was missing Angela and he was feeling like this would help him, to walk on the beach. He knew that Angela used to love the beach so much. He was walking on the beach and he was feeling bad, because he wanted to be walking on the beach with Angela. You know, these were the sorts of feelings he was having. He started to walk back toward his truck, and he has tears in his eyes, so he can hardly see, and then he sees a butterfly in the air, struggling against the wind, flying toward him. The butterfly flutters around him, like it's paying him a visit, then flies away – high, high, high up in the air until it's out of his sight."

Lynne paused, perhaps to give me a chance to respond, or perhaps so she could restore herself, because I heard her take a deep breath.

I said, "I don't know much about butterflies, but isn't it unusual to find butterflies on the beach? How did Ron react to this?"

"He called me on his cell phone, as soon as he got back in his truck. But he's still thinking, even now, as far as I know, that it's just a nice coincidence. I don't know Professor, maybe you can understand these things. I *feel* Angela's presence, I *can see* the way she is reaching out to let us know that she is with us. She is coming to us as a butterfly. But he can't see this yet. He is still so distrught. Maybe you can talk to him, so that he can see this."

I said, "He will see what there is to see when he's ready to see it, right? I don't know, exactly, right now, what I could say to him. But Ron and I will be speaking again before too long, I'm sure."

Lynne and I exchanged our e-mail addresses, and she gave me some other mailing addresses and phone numbers, where I would be able to contact her, or her ex-husband. She reiterated her confidence that I would get Angela's ashes in the mail within the next day or two. Then we said au revoir gently to each other.

When I got off the phone avec Lynne I went into the bathroom. I was thinking about the butterfly synchronicity story, the mounting of meaningful coincidences, one after another. On the shelf above the bathroom sink, which is rarely used by anyone other than myself, I found something that was not there before. It was a piece of jewelry, une petite pin. A butterfly. Un papillon!

8 Octobre 2008

"Depression Radio"

As soon as I finished teaching my sociologie class yesterday afternoon, I got in my car and headed out for Stafford. At 21h, when the Obama/McCain debate got   underway, I was on I-89 in Vermont, juste past White River Junction, et a couple of hours from Stafford. Normally, I fill up my gas tank in Greenfield Mass., et drive for a couple of hours before I stop prochaine in Randolph, Vermont, off I-89. I still had not reached Randolph at 21h, mais I decided that I would not stop encore jusqu'a après the debate. I can usually time when I will get to Stafford within 15 minutes, so I figured that I would be stopping for gas at the Pinnacle Peddler in Richford, Vermont, before 23h – their closing time, je pense.

Quite an experience to listen to this historic debate while driving through the Dark Mountains of Vermont. Et it was dark, *vraiment noir*, as the mountain roadway was lighted only by a prophetic half moon, et there were few cars and trucks traveling at the time. It was comme une scene de un film noire. I had a sense of what it must have been like in rural America during The Great Depression, to turn one's ear to a radio and listen with great care to the words of an FDR.

I had to fiddle avec le radio as I drove through les montagnes. I switched from one AM station to another, trying to listen to the broadcast avec a minimum of static. What came through loud et clear was that Barack Obama sounded like un nouveau Franklin Delano Roosevelt et John McCain sounded like an old, et une noire, Sarah Palin.

McCain was pathetic. I was feeling a bit sorry for him at times. Mais his blind aggressiveness blunted that emotion within me. Et Barack Obama presented himself as the person this world needs to be the President of the United States.

The contrast between McCain and Obama could not have been any clearer if it had come out of a script written to be a farce. McCain spoke to an audience that he apparently visualizes as naive children, or hate-filled people, or people carrying serious dysfunctions from their childhoods. My sense is that McCain is no different than the audience that is his often-referred-to, "base." No matter how gray, McCain & his basest base are essentially immature, hate-filled, dysfunctional. And they know not that they know not. Quintessential fools, waving flags and marching into battle for hamburgers and freedom fries. Bien sûr, these people are characterized on FOXNews as patrioitic and god-loving Americans.

Bien sûr, the Canadian election for Prime Minister will be carried out in Octobre, a couple of weeks avant the presidential election in the states. Harper, a conservative in Canada – and a Mahatma Gandhi compared to his republican counterparts in the states – is favored to be re-elected, mais stay tuned on that one, as a coalition could change the outcome at the 11th hour, non? Regardless of what changes come forth after the Canadian election, the system of government is not going to be appreciably altered. Je ne pense pas. Mais, in the states, if Obama wins, health care will be considered a citizen's right, and if McCain wins, health care will be considered a citizen's responsibility.

At this point, j'espere, je pense, je crois, I've got my fingers crossed, that McCain sealed his defeat during the debate, when he could not find a way to talk around the question of whether health care is a citizen's right, or a citizen's responsibility. If McCain had held true to form, he would have answered immediately (like a, "Real Man," in the fantasy world that McCainittes live in): "*Health care is both a right and a responsibility, my friends, because blah, blah, blah, the red-white-and-blue American Flag God says so somewhere in the Bible that health care is both a right and a responsibility and you know I'm telling you the truth when I say this because I was a prisoner of war in Vietnam, an American Hero, who God wants to be your President, so make sure, my friends, that you are not fooled by that one, that one, that one – that...Other...who is called by the un-American name of Barack Obama, my friends.*"

McCain *would* have said something like that, if he had held true to form, non? Mais, for this question he had to think on his very unsteady feet, and he couldn't hesitate more than the nanosecond that he did hesitate, so he went on with saying what was in the deepest and darkest recesses of his noir heart: that he believes health care is not a citizen's *right*, but a citizen's *responsibility*. I'm sure the quote-unqoute, "*Christian* Right" – the every-man-for-himself Christians, Bible in one hand, gun in the other – just loved his answer.

The debate ended environ one-half hour before I got to the border, while I was around Enosburg. Funny thing is, for the rest of the drive to the border, my thoughts were not on the debate, but on how dark the road was. In more ways than one.

11 Octobre 2008

"Angela's Ashes"

Aujourd'hui was une belle day. Une trés belle autumn day. A beautiful day to die on. Oui, a beautiful day to die on. I ruminated on cette pensée while I stood outside, having ma premiere tasse de café, ce matin. Bien sûr, my mind went to these thoughts parce que I knew that this was le jour that Paddy et I would be casting Angela's ashes.

By the time I had ma deuxiéme tasse de café I was standing at the kitchen counter, facing across le chambre in the direction of the front window, when Paddy juste materialized at the sliding door, environ two meters away from me, à ma gauche. At the time, my thoughts happened to be on Paddy, wondering if he was going to phone, ou if he would be coming up the road soon. Encore, there he was, encore. Je ne sais pas how he drove up the road to my place without me hearing him. Et je ne sais pas pourquoi I did not hear him slam his car door shut. I pondered these questions for environ one moment, et then my thoughts were distracted by Paddy's fiddling avec the handle of the sliding door.

I put down ma tasse de café to go to the door, mais Paddy figured it out before I got there. He stepped inside, gave a quick brush of his Converses on the mat, et absent-mindedly left the sliding door open behind him. I put my arm on his shoulder et gave

69

it a bonjour squeeze, then I reached around him, slid the screen door shut, et left the glass door open, parce que the morning air was trés fresh, and not cold. To explain my haste in sliding the screen shut, I said to Paddy, "I'm trying to keep the ladybugs out of the house."

Paddy responded rapid-fire, avec a smiling, presque laughing voice, "You're not going to let them winter inside? What was it Einstein said about the ladybugs? Something about the planet would be in really big trouble when we start losing the lady bugs, wasn't that it? Or was it the bees he was talking about? It was Rachel Carson who talked about the ladybugs, right? She's the one who wrote *Silent Spring*, isn't that right? She was the mother of Harry Carson, the linebacker for the New York Giants, wasn't she? What do I know, I'm a retired bookie, and now I'm just a – what can I call it? – I'm a semi-professional Texas Hold'em player, eh? You're the professor, eh? Anyway, you ready to go, for Angela?"

I said, "I'm ready. But there's no need to rush, is there?"

Suddenly dead serious, Paddy said, "No, there's no need to rush."

He took a few steps over to the kitchen counter et put down the things he was carrying in his hands – candles, a box of wooden matches, et a piece of paper. Pointing to the candles, he said, "These will float, I think."

I picked up the candles, six petite blanc et pink candles, shaped comme flowers, comme lilies. They were packaged in a small tray avec a see-thru plastic cover. They were labeled bi-lingually, bien sûr: "Floating Candles…Bougies Flottantes." I said, "These look good, Paddy. Very nice."

He handed me the piece of paper he had brought in avec lui, which was a copy of the Hesse passage from *Magister Ludi*. J'ai oublié that he had taken it avec lui hier. He said, "Here's 'Stages.' I can't think of anything else we need. We don't even need this stuff, eh? We just need to be present, with Angela. But this poem is just beautiful, eh?"

"It certainly is," I said quietly, as I recalled that Paddy recently told me that he wouldn't mind if I read, *"Stages,"* as part of his going-off.

Paddy was not moving to take a seat. I wasn't sure if he wanted to go to Triple Falls right away. I said, "I just want to have a

70

bowl of oatmeal before we go, or maybe a piece of toast. Do you want some oatmeal, or toast? Would you care for some eggs?"

"I'll have eggs if you're going to make them for yourself," he answered, while he took a seat at my worktable. He began flipping through the book that was on the table, *After the Ecstacy, the Laundry.* I poured myself une autre tasse de café, et I microwaved une tasse de Tetley tea for Paddy.

I said, "I'm going to fry three egg whites with just a little olive oil, in a non-stick fry pan. For myself, I sprinkle a little grated cheese, instead of salt. But I can make your eggs in a different way."

Paddy said, "No, no, I'll have it whatever way you're making it for yourself. Make it whatever way you're making it. It sounds good." I could see he was preoccupied avec the book, reading one of the passages I had put in brackets. Then, suddenly energized, he said in a raised voice, avec his finger tapping on the opened page, to punctuate his words: "Okay, this is good. This is very good. I didn't put many notes in this book before I gave it to you, but I did make this note on page 103, about Bede Griffiths. And I see you made a note on the top of the page. What did you write here? 'Be your...' What the hell is this? 'Be your...' *Wow.* I can't read your writing..."

I said, "I'll make sure I print from now on." Mais Paddy didn't hear the joke. I continued, "You don't always print when you leave *your* notes in the margins. You get a little scribbly – not as much as I do – but you get scribbly every once in a while. And you don't put many notes in the books you read, Paddy. At least not like I do."

"Well, not compared to you, Mario-Jacques...Hey, you know sometimes there's a lot of ego stuff in note-taking. It's our intellectual ego, taking us out of the present, thinking ahead to the future, that thinks it's so important to get this stuff underlined, eh? I'm not saying that's what you're doing. Only you can answer that." He said this gently, sans harshness from his mouth to my ears.

I said, "I think there's a lot of truth in that. C'est vrai. I am making a mental note of that." He missed my joke, je pense.

Paddy said, "As long as you stay in the present, I guess that's good, but at the same time make sure you stay in the present on those fried eggs, the scrambled eggs, the olive oil eggs, whatever eggs you're making – which I will be happy with, no matter what they are. But you don't want to burn them. Oh, you can burn mine, I

71

don't care. Jesus Christ, I'm happy you're giving me the egg. Even if I don't eat the egg, you're still giving me nourishment, Mario-Jacques."

We had our eggs and talked environ a number of things, mais in the next one-half hour we did not discuss how we were going to cast Angela's ashes. It was not jusqua we were outside, walking down the front steps, to get into ma voiture, that I remarked to Paddy, "Are we set? You're the shaman."

"We're set," was all Paddy said. Then he looked up at the sky, et if he had not fallen pensive at that moment, je pense he would have said aussi, quelque chose comme: "It's a beautiful day to die on."

During the 10-minute drive over to Triple Falls we listened to our thoughts plus tranquillement que usual. I parked on the side de la rue, parallèle à la rue, in front of le *non defense* signe. Je pense Paddy was out of la voiture et in stride avant I turned off le moteur.

As we walked from ma voiture into the woods, avec Paddy walking trés rapide ahead of me, my thoughts went to Angela, as if she was there avec moi. In what form, je ne sais pas. Mais I could almost hear her laughing when Paddy stopped walking, once we got peut-être 20 feet into the woods, so that he could pee. I stopped un métre derriére his derriere, next to a small statue of Saint Francais that marks the best entry path to Triple Falls. Aprés Paddy's quik pee, we walked dans le silence. I followed in Paddy's footsteps, on a serpentine path, first on flat ground covered inches high avec rouge et pale vert et golden fallen leaves, then up a gently rising slope, where tree roots were spread out among the rocks, like the veins on the back of an old man's hands, or like the veins on my hands at times, bursting on the surface, spread out over bones.

At the top of the ridge, where the forest becomes enchanté, where the pine trees stand wide apart, like poles holding up a canopy way up high, I stopped walking, as I do whenever I approach cet espace. I turned my head lentement, scanning les environs. I saw the enchantment, I felt the magic. I felt in communion avec quelque chose. I thought to myself, *peut-être I am standing where an Abenaki native once stood, who aussi felt le même communion.* I am as sure as Paddy is that this ground was considered by the Abenaki to be a place where sacred energy resides.

Much of the ground that was ahead of me, leading to where the brook falls, is covered avec deep vert, trés cushiony moss. Le velour dans l'eglise forrest runs on the ground, over small rocks, large boulders, up trees. I stepped softly, et sometimes walked around the moss, comme it was a carpet that I did not want to soil. I caught up avec Paddy at the top of a steep path that leads down to the stream. He was holding back a tree branch, clearing the way for me to follow him down the path. It occurred to me that if I could have taken a photograph of Paddy standing there, it would have captured, in microcosm, his care pour moi, and for others. Peut-être some day a maybe-ist will mark a path with a small statue of Paddy O'Brien.

Paddy passed the tree branch to me as if it was a baton, et then he moved on down the path ahead de moi. Après I stepped avec grand attention, et slid down the last 20 feet of the path to the stream, I paused to survey la belle scène.

To my left, as I faced the stream, was le first of three waterfalls. This waterfall is vers 15 feet wide, et pours water smoothly into a pool vers 15 feet below, that is deep enough for Paddy et quelques amis to wade in. The rocks within et vers the waterfall have obviously been sculpted by an ancestor of Michaelangelo, long before the Renaissance. They are not shaped to look comme humain figures, mais la mainière in which they are shaped emphasizes the life within them. L'artiste was méticuleux au sujet turning la chute, so that it faced the shore where I stood, et heightened the dramatic effect of waters falling out of the forrest background. I wonder what it would look like si un artiste tel que Maxwell Parrish painted the scene I was looking at; I wonder what it would look like si un Staffordian comme Niente were to paint this scene; Et je vraiment wonder what it would look like if Gaston Briere were to paint this scene.

Paddy squatted down next to the water et began unwrapping the candles. I took the Hesse reading from my pocket et unfolded it. We remained dans le silence jusqua Paddy asked me for the vessels avec Angela's ashes. Les petites vessels appeared à moi to be lovely, ornately carved, smoked glass vials of perfume. Wholly appropriate. Un autre mot pour le parfum est essence, non?

Where we stood, the river was vers 30 feet across to the other side. The waters flow gently ici, et at our feet the rocks created un petit pool de presque still water. Paddy said, "After you do the reading, I'll light the candles."

Paddy et I stood shoulder to shoulder, our eyes and our hearts only slightly down, facing the waters. I felt les mots come from my mouth avec a palpable weight, comme the weight of wafers de communion. The sounds from the water playing on the rocks became more noticeable as I read, mais remained in the background, a perfect accompaniment. Je sais the reading took vers a minute, mais it was one of those timeless minutes that one sometimes experiences.

Après I finished the reading, I squatted down next to Paddy et watched him sprinkle Angela's ashes on to the wax flowers. He put la premiere candle in the water alone. We watched the candle float avec juste un petit mouvement pour un long instant. While we watched, Paddy said to me, "She doesn't want to go yet." Et then, as if responding to his words, the candle swirled in a small circle, then drifted slowly toward us, avec un mouvement that was scarcely perceptible. Encore, Paddy gave a commentary. "Come on, Angela. Let go." The candle entered a current that was not visible on the surface of the water, et began to drift away from us, downstream. We watched it slip down through some rocks into a lower pool of water, where it remained lighted, somehow. It swirled again, then found a way to continue floating downstream. We stood to watch it go over the next waterfall, out of sight. Then Paddy said, "Good."

He lighted three more candles et put them in the water. Deux of the candles acted as le premiere candle did, circling et then moving downstream après some initial hesitation. The third candle held much longer avant moving on. We watched that last candle pour plus than a minute, jusqua Paddy said, "I might have to move it on, eh?" Mais, juste avant it was starting to look like he would have to do that, the candle swirled in a circle, stopped, then moved into the invisible current et floated downstream. We watched as the candle made its way through the rocks, jusqua it went over the middle waterfall.

Paddy then lighted one of the two remaining candles et set it next to his Buddha statue, which sits on a moss-covered rock ledge that was juste to his left. The Buddha is environ two feet tall. The rock that enshrines the Buddha is un autre one of the features of l'espace that is evidence pour this being la terre sacrée des indigènes. The rock, environ five feet tall et three feet wide, looks comme un gris scallop shell, et un centerpiece in a garden of earthly delights. In times past, long avant Paddy set his Buddha ici, the scallop rock contained an Abenaki shrine, peut-être. Probablement. I remember seeing Angela's spirit touched when she looked upon this Buddha for the first time, juste a few months ago. Après Paddy set the lighted candle next to the Buddha, I said, "That's good, Paddy. Perfect."

To the left of the open side of the scallop rock, at the same height of the Buddha, there is a two-foot round basin carved in the rock, which fills when it rains, as it had over night. Paddy lighted the sixth et last candle, et floated it in the basin. Encore, I said, "That's good, Paddy. Perfect."

Paddy took a step back from the altar et began meditating avec his eyes open. I closed my eyes et did not try to do anything mais feel what there was to feel in the present moment. My eyes filled avec bonnes tears.

8 Novembre 2008

"Peut-être Un Maybeist Manifesto"

Paddy phoned me at 10h50m. He can talk up a storm when he is avec someone in-person, mais when he is on le téléphone, brevity is his watchword.

I answered mon telephone, "allo," avec quelque chose entre un anglophone et un francophone pronunciation, and this was probably the reason why Paddy delayed speaking for a moment, before he said, "Hey you going to be around, be okay for about an hour? I'm going to run over in about 10 minutes, but I got to leave in an hour."

Avec enthusiasm et brevity, I said: "Sounds good!"

Paddy said, "Okay," then hung up.

Sure enough, 10 minutes plus tard, il y a Paddy. His attire ce matin would been perfect for an athletic and very hip genie, and was close to perfect for Paddy, as he is close to being an athletic and very hip genie. He was wearing neon psychedelic workout pants slash/pajama bottoms. Bien sur, the look suited him – a one-of-a-kind outfit for a one-of-a-kind man.

I said, "Yo Paddy, I like your rags man! They remind me of the bad boys that the karate instructor in *Napolean Dynamite* wore. Did you see that movie?"

Paddy's Shadow ignored or didn't hear the question, but he gave me a big hug and I could see he was in good spirits. He said: "Congratulations! How are things down there in the states? Big celebrations, eh? There were about 25 people down at Kenny's Tuesday night. When Obama won, Kenny broke out the champagne. I guess everyone was happy down your way, eh? You see people acting different? It's been different here. Everyone's walking around smiling. The world has changed, eh? The United States gained a lot of respect all over the world, eh?"

Paddy does not like to parle au sujet la politique ou manger corn, presque de les même raisons. So I was un peu surprised to see that he was bringing up le sujet maintenant. I said, "I have never seen people acting the way they are, in public. As you say, people are walking around with smiles, and actually being kinder to each other. I have never in my life seen anything like it."

Paddy took une chaise at my work table, la chaise that I normally sit in, in front of mon ordinateur screen. We talked au sujet la politique while I made le thé pour Paddy et le café pour me.

Paddy said, "How about all this stuff from McCain and Palin about Obama being a communist? Or are they saying he's a, 'socialist?' Nobody down there knows what the hell the difference is anyway, eh? Jeeezus, I mean, they just about said that, didn't they? Obama wants to take some more tax money out of the rich, so they call him a, 'Marxist,' eh? What's wrong with the people in your country? Obama talks about redistributing the wealth and right away people act like he's replacing the American Constitution with *The Communist Manifesto*…Jeeezus! What do you guys say, how do you say it? 'Jesus *H*. Christ?' What does the 'H' stand for? I always wanted to know that. Pooh-tit that's why Bush wants everyone to call him, 'George *W*. Bush, eh? Well, you got rid of a guy with a messiah complex, and you replaced him with someone who a lot of people think is the new messiah, for real…Obama's got one hell of a job…Anyway, enough talk about Bush, Obama, and *The Communist Manifesto*…"

Paddy finished as I brought le thé over to la table. He shifted from ma chaise to l'autre chaise. We both took sips from our tasses, et we both crossed our legs, synchronistically. I said, "Okay, enough about Bush, Obama and *The Communist Manifesto*. Let's get to *The Maybeist Manifesto*."

Paddy laughed, et avec equal pièces humour et seriousness he replied, "You want to continue on the subject of *The Maybeist Manifesto*? There's not much more to say than what I said the other day. All the book would say is: 'Everything is maybe.'"

I thought to myself, this is the watchword of radical reductionism: "Everything is maybe." I said to Paddy: "Which means that even the idea that everything is a maybe is, in itself, a maybe."

Paddy replied: "Maybe."

Bien sûr, mon plus grand motif for wanting Paddy to sit avec moi et écrire was parce que he never, never, jamais, allows me écrire des notes. C'est son syndrome de Gurdjieff. Mais oui, toujours, as soon as je commence to take notes quand he's talking, he makes moi arrêt. J'ai pensé that writing *The Maybeist Manifesto* would be une manière to circumvent this. Bien sûr, leave it to Paddy to write un manifeste dans une phrase. Paddy is a tough nut to crack.

I relented. Mon jaune writing pad was on la table, entre us, et I took un stylo from la collection de vers 20 that I keep dans une tasse café sur la table. I tapped le stylo on the pad et said, "That's it? 'Everything is maybe?' Come on, we have to elaborate on that. We'll never grow beyond our cult of two. We need to give our movement some structure."

Paddy re-crossed his legs. Alors he said, avec a smile, "I'm happy with our cult of two. If you want to bring more people into our cult, you'll have to write the manifesto."

I said, "Peut-être I can contribute some ideas, but you're the leader of the cult, the High Llama."

Paddy replied, "I don't want to be the High Llama. I don't want to be put on a pedestal. Pooh-tit that's where they'll want to put me on a cross." At least Paddy was still smiling quand he said this.

I relented. Encore, I tapped on mon writing pad avec mon stylo, et said, "C'mon monsieur, we need some more words for *The Maybeist Manifesto* than: 'Everything is maybe.'"

Paddy said, "Okay. I see you really want to do this so badly. Pooh-tit I'll take you out of your suffering. Write this down: 'This is the sitting-on-the-fence doctrine.' It's based on the teachings of my mentor. You know who that is, don't you?"

"Bede Griffiths?" I asked.

Paddy said, "No, not Bede. We're talking about the maybeist doctrine. That's not Father Bede. What's the name of your mentor, from East End Bay?"

"I don't know who you're referring to," I answered, vraiment puzzled.

"What's the name of that psychologist you think so much of? Bob O'Connor, right?"

I nodded ma tête dans la confirmation et leaned farther back dans ma chaise.

Paddy said, "I was just reading a book this morning by my mentor Sam O'Connor, the poker master. There's another synchronicity between us, eh? Our mentors both have the same last names: Bob O'Connor and Sam O'Connor. What's the odds of that, eh? They're both common Irish names okay, but still, what's the odds, eh?" Paddy laughed, alors took another sip from his thé. Mais he stopped talking.

I wanted to get him back to *The Maybeist Manifesto*, et he could see that. Encore, he laughed, alors said, "Put this in *The Manifesto*: 'A 2 and a 7 in the hole is the worst hand.'…It's all tied to poker. There's certain hands that you don't want to bet on, and there's certain hands that should win – but you never know."

Alors Paddy took one of my books from the pile in front of him, on the table. It was *After the Ecstacy, the Laundry*. He rifled through the pages, looking for a passage he wanted to read to me. He said, "Jesus H. Christ, Mario-Jacques. I thought I was overdoing it with the notes I put in this book. You've got notes in the margins on almost every page! I'm looking for the part where Kornfield writes about the man who asks the guru what happens after we die, and the guru says something like: 'How should I know? I've never been dead!' That's good, isn't it Mario-Jacques?" Paddy finished, avec equal pieces humour et seriousness. Then he had to take a sip from his cold tea, in order to stop himself from continuing to laugh at his humour and DaVinciesque wisdom.

I smiled et contemplated his words. I wanted to fuel more thinking from Paddy au sujet Maybeism, so I asked him if he wanted une autre tasse de thé. Paddy shook his head non. Mais, he could see that I was hoping to elicit plus pour la doctrine. He smiled his forever young Paddy O'Brien smile et said: "Here's something for the book, pooh-tit: 'Buddhists say they don't believe in God, but they don't know; I *believe* in God, but I don't know.'"

I can see that *The Maybeist Manifesto* is not going to be a thick book.

9 Novembre 2008

"Juste une question de what we choose to notice?"

I went over to The Lie vers 20h30m la nuit dernière. I parked ma voiture derrière le bâtiment, prés l'entrée à la cuisine. This is where Jeannine, le propriétaire of l'Oeil parks sa voiture, which is une noire Toyota, la même as mine. Et la nuit dernière I parked dans l'espace right à côte de hers. As I was getting out de ma voiture Jeannine came out the back porte et shouted to me in English, with her Quebecois woman accent: "Hey, if you park there, when I leave, people will still think I am here. I do not know if that is good." Alors elle gave me her hearty Quebecois woman laugh, juste to make certain that I knew elle was kidding.

I stopped in my tracks et stomped my right foot on the ground, to accentuate mon retort. I shouted, "Yo, Jeannine! Pas grave, girl. Not only do I have New York plates on ma voiture, mais I have a Barack Obama bumper sticker on le derrière de ma voiture."

Elle shouted back her reply theatrically : "Hey, Mario-Jacques! I am happy to hear that Oba-ma won, and I am happy to hear that your French is getting better!"

I replied, "Mais oui. Merci et merci, mademoiselle. Je pratique mon français. Especially parce que I was concerned that McCain et Palin could have actually been elected. Peut-être I would have been seeking asylum."

She said, "I understand! Aaah, ciao Mario-Jacques. They are calling me inside. I must go. Je suivre la parade," elle said, as elle turned back dans la cuisine.

I walked gingerly sur le trottoir, which had patches of ice on it. If I was in a New York state of mind I would have considered le trottoir a lawsuit waiting to happen. Mais, depuis I was in a Stafford state of mind, it felt bon to have this taste of the Québec winter coming on. Jusqu'à Stafford took its place in moi heart, I didn't like winters. Mais maintenant il est différent. J'aime the winter in Québec, ici in the Eastern Townships.

I realized that I had left the Barack Obama campaign pin that I had promised to Jeannine dans ma voiture, so I decided to go back for it. Juste as I turned around, I looked dans the headlights of une voiture driving toward the parking lot. I saw that it was un Ford Echo rouge, et it was Pat Barkley driving. I wasn't certain if elle saw me while elle was driving dans the parking lot, mais quand elle got out of sa voiture elle waved bonjour à moi.

I waved back, et called out à elle, "I'll give you a hand with your equipment." Mais first I hustled to ma voiture et got the Obama pin, which I had left in the coffee holder on the console, alors I went over to Pat, to help her.

We said bonjour avec pecks rapide on both cheeks. Elle was not wearing un chapeau et I noticed that her hair was différent, encore. This time shorter. Elle looked comme elle had lost some weight, mais I did not see un visage stressed. I asked, "Ca va?"

Elle responded, "Ca va bien. Et tu? (Dear Diary, I think she said, "et tu?" mais peut-être it was, "et toi?" I have a hard time getting "tu" et "toi" right.)

I replied, "Ca va."

"Congratulations on your new president, Mario." Her words were spoken with a tone that was not noticeably serious, but emanated from her heart.

"Merci beaucoup. C'est fantastique," I replied.

Being kind, Pat said, "Your French is improving, I see."

I replied, "Un peu, juste un peu. Mais, I am working very hard on it. I keep playing my French lessons on a CD in ma voiture. I have to immerse myself, you know what I mean? My only alternative is to move to Granby, or somewhere in Québec outside of the Eastern Townships, where the only way I'm going to eat is by speaking French."

Elle said, "You know, that could work for you. But go north, because I don't think you would want to live in Granby." Je ne sais pas pourqoui Pat said this. I like Granby. Elle opened the hatch of sa voiture et began reaching dans pour son equipement, which consisted of a music stand et a briefcase avec elle sheet music.

I took the music stand from her hands avant elle could lift it up. "Granby isn't that bad a place to live in, is it?" I asked.

"Je ne sais pas, Mario. I've never lived there. I have some friends who live there and they seem to be reasonably happy there. But it's not like Stafford. And I know you're so keen on living in Stafford."

I laughed. "There's that word again: 'Keen.' What is it avec anglophones in the Eastern Townships and that word? 'Keen,' is extremely retro. I mean, retro to the *nth* degree. Know what I mean?" I asked.

She replied, "No, I don't know what you mean. 'Keen,' is, 'retro?'" Elle looked vraiment puzzled.

Anyway, elle slammed the hatch of la voiture, and this turned the page of our talk. We began walking toward the side door of The Lie. Even though elle was walking in heels, je pense elle had to walk un peu slower comme elle wanted to, parce que I was less certain comme elle vers walking on the frozen ground avec quelques patches of ice.

La première personne we saw quand we walked in la porte du café was Christine. She came from around derriere the counter to greet us, with hugs and kisses. She pointed to the music stand in my hand and said, "What's this? I wanted you to be *my* roadie!"

I replied, "I'm just trying to be un americain-quebecer gentleman, helping the lady with her equipment."

Christine said, "Yes, I know you americain-quebecers are a civil lot. After all, you come from a nation that just elected a Barack Obama."

I said, "C'est vrai." Alors I told Pat I would put the music stand près de elle microphone, et I left Pat et Christine to confer au sujet their work.

Then I saw Carnie Jack, waving to me from his favorite place at The Lie – sitting on one of the two synchronicity stools at the turn of the counter. I took the stool à côte de lui, l'autre tabouret de sychronicity. Carnie told me that he had heard from Luci, Paddy's granddaughter, that we had cast Angela's ashes at Triple Falls. Carnie had met Angela while elle was in Stafford with other students from Suffolk for the conference, et he had made quite a connection avec Angela et some of the other students. He was quite saddened when I told him about Angela's tragic death. He told me that he was touched when Luci told him about Angela's ashes. He also told me that he had this feeling when he met Angela that elle was someone who vraiment fit in ici, that she was un vrai Staffordian spirit. Et he told me that he had this feeling maintenant that elle was going to remain part of the community in Stafford, somehow. Je comprends.

It did not look like Christine et Pat were about to commence la musique, et depuis we were sitting dans The Synchronicity Stools, I began telling Carnie l'histoire de papillon. Peut-être une minute plus tard, Pat Barkley came et joined us. Elle stood at the end of the bar, facing me, with Carnie between us. Elle told us that Christine was going to begin the 1st set by singing a birthday chanson to someone, et she would introduce Pat après 1 ou 2 plus numbers. Pat ordered un Boréale Noire et while she waited for la bière she listened in on notre conversation.

As I told l'histoire to him, I could see that Carnie was très interested, et Pat considerably less interested. Actually, I shouldn't say elle wasn't interested, it was plus comme elle did not find the coincidences dans l'histoire to be meaningful.

Avant I finished l'histoire, Carnie received un appel on his cell phone et he had to go outside to talk. I finished telling l'histoire to Pat, mais rapidement. Alors I put my fingers over my lips while I looked at Pat's visage, pour elle response to l'histoire. Anyone I've told l'histoire de papillon to has been struck by the many and rather remarkable coincidences…among them: that la mère d'Angela read in Angela's magazine, "*I will come to you as a butterfly*," et ensuite elle decided to look up a counseling center on le Internet et found, a few minutes plus tard, *"The Butterfly Counseling Center."* That la mère d'Angela noticed pour le premiere time, while elle was telling Angela's father au sujet this, that there was un papillon dans le photo of Angela on the wall; That Angela's father was walking on a beach a few days later, despondent avec grief, et un papillon fluttered to him, through the wind on the beach…et this was une plage d'océan, which butterflies do not frequent; Et that immediately après la mère d'Angela told me au sujet these coincidences on le téléphone, I went dans ma salle de bain et found a piece of jewelry that I had never seen avant, et it was un papillon pin; et just before Angela crossed the border to enter Québec pour le premiere time, she had stopped at The Pinnacle Peddler in Richford for lunch, and while she was sitting at the picnic table a huge butterfly – the biggest and most beautiful butterfly she had ever seen in her life landed on her hand...and she took a picture of it, which she kept showing to everyone.

Mais Pat seemed to shrug off these coincidences, as facilement as elle finished the rest of sa Boréale. Elle said à moi, "I don't know Mario, I just think it's a matter of what we choose to notice." Her words were not spoken with a tone that was noticeably serious, but they did not seem to emanate from her heart. I wasn't quite certain how to interpret her remark, or how to respond to it. In any case, Carnie Jack returned to the other synchronicity seat, à côte moi, et Pat went to sit près du bandstand.

I told l'histoire de papillon to Carnie encore, in abbreviated form, et he was quite taken by the synchronicities. Bien sûr, we were sitting in The Synchronicity Seats, a.k.a Les Sièges de Synchronicité. Quand I concluded the story, Carnie said, "That's synchronicity, for sure. Mais oui, that's sychronicity for sure," he repeated, shaking son tête avec a Carnie Jack/Alfred E. Newman benevolent madman smile.

I said, "You've been noticing synchronicity for a long time, haven't you, Carnie?"

Carnie took un sip de son verre de Boréale Blanc, while nodding son tête up and down, which isn't facile to do. Après he wiped la bière from the corners of his mouth, he said, "You know, I've had so many experiences with synchronicity, and people tell me about it all the time, but I never heard the word before, or at least I don't remember hearing the word before, until you told me that's what you call it, Mario-Jacques. Now I know I probably hear...in fact...I'm sure I *must* have heard the word, 'synchronicity,' used, but I guess I never paid attention to it, eh? I used to use the word, 'coincidence,' or, 'weird.' Tu comprends, Mario-Jacques?"

I replied, "Je comprends, je comprends."

83

Encore, Carnie wiped la bière from the corners of his mouth, avant speaking encore. "You know Mario-Jacques, c'est vrai, there is some synchonicity going on. That would be a great title for a song, eh?" Carnie leaned forward, toward me, et he sang les mots, *"There's synchronicity going on..."* Encore, the Carnie Jack/Alfred E. Newman benevolent madman smile. He continued, "What was the name of the song...Oh, I can see his face now...Marvin Gaye...right? That was his name, mais oui! Marvin Gaye sang *"What's Going On?"* Big hit in Montreal during the Vietnam War. I know it was a big hit in the states too, eh? Mais oui...somebody like Marvin Gaye – oops, he's dead now, right? Yeah, well okay, somebody with a silky voice, like Pat Barkley, could sing a song about synchronicity going on. Nice and soft, très tranquille."

Carnie stopped parce que Pat Barkley started singing la première chanson. It was *"The Nearness of You."* Carnie and I both felt it was synchronistic that Pat began to sing in the instant after Carnie said, "Pat Barkley."

When Pat finished singing la chanson Carnie tourné à moi et said, "When Pat sings a song like that, it reminds me of this song I used to love listening to on the radio, in the old days...It started with an 'r' I think...I can't think of the name of it. It was a blues singer who did it...I can't think of her name." He put his tête down et tapped his forehead avec his fingers, in much la même manière that he used to tap his fingers on the top of his radio in the old days, quand all he could hear was static.

I offered: "Etta James?... Ella Fitzgerald?... Billie Holliday?"

Carnie shook son tête, "non"..."non"..."non." He said, "I can't remember who sang the song, but she sang a lot like Pat. I used to love to listen to her sing the first song that they would play as the theme song for this radio program on NPR Vermont called, *"The Glass Bead Game."*

I stepped off the bar stool, my synchronicity seat, and then back onto it avant I said, "Whoa! Tu comprends, '*whoa*,' monsieur Carnie?! Did you say: *'The Glass Bead Game?!'*"

Carnie said, "Yes. That was the name of the show I used to listen to on NPR, from Vermont."

I said, "This is wild. Je pense The Synchronicity Seats have struck encore."

Carnie turned on his synchronicity stool to fully face me. "Pourquoi?" he asked, avec vraiment interest.

I asked him, "Do you know why the show was called, *'The Glass Bead Game?'* Do you know what, *'The Glass Bead Game,'* is?"

Carnie answered, "No," avec his Alfred E. Newman smile.

I asked, "Have you ever heard of Herman Hesse, the writer?"

Carnie rubbed his chin, et thought pour un instant, alors he answered, "I'm sure I've heard the name. I hear the name from time to time. But I haven't read any of his books."

I said, "Well, Hermann Hesse won the Nobel Prize for literature in 1946 for his book, *Magister Ludi.* When Paddy O'Brien and I cast Angela's ashes at Triple Falls I read a passage from *Magister Ludi.* The book is also known as... *The Glass Bead Game.*"

Carnie said, "I see. That *is* pretty wild. Especially seeing that we were just talking about Angela, and I was saying that when Pat sings the blues it reminds me sometimes of the theme song from the radio program I used to listen to: *The Glass Bead Game.* And you say that, *"The Glass Bead Game,"* is another name for the book that you and Paddy read from when you spead Angela's ashes at Triple Falls? Okay, here you go, Mario-Jacques. We're sitting on The Synchronicity Seats, and we are experiencing synchronicity again. We've got to tell Pat about this. I'll bet she'll be interested in hearing about this."

I replied, "Je ne sais pas, Carnie. She may not think it's as interesting as you and I do. She might say it's just a matter of what we choose to notice."

Carnie rubbed his chin et said, "How do you *not* notice something like this, Mario-Jacques?"

East End Bay
November 29, 2008

"Twas Le Jour Après Thanksgiving In The U.S.A"

85

Hier, le jour après Thanksgiving aux États Unis (et a month après Thanksgiving au Canada) was un Vendredi Noir, vraiment. A 34-year-old homme, a part-time worker at a Wal-Mart magasin on Long Island, was killed by shoppers who knocked down les portes et stampeded over him quand le magasin opened at 6h. The shoppers were frénétique to save a few dollars on cadeaux de Noel.

Après removing the man's body, et quelque investigation by the police, Wal-Mart opened encore at 12h, midi. Yes, at noon. Closing the store for a few hours while the police investigated was the quote-unquote "respect" that this so-called Great American Enterprise gave to a man in uniform who died in the line of duty. He was a Black man, capital "B," working a second job as a security guard, to save some extra money to buy, Jesus Christ(!), Christmas gifts. It is rather disgusting, the materialism that operates under the pretense of being a Christian celebration. What would the Christ of the Bible say about the shoppers? Peut-être : "Forgive them, for they know not what they do."

I think four of the ten wealthiest people in the world are members of the Walton family, the owners of Wal-Mart. What happened yesterday provides another example of how they make their money, and how much they care about the people who work for them. Jesus, they could have closed the store for the day.

What people do for money. Wal-Mart, and some of their most avid customers.

Though the killing of this man will not have ramifications comparable to the killing of JFK, et the viciousness of the violence was not of the magnitude of 9-11, this was un jour, a Black Friday, that should live in infamy, je pense.

1 Janvier 2009

"Bonfire Bonne Année"

La nuit dernière, New Year's Eve, I spent à la maison de Merlin The Magician et Gwen Beckett, et chez Diana Stuart. Gwen e-mailed an invite à moi il y a quelques jours. Elle a dit there would be un ou deux couples coming pour le dîner et I was bienvenue pour venir pour tout ou une partie de la soirée. Diana's invite, e-mailed aussi, was la même, in terms of inviting me pour venir pour tout ou pour une partie de la soirée. Quand j'ai regardé Diana's e-mail, j'ai vu que elle had invited beaucoup de personnes. La liste était long. La plupart des personnes Diana invited were acteurs, théâtre people, performers de une sorte ou un autre, artistes. Diana's invite mentioned aussi que there would be une cérémonie bonfire à minuit. I decided I would go à la maison de Merlin et Gwen pour dîner et chez Diana après le dîner et avant minuit.

Via e-mail, I let Diana et Gwen know that I planned on going out to the farm première, et ensuite chez Diana. Mais hier après-midi Diana sent me un autre e-mail et invited me to stop à sa maison to have un verre de vin avec elle et qulques autres, while I was on my way to Merlin et Gwen's place. That's what I did.

I got to chez Diana environ 19h et was surprised to find que I was la première personne à arriver. At least 50 personnes were invited, je suis certain, et I expected que cinq ou six personnes would be à sa maison at this time. La dernière fois que j'ai vu Diana, il y a quelques mois, early autumn, et elle était going bientôt pour visiter ses frères, et elle parents, à England. This was maintenant un bon temps pour nous to catch up avec each other.

Avant Diana was going à England elle told moi que this was going être a significant voyage pour elle. Je pense elle a pensé au le voyage as the one steppingstone dans l'eau that would get elle onto the path elle aimed to take. Mais elle gave me *Les Readers Digest* version de l'histoire de son voyage, et it sounded comme *Les Readers Digest* version de l'histoire – sans depth des emotions. Je pense elle juste wanted to keep it light, et elle was anticipating le voyage comme Thorcau waiting for company. Mais oui, not with great excitement.

Après une autre heure, une autre personne est arrivée. Il était Helga Ruskowski, une actrice que j'ai vue l'été dernière dans *Le Banc de Parc,* un jeu merveilleux que Diana wrote et directed. Je suis resté pour un autre dix minutes, ensuite I headed out to Merlin et Gwen's place.

I had a nice dîner avec Merlin, Gwen, et un autre couple. We talked au sujet comparisons entre les États-Unis et Québec, et entre the East End of Long Island et the Eastern Townships de Québec, et entre East End Bay et la ville de Stafford. Avant I knew it, j'étais out la porte encore, sur la route encore, pour retourner à chez Diana.

Quand I got back à chez Diana j'ai trouvé plus six guests pour la fête. Diana introduced me to everyone – who seemed to be speaking anglais avec each other. Ensuite elle escorted me à l'entrée de sa maison, to show me une pile des branches d'arbre, layed out sur the floor à côté de la porte. Elle told me to pick out the stick that was le correct pour moi. This would be the stick that I would burn à minuit – to burn what I wanted to leave derrière de 2008. Elle a dit that quand I toss the stick in the bonfire I should aussi pensez au sujet mes intentions pour 2009. J'ai vu une branche dans la pile that was split dans demi, lengthwise. Pour quelque raison, that seemed comme le correct pour moi.

À juste avant minuit we went out to the bonfire. Il était entre 23h45m et 23h55m. All of us wore bonnes footware pour les sub-zéro températures outside, mais not one of us was wearing a watch on this New Year's Eve. Which says quelque chose au sujet this collection de personnes, et les temps. Et je ne sais pas if there was a clock somewhere dans la maison de Diana. No one seemed to care si nous would be able to acknowledge minuit avec a shout à la precise temps quand clocks calibrated à Greenwich Mean Time indicated il était minuit. This was la première temps dans ma vie that I had witnessed – et participated dans – such disregard pour clock temps. Einstein should have been there.

Us six watchless personnes hiked up la montagne derrière la maison, through a path dans la niege, created by Diana. It was a winding path avec sure footing, lighted by la lune.

Juste off le droit side of the path et dix mètres down mountain of the bonfire, I noticed what looked être what américain-quebecers call, "monkey bars." I stopped walking, to get a better look à la structure, et I considered that la structure might be monkey bars – formé comme un Buckminster Fuller conception pour un igloo. Ou peut-être it was Diana's sweat lodge! ((Plus tard I learned that il *était* Diana's sweat lodge, quelque chose that intrigues me.))

The bonfire was built dans un concave rond pit lined avec les roches, environ deux mètres wide. This bonfire, comme the sweat lodge, reminded me d'une variation of a geodesic dome. Round chunks of unsplit logs, all the same exact size, were piled dans un dome, on top of un chaud rouge fire. L'air de montagne billowed the fire perfectly. A Hall of Fame fire.

I took my place around the bonfire, du nord et à la gauche de Diana, juste à la droite d'ou les longues flammes were pointing. J'ai pensé que c'était un bon signe que les flames were pointing au nord, parce que le nord est ma direction. Diana told me que mon direction est le nord. Je pense she is right.

Environ minuit, environ dix minutes après minuit à la East Coast Rolex temps, we began le cérémonie bonfire. Diana et la artiste Helga, et a married couple, Kathryn Davis et Jeffrey Liebmann, who are makers of documentary films, began a chant. It was repetitive, as chants tend to be, et I joined dans après le 6ème ou le 7ème chorus. Fortunately, le chant était bref. Il seulement went environ huit ou neuf choruses. I cannot chanter ou chant much better than I can parler Mandarin, ou Français.

Les deux autres personnes standing around the fire were Jeannette Tardif – a friend and neighbor of Diana, et son fils – the maker of the fire, 20-year-old Yves. Jeannette should have named son fils Prometheus, parce que c'était a fire incroyable. En anglais, this was one *hell*(!!!) of a fire. Et c'était performance art. L'esthétique de the chunks of logs, cut la même size, et stacked in a mound, était a work d'art. Une sculpture to be burned.

Quand le chant ended, Diana a dit quelques mots au sujet ce qu'elle was burning 2008, et intentions pour 2009, et ensuite elle tossed sa branche dans the fire. It was a declaration que elle était letting go of the past, et not reaching pour le futur, to live dans le present. We all took a turn at doing this, dans no particular ordre. Je ne sais pas exactamente ce que j'ai dit avant I tossed my stick dans the fire, mais c'était au sujet following a path allumé.

20 Janvier 2009

"20-1-09"

Aujourd'hui était Inauguration Day dans les États-Unis. I had been wanting pour observer the inauguration avec un groupe des

Quebecers/Quebecois, mais quand I got up ce matin, which was environ 5h, j'encore had not figured out comment faire ceci.

Le premier chose I did après I made myself une tasse du thé, was to go on le Internet to check the schedule of events pour le jour. It looked comme Barack would be giving his speech environ 12h. I had thought I would be able au ski pour deux ou trois heures le matin, donc maintenant I realized that that would not be possible.

I checked my e-mails et j'ai vu un courriel de Jillian Lafleur, which was not là quand I put mon ordinateur to sleep la nuit dernière. I opened it et j'ai vu elle had e-mailed juste il y a quelques minutes. The subject line read: *"Happy Obama Day."* Elle wrote:*"Salut Mario-Jacques...My friend Murray (the man I was telling you about who teaches philosophy at Édouard-Monpetit) is interested in talking to you about educational exchanges. If you see this e-mail this morning, then may I be the first to wish you a **Happy Obama Day!** It is a great day with the inauguration. Exciting. I am going to bring an American flag to our meetings at Dawson. J."*

Tandis que je était on my way to town vers 9h, mes pensées were sur how différent le monde est aujourd'hui. Mes pensées were interrupted quand I came à un signe d'arrêt at Rue Pin et une voiture avec a license plate de Virginia drives past! J'ai vu that the license plate had, instead of the state motto, les mots: *"Fight Terrorism."* What?! This is what they are putting on license plates now?! In *Virginia*! The motto for Virgina was: *"Virginia is for Lovers."* En tout le mois de Janvier I have not seen une voiture dans Stafford avec a license plate de Vermont, que est 30 minutes away, et maintenant je vois une voiture de Virginia(!) avec a, *"Fight Terrorism,"* license plate. This was more than a license plate, this was a *sign* on the back of that car.

Wow. « *Fight Terrorism,* » inscribed onto the state of Virginia license plate. Did the driver pay a fee to have that put on the license plate? Do all the license plates in Virginia actually display these words? Why not, instead, have, *"Get Bin Laden,"* on the license plates? In a few years, the way things are going, the plates may read, *"Shop Wal-Mart."* Yeah, Wal-Mart will pay a fee to advertise on all the state license plates, just like corporations buy the right to have their names put on stadiums paid for by taxpayers. En tout cas, I would love to see the day when the words on the Virginia license plates only say, *"For Lovers,"* instead of, *"Fight Terrorism,"* or, *"Shop at Wal-Mart,"* if you know what I mean. Peut-être that will be après the license plates for Québec have les mots: *"La Belle Pays."*

As I write these words, my thoughts go to imagining a Québec avec license plates that read, *"Fight Terrorism,"* au lieu de, *"Je Me Souviens."* Mon dieu, imagine Québec avec McDonald's, Subway, Starbuck's, Wal-Mart everywhere. Imagine Québec Americanized. Dans *that* corporatized Québec, it would not be incongrous voir voitures avec license plates that read, *"Fight Terrorism."* Mais maintenant, c'est sooooo incongruous voir un, *"Fight Terrorism,"* license plate sur une voiture dans Québec.

I went to Café Dumont, where I had mon petit dejeuner, et saw today's edition of *Le Devoir*. The lead story, run à la gauche côté de le page, deux columns, was headlined: *"Péréquation: Ottawa contredit Québec...Charest doit se retirer du conseil de la federation dit Marois."* Du côté droit de la page, avec un font mois en evidence comme le font utilisé à le péréquation headline, il y avait the one-column headline: *"Le jour J pour Obama...Au moins deux millions de personnes attendues á l'investiture."* Entre les deux histoires était une photo de Barack, wearing jeans et d'un chemise simple, et casual shoes, avec un rouleau de peinture dans des ses maines. It looks comme il est having fun, painting une salle. La légende sous la photo à dit: *"Barack Obama a aide hier à repEndre un foyer pour adolescents sans abri, à Washington, à l'occasion de la journée d'hommage à la Martin Luther King, une journée fériée aux États-Unis qui est aussi consacrée au benevolent dans les organisms de bienfaisance. Il prendra part aujourd'hui sur les marches du Capitole à la cérémonie d'investiture qui fera de lui le président des États-Unis et le premier président noir de l'histoire américaine."* Here he is, the most powerful man au monde, painting un abri pour homeless teenagers. Voila...une idée whose time has come...une idée whose time has come...

Linda Hickey came into le café, juste comme I had finished eating mon petit dejeuner et I was about to head out, pour observer l'investiture. Linda a dit à moi qu'il looked comme beaucoup de quebecers were staying à la maison pour observer l'investiture. Elle a dit les conditions pour le ski were très bonne, mais non trop des personnes were sur la montagne. Pas surprise, Café Dumont et Rue Principal was aussi unusually quiet, avec few people out and about.

Quand je suis arrivé à chez Christine, j'ai trouvé that she had moved la table de cuisine afin que we could watch sa nouvelle grande télévision, 47-inch(!!!), tandis que we sat à la table avec nos tasses de café.

Cette télévision est une semaine vieille dans la maison, et c'est la première télévision Christine has owned dans sa vie adulte. Christine Neumann buying a 47-inch télévision is the Eastern Townships version of Mother Theresa buying a Rolex. What can it mean? Time will tell.

As I was taking my boots off I kept one eye à la télévision, which was showing Barack et Michelle Obama stepping out of a limousine at the White House, avec George et Barbara Bush standing up quelques steps, to greet them.

Christine a dit, "I've got MSNBC on. Cool?"

J'ai dit, "Definitely. That's what I watch all the time in New York."

Christine a dit, "Yeah, I like this better than CNN. "

Quand I put my coat over une des chaises de cuisine, Christine suggested rapidement que je deplace il, parce que le mur près the coat was humide avec la peinture. Comme partie her nesting behaviour avec Camille, Christine et Camille sont peint la maison. Pas une histoire worthy de la première page de *Le Devoir,* mais peut-être the *Brome County News.*

I reached over la table to move my coat, ensuite I froze in my motion, comme Christine a dit, avec une excitation bubbling, "Oh! Obama gets out of the limo and he opens the door for Michelle, so Brokaw says, 'Barack Obama has just ramped it up for millions of men around the world.'"

J'ai observé Barack et Michelle Obama approaching George et Barbara Bush. The Bushes remained stationnaire tandis que les Obamas approached them. Barack et Michelle kissed the Bushes, pas l'autre manière autour. I laughed avec Christine et j'ai dit: "Brokaw said, *'ramped it up*?'"

Elle a répondu: "No, he didn't use those words, but you know what I mean."

Encore, we laughed. J'ai dit, "Brokaw is good. He is not a Keith Olbermann – in terms of being humorous, or being risky – but he's good. He has integrity."

Christine a dit, "Brokaw is good. He did a nice rap before on post-modern politics, referencing the bloodless cessation of Czechoslovakia."

Christine is an aficionado of broadcast news à Les États-Units. Ce qu'elle observe will be différent maintenant qu'elle y a une télévision dans la maison, hooked up to satellite. She has been on a heavy diet of Keith Olbermann et Rachel Maddow, who happen to be my favorites on MSNBC. Jusqu'à maintenant, ce qui Christine observe has been limited to Olbermann, Maddow, et quelques autres on YouTube.

Bientôt, la télévision camera focused sur un vieil homme, hunched over, walking lentement à un siege près d'ou Barack would be speaking. I told Christine que j'ai pensé qu'il était l'oncle de Barack. I was shocked pour entendre qu'il était Muhammad Ali...Oui, Muhammed Ali.

I once met Ali, sur les rues de New York City. Oui, on the sidewalks of New York. Il a ressemblé The Heavyweight Champion du Monde. I remember looking at the size of his hand, et pensée qu'il could knock someone's tête clean off avec il. Mais il a semblé comme un homme doux. Oui, maintenant I see sur le télévision que Ali is hunched over...Je suis certain que Barack knows qu'il stood on the shoulders of the world's champion fighter, and then others, in his climb up, to become the most powerful man au monde. J'ai dit quelque chose to this effect à Christine, et elle a répondu avec: "Amen, brother."

All of a sudden, le signal satellite was lost. La télé went post-moderne, avec une matrice des milliers de rectangles verts au neon de palpitation, sur un fond de noir. Les images d'hésitation à la télévision were intéressant pour observer, mais j'était plus intéressé à voir les images de l'Investiture.

We listened to le commentaire et observé la matrice dévoilent pendant environ 15 minutes, et ensuite I tried to convince Christine de venir avec moi à St. Benedict's Pub sur Rue Principal. Mais elle a voulu rester à la maison – avec moi, ou seulement. Elle a dit, "No, you go. I'm a radio woman. I'm cool listening to it."

Mindful du fait that Christine has, à plus d'une occasion, listened to a recording of quatre minutes et trente-trois secondes de silence a la John Cage, I took her at her word. I decided to go to St. Brendan, sur Rue Principal.

J'ai garé ma voiture derrière l'Oeil et coupe à travers le passage couvert, entre le café et le musée du chocolat, to get to St. Brendan sur l'autre côté de la rue. J'ai noté il y avait hardly any voitures garées sur la rue.

J'ai espéré que St. Brendan would have beaucoup de personnes watching l'Investiture, mais as soon as I got there j'ai vu qu'il y avait seulement cinq hommes sitting à la barre, consommation du déjeuner tandis que watching l'Investiture. They were watching la télé attentivement, et ne disant pas beaucoup. Quand ils ont parlé, il était en français. Il y avait aussi trois ou quatre femmes et un homme sitting aux tables devant une télévision géante d'écran, observant l'Investiture sur un canal de langue française.

J'ai demandé à la femme travaillant derrière la barre – who is l'éspouse du propriétaire de St. Brendan, je crois – si elle pourrait pouvoir mettre une des télévisions on en Anglais, si il would not interfere avec le visionnement des canaux français. Elle était assez aimable pour faire ceci pour moi.

La barre, le secteur dinant, un bandstand, et la télévision géant d'écran – ce qui est la taille du mur – sont tous dans une grande salle. Outre du coin de la salle, à la droite du grand écran, il y a un salon, comme une salle de séjour confortable, avec leather divans, et une cheminée artificielle. Elle a mis la télé dans cette chambre sur le canal d'anglais. I sat avec une tasse de café sur le divan for a while, et alors I took un siège à une petite table de cocktail, entre le salon et le grand écran. Ceci a signifié que mon oreille droite a été tourné vers le bruit de la télévision d'anglais, et que mon oreille gauche a été tourné vers le bruit de la télévision français. Bienvenue au Québec, monsieur Mario-Jacques.

J'ai principalement regardé le grand écran. J'ai entendu les mots parlés trois fois – premier, vivez en anglais ((du canal d'anglais)), la deuxième fois en français ((du canal d'français)) et pour quelque raison le bruit ((et image)) ont été retardés, du canal français. Alors j'entendrait la traduction française, habituellement juste avant les prochains mots de phrase de anglais TV. C'était un peu fou. Mais c'était une experience. Un Américain-Québecer experience.

Bien sûr, un moment dans l'histoire. Pour moi, c'était le prochain clic de l'horloge après ce moment les Américains se réfèrent: *"9-11."* Un oscillation du pendule – des ténèbres à la lumière du soleil.

J'étais joined à mon table de cocktail pour ceci momentous occasion by Georges Simoneau, who was one of the first Staffordians who I came to know, back a few years ago, quand he was the chef and owner of a terrific restaurant in Stafford. J'étais heureux to have Georges join me, mais il á commence à parler au-dessus du bruit venez du canal français. Though Georges est tout à fait bilingue and his mother tongue is french, he kept saying choses comme: "Why don't they have the English subtitles on the TV?" et, "This is about the American President – we should be watching this in English!" At this point I realized that I wanted to watch the proceedings sans talking to anyone.

J'ai dit à Georges que j'étais moving to the Anglais salon parce que j'ai voulu to concentrate on Barack's speech. Georges came avec moi. He continued talking. Il a parlé tandis que we stood, shoulder to shoulder, avec our eyes à la télé haute sur le mur devant nous. Il a dit: "I used to like my name until George Bush became the President of the United States. I have not liked having the name, *'Georges,'* during the last eight years – you know what I mean? Even though it is spelled with an, *'s'* ... only some silly Anglophones pronounce the 's'… it is still *George*, you know what I mean? Same as George W. Now, come to think of it, I would like it if people would start to call me, 'Barack,' or, 'Obama.'" Bien sûr, j'ai fait une note mentale appeler lui 'Barack' la prochaine fois que je vois Georges.

Dans réponse, j'ai incliné ma tête en haut et en bas pour dire, 'yes,' sans speaking out loud. I tried pour écouter à Tom Brokaw à la télévision devant nous et be aussi poli que je pourrais être à Georges. J'ai su he had been drinking – combien, je ne sais pas – mais je suspecte que ceci pourrait have contributed à Georges being un peu chatty.

Quand I sat down sur un des divans, Georges sat down on l'autre. Mais ensuite, mon dieu, The Queen of Soul appeared on the television screen, pour chanter: *"My Country Tis of Thee."* Georges got up outre du divan, juste après que j'ai fait. Et I got up from le divan juste après Ray Charles was stepping out of another universe, pour observer Miss Aretha Franklin chanter. I wonder combien black people were watching à ce moment et reciting to themselves les mots

95

d'un nouveau, edited, national anthemn: *"R-E-S-P-E-C-T, tell you what it means to me..."*

Georges put sa main over his heart, comme si il était pledging. Il a dit à moi, solemnly, "I am standing up out of respect for you, Mario-Jacques."

I was standing avec my arms folded across my chest. Georges nudged me, to get me pour mettre ma main over mon coeur. J'ai répondu rapidement à Georges parce que j'ai voulu ècouter à Aretha. "The pledge is for the flag, Georges. You don't have to do that ici, in front of the TV, for this song."

Georges relented, "I am doing out of my respect for you. I am honored to be sharing this moment with you, Mario-Jacques. And I am doing this for your great country, the United States of America."

Je n'ai rien dit, mais j'ai touché his shoulder lightly, to express merci. I did not speak, je suis retourné mon attention to the télé.

Mon attention was drawn to Aretha Franklin's Chapeau. Mais oui, c'est, *"Chapeau,"* avec a capital, *"C."* Aretha's Chapeau was this textured gris matériel – velour, ou felt peut-être, je ne sais pas – that looked à moi comme a stylized scarf worn around sa tête, avec un grand bow. Whoever designed that hat designed a *Hat,* avec a capital, "H." Aretha's Chapeau answered une question familiar à un couple de millards femmes dans le monde: *"How can one wrap cloth around the head, tie a bow or two, and make a beautiful hat?"* Parfait. Peut-être, dans un facon, c'était le personification de the transition of the Black woman in the U.S.A from the slave auction block to standing on the most important platform in the world on this day. Mais oui, the *audacity de hope.*

Après Aretha a chanté, we settled down to watching l'Investiture avec peu de conversation. Pour moi, il était tout comme observer l'evénement par un télescope. Je me rappellerai de regarder par mon télescope at George W looking comme le père de l'homme que est devenu président il y a huit ans, and to le Dick Cheney, dans his wheelchair, looking comme la réincarnation of Président Franklin Delano Roosevelt, réincarné par le diable.

Aussi, je me rappellerai qu'un ministre did not ask Dieu pour bénir les soldats américains, mais pour que les gens à battre tanks dedans tracteurs. When will we hear the Christians in the states saying, "Let us beat tanks into tractors," more often than they say: "Fight terrorism?" This would be un changement de paradigme des proportions bibliques.

Après Barack Obama a présenté son discours, je suis retourné à la maison. Je suis immédiatement allé dans l'Internet trouver une copie de son discours. J'ai lu le discours et I recalled the parts quand I was brought to tears. Le temps quand Barack a dit qu'il était un homme, "...whose father less than sixty years ago might not have been served at a local restaurant [mais] can now stand before you to take a most sacred oath." Et un autre temps, quand Barack a dit: "...to all the other people and governments who are watching today, from the grandest capitals to the small village where my father was born: Know that America is a friend of each nation and every man, woman and child who seeks a future of peace and dignity...and that we are ready to lead once more."

We shall see what we shall see. Quelque fois, plus ca change, plus c'est la même chose. Mais les mots de Barack Obama sont les mots d'un homme qui est exceptionelle. This was a day for U.S.A America to be proud.

2 Mai 2009

"Déjeuner Avec Le Maire"

Met Ben Lamontagne au Café Dumont ce matin pour le déjeuner. We met environ 8h30m. C'était un dimanche matin tranquille dans le café, et dans la ville. Il y avait peut-être dix personnes, à trois ou quatre tables, dans le café.

As we sat down, Ben a dit a moi, "I took my morning walk and I'm like an old dog who has to pee at every post, because everyone who sees me has something to say to me, Mario."

Our waitress, Nicole, came over to la table et began parler avec nous en anglais. Ben interrupted elle, et il a dit à elle en français que elle should not parle avec moi en anglais parce que je veux pratiquer mon français. Je pense this is what il a dit. En tout cas, Nicole turned toward me, avec un grand sourire sur son visage, et elle began parler à moi en français. I figured elle parlait du menu, peut-être asking for my order. J'ai dit, reflexively: "La même chose."

Nicole's sourire turned dedans a laugh, donc I asked elle parler en anglais, et j'ai dit que I would speak en français, ou franglais. Ensuite Nicole a dit, in a lovely sing-songy manière, "Le maire is just going to have toast. Would you like to have the toast? Ou peut-être you will have the *muesli and the yogourt,* as you did yesterday, and which you seemed to like, very much?"

J'ai dit, "Oui. C'est une bonne idée, *muesli et yogourt.* C'est bon. Merci."

Ben a dit, "What's going on, Mario? You're not ordering *la même chose* today. You love the même here." He laughed at his own joke. Ha, ha.

J'ai dit: "Je sais, Ben. Mais je pense Nicole understood I would like *muesli and yogourt.* Mon français is getting better, non? Je suis certaine I will be able to speak français by my next incarnation."

Ben gave me quelques mots of encouragement et puis we segued dedans une conversation au sujet la politique. Plus prècis, we talked au sujet la décision Ben has made to run encore pour le maire. Pas vraiment une surprise, depuis Ben has been le maire pendant 22 années. He lost une election, il y a six ans – parce que beaucoup personnes blamed him pour l'expansion d'un Ultramar gas station/depanneur dans la ville. Bientôt après that election, les gens realized they had made une erreur. Quand Ben ran for office la prochaine fois, il a gagné in a landslide.

Ben Lamontagne est une instituition en Stafford. En une manière, la seule institution réel plus enduring dans la ville que le maire Lamontagne est Mont Stafford.

J'ai dit a Ben, "Here is a campaign slogan for you: *'Ben Lamontagne and Mount Stafford. Their names are almost synonymous.'*"

Ben a dit, "I think I'll stick with, *'Ben Lamontagne for le maire.* Don't you like that Mario? It's good Franglais!'" And he laughed at his joke. Ha, ha, ha.

En tout cas, Ben seems to be feeling bon, même excited, comment choses are shaping up for his prochaine run pour le maire. Il sera running avec deux personnes qui seront bons pour la ville, et

Ben is looking forward to campaigning avec eux, et working avec eux on the town board.

I asked le Maire if he was consuming stress, ou s'il était setting himself up pour tomber the workaholic bandwagon, et he seems to be comme sobre au sujet ceci comme a recovering workaholic can be.

Si quelqu'un possesses les energies Staffordian, c'est le maire. Ben exudes passion pour les choses he speaks about. Quand he speaks avec moi, au sujet la ville, ou au sujet the Eastern Townships, ou Québec, ou we speak au sujet Barack Obama, ou Sarah Palin, ou les deux solitudes, ou vie et mort dans nos familles, il parle avec passion, et il energizes mes passions.

During breakfast hier I learned that Ben's father, Ken Lamontagne, never owned a car until the late 1950's. He didn't need one, parce que he walked to work. Ben's family lived dans trois maisons différentes en Stafford, et chacun était dans une promenade de cinq minutes de Rue Principal. Ken Lamontagne was the accountant for la cour à boir Stafford Lumber. When Ken Lamontagne was 35-years-old, he was making 35$ par semaine. Bien sûr, c'était les 1950's, around the time Little Richard had invented rock and roll.

During dejeuner aujourd'hui I learned that Ben's father et Ben's uncle, Henry, donated la terre où la ville de Stafford maintenant has the town pool and ball fields. Ben's uncle Henry, who also worked for Stafford Lumber, didn't have any more wealth than Ben's father. He was making less than 35$ par semaine in the late fifties, et il était 50-quelquechose in age. Yet, in 1959 the Lamontagne frères bought the land from two different farmers, pour environ 1500$, et en suite turned la terre over à la ville. Comment the brothers Lamontagne were able to do this is beyond me, et Ben says he has never been able to figure it out. C'est aussi remarquable que son pàre et son oncle were si inclined pour donner à la communauté, n'est-ce pas ? Quand j'ai dit à Ben que son père et son oncle must have been a special breed to be so giving, he seemed to think that I was making plus of it than it was. Bien sûr, il est un vrai Quebecer. Très modeste.

Aussi, Ben m'a dit que sa mère et sa tante had established et ran a free violin school, on the second floor de l'hotel de ville, pendant beaucoup d'années. En fait, encore l'ecole est operating on

99

the second floor de l'hotel de ville, as a service sponsored by la ville..

La mère de Ben était un francophone avec le sang d'Abenaki et son père était un anglophone avec le sang Iroquois. Sa famille maternelle extends from Vermont nordique au Québec nordique. La même chose pour son famille paternelle.

Pendant notre dejeuner, je pensais au sujet how incroyable il était que Ben has plus les compétences que le governeur du Texas ou le governeur de l'Alaska. Voici Ben Lamontagne, le maire de la ville de Stafford, a town which Tom Inghalls says exists only in the minds of a few people. The mayor of this little town in Québec could govern states from below and above the 49th parallel better than their present governors. He would at least start to unravel the gordion knot of problems in Texas and Alaska – les deux plus grands états aux U.S.A. Ironique, n'est-ce pas, if the governor of Alaska tried to be le maire de Stafford, elle would be *sans indice*, clueless in Seattle. Et si le governeur du Texas tried to be le maire de Stafford, probablement he would think c'était une bonne idée pour Stafford á séparé du Québec, mais pas Canada. Pourquoi pas, après tous? Le governeur du Texas croit que peut-être c'est une bonne idée pour Texas séparé from the U.S.A. Comment dit-on, *"nincompoop,"* en français ?

15 Juin 2009

"An Invitation To Chez Sweat"

I received un courriel from Diana Stuart aujourd'hui, part of a group e-mail, asking if I would be interested in participating in a sweat lodge cérémonie. Je ne sais pas beaucoup au sujet sweat lodge ceremonies, mais the most vivid image I have of a sweat lodge cérémonie est du film, *A Man Called Horse*. C'était le film in which a British aristocrat decides to apply for dual citizenship in a Native American nation. He was required to go through a rite of passage, carried out in a sweat lodge. It would have been a heck of a lot easier for him to convert to Judaism, in which case a rabbi merely cuts off un petit piece of your penis, and the worse thing that can happen is that you are in excruciating pain for a while. In the sweat lodge ceremony depicted in *A Man Called Horse,* the aristocrat ((played by the British actor Richard Harris)) had to sweat enough to fill a baker's dozen of pottery bowls, and hallucinate for two or three days, and then hooks were put into his breast skin, and then ropes were fastened to the hooks, and then he was hoisted up with the ropes to the top of the teepee sweat lodge, where he had to hang for a good while longer. Having to go through that last part of the ceremony is the major reason why some people I know, who happen to be Jewish, refer to the Richard Harris character as, "*A Man Called Schmuck.*"

But I saw the sweat lodge that Diana has behind her house, and it does not look at all like the sweat lodge that I saw in *A Man Called Horse.* And I'm sure the ceremony that will be carried out in the sweat lodge that Diana has will be nothing like the ceremony that was shown in *A Man Called Horse.* At least I hope not. Peut-être I should have given more thought to it before I sent un courriel back to Diana, saying that I *would* be interested in participating.

My intuition is telling me that this is a thing for me to do. Not a, "no sweat," thing to do, but something is drawing me to do this. We shall see what we shall see.

28 Juin 2009

"*Non Sweat*"

Je ne sais pas what happened avec le sweat lodge cérémonie à la maison de Diana Stuart. J'ai pensé que it was going to be ce soir. I have not drank any café ou thé ou vin dans les 24 dernières heures. I have been drinking beaucoup d'eau sacrée de Stafford du robinet près du IGA, et Perrier. Mon esprit est disposé et mon coeur est ouvert. Je crois que je prépare. Mais I have not received un courriel ou un appel téléphonique concernant le sweat lodge cérémonie. Peut-être Diana was not able pour trouver a fire keeper. Peut-être c'est la pluie. Peut-être the sweat lodge est dans mon futur, dans le nord.

5 Juillet 2009

"La Frontière À Richford, Vermont"

J'ai traversé la frontière environ midi aujourd'hui, pour acheter le gaz dans Richford, Vermont, at The Pinnacle Peddler. Aussi, j'ai voulu acheter Claritin D au pharmacie dans Enosburg Falls. J'ai oublié qu'il y a une pharmacie tucked away sur le deuxieme étage du centre médical dans Richford. So I drove environ 30 minutes round-trip sans raison.

Quand I got to la frontière il y avait six voitures lined up devant de moi, waiting to pass through la douane américain. D'ordinaire, quand je traverse la frontière à Richford, il est rare for there to be plus d'une voiture devant de moi.

I had to wait environ 20 minutes sur la ligne. Je ne sais pas pourquoi they did not open une deuxième ligne pendant ce temps occupé. Peut-être ils figurent que les canadiennes sont les personnes patientes, ainsi pourquoi être concerné? Ou peut-être this is juste the impatient New Yorker in me talking.

I could not listen to my French language lesson on the CD while I waited. Comme le bon Américain-Quebecer que I try to be, I did not want to idle the car engine for so long et I also did not want to wear out the battery in the CD player while I waited at the border crossing, so I occupied my thoughts in contemplation of my surroundings, and it occurred to me that I was in no-man's land between the two border crossings – out of Canada, but not officially in the USA. For the moment, existing outside of any country. Plus comme un citoyen du monde que normale.

What if I ran out of le gaz tandis que I was waiting? I daydreamed que les américains would probablement let me téléphoner pour un camiòn pour towing, mais I would have to pay un bras et une jambe pour le camiòn. Juste comme health care dans les

102

états. "Vous avez un problème? C'est *votre* problème." And it costs an arm and a leg, et les yeux de la tête.

Aussi, I daydreamed au sujet what would have been done at the border crossings si John McCain et Sarah Palin had been elected en novembre. By now, they would not have had time to put up an iron curtain across the border, similar to the one being erected en Mexique. But by now McCain and Palin would have made a deal with Stephen Harper to split no-mans land at all border crossings 50-50, so that the United States could lease advertising space, and Canada could also, except for in Québec. La Belle Province would keep the no-mans land between the border crossings as is. Plus écologique.

Aussi, pendant I waited, j'ai lu les signes. "*Proceed to Inspection on Green Light,*" and written below that: "*Avancer À L'Inspection Sur Le Vert.*" Et écrit sur le signe hexagone rouge familier d'arrêt: "Stop," over un miniscule "Arrêt." Un autre signe a dit: "Proceed," over, "Avancer." Above the customs building, I took notice du signe qui a indiqué, en noir et blanc: "US Border Inspection Station."

Aussi, j'ai tourné autour et regardé over my shoulder à les douanes canadiennes. Les signes aussi looked official, et they were tous bilingues. Quand you enter the U.S here you feel like you are being inspected. Quand you enter le Québec you feel comme you are being welcomed. I sat there contemplating les différences entre traversing la frontière d'un côté ou l'autre jusqu'a it was mon tour à passer.

I recognized the american customs officer, mais je ne suis pas certain s'il recognized me. Il à posé les questions standard. "Where do you live? What do you do? Anything to declare?" And then they usually slip in one trick question, such as, "Who is the third baseman for the New York Mets?" or, "Do you have any tomatoes?" As much as I wanted to, I did not give any funny answers to the questions.

C'est ne pas une bonne idée to joke avec the customs officers on the American side. I should say, most of these men and women are appropriately professional and also manage to be friendly, as on the Québec side. But I think there is a certain militaristic attitude that intrudes on the performance of some officers. The cloud of residue from the 9-11 fall of the Twin Towers is still settling at the border crossings. It's going to take a few more years before this over-reaction diminishes, non? Anyway, I passed inspection in less than a minute, and was on my way dedans les états via la ville de Richford, Vermont, home of The Pinnacle Peddler.

Après la douane, le route winds up a hill. At the top of the hill, à la droite, il ya une belle vue – il ya un cornfield, une vallée, et les montagnes dans la distance. They should put up a big picture frame at that spot. It would become une attraction touristique. Richford would be thought of as: "That little town near the border, with the big picture frame on the hill." Not the worst way to be known as a town, on the Vermont side of the border.

If you look at Mont Pinacle from the road that leads up to the border crossing near Richford, the mountain range forms the silhouette of a pregnant native princess lying on her back. According to legend, the Mont Pinacle Princess is a monument created by Mother Nature, and welcomes people to continue north, where a new species of human beings will be born, and l'Age de Gaia will commence.

The first or second house I passed on la gauche had a long clothesline avec bed sheets hanging, and such an assortment of multi-colored clothes hanging that it looked artistique. In front of the next house there were hanging plants for sale. They use the honor system – anyone can take a plant and leave money. It occurs to me that Long Island, all over Long Island, used to be a place where the honor system operated. Now there are just a few spots on the East End of Long Island where the honor system operates. Je pense que le comportement des gens de Long Island ne sont pas comme honorable comme le comportement des gens de Vermont ou des gens du Québec. Anyway…the only cars that would drive past this house, other than those of their next-door neighbors, would be going to ou from the border. The people selling these plants must take Canadian money. But they have a sign written en anglais, seulement. Evidently, they are not trying to cater to french-speaking people, ou they are confident that so many québécois who pass through here parlez anglais. Mais, it is also as if Canadians do not also speak French. Je répète journal intime: *comme si les Canadiens ne parlent pas le français.* And by car, it is about 60 seconds from la province du Québec.

I pulled my car over to the side once I got past the top of the road, to view the surroundings and to consider what the people from Quebec look at, as they enter the U.S.A from ici. Vers ma droite, et downhill, il y a le Blue Seal production center. The invisible hand of capitalism has not yet moved Blue Seal to China or Mexico. They must sell beaucoup feed for livestock. I counted 28 tractor-trailers lined up, facing the loading docks. The last time I saw so many tractor-trailers lined up was a few months ago, in Brooklyn. They were parked in an environment of decrepit warehouses that use barbwire to control people, and not to control livestock.

Richford, Vermont, et Brooklyn, NY. Slightly different cultures, eh? I gazed at the backdrop for the Blue Seal loading docks – a low range of pastel-green mountains, a thing of beauty stretched across the entire horizon. This landscape around Blue Seal est une paysage that someone should paint.

I noticed that above the roof of the tallest Blue Seal building is a metal scaffolding, that looks odd to me. The ironwork looks like it could have been transplanted from the bridge of a submarine or a battleship. This, bien sûr, is extremely unlikely. Mais, qui sais? Ma perception est influencée par un drapeau américain that flies from the top of this scaffolding. This is *literally* a high-flying red, white and blue.

Je ne sais pas how to feel au sujet cet affichage du drapeau. Aujourd'hui, c'est difficile to clearly understand what is being expressed lorsque le drapeau américain est affiché. As far as I am concerned, no matter how tall the pole, the American flag does not fly high when it is degraded to being a device to beckon shoppers. Ici, à Blue Seal, je ne suis pas certain what the flying of this flag means. Peut-être c'est un memorial pour Blue Seal people who died in combat?

Un maison à travers la rue du Blue Seal aussi flies un drapeau américain. It is le jour après le 4ème de juillet, Independence Day aux États-Unis. Mais ce drapeau at Blue Seal flies plus que juste national holidays, je suis certain.

I parked ma voiture encore, devant une autre maison à travers la rue du Blue Seal. Ce maison has a red tin roof over an open porch, painted gray. Trim on the house is painted juste vers la même couleur comme le mulch rouge dans le lit de fleur. The flowerbed has yellow flowers. Each flower stands alone, at equal distances from each other, in exact rows…comme bonbons in a box, ou comme les voitures stuck dans la circulation.

Bricks rouge sont buried dans le terre et circle a bush et deux arbres. Petit plants aussi circle les arbres. They are planted equal distances apart from each other. Toy américain drapeaux on wooden sticks are pushed dans le terre, centered sur le porch et le jardin. Sur le porch il y a trois posts, which are set equal distances from each other. The four front windows de l'maison are centered, bien sûr. Il y a une précision géometrique à cette maison.

Vers la gauche, où je peux voir vers the back de la maison, il y a un camion rouge de *Chevy*. Les routes autour d'ici can be mighty dusty, mais ce Chevy est brille brillant. Le camion is parked derrière un above ground piscine. The wooden steps et platform for the pool have not yet been painted rouge, they remain naturel. Vers la droite, au coin de la propriété, quatre grandes roches have been strategically placed, peut-être to prevent cars from taking a short-cut across the lawn. Les gens font ceci dans the suburbs de Long Island, mais je ne sais pas au sujet ici. Aussi, les rochers en face du maison ici could stop a tractor-trailer.

I know that Vermont elected Bernie Sanders, the only senator in the United States who is a socialist ou a social-democrat, but my sense is that the Chevy parked in the back of this house does not have a Bernie Sanders bumper sticker, or a Frank Zappa window decal. Bien sûr, I could be totally wrong. Mais oui, this house could be owned by some flatlanders who just moved up from Connecticut, and are Zen Buddhist fundamentalists, but I don't think so.

13 Juillet 2009

"Sweat Lodge Question Answered"

J'ai vu Diana Stuart ce matin à l'IGA et elle m'a dit que la cérémonie sweat lodge occurred. Apparently, quelque chose was miscommunicated entre nous avec les courriels we exchanged. Elle a dit que la cérémonie était un grand succès, et there will be plus. Je serai prêt pour la prochaine cérémonie. Je pense.

12 Aout 2009

Cet après-midi j'étais en ville et crossing the street at the crosswalk qui est près du bureau de poste et en face du Goût de la Vie. I must be plus prudent, parce que je sens tellement sûr traversant la rue ici, que il est dangereux. Je ne veux pas être over confident. If I was crossing a street in any of the towns south of la frontière, just a few miles from here, I would not cross their rue Principals, their Main Streets, avec la même confiance que j'ai quand je traverse rue Principal à Stafford. Soooo, j'ai vu from *the corner of my eye* un petit camion driving vers moi, vers the crosswalk. Je n'a pas remarqué que c'était Merlin The Magician, who probably came into la ville to buy alchemical supplies.

Merlie shouted to me, "Monsieur Mario! Salutations!" Je me suis arrêté et tourné while I was still in the crosswalk, not quite across la rue yet. Merlin a ajouté, in a lower voice, just about mouthing it, so no one else could hear what he was saying sauf moi: "I want to talk to you about 2012."

J'ai répondu, "D'accord. I will call you."

I was hoping I could call Merlin ce soir, et peut-être visit avec lui ce soir, mais I am trying to hike entre two and four hours chaque jour ce mois. Mais, après my hike ce soir c'était trop tard, way too late to call him. I am intrigued. All of this au sujet 2012 is becoming more noticeable.

27 Aout 2009

"Breakfast Pizza At Le Pinnacle Peddler"

Ce matin, while on my way to St. Albans, to pick up a book at The Eloquent Page, I stopped at the Pinnacle Peddler, dans Richford. J'aime le Pinnacle Peddler. Il y a quelque chose au sujet de cet endroit.

I got there environ 6h. C'était le premiere temps I was able to get there at the crack of dawn et be able to sit down. D'ordinaire, quand I am in le Peddler à six le matin, I am on my way back to New York, et I just grab quelque café après I fill up avec gaz.

Le Pinnacle Peddler est environ cinq minutes de la frontière. Quelque people, peut-être, think of it as a Mobil gas station avec une depanneur/quik-stop attached. It is plus comme a late 20th century Vermont general store avec a Mobil gas station attached. Il y a aussi a hair salon et une boutique de cadeaux, all connected, in the same building. Weird mélange, non? Mais, le Pinnacle Peddler is a gathering place for good spirited people.

There are six pumps et three petit islands pour gaz là. You can pump your gas first, et then, *et ensuite(!)*, go inside et pay. Oui, oui – *puis(!)*, you can go inside et puis payer. You do not have to leave your carte de crédit ou a child who is a close relative to you avec le caissier first. Maintenant, in the year 2009, it is plutôt amazing that I can stop at this place five minutes from la frontière du Québec, avec New York plates sur ma voiture, et be trusted to pay *after* – encore, *après(!),* I have pumped.

Change, for the worse, is not far from here. Stay on Route 105, the road that le Peddler is on, et you will come to un autre station in St. Albans, Vermont (je pense it is an Exxon, peut-être a Mobil, whatever). Là, you pay avec credit card ou cash *first,* Charlie Brown. Here, ici à le Peddler, a stranger with New York license plates is trusted. *There* (à Mobil-Exxon-Starbucks-Taco Bell-Whatever) where corporate culture has replaced local culture, it is: *In God we trust, et all others: Fuhgeddaboutit.*

There, in that other world, that is not so far down the road from Richford, Vermont, you can buy a breakfast, as the Exxon-Mobil signs say: *"on the run"* – in some cases prepared and prepackaged in some far away place that is far more like a laboratory than a kitchen. Ici, au Pinnacle Peddler, you can sit at a little counter avec four stools, et see food prepared right in front of you, in a kitchen that smells like a kitchen, instead of a laboratory or a McDonald's.

When I got to the Peddler ce matin, encore, at 6h, there was no one sitting at the counter, so I put my note pad on the stool at the end of the counter, et drew myself a medium Green Mountain coffee, "house blend." I took a sip, et decided that it was d'accord, mais not as much to my liking as le café au Café Dumont ou The Lie dans Stafford. I would say that Green Mountain coffee is to Vermonters what depanneur *7-11* coffee is to New Yorkers, et what Tim Hortons coffee is to Canadians.

Quand you sit at the counter at the Peddler it is a lot like sitting at a kitchen counter in a home, which is where people most like to gather as a group, non? I thought about this as I looked at the heart-shaped plaque à côté de counter that said: *"Friends gather here."* I did not doubt that these were true and heart-spoken words. I was not looking at a sign mandated for a franchise, by some corporate fiat. If some corporate chain were to take over the Pinnacle Peddler, that sign would go, or it would soon become meaningless, je pense. Customers anonymous to each other would gather there…if people gathered there at all. The family and friends who work there would be wearing name tags, which would clearly identify that the sense of community was being replaced with corporate nonsense.

En tout cas, on the counter, à côté du mur, il y avait an assortment of large flowers, placed non-pretentiously in a non-pretentious plastic container, not a vase. Stacked on the counter were also breakfast sandwiches – eggs avec sausage patties in muffins, eggs avec bacon, et avec cheese ou without, it looked like. These are the kinds of breakfast sandwiches that McDonald's and the other fast-food joints imitate poorly and profitably.

Also on the counter was a copy of today's *Burlington Free Press* – which is not a tabloid, et a helluva lot better paper to read with a breakfast sandwich than the *New York* tabernacle *Post.* I turned the paper so I could see the front page headline, which read: *"For America, he was a defender of a dream."* I thought to myself: *Aaah, il est mort hier.* Ted Kennedy. Et juste hier, while listening to a French lesson on a CD, I learned that the way to say, "he died yesterday," en français, est: *"Il est mort hier."* Ironique.

Synchronistique aussi, parce que mon ami, Babette, a dit à moi hier: "When will you get a chance to use that phrase?" Et when she said that, it flashed through my mind that I might be using it bientôt. Not the sort of synchronicity that brings a smile to my face.

Anyway, while I was reading the story about Ted Kennedy, three men, one at a time, came into the Pinnacle Peddler, poured their coffees, et sat down on chairs that were set in a semi-circle, a few feet from where I sat at the counter. They looked like farmers to me, parce que they were wearing coveralls, soiled baseball hats, et they walked slow, like they were used to walking through crop fields, ou in mud. Et they had farmers hands. For a few minutes I focused on listening to their conversation, mais they really did not have much to say to each other.

One said: "Kind of cold today."

After a period of silence, one of the others responded quietly: "Yup, had to turn the heater on today."

More silence, then one of them said: "Thirty-eight in the hole."

My guess is that he was referring to the temperature being thirty-eight, Fahrenheit, in a valley, ou in some kind of ditch or a hole on his farm. Whatever he was referring to, it took a while for a response to come from anyone in the group, and when a response did come, it was only: "Thirty-eight?"

This was quite a scene. *Waiting for Godot* made more sense to me the first time I saw it. I thought I was going to be taking all kinds of notes on les choses these men would be saying to each other, mais they had little to say. Mais, somehow, I could tell that they just felt good et confortable avec le dialogue minimal.

Mon attention went to the chalkboard on the wall in the kitchen area. The kinds of meat et cheeses that could be ordered on a sandwich were listed. Pour fromage, you could order: *Provolone, American, cheddar, swiss, ex-sharp*, et *muenster*. What?! No brie?! No camembert?! The border is only minutes from here, et on l'autre côté you are not going to find *American, provolone, cheddar, swiss, muenster*, on the chalkboards there. Cinq minutes, culture différent.

While I was looking at the chalkboard, the cook – a très occupé grandmotherly sorte – walked into the cooking area, carrying toward me an oven pan avec a pizza on it, sans topping. Her eyes seemed to follow mine to the chalkboard, mais très rapide, parce que she could not afford le temps to be distracted by this *I*-talian looking flatlander sitting at the end of the counter, who was looking at the chalkboard and writing quelque chose on a yellow pad.

I watched her slip the pizza into the oven, which was not a pizza oven comme you would find in any pizzeria in the greater metropolitan area de New York. It was a commercial pizza oven, mais it was not that much bigger than an ordinary household wall oven. I guess that's all they need for the volume of business they do here. The pizza that I've seen on the counter at the Pinnacle Peddler always looks good. Over the years I've found that in Vermont they make pizza as if their real specialty is maple syrup, if you know what I mean. Mais the pizza in le Pinnacle Peddler would be respectable in any pizza place in New York, even on Staten Island – where the standards for pizza et cannolis are as high as the standards in the mother country, Italy.

Not only does it look like they have good pizza at Pinnacle Peddler, mais they have a selection, a variety of pizza. Après que j'ai observé le très occupé cook put the pizza in the oven, I looked at the chalkboard et saw that there were about six different kinds of pizza listed. I read down the list: *"Hawaiian," "Tuscan," "Greek," "Veggie"*... *Hmm, this is something,* I thought to myself. *Plus de something, c'est: quelque...chose !* Somebody (Paulette Legault – the owner, le propriétaire) decided to do pizza right ici.

I looked up at the chalkboard encore et saw that I had overlooked one of the kinds of pizza offered. First on the list was: *"Breakfast."* Oui, *"breakfast* pizza!" What a concept: *Déjeuner pizza.* It would sound better, peut-être, si it was called: *"Pizza déjeuner,"* je pense. Mais, c'est ne pas importante.

Bien sûr, I have had cold pizza for breakfast more than a few times. Mais it was not, *"breakfast pizza,"* it was just leftover pizza. Call me culturally illiterate, call me a lapsed Italian, mais I never heard of, "breakfast pizza," before. I wanted to ask the cook if, *"breakfast pizza,"* was *actually* breakfast pizza, mais it did not seem like the sort of metaphysical question she would have wanted to hear right then, while she was busy shuffling back and forth avec things from the food pantry. So I waited a while, until she came near me to stack more egg muffins on this huge pile that was just to my side, on the counter. Encore, these are the *real* egg muffins that McDonald's poorly imitates avec their, *"Mc"* muffins. The egg muffins at

111

Pinnacle Peddler are the egg muffins that Vermont *farmers* eat, not shoppers in indoor malls, if you know what I mean.

I foolishly thought I might strike up a conversation, however short, avec le très occupé cook. Tandis que she was stacking the egg muffins, j'ai dit: "I see '*breakfast pizza,*' is listed."

She did not say anything in response, mais I did not feel any negative energy coming from her toward me. Je ne sais pas, peut-être she did not realize my statement was a question, ou peut-être she felt there was no rush to answer my question, which there was not. Ou peut-être it was just parce que she was operating on Vermont Time, which is très différent from New York Time, ou temps Québec. After she finished stacking the muffins, I quietly asked: "It's pizza? I don't think I've ever seen, 'breakfast pizza,' before."

After a time, as if she was driving in Burlington and was just asked a question by her grandson in the car seat behind her, elle a dit: "Yeah, it's pizza…We put breakfast stuff on it…eggs, bacon."

D'accord. She talked me into it. J'ai décidé I would try the breakfast pizza – as long as it did not look unappealing quand I saw what it looked like.

I had a second tasse de café tandis que I sat at the counter reflecting on les environs. A steady stream of people – mostly men, alone – came in and payed for gas at the counter à côté de front door. The pretty young woman behind the counter, Linda, gives everyone a smile. The men notice that her soft bleu eyes match her sweater. The men say nothing about her eyes, mais they make comments on the weather. She is friendly with them. Neighborly friendly. Il est evident que she is a giving person. Ici, in the Pinnacle Peddler, she does not have to wear a nameplate, as they do in the corporate stores.

A steady flow of people – mostly men, mais les femmes aussi, entered. They took their coffee from the row of Green Mountain thermoses derrière moi, et ensuite grabbed an egg muffin from the pile à côté de moi. I noticed a lot of potbellies. Not too many *muesli et yogourt* people among les habituées.

A man who looked to me like a farmer came in et began talking to the circle of men près de la café, au sujet having the lens cut out of his eye et having it replaced avec a plastic lens. Il a dit que it probably cost seven or eight thousand dollars to do this, et it was a good thing that he had insurance. His words gave me more of a jolt than the Green Mountain coffee I was drinking. Unless I misunderstood, he had to lay out seven or eight thousand dollars from his own pocket, even though he *had* insurance! He *had* insurance and it still cost him seven or eight thousand dollars! American private enterprise health insurance: What a concept. And not as good as breakfast pizza for someone with a stomach problem. En tout cas, none of the men in this circle said to their friend, "Yeah, we need to change things," after hearing what I heard.

These were men of few words, at least on this morning. No one referred to Ted Kennedy, who evidently spent many hours of his dying days trying to do what he could do so that every person in the states would have health insurance, like in Canada. My thoughts went to Kennedy, and I decided to read the story about him in le *Burlington Free Press.* Then my thoughts went to the breakfast pizza, which had been placed on a special rack, right in front of me, on the counter. I decided I would try a piece of the breakfast pizza.

...Cher Journal Intime, I see my long lost friend, Paddy O"Brien, parking his car en face chez moi. I will have to continue this entry plus tard...

27 Aout 2009

"Circumambulating Kalish et Stafford"

Paddy O'Brien finally reappeared. I have not seen him for any length of time since July 9 (which I know from checking my diary entries). En fait, je pense I have only seen him once since July 9, when he was dancing up a storm at La Cantina, quand Tap-Tap was in town. This morning, as I was writing about the Pinnacle Peddler, I heard a car coming up the road, looked up, et saw that it was Paddy. I went outside to greet him. From le terrace dehors the sliding door, I yelled down to him as he was getting out of his car, avec my best Sicilian accent, et avec my fingers pursed and shaking Sicilian style: *"Finalmente!"*

Paddy's response was: "You still practicing your French? Give it up already. Practice detachment."

Before I got a chance to tell Paddy that the, *"finalmente,"* I yelled was not français, mais le mot sicilien that kinda means: "Where have you gone, Joe DiMaggio?" Paddy was already saying quelque chose au sujet I needed to meditate. I could see that he was emitting a lot of energy.

J'ai dit à lui, "I have been meditating more in the past few weeks. Not enough, but getting there, especially while I have been hiking. And I've been doing some zen walks lately, up to Lac Frog, up to Abenaki."

I was saying this while he was walking up the front steps, from the road. Encore, I could see he was emitting beaucoup d'énergie. He was not looking at me, mais talking, going on avec questions about the meditation I was doing. Quand he was in Montreal – back in the day in Montreal, this was quelque chose comme le mindset Paddy would be in quand he was approaching a guy who owed him some money, je suspecte.

He was talking quietly, almost under his breath, mais he was shooting the questions at me, shooting avec a silencer. "Have you been meditating in the house, too? You setting aside time every day to meditate? Do you realize this is the most important thing for you to do? You know that? Annick and I been meditating an hour in the morning an hour at night for 25 years. Now I'm running around back and forth to Montreal on account I got to take care of my mother, so that's getting in the way a bit, but I'm doing the work, and that's what I'm trying to get across to you, you got to do the work and stop taking all the notes." When Paddy is stringing his sentences et his thoughts together like this, he is either in a state that is very good, or not very good. Il était très évident that he was in a state this morning that was not very good.

This all had a lot to do avec le fait that he has been mad at me, ou quelque chose has been bothering him, et he has not talked to me about it. This has been building for months. My sense was that it was about my energies being spread in a lot of different directions in the last six months, et Paddy et I have lost intensity in the energies we have been exchanging, pendant les temps we have been avec each other. Aussi, Paddy has had his energies consumed by a lot of people around him, more so than usual. He has had friends et family dying, friends et family sick. He has spent a lot of time this year in hospitals et at funerals.

I gave him a hug before he could squeeze by me through the sliding door into the house. As soon as he stepped inside, j'ai dit:

"You have to take your shoes off. I just bought some new rugs. I want to keep them clean."

Paddy stepped tentatively into the room et onto one of the little carpet squares that I bought at Canadian Tire in Cowansville, et was using to create a footpath over mon nouveau tapis. I had the little carpets strategically placed by the sliding door, leading around my little dining room table. Anyone, including Paddy, could step on these small rugs, et get to the bathroom, sans stepping on mon nouveau tapis.

Paddy glanced down at the tapis for only a nanosecond. Bien sûr, he has no interest pour des choses matérielles, excepté des livres et CD's. Sans removing his shoes, he walked across the afghani tapis que j'ai acheté à la flea market Samedi – which I had been maintaining by kneeling down et picking pieces of lint off it, one at a time. He turned around, so that his back was to mon divan et he was facing la fenêtre avant de mon bureau. He planted his feet, as if he was going to commence tai-chi. Mais oui, for a nanosecond j'ai pensé he was going to do une certaine sorte de rite pour mon nouveau tapis, ou possibly commence le tai-chi. Instead, il a commencé to jump up et down sur mon tapis, comme un enfant jumping up et down on a bed. Pendant he is jumping up et down, he is saying, un – mot – par – jump: "Is – this – what – you – want – to – keep - clean?"

The man is *at least* 83-years-old. He tells *me* that he is 79. He tells other people he is 75 ou 76, depending on when he last told them how old he was. Anyone who asks him maintenant, he says he's 75. If he told the person three or four years ago that he was 75, he says now that he is 76. En tout cas, the calendar years of this man is in the octogenarian range mais *les années émotionelles* de cet homme, c'est une autre affaire.

According to the way the famous psychologist Erik Homberger conceptualizes the nine stages of psychosocial development, Paddy is in the 9th stage, which very few people reach. He is a living example of someone who has reached what Homberger calls, "The Shangri-la Age." This may be sacrilegious to say dear Diary, mais je ne sais pas si le Dalai Lama has reached Shangri-la Age yet.

En tout cas, I am standing là, watching cet homme, cet home-garcon, cet hippyish, shamanesque, Abenaki-ish, streetwise High

Lama, jumping up et down sur mon nouveau tapis afghani. I am practicing detachment. Mais oui, je pratique le détachement. Et je dit à Paddy, "Peut-être this is your way of getting me to learn *détachement* ?"

Paddy just smiled et a dit, "I don't know what you're saying, Mario. I think you want to say, *'pooh-tit.'* You gotta learn the right way to speak French and I'm trying to show you the Montreal way – at least the Montreal way I know. I'm telling you, pronounce it, *'pooh-tit,'* and everyone will know what you are talking about."

Je pense there was une certaine sorte de plaisanterie sexuelle connected to what he was saying, which is quelque chose not très, très, très unusual avec Paddy.

En tout cas, this set the stage for Paddy et moi to talk au sujet not seeing each other beaucoup pendant l'été. There have been circumstances for both of us, is the way I look at it. En tout cas, I let Paddy know that I have missed him a great deal.

My living space has changed quite radically since Paddy was last here. He could see that I did a makeover of my living space, from contemporary to américain-québecer, mais he did not have much to say about it. He did, however, do a couple of walks around the room, comme un chat orienting to a new environment.

Finalement, he sat down on one of the two chairs à ma table de salle à manger, which was a signal à moi that he was ready to get down to business, encore. J'ai dit à Paddy, "Je suis prêt. We have to get back to work on *The Maybeist Manifesto*."

Paddy a dit, "Yeah, maybe. Pooh-tit." He laughed at his own joke, ensuite il a dit, "I tell you about my Mount Kalish synchronicity?"

J'ai dit, "Kalish? Where is Mount Kalish?" J'ai pensé he was referring to un des montagnes près d'ici.

Paddy a dit, "You don't know where Mount Kalish is? What the hell do they teach you people in the states? Aren't you supposed to be some kind of professor? You don't know that Mount Kalish is in Tibet? Sacred mountain. Called the, 'precious jewel of snow.' Takes three days to cir-cum-amb-ulate Kalish. How do you like that word, Professor? *Cir-cum-amb-ulate*. Not the easiest word for me to pronounce with these choppers, but a good word, eh? Almost as good as that word you taught me, *an-an-an-anthro…anthro-po-mor-phism. Anthropomorhism!* Yeah, takes three days or three years to circumambulate Mount Kalish, depending on how many prostrations you do...Make me a tea, will ya?...Yeah, I might have gone there. Dog at the train station in India bit Annick so I haven't gone there yet...Well, anyway, I have known only one person who has been to Kalish, and that's Ronnie. Then, last week, I meet this kid who has traveled from Taiwan to Abercorn, to work as a servant – well, not to work as a servant, but to work as a servant for the Cronin's in Abercorn, so that he can circumambulate Mount Stafford. How do you like that? This kid been around the world, been to Kalish, but he comes to Quebec, because he has to visit Mount Stafford."

J'ai dit, "Paddy, this does not surprise me. You've told me about the Buddhist monks who traveled here from Tibet – 15, 20 years ago, wasn't it? Kornfield and Ram Dass have been through here. This does not surprise me."

Paddy continued, "You forgot to mention Scotty Bowman. He was here and a lot of people think he's a guru, too. Anyway, this Taiwanese kid told me that he heard about Stafford while he was in Tibet! Can you imagine that? A monk in an ashram over there was talking to him about Mount Stafford. Talking about the quartz in the mountain. Yeah, now listen to this...The day after I meet the kid from Taiwan, I start my four-day retreat up at the lodge on Livingston, and I find out that seven of the eighteen people at the retreat have been to Kalish! These people are from Boston, Connecticut, Texas. Minnesota, for Chrissakes! Seven out of eighteen been to Kalish. What's the odds on that? Take it from somebody who knows something about odds-making: One hell of a long shot. And they're all talking about the quartz in the mountain. When they weren't meditating, I think that's all they talked about – how the quartz in Mount Stafford resonates. I'm telling ya, Mario, the quartz in this mountain is powerful. You gotta talk to Merlin The Magician about this. He knows a lot about quartz. Talk to Merlin, and tell him about this kid from Taiwan been to Kalish then come here, and about the seven out of eighteen people at the retreat at Livingston who were at Kalish, then came here to Mount Stafford – and they never met each other before – but they were all drawn here! Tell Merlin what I told you just now about what they were saying about the quartz."

J'ai dit, "D'accord, Paddy. I'm probably going to see Merlin and Gwen tonight. I would be interested in hearing what Merlie has to say about the quartz." With that, I walked over to the fireplace and picked up a chunk of quartz that I had dug up in the backyard last week.

28 Aout 2009

"Talking Crystal Avec Merlin"

J'ai visité avec Merlin The Magician et Gwen Beckett la nuit dernière. Je suis arrivé à la ferme vers le coucher du soleil, environ 20h, et j'ai vu Merlin come out of the greenhouse as I was parking ma voiture devant la grange. Avec un accent brittanique crisp comme l'air de nuit, il a dit bonjour de sa manière habituelle: "Greetings, lad."

He was carrying deux objets en ses mains, que looked to me like, peut-être, they were grapefruit, ou les melons de quelque sorte, mais je n'étais pas sûr s'ils were un ou l'autre, ou neither. He plopped un dans ma main, et il a dit, "Here you go, lad. One avocado like this every day will keep the proctological cancer specialist away. Loaded with vitamin E."

J'ai dit, "Tu plaisantes ! This is an *avocado*?"

Merlie a répondu, "That it is. The fruit that was recognized by the Aztecs for its   power to promote fertility. Do you know that the word, 'avocado,' comes from the Aztec word for testicle ?" He paused to evaluate my expressionless et unblinking reaction, before he added, "I kid you not, my friend."

J'ai dit: "It looks like a green grapefruit. How did you do this, Merlin !?

Il a dit, "The phrase, 'thinking outside the box,' or, 'outside the circle,' applies here, Mario. A few years ago I began to think about avocados outside the normal parameters – 'outside the skin,' if you will, of the normal California or Florida avocado that is ubiquitous in parts of North America. Beyond conventional horticulture, there is what one might call, 'alchemical gestation.' That's the short form answer to your query. It would be my pleasure to return to the greenhouse with you, and provide you with a more

118

comprehensive and visually-enhanced answer to your question, but that would mean postponing, once again, our sit-down to talk about 2012."

J'ai répondu, "D'accord. But I have to tell you, I am *very* interested in hearing how you have managed to grow avocados like this." I felt the weight of the avocado, as I tossed it back and forth between my hands. J'ai dit: "This has the weight of a *bocci ball* ! And it must be worth its weight in gold, Merlie. What are you going to do with this avocado?"

Merlin a dit, "*That* avocado is yours, Mario. And this one, in my hand, is the sample that I will give to Chantal at La Bonne Terre tomorrow morning."

As we walked to the house Merlin explained that he was not ready to bring giant avocados to market yet. He has not yet succeeded in growing the giant size with enough consistency and with the crop yield he is seeking. In short, *Merlin The Magician Avocados* are not quite ready for prime time, but it looks like they will be making cameo appearances soon, at least in Stafford at La Bonne Terre.

We got so absorbed in talking au sujet the avocados that Merlin insisted we return to the greenhouse, "for a few minutes," so he could show me what he was doing to cultivate them. We wound up spending a half-hour in the greenhouse before we went à l'intérieur de la maison.

Gwen did not sit avec nous parce qu'elle était un peu malade. Head cold.

Merlin a fait le thé avec leaves des thé, et basilic(!), et citron, et miel. He calls this creation his, « *Italian tea.* » It is but another of Merlin's creations that he could market to millions of people, if he were a lesser man. Merlie carried the tea sur un tray mahogany that is un objet d'art que il a fait, and we retired to Merlie's den, a low ceilinged, beautifully appointed, book lined, mortar and pestle-filled chambre. C'est un chambre fitting for a thoughtful English gentleman, such as Merlie. We sat down where we normally do quand we have a fireside chat – Merlie at his desk, comfortable there in his wooden swivel chair, myself comfortable in a cushioned antique chair à la gauche du bureau, facing Merlie.

We sat dans une John Cage silence. Juste listening à la musique de ambient sounds. Je pense que tous les deux nous were

119

waiting for l'autre pour parler. Merlie lit his long-stemmed pipe, the foot-long jobbie he uses for big thinking, ensuite il a tourné et commencé au contempleate un des crystaux sur son bureau. I watched him reach for the crystal and pick it up. Il a tourné dans sa chaise to face me, mais his eyes remained fixed on le crystal qu'il a tourné dans sa main, comme il la recalibrait. Which he was, d'une certaine manière.

He was holding one of the three crystals qu'il garde sur son bureau que j'appelle: *"The Superman Crystals."* They remind me of the crystals que Superman a utilisé dans les films de Christopher Reeve et Marlon Brando.

J'ai dit, "Ah ha ! That reminds me. Paddy told me to make sure I spoke with you au sujet quartz. About the quartz in this region et especially au sujet the quartz of Mount Stafford."

Merlin a dit, "'*Ah ha*,' indeed ! An *ah ha* moment and a synchronisitic *ah ha* at the same time." He leaned back dans sa chaise, à pris un sip de son thé et de son pipe, alors ajoutée: "What has just been demonstrated is how our energies – yours, mine, the crystal – resonated in such a way that my attention and hand were brought to this crystal, this piece of quartz from Mount Stafford, as soon as we sat down. One might say, Mario, that the *intentionality principle* was demonstrated."

"Je comprends," j'ai dit.

Ensuite, Merlie went from 0 to 60, très rapidement. I put my seat belt on and sat back in my chair as soon as il a commencé à parler. « There is much quartzite and quartz crystal in Mount Stafford. In this whole area there is a wonderful amount of crystal. Various forms of crystalline solids generate a frequency, just as we generate a frequency. We humans are little more than a liquid crystal display, ourselves. We're 85% liquid or something. So, we're a liquid crystal display. My eyes are what? 90 percent water? Take a drop of blood and look at it closer, closer, closer. The more closely you look at a liquid the more you will find that it is of a crystalline nature. A fluid crystalline nature. »

He paused, et I made sure that I did not speak un mot, parce que I know his thoughts were moving forward like a train, et he cannot get up a good head of steam unless he is allowed to stay on one track.

Après un autre sip de thé, Merlie continued. « Hold a prism by the window and as the light comes in, the light is broken into colours. Well, each of us brings the light through in a different hue. Isn't that true? We generate a hue as we move around. Some call it an, '*aura*.' Edgar Cayce could see the aura of a person as easily as you or I can see someone's shadow. Maybe that's because we are conditioned to look for the shadow, and Cayce was one of those people who re-conditioned himself to look for the aura, instead...Be that as it may, some people are better able than others to perceive that crystalline display of ourselves that we call the, '*aura.*' Nicolas Tesla could see the aura. Heavens, I almost forgot Mario, you know Aileen. She is a real-deal native medicine woman. She saw your aura almost as soon as she laid her eyes on you. In fact, you were sitting in that very chair weren't you, when you two had a rather astounding experience with resonance?"

I nodded my head in the affirmative, and Merlin continued on. « A great deal of us is crystal. And we react to crystal...Being attracted to the Stafford mountain range – which is a small range among the Appalachian Mountains that has a quite unusual crystalline nature – your frequency and the frequency emitted from the mountains resonate. Your frequency is generated by the nature of your being. The nature of your being generates your attitude. Your attitude creates a frequency that attracts you or repels you to or from various situations. »

Merlin a tourné vers The Superman Crystals sur son bureau. « These crystals have been around for 50 million years. Crystals have memory and they have recorded the history of their time. Our brain, crystalline in nature, is a huge storehouse of information that is stored consciously and unconsciously, for all of our lifetimes – which are there, in memory. Which brings us to the *akashic record*. It also brings us to what Carl Jung called, 'collective unconscious.' *There's* something you have learned quite a bit about Mario, from your studies, and from your experiences with synchronicity here, in Stafford. »

When I finally interjected some of my thoughts, in reaction to what Merlin was sharing avec moi, I sent his train of thought to other directions. Avant que je le savais, le conversation segued north, south, est et ouest, et another hour passed.

I was getting très fatigué quand Merlin abruptly stopped speaking, to look across the room at Gwen, who suddenly appeared on the landing near the front door, and was looking in on us. Neither one of us had noticed Gwen standing there until that moment, mais she had apparently been waiting patiently for Merlin to pause so she could say quelque chose to him, or us. Elle a dit à Merlin, « Il est mort hier ? »

D'accord. Here we are, in a conversation that winds around and leads up to the point where Merlin makes a reference to synchonicity, et Gwen enters the room, like an actor stepping on stage, on cue, et she asks a synchronous question.

My mouth was open, parce que it was only two days ago that I heard and repeated le phrase, *'Il est mort hier,'* from my French lesson CD. Et it was only yesterday morning that I had repeated those words to myself, unconsciously peut-être, mais certainement sychronistically, quand j'ai lu the headline on the front page of the *Burlington Free Press* au sujet the death of Senator Ted Kennedy, pendant I was at Le Pinnacle Peddler, in Richford. Maintenant, Gwen Beckett is fluent en français, mais she does not parle en français avec anglophones, as I do. Certainement, she does not parle avec Merlin en français, ou moi. Mais elle a posé la question, « Il est mort hier ? » en français !

Merlin a répondu, « Who is it that died yesterday, Gwen ? And why are you speaking en français ? » Ensuite, avant Gwen could answer either question, Merlin a dit, « Oh, you are referring to Mortimer. »

Mortimer Adler is one of the family cats. Ou should I say one of the cats in the *family,* parce que Merlin et Gwen sont animal lovers. Mortimer went AWOL, once again absent without leave, disparu il y a deux jours. Gwen was concerned that he may have been killed by the same red tail hawk that got one of their other cats a few weeks ago.

Merlin is a magician who can do more than pull rabbits from hats. Sans un autre mot, Merlin got up from his chair and walked straight past Gwen, through the kitchen, opened the front door, and let Mortimer in! Bien sûr, les deux de nous, Gwen et moi, wanted to know how Merlin knew that Mortimer would be at the front door. Merlin a dit que he, "followed the lighted path."

That was my cue to follow the lighted path home. J'étais très fatigué. Je suis partí avec la pensée que il était plutôt incroyable que le phrase, "Il est mort hier," keeps coming up, and **noticeably** in the past three days. « Il est mort hier » n'est pas une phrase que je prononce chaque jour, ou entendre. Mais la synchronicité que I have experienced avec this phrase in the past three days has been incroyable. Merlie et Gwen agree with me.

J'espère l'idée que, "everything happens in threes," will hold up ici…Hmm, je pense this may have been le troisieme straight time j'ai visité avec Merlin pour parler au sujet 2012 et it did not happen.

30 novembre 2009

« La Coupe Grey 2009 »

Je suis allé à la Pub Cantina hier soir, pour voir la Coupe Grey football game. To us américain-quebecers, the Super Bowl is the U.S.A version of the Grey Cup championship game.

Je suis arrivé à Kenny's environ 6h45m, après que le jeu ait commencè, qu'ètait vers de 6h15m, je pense. Il y avait vers 20 personnes là, presque tous les hommes. Bien sûr Kenny ètait là, et mon voisin Siegfried ètait là, et Dave Brown, et David McCully, the lead singer of l'Appalaches.

Kenny, Dave Brown et David McCully were sitting proche the flat screen television at the back of the room, proche de la salle de bain, et le Loto machines. There were not any seats left there, in front of the screen. Donc, I leaned against the half-wall devant le Loto machines, et that turned out to be where I watched the whole game.

Kenny had a pool set up for the game. He had a sheet of poster paper taped on the wall under la télévision, avec lines drawn en grid, so that there were the necessary hundred boxes, to represent every possible score for the game. Even though the game had already started, Kenny had not yet put any numbers over the boxes. I had paid 5$ hier for a box, et I had selected the box in the top left corner, where I staked my claim by writing, avec un rouge marker: "Mario-Jacques." Je pense it was le seule américain-quebecer name on the board.

Kenny told me that they had 240$ in the pool, et he was going to give everyone jusqu'à the end of the first half of the game to get into the pool. It was going to be winner-take-all. The way I have seen this done in NY, toujours, is to have a winner après chaque quarter. Mais Kenny wanted to have une plus grande piscine. He wanted a big payoff.

Bien sûr, j'étais très intéressé à voir les différences entre la Coupe Grey et le Super Bowl, comme présenté à la télévision. La première différence that I noticed was that il y a plus Rona annonces publicitaire pendant la Coupe Grey que le Super Bowl. En fait, I have never seen a Rona annonce during a Super Bowl. Je ne sais pas combien de fois they played le même Rona annonce, encore et encore. Aussi, that commercial would have been trop sexuelle pour Sears, which I would say is quelque chose semblable à Rona dans les états. ((Peut-être Sears is Rona on steroids.))

In the Rona annonce, une femme est dans la baignoire et un homme ((son mari, ou son petit ami, ou a workman – c'est nébuleux)) est dans la salle de bains standing à côté du femme dans la baignoire. Je ne sais pas what was said between them, mais l'homme soudainement moved avec très vitesse, fast foward speed, to completely renovate la salle de bains – avec produits de Rona – et ensuite he jumps dans la baignoire avec la femme.

In the states, the Super Bowl commercials are normalement plus intéressant que le jeu. Bien sûr, la raison d'être de la Super Bowl est les annonces publicitaires. La raison d'être de la Coupe Grey est le *jeu*, *pas* the commercials ((au moins, for those who watch le jeu)). C'est une bonne chose. It does not appear to me that Canada has sold its soul aux Fondamentalistes d'Argent. Pas encore. ((Mais, a deal seems to be near.))

Oui, some parts of Canada are smelling more like McDonald's hamburgers than fresh clean air, mais in most of Canada les gens can still smell the breath of Mother Earth. Dans la belle province de Québec, l'air sent le frais excepté où vous trouvez le McDonald's, et McDonaldization, creeeeeeeeeping dans la belle province. On Fox News ((a.k.a Hate TV)) they talk about, "creeping socialism." LaughOutLoud. Au lieu, we should be talking au sujet, "creeping McDonaldization," ou, "creeping McDonaldism."

En tout cas, the commercials for the Grey Cup do not cost the sponsors millions of dollars per minute – as they do in the states for the Super Bowl version – et the Grey Cup sponsors repeat la même commercials. Even Coke a utilisé la même annonce, encore et encore pendant la Coupe Grey.

I do not watch américain football ((*U.S.A* American)) very much anymore. I used to watch it every Monday night, et beaucoup on Sundays. Maintenant, the thing I like about américain football the most, is that I can take a nice nap pendant un jeu à la télé. Many of my fellow Americans like to drink beer while they watch football. Were that not the fact, where would American football be? Canadian football is much more exciting than américain, pour moi. J'aime le champ plus grand. Compare le canadien football field à le américain gridiron et it is like comparing the wide open spaces of Canada avec la terre de les États-Unis – where more people utilise the elevator than any other form of transportation. Canadian life et vie américain sont reflétées dans leurs football. Nord du quarante-neuvième parallèle vous trouvez plus de mobilité. Dans plus d'un sens du mot.

Anyway, en tout cas, il était formidable to watch le jeu à La Cantina. As le propriétaire et internationaliste Kenny Grudman m'a dit while we were watching the game: "*This* is what we should be doing, playing games and watching games, instead of engaging in war. Games are necessary."

David McCully tapped Kenny on the shoulder quand il a dit cela, et a dit: "Talking about *necessary*, you need to fill in the numbers for the football pool before the first quarter ends."

Ken was still taking an extremely laissez-faire attitude about the football pool. Il a dit à David: "Don't sweat it."

Mais, David kept it up, talking about how, '*messy,*' it was going to be if Ken didn't start to fill in the numbers across the top et side of the grid. Finalement, Kenny a dit à moi, "Okay. I guess I'll need to regulate the money pool." And added, "I hope I can do a better job than your man – or your ex-man, Greenspan – did in the states, regulating the banks."

J'ai répondu, "mais oui, " but we did not segue into a political conversation. From this point on, mes pensées et les pensées de tout monde dans le pub était focused sur le match.

Choses went très mauvais for the Alouettes, for the whole first half of the game. Elle a ressemblé, peut-être, un massacre in the making. Peut-être a slaughterization. Mais, le jeu n'était pas out of reach for the Alouettes. Pas encore.

The score was quelque chose comme 17 – 3 at the half, in favor of Saskatchewan. If you are playing ping-pong ou badminton, say: "bad news." Mais, this is football. Mais oui, le football Canadien. I still had this feeling that les Alouettes were going to prevail. I was hoping to see the Alouettes pull off a come-from-behind victory, so they were following the script, as far as I was concerned...Which is not to say that I was 100% certain they were going to pull off a storybook, come-from-behind victory. Mais, I had a feeling...

At half-time I chatted avec Dave Brown et David McCully. We got into a rap au sujet les différences entre le canadien et le football américain, et les origines du football. Ils tous les deux agreed that football must have come from rugby, et that the game was invented in Canada – not in Cantonsville, Ohio, comme l'histoire du jeu is told dans les états.

Brownie et David McCully jouent rugby. Et ils regardent comme ils jouent au rugby. They are très fit. Brownie est un grand homme, très musculaire, très fort. C'est drôle, if you just heard him speak, his squeaky voice would convince you qu'il est environ three feet tall. Even though he is pushing soixante, Brownie is a chick magnet, et an electric magnet for women named, "Natasha," for some reason. David McCully est un ectomorphique, musculaire, avec flaming red hair. Avec a personnalité qui est tranquille, pensif. Aussi, he has a prominent tattoo on the side of his neck. De un papillion.

J'ai su que Dave Brown a joué au rugby. J'ai su qu'il était presque un professionnel. Mais, je n'ai su pas que David McCully était un jouer tellement avide. David told me that just last year his team played a team from Montauk, Long Island, in a tournament in Massachusetts. I told him that I knew a lot of people from the small town of Montauk, but he did not remember any names of the people he met from Montauk.

David asked me if I knew anything about the buried pyramids in Montauk, or anything about secret experiments carried out by the United States Navy là. He was surprised to hear me say that I had never heard Montauk people talk about the pyramids, except for a librarian I know. Toutefois, I told Dave that I *have* heard many Montauk people make references to secret experiments at the old Navy base là. I was about to tell David that I have heard a lot about the Montauk experiments ici, in Stafford, from Merlin. Mais puis le deuxième half began. I should say, the *real game* started in the second half. En fait, the 2e half made this *A Game for the Ages.*

Anthony Calvillo, the quarterback, the field leader of the Alouettes, was born to slay giants. Mais Anthony Calvillo does not look to me like a football player, ou an athlete of any sorte, except, peut-être, a bowler. He has the tummy of a jeudi soir bowler. Et skinny legs...I saw him play only a couple of times before I saw him play this game, mais I knew that he was the type of player, the type of leader, who never says die. He has *It*. Ooooooh yeah. He has *It*. Alan Watts could have written a book about the "It" that Anthony Calvillo has. En raison de Calvillo, despite the 17 to 3 score at the half, I still would have bet anyone a large Coke that the Alouettes were going to somehow win this game.

The turning point came, as it so often does, when hope was almost lost. Key word : *almost.* L'espoir a été *presque* perdu. Le moment précis of the turning point came quand Kenny tourné a moi et dit : "It's time for an interception, Mario." He said this avec la même inflection he would have had in his voice if he had said: "The bus from Montréal is due at the Ultramar.*"*

J'ai répondu, "Oui. Time for an interception !" J'ai dit ceci avec my eyes wide open, et avec measured words...mots measurés. If ever, in the history of football, on either side of the 49th parallel, there was a time for an interception, *this* was such a time. Et if ever, in my lifetime, I have had a feeling that my team was about to rise up from the ashes, *this* was such a time.

I really knew the planets were lining up parce que à ce moment précis Paddy O'Brien materialized à côté de moi, from out of nowhere. Something had happened to his television or his television transmission during the game, so he drove down from his chalet on the mountain to catch the rest of the game ici, à la Cantina. He was a little crotchety. Aucun sourire. He did not say allo to anyone. He just wanted to know the score.

Paddy put his hand on his toque to take it off, mais kept his hand right there on his head as the next play went off. This was *it,* that loooooooooooooooong moment in time quand choses slooooooooooooow down...to...a...stop/arrêt. Tout monde dans Pub Cantina was leaning forward, avec their eyes on the television.

Et…et…et…*IN-TER-CEPTION* ! IN-TER-CEPTION ! IN-TER-CEPTION !

Irish, the barmaid, let out a scream that made me think that peut-être quelqu'un had passed out, ou tombé, dans toute l'excitation. Mais, Irish had just gotten caught up in the moment. I grabbed the scarf that Kenny had around his neck avec both my hands et started choking him. J'ai dit à lui: "We called the shot !" Dave Brown et David McCully jumped off their stools et were hugging each other, et two ou three women came from the other end of the bar to hug the two Davids, as if they were Michaelangelo David's. Tout monde went fou-fou farfelu crazy.

Paddy took a seat on the chest freezer, on the wall facing me. Choosing the Way of Zen, il a dit à moi, dans une voix au-dessous du vacarme, "Glad I was listening to the Universe and drove down here. Good timing Mario, eh ?"

Ken announced that he would buy drinks for tout monde, if the Alouettes win the game.

Il était très excitation jusqu'à la fin. This was not a game that went down to the final seconds, it went down to secondes *zero* ! Je veux dire, the clock read, "0:00," et they were playing encore ! Quand the clock reads, "0:00," the game is supposed to be over, non? Zero means rien, non? I asked Paddy about this, how this could be, et il a dit à moi: "They are in the *bardo*, Mario."

Ken et Dave McCully heard Paddy say this. Dave McCully a dit, "This is true, Paddy. Between an inhale and an exhale. Eckhart Tolle would call that, 'being in *The Now*.'"

Ensuite Ken a dit: "That's the third time today that someone sitting on that freezer has said something to me about being in the *bardo*."

Et juste at that moment, Damon Duval, the kicker for the Alouettes, was set to kick the ball for a field goal. If he kicks the ball between the goal posts, the Alouettes win. If he does not, they lose. Maintenant, ici est la chose, up until now, Duval has been the goat dans le jeu. Earlier in the game, instead of kicking the ball up the field, he kicked it almost straight up in the air. Tout le monde who was paying attention should have taken that as a sign of things to come. That is, the game was going to be a disaster, ou Duval was on The Jack Kerouac Road to becoming A Redeemer. Moi, being a

128

believer in redemption, felt Duval would play his role as A Redeemer in this game…

Mais, Duval kicked the ball avec the game on the line…et……….. he *missed!*

Game over…Alouettes lose. Duval does *not* redeem himself. Instead of winning 28 – 27, Alouettes lose 27 – 25.

Mais wait ! It is not over ! Pas encore. The Saskatchewan Roughriders are penalized for having too many players on the field ! What ? ! Quoi, quoi, quoi ? ! To the fans of the Saskatchewan Roughriders, this was presque as unbelievable as getting penalized for having a team name avec too many letters. Damon Duval is going to get a chance to kick the ball encore ! He can still fulfill Le Destin d'Un Rédempteur. The Alouettes can still win the game !

Personne dans le Pub Cantina inhales ou exhales jusqu'à Damon Duval kicks la balle entre the goal posts ! Les Alouettes win 28 – 27 ! Tout le monde dans le Pub Cantina vont fou. They go absolutely fou-fou. C'est : *Joie de vivre !*

Ken buys les boissons for the house, environ 20 personnes. Dans le futur, 100's des personnes will say that they were at le Pub Cantina cette soir.

18 janvier 2010

"Le Homme de Mystère de Stafford"

Cet après-midi je suis allé au Café Dumont pour rencontrer Simone Tetrault ((à ses amies : "Simone de Beauvoir")). Simone is going to be in a Michel Tremblay play à l'Esprit du Village ce week-end, et she gave me une copie du manuscrit, en français. Je dois traduire ceci à l'anglais avant the performance, ou je ne vais pas à comprendre quand je le vois.

Simone est le classique Beau Blonde. Elle has significant financial wealth, even though she does not flaunt it. Elle était une modèle, à Montréal et à Paris. Maintenant elle médite, fait des bougies, et elle commence une nouvelle carrière comme une actrice.

Pendant que je parlais avec Simone, mon ami, my long lost friend, Pierre Roy, est entré dans le café. Pierre est venu de France au Québec il y a deux ans. I have been wondering where he has been, parce que je ne l'ai pas vu en six mois. En fait, il était seulement ce matin que j'ai demandé à Susan Wright, à la Tête de l'Ordinateur, si elle avait vu Pierre. She said that she had not seen Pierre dans un mois.

Simone et moi se reposent sur de tabourets à la longue table rectangulaire au mileau du café, où environ 12 personnes peuvent s'asseoir sur des tabourets. We sat parement de la fenêtre avant du café. Donc, j'ai vu Pierre entrer le café tout de suite. He seemed to be in good health, en forme, a perdu un certain poids.

J'ai dit à Pierre, "Yo, Pierre ! Ca va ? I did not recognize you, presque. Ca va, Monsieur ?"

Pierre a répondu, "Ca va. How are you, Mario?"

J'ai dit. "Ca va, et *molto bene*. You look fantastique, mon ami. I have missed you. Where have you been? I have not seen you since we hiked in the spring."

Il a dit, "I moved to just outside of Knowlton."

J'ai dit à Pierre, "Incroyable! Knowlton!"

Pierre se mit à rire, et il a dit. "Yes. I know. I find it is, I must say, 'strange,' in Knowlton."

I would have been less surprised to learn that Stephen Harper had moved to Québec. La *ville* du Québec. Je veux dire, le Québec n'est pas assez de français pour Pierre. Et la ville de Knowlton, not Montréal, est le capitol de la colonie brittannique au Québec, still hidden in the open.

J'allais présenter Simone à Pierre, puis I remembered that they had met before. I remembered being dans une conversation avec les deux environ il y a une année, au Café Monet. Aujourd'hui Simone et Pierre looked at each other et seemed to remember meeting each other en même temps.

Simone stepped off her stool et Pierre walked around me, so that they could exchange bonjour kisses on the cheeks. Plus rapide qu'un cligne d'oeil, l'attention de Pierre est allée de moi à elle. I should mention, Simone portait une robe de la Boutique Patrice, qui a étreint son corps.

Les trois de nous chatted en anglais pendant quelques minutes. Puis, Simone s'est excusé, parce qu'elle a dû aller à une lecon de piano. Elle est cinquante années et elle apprend à jouer le piano. She plays la guitare, presque professionnelle.

J'ai écouté attentivement tandis que Pierre et Simone ont parlé, pour voir si je pouvais comprendre quelconque de leur français. J'ai entendu Pierre dit à Simone : "Bravo." C'était le dernier mot que j'ai entendu que j'ai compris, pendant quelques minutes.

Après quelques minutes, Simone a dit, "Ciao," à moi et à Pierre, et alors Pierre a pris son tabouret et il a installé son ordinateur laptop sur la table. Il est allé sur l'Internet, vérifier ses courriels et surf websites de nouvelles. J'ai vu que il était allé à *Le Monde, Le Devoir* et BBC, dans cet ordre. Sauf BBC, tout était français, donc j'ai scanned seulement les gros titres, un peu. While he surfed the web, we talked au sujet the earthquake en Haïti. Le tremblement de terre en Haïti est la nouvelles manchettes dans le monde occidental.

Pierre a dit à moi, "Who is this crazy minister, this Pat Robertson ?"

J'ai dit, "Tu ne connais pas Pat Robertson ?"

Il a dit, "I know he says that Haiti is punished for their sins by this disaster."

J'ai dit, "Mais oui. C'est vrai. Je sais que il dit... this fou thing." J'ai voulu continuer de parler français mais je pris la moyen facile: en anglais, avec un peu français. "Oui, Robertson is a lunatique minister who has run for President of the United States, un ou deux fois."

Pierre se mit à rire, et rolled back on his stool, presque falling off. "*Robertson ran for President of the United States?!* I did not know that! This means, I think, the people in your country are just *sooo crazy*. Because he is a minister they think he is a good person? How could people vote for such a crazy person?"

J'ai dit, "Sarah Palin just ran for Vice-President. She would have been a breath away from being President. Sarah Palin for Vice-President was more surreal than anything Salvodor Dali ever painted."

Pierre a dit, encore avec un rire, "Yes, I see what you mean. That is true."

Pierre et moi avons parlé la politique pendant environ 10 minutes, et alors la conversation s'est tournée vers nos vies de désespoir tranquille.

J'ai voulu savoir pourquoi Pierre était ici, dans l'Estrie, en Québec. Ce qui est loin de la France. Alors, je lui ai demandé : "Do you ever have a hard time understanding the French that is spoken ici ? Is it much different than français en france ?"

Pierre m'a indiqué que parfois il est plus facile pour il comprenne l'anglais qu'il est pour il comprenne le français au Québec. (Peut-être he hears les gens comme moi speaking français, too much.)

J'ai répondu, "Do not tell me that! I am trying to learn French and you have been speaking French all your life, and YOU cannot understand the French spoken ici ? What hope is there pour moi ? Jeeez! Si tu voir ce que je veux dire, Pierre : *Jeeez!*"

Bien que c'est vraiment la belle province, j'ai voulu savoir pourquoi Pierre a décidé de venir ici, au milieu de sa vie, pour résider parmi les étrangers, pour être un étranger dans une terre étrange ? Donc, j'ai demandé, somewhat circuitiously : "So, what have you been doing?"

Pierre a répondu comme un homme vivant une vie de désespoir tranquille pourrait être prévu répondre. He told me that he normally rides his bike for hours every day. Mais, he also told me that he has not been on his bike for at least the last six weeks, because of the snow. Donc, he told me nothing. Rien. Il est, toujours, mysterieux. Pierre does not work, but he appears to live well. Mais je pense qu'il est en Québec to get away from something, je ne sais pas. Toujours, I see him dans les cafés, reading the Québec newspapers, et il lit les journals du monde sur le Internet. Je sais qu'il a un grand intérêt pour la politique, l'économie, la finance.

Mais oui, Pierre est un homme de mystère. Peut-être il est l'Homme de Mystère de Stafford. Et, alors même que he has moved to Knowlton, he is encore The Mystery Man of Stafford. There is one in every town, non ?

C'est un long chemin de venir au Québec, à travers l'océan, de France. Je sais, je traverse presque un océan des personnes pour venir à Stafford de Long Island. (Et ce n'est aucun mystère pourquoi je suis ici. Je suis le chroniqueur de Stafford.) Mais quoi attiré Pierre au Québec, à l'Estrie, the Eastern Townships of Québec, et en particulier, Stafford ?

Il aime à monter son velo, hiking les montagnes, camp-ing. Il est évidemment un homme éduqués qu'est très intéressé par les affaires mondiales. Il sait que le Canada a 2000 soldats en le Haïti, 3000 soldats en Afghanistan, et aura 4500 soldats pour les Olympiques. Il a un intérêt spécial pour la botanique. Quand I hiked avec lui up to Lac Frog, he kept stopping along the way, to take photos de plantes. Il est environ 40 ans. L'année dernière, pendant un moment, il a eu une petite amie de Rimouski – Gisella, qu'était environ 22 ou 23 ans.

Quelle est la somme de tout ceci ? ((Et oubliez qu'il habite au périmètre de Knowlton. C'est une aberration temporaire.)) Est Pierre dans une programme de protection de témoin ? Est Pierre a hit man pour un syndicat de crime ? Oui, he could be a hit man, mais je pense, peut-être...peut-être...il est un Staffordian, et il est attiré ici par ce qui résonne de Mont Stafford.

14 février 2010

"Saint-Valentin était un Soldat ?"

Aujourd'hui est la Saint-Valentin. Au Québec, drapeaux flottent en ce jour de la manière que les américains sous le parallèl 49e flottent les drapeaux à commemorate guerre. Considering the manner in which la ville de Stafford is decorated, most Americans would think that Saint Valentine was a military hero or something.

Ce matin I stopped at The Lie pour acheter un croissant. That is, to buy a melt-in-your-mouth croissant que Jeannine a fait d'une recette de famille qu'est vieux de plus de cent ans. This is not a Dunkin' Donut make-believe version of a croissant that I am talking about.

J'ai dit à Jeannine: "Will you be très occupé ce soir, for Valentine?"

Jeannine a répondu, "Peut-être. But probably not, Mario. I do not know why it is, but on the week of Valentine we are busy always, on every day of the night, unless it is a Sunday. I do not know why this is so, but this is the way it is always. Yesterday night was very busy. It was Saturday. Tonight? Who knows?"

Antoine, le frère de Jeannine, se tenait tout près, faisant un café d'expresso, quand elle a dit ceci à moi. Il a ajouté, "Mais oui, c'est vrai, Mario. Sunday night is the only night that we are not so busy for Valentine. But, we might be busy tonight anyway, because all of the Americans are coming for the Washington Day. Carnie Jack was here this morning, to pick up the croissants for the workers at the ski station. He bought 24 croissants. My sister, she has many fans for her croissants, eh Mario? I think the men would do better to buy croissants for their sweet hearts than to buy the chocolates."

J'ai répondu, "Peut-être. Put the croissants in heart-shaped boxes!" Ensuite j'ai ajouté : "C'est incroyable à moi – that there are so many decorations in the town for Valentines Day. This is a very big holiday ici. Mais, there is another big holiday maintenant. Demain. Dans Québec. Dans Canada. Do you know what that is, Antoine?"

Antoine et Jeaninne les deux pensée que je plaisantais. Jeannine a dit, avec un rire, "Okay Monsieur Mario, we give up. What is the other big holiday in Québec and in Canada tomorrow?"

J'ai dit : "What? *Holy Che Guevara caramba!* You guys do not know what the other big holiday is tomorrow?"

I could not get over it. J'ai dit, "Wow! This is sooo telling about Québec. So telling about the Eastern Townships, so telling about Stafford."

So telling, mais I just stood là, avec a loss pour mots. Antoine a dit, "Okay, tell me, Mario. I have to grind the coffee beans. What is the big holiday tomorrow that you say we do not know about?"

I was going to tell them to consult leur calendrier, mais ils ont utilisé un calendrier de Che Guevara, de Cuba

J'ai dit: "Tomorrow is *le Jour de Drapeau* ! Flag Day!"

Antoine walked away, to grind some Columbian coffee beans. Speaking to me over his shoulder, il a dit: "Flag day? Which flag? The Canadian flag or the Québec flag?"

I had the distinct feeling that he could care less about Flag Day. Jeannine, who is Parti Québécois – all the way radical PQ – a dit: "You are serious, Mario? Mais, is this the flag of Québec that we are supposed to celebrate, ou le drapeau canadien ?"

I informed her that it was le drapeau canadien. Jeannine et Antoine both laughed, et ensuite went about their business.

Il y a beaucoup de drapeaux de Valentine, avec des coeurs rouges, volant dans Stafford maintenant. Je ne pense pas qu'il y aura autant de drapeaux de canadien volant demain, ici dans Québec.

Drive over the border to Vermont on Flag Day, sur le jour de drapeau américain. Go to Richford, Vermont. Si vous conduisez vite, une demi-heure d'ici. You will see many red, white and blue flags there. It is not just another country thirty minutes away, c'est un autre monde. Mais oui, a different world. Et combien de difference existe entre le reste de Canada et Québec?

17 février 2010

"Gaston va PQ"

Hung out avec Gaston hier, pendant environ une heure, or so, à la galerie d'art. He drove out from Montréal ce matin, et il est retourné à Montréal à la fin du jour, quand il a fermé la galerie. It was good to see Gaston.

Il est juste retourné de faire un vernissage à Toronto. Three of his paintings were sold at le vernissage, so he is excited about having his work in Toronto now, even though he is not an aficionado of Toronto. La galerie de Toronto a vendu les peintures aux prix trois fois plus haut than they would have fetched ici, dans Stafford.

Quand j'ai marché dans la galerie, Gaston m'a salué avec : "Ca va ?"

J'ai répondu, "C'est tiguidoo Monsieur, tiguidoo ! Et mon ami ? En forme ?"

Gaston was setting up his easel, au fond de la galerie. Pour la première fois, il allait essayer de peindre dans la galerie, avec les gens marchent autour.

Je pense que c'est une bonne idée. I have only watched Gaston paint un peu. Pour moi, c'est très intéressant. Je pense, observant le processus d'un artiste dévoile, visuellement, is a kin à observer une exécution art, performance art, comme une pièce de théâtre. En tout cas, I think people will like watching Gaston and the other artists do their painting. Et je pense que plus de peintures sera vendus.

I was wearing my Kamik rubber boots, ones that I bought en décembre, at Canadian Tire, in Cowansville. These boots are fantastique. In my Footware Hall of Fame, pour certaine. They look nerdy, in the best sense of the word, si vous voyez ce que je veux dire. Classique. Nerdy/Cool, comme Converse high tops. Rubber. Bonne caoutchouc. Demi d'haut le mollet. Une isolation thermique qu'est très douce, très chaude. Très facile à mettre dessus, pour enlever. Staffordians are very partial to these boots. Tellement fonctionnelle. Viva Kamiks.

I took the boots off and carried them au fond de la galerie, pour les mettre sur le plateau, proche de la porte arrière. Quand Gaston a vu les bottes, il a dit : "The rubber boots! A true Staffordian."

J'ai dit, "Mais oui, Monsieur."

Gaston a dit, "Heille, garcon de la maison, can you believe it? You see that the inukshuk is so prominent in Vancouver? Well, actually, I found out that when the figure is of a man, it is called an, *"in-unn-guaq."*

J'ai répondu, "Is that le français ou un anglais translation of the Inuit mot?"

Gaston a dit, "I think it is the franglais word, which originated with your people, the américain-quebecers."

J'ai dit, "Ha, ha. Très drole, Monsieur. But think about it. If there was ever a word that was begging to be translated, it is the one you just said, that I cannot pronounce."

Gaston a répété, avec plus fluency this time : *"Inunnguaq ?"*

J'ai dit, "Oui. *That* mot."

Gaston a dit, "Well, Mister Mario, I don't think there is any translation for that word. Not in french."

J'ai dit : "How about: *'homme de roche?'* It is a, *'rockman,'* non ?"

Gaston a eu assez de ma blague. Il a dit, "Oui, et Mick Jagger is a rock man."

En fait, Gaston était un peu ticked off au sujet des Jeux Olympiques de Vancouver. Et I had just reminded him pourquoi he was ticked off.

Il a dit, "They forgot about Québec in the opening ceremonies. They forgot that the Olympics is *French.*"

J'ai dit, "French?"

Gaston a dit, "Oui. It was a french man who revived the Olympics, in something like the late 19th century. That's why we have the Olympics today. So, what did they do? They spoke a few sentences in French, and they had a little scene, for 30 seconds, about French explorers in a canoe. They make it look like, 'oh yeah, we also have french people in Canada. They forget *all* of Canada was settled by the French. From watching the opening ceremonies you would not know that the French made the Olympics, made Canada. That's it, I've had it, Mario. Now I think we should separate."

He spoke quietly, actually. Mais even sans vociferous emotion, it was apparent that strong feelings were attached to his words. C'était la première fois que j'avais jamais entendu Gaston avocat pour séparation.

J'ai dit, "Wow, you would support separating? I have never heard you talk like this before."

Il a dit, avec a sweeping motion of the paintbrush in his hand, "Yes, I would. We're better off. They just… don't… get it."

Il était pissed. Ce n'était pas un problème pour Gaston que Paul McCartney était la vedette pour le 400e anniversaire du Québec. He saw it comme un concert de célébration qui devrait avoir un superstar, tel que Paul McCartney. Mais les Jeux Olympiques, à Vancouver, c'est quelque chose d'autre.

Gaston told me that *Le Devoir* wrote a very good editorial about this, this trivializing of Québec et le Français during the Olympic games in Vancouver. Dans un meilleur monde, le monde regarderait à Québec comme culture plus digne de l'émulation que la culture de U.S.A, Inc. Dans un monde meilleur, *Le Devoir* aurait plus d'impact sur le monde que FoxNews, et les autres sleazoids, en Amérique du Nord et autour du monde. Mais, je crois que c'est vrai, ((pour citer Victor Hugo)) : "Il existe une chose plus puissante que toutes les armées du monde : c'est une idée dont l'heure est venue." Peut-être we are nearing the time in which a New World will be born. Non ?

18 février 2010

"God: The Great Mystery; Oui, le Grand Mystère de Dieu"

Je pense Paddy is thinking about going to press with his first book: *God: The Great Mystery, Oui, Le Grand Mystère de Dieu.*

Unless the book is edited between now and the time he ultimately goes to press, the book will open and close with these words: "I told you it was a mystery. Now give me the 10 bucks, stupid! Et en français : « Je vous ai dit que c'était un mystère. Maintenant donnez-moi 10$, stupide. »

I am going to buy a stack of first editions, and get Paddy to sign them. À l'avenir, ces livres vaudront plus que des cartes d'hockey de Sidney Crosby.

20 juillet 2010

"Elvis, Michael Jackson, Georges Simoneau"

Tard cet après-midi, je marchais sur la rue Principal et j'ai entendu la musique jouer des haut-parleurs. The volume of the music was low, and even though there were few people walking on the street, it was a bit windy, so I could not hear the music very well.

Plusieurs fois, j'ai cessé de marcher, pour écouter la musique plus soigneusement. By the time I walked from Pub Cantina to la Cascade, je pourrais entendre que c'était la musique de Georges Simoneau qu'était jouée. J'ai reconnu la musique d'un CD que Georges m'a donné. The music that was being played on the speakers was the music that Georges has played many times on the streets of Stafford, avec his guitar.

J'ai acheté un café à Boni Soir et puis je suis allé au gazebo à boire le café. Toujours, parce que du vent, j'ai dû écouter très attentivement. One might say, I was *compelled* by nature to listen more carefully. The more carefully I listened, the more I had this strange feeling that Georges had died.

Oui, j'ai écouté trés attentivement. C'était comme si Georges m'a chuchoté, doucement, me disant qu'il était mort.

J'était lent à réagir. I was slow to react in the same way that I was slow to react, quelque fois, when Georges would tell me a joke that I did not understand. Oui, c'était comme Georges me disait une blague, que je ne comprenais pas, encore.

I knew Georges had been in the hospital, à Montréal. Mais je ne savais pas s'il était mort.

Puis, je suis allé boutique Defpotek et Lieve Jovie m'a dit que Georges est mort.

...His music, only his music, was played all day. It was like when Elvis died, ou Michael Jackson. Je pouvais voir le sourire de Georges.

23 juillet 2010

"Mémoires de Georges"

Cher journal intime...Mes pensées se sont tournées vers Georges beaucoup en derniers jours, depuis sa mort. A part of Stafford died with Georges.

I was thinking back to when I was first getting to know Georges, il y a environ quatre ans, quand he took me on une petite tournée de marche de Stafford, près de rue Principal. Je me souviens, c'était après que nous ayons eu un ou deux conversations au sujet de synchronicité, et des roches, et des légendes de Stafford. In fact, it was just after Carnie Jack et Antoine had first talked to me about the synchronicity stools at the corner of the bar in The Lie. If I had a dime for every synchronistic experience I have had while sitting on one of those synchronicity stools, I could buy more than a large egg cream.

Je me souviens que Antoine m'a parlé de la légende de Abénakis, qu'il y avait un triangle d'énergie particulière, et le point bas du triangle est rue Principal, où l'Oeil est situé. Antoine m'a dit pour parler à Georges de la légende de l'énergie. I had known Georges for, peut-être, a year at this time. Mais, I did not know he had this interest and knowledge concerning the Abenaki energy legend.

Georges brought me to the cemetery on rue Pin, up the mountain, juste outside of town. Dans le cimetière, il m'a montré quelques symboles – Masonic symbols, qu'ont été caché loin. Il m'a montré quelques fleurs au cimetière. These were flowers that were not known to grow in Québec, ou Canada, ou North America. Georges m'a dit qu'il y a environ trente ans, les fleurs ont été remarqués par une femme Stafford qu'était un botaniste, et sa recherche ont constaté que les fleurs sont connus pour grandir seulement au Tibet.

Georges brought me to a grassy spot, under a tree, facing downhill, toward rue   Principal. The terrain is concave. Un aide à l'écoute. Je peux facilement imaginer Abenaki, ou colons, s'asseyant dans cet endroit. Peut-être sound waves are caught là.

Georges m'a dit que l'Abenaki a appelé cet endroit : "L'oreille du village." Et Georges m'a dit que the original British settlers, les loyalistes, also referred to this spot on the mountain as, "the ear of the village."

Je me souviens, we sat on rocks, which had apparently been placed there to serve as seats, perhaps hundreds of years ago. Il y avait environ six ou huit roches, arrangé dans un arc. Je me souviens, nous avons écouté. We actually heard chatter from rue Principal, et Georges a dit qu'il pourrait entendre les gens au parc, de l'autre côté de la ville. J'ai écouté. I heard shouting. J'ai entendu des cris, acclamaient, au parc. I heard them clearly. *Clairement.* C'était incroyable.

The funny thing is, I have not gone back to that spot in the cemetery. Mais je vais retourner là, bientôt. Je veux m'asseoir au nouveau où je m'assis avec Georges. Je vais peut-être entendre les echoes de la voix de Georges. Oui, he might be quoting Felix Leclerc. Ou peut-être il va citer les mots de Denis Boulanger, du *Tour.*

Je me souviens le jour de l'investiture de Barack Obama, quand Georges et moi avons regardé beaucoup de l'investiture ensemble à St. Brendan. C'était drôle, we sat entre les télévisions qu'ont été syntonisés à différentes stations, en français et en anglais.

20-1-09 est un jour que je me souviens. Juste comme je me souviens 9-11. Georges and I both knew that we would always remember that we watched l'investiture ensemble. Bien sûr, quelle est la signification de, "toujours?"

Now I am thinking back to when Georges introduced me to Paddy O'Brien. En fait, il était au café, l'Oeil, où j'ai rencontré Paddy pour la première fois, présenté par Georges, who had set up un rendezvous pour nous. Rencontrer Paddy était un moment pivotal dans ma vie.

Oui, I have good memories of Georges. Merci Georges.

15 août 2010

"A magic mushroom comme grand que Mont Pinacle ?"

Grace Terranova paid me a surprise visit hier. Elle a dit qu'elle était en route au Boulder, Colorado, de Long Island, et Stafford était sur son chemin. She took a long ride nord avant d'aller à l'ouest. Elle m'a dit que le chemin de Long Island à Colorado traverse Stafford n'était pas la distance la plus courte en termes de miles, mais la distance la plus courte en termes de suivre un chemin allumé.

Elle est venue avec son petit ami, Cristofal. The both of them will be going to school at the University of Colorado, Boulder. Grace will be working toward a Ph.D. in anthropology, et Cristofal will be working toward a Ph.D. in physiques quantum.

They met in Ecuador this past winter, tandis que they were working on a project in the Amazon, using certain mushrooms to consume oil waste that has been dumped in the Amazon by American oil companies.

En juste quelques heures courtes ils ont établi un rapport avec beaucoup de gens dans Stafford. Et they made quite a connection avec Paddy et Merlin.

Paddy took Grace et Cristofal to Triple Falls. Bien sûr, ils ont été enchantés par la beauté là. Enchanté.

Ils n'ont pas été surpris quand Paddy leur a dit au sujet du moine de Shoalin qui a vu Triple Falls il y a quelques mois, et a été enchanté par la beauté là, aussi. This monk would like to buy Triple Falls from Paddy, to build a Shaolin temple there. Il y a maintenant un temple peut-êtrehiste là. Fittingly, for Maybeists, Paddy's pagoda is open on all sides, symbolisant l'openess du Maybeisme, sous une influence mystique tibétaine.

Later in the afternoon we drove over to see Merlin et Gwen. Quand j'ai téléphoné Gwen, pour vérifier si c'était correct pour nous de visiter, elle m'a dit : "Come on over, love to see you, Merlie's in the greenhouse, doing one of his Tesla things on the plants. It's working, believe me!"

As soon as they met, Merlin took a liking to Grace et Cristofal, and vice-versa.

La première chose Grace dit à Merlin était : "Ah, now I see. You look like yourself, as Mario said you would, Merlin."

Merlin dit à Grace : "That, my dear, is unquestionably a true statement. I will have you know, I have spent many years looking like myself."

Grace et Cristofal ont été étonnés quand ils ont vu la taille des tomates dans la serre. Astonished. *A-ston-ished.* Les tomates approchent pamplemousse-taille maintenant, et Merlin indique que ses tomates va deviendront plus que doublent cette taille.

Il nous a montré ce qu'il faisait avec le dispositif Tesla. Seulement Christofal pourrait entièrement comprendre Merlin quand il a commencé à fusionner de théories au sujet la physique quantum et l'électricité, pour expliquer le dispositif Tesla.

Merlin shared with Grace et Cristofal the basic formula for his fertilizer, they told me later. This is a fertilizer that makes Miracle-Gro look like weed killer. Gwen gets mad at Merlin, because she wants him to put his fertilizer on the market somehow. She says Merlin should call it, "Magic-Grow." Gwen's idea is on target, je pense, in terms of challenging a corporate giant who could be knocked off his feet by the far superior quality of Merlie's product. Engrais Merlin est le vrai miracle. Take a look in Merlin's greenhouse and you get an idea of what plants looked like during the age of dinosaurs. Merlin grows tomatoes that are as large, sometimes twice as large, as grapefruits. Et ils sont délicieux. *Dé-li-cieux !* Tomates par Merlin, pas Monsanto.

Gwen gave us a quick tour of the bar and the art gallery. Merlin was too immersed in work – immersed in resonating devices, and fertilizer – to leave the greenhouse.

First, Gwen took Grace et Cristofal to see her son John's trampoline. This is a trampoline that Merlin and John made. Themselves. Using specifications for a trampoline that is used by the Hungarian olympic gymnastic team.

The art gallery, the second floor of the barn, is enormous, et idéal for showing large paintings. Mais la galerie était vide, avec rien sur les murs, excepté deux grandes peintures. Tous les deux peintures étaient très frappantes. Fait par un artiste qui s'est juste déplacé à Stafford, de Frelighsburg. Gwen a décrit les peintures comme étant, "close to Chuck Close," et je pense il est une bonne description du style et de la technique de cet artiste. Pas photo-réalisme, mais hyper-réalisme pour moi. Toutes les deux peintures que nous avons regardées étaient des portraits. Gwen a indiqué que cet artiste avait travaillé à sa technique pendant des années, et elle a vendu seulement quelques peintures, parce qu'il est si dévoué à perfectionner son travail. Ils n'ont pas encore décidé quand il y aura un vernissage.

Gwen insisted that we all go in the house for une tasse de thé. Mais, we ran out of time for le thé, parce que Grace et Cristofal étaient tellement absorbé en regardant la bibliothèque et tous les cristaux que Merlin a dans sa collection.

Merlin came out of the greenhouse to say au revoir et, bien sûr, ceci a mené à une autre conversation sérieuse, cette fois au sujet des champignons étant employés pour aider sauver le monde.

Ils ont commencé à parler d'un livre appelé : *Mycelium Running… How mushrooms can help save the world.* Merlin was not familiar with the book, mais I just ordered two used copies of the book from *Amazon.com,* for him and I.

Somehow I get the feeling that mycelium mushrooms will be growing in Stafford soon. Oui, j'ai un sentiment très fort que les champignons de mycelium pousseront dans Stafford bientôt. Ce n'est aucune petite matière. Tout ce Merlin grandit, il grandit grand. Bear in mind…pensez cela ! Il y a un mycelium croissant dans Orégon qui pourrait être le plus grand organisme au monde. Il est plus qu'un kilomètre long, plus qu'un mille long. Merlin pourrait cultiver un champignon qui est plus grand que Mont Pinacle. Stay tuned.

24 aout 2010

"Une Question Pour l'Univers"

I have gotten into a routine of meditating. J'ai médité tous les jours, dans une forme ou une autre, pour ces dernières deux semaines. I keep forgetting to tell Paddy que j'ai maintenant cette habitude. Peut-être he will stop bragging about having meditated every day for the past 44, *quarante-quatre*(!), années.

Ce matin j'ai médité aux environ de 4h, juste avant de sortir du lit. À la fin de ma méditation, j'ai posé une question à l'univers : *"Why am I here, in Stafford?"*

Il y a quelques jours, au Marché du samedi, j'ai vu Aileen, Medicine Woman, whom I had not seen depuis l'été dernier. Après we hugged each other, elle m'a dit : "When you meditate, ask what you can do for the universe, Mario-Jacques. Also ask the universe why you are here, in Stafford. Ask soon." C'était tout ce qu'elle m'a dit. Alors elle a regardé profondément dans les yeux, m'a embrassé sur les deux joues, et elle s'éloigna.

I forgot about that until yesterday. Hier je causais avec Simone Deblois et Linda Hickey au Café Dumont, et Simone a raconté une histoire au sujet de sa pratique de méditation. Elle a dit qu'à la fin d'une méditation, elle a demandé l'univers : "Why am I here?"

Linda Hickey a répondu qu'elle savait déjà pourquoi elle était là: pour une tasse de café et to do the crossword puzzle in *The Gazette*. We all laughed, mais alors, Simone a regardé profondément dans mes yeux, et elle a dit : "After you meditate, ask the universe why you are here, Mario."

Once again, once again, encore un fois, some things happen in threes, so I was now waiting for someone else to say: "Ask the universe why you are here, Mario-Jacques."

Plus tard de l'après-midi, il s'est passé pour la troisième fois.

Tandis que je marchais vers le haut au Lac Frog, j'ai rencontré Femme de la Montagne. Elle était assise sur un banc, à une intersection de trois sentiers. Elle balançait ses jambes, comme une petite fille.

Nous avons embrassé sur les deux joues avant que nous ayons dit bonjour, out loud. Puis elle m'a dit : "Mario-Jacques, I was just meditating. I asked the universe what I can do for it today, and you appear. *Pourquoi ?"* Elle a souri tandis qu'elle parlait et son sourire élargie quand elle a demandé, *"Pourquoi ?"*

J'ai répondu, "Je ne sais pas. Mais, I am happy that our paths have come together. I am so happy to see you!" J'adore Femme de La Montagne. Elle est énergisant.

Elle m'a demandé de m'asseoir à côté d'elle sur le banc, où la lumière du soleil traverse les arbres. Dès que je me suis assis à côté d'elle, elle a fermé les yeux et son visage détourné de moi, et s'est tourné vers la lumière du soleil. J'ai pensé qu'elle ait recommencé à méditer. Puis, je suis resté dans le silence, et j'ai aussi fermé les yeux et me suis tourné vers la lumière du soleil.

J'ai commencé à méditer. J'ai écouté la respiration de la montagne. I smelled the scent of the mountain. Un parfum d'épinette subtil. Alors Femme de la Montagne m'a parlé, dans un chuchotement. Elle a dit : "Our paths meet today for a reason, Mario-Jacques."

Time stopped....................................Après une pause que je ne peux pas dire était court ou long, elle m'a dit : "Ask the universe why you are here, Mario-Jacques."

Okay, j'ai ouvert les yeux et me suis tourné lentement vers elle, pendant qu'elle ouvrait les yeux et tournait lentement vers moi. J'ai dit : *"Synchronicité !"* I explained to her that I was waiting for someone to tell me, pour une troiseme fois, to ask the universe why I am here. J'ai dit à Femme de la Montagne que je pensais à ceci juste avant de commencé ma marche sur les sentiers.

Femme de la Montagne a dit, "Now we know the reason our paths have come together. À la prochaine." Elle m'a donné un sourire qui a résonné avec de l'énergie de Mont Stafford. Alors elle s'éloigna, sur un sentier que la plupart des gens ne remarquent pas, mais un sentier de lumière pour La Femme de la Montagne.

…Donc, c'est pour tout ca que j'ai demandé à l'univers ce matin *: "Pourquoi est-ce que je suis ici, dans Stafford ?"*

Would I somehow get, une réponse à cette question de l'univers ? Je ne savais pas, mais j'ai décidé que j'allais prêter l'attention.

The first thing I did after my meditation this morning was to sit at my desk and turn on my computer. C'était encore aube. Sombre encore. Les yeux sont allés à la petite note sur le coin de mon écran d'ordinateur. I was looking at an orange stickee note that was given to me a few days ago by my new artist friend, Sophie Picard. I had asked Sophie to give me a new word to learn, en français. Sur le morceau de papier minuscule, elle avait écrit : "Épanouisse-ment." A word so long that Sophie had to write it on two lines, sur le stickee. She could not quite explain to me what the word meant, en anglais. Elle m'a dit de chercher le mot dans un dictionnaire.

I looked up le mot. Le dictionnaire a indiqué : "1. blooming; 2. brightening, lighting." D'accord, okay. Un signe de l'univers ? Je ne le juge pas. Au lieu de cela, j'ai fait le café.

When I went to have my first cup, à côté de ma machine de café, j'ai trouvé un sac qui m'a été donné hier, par une amie, Monique Kassem, le seul Staffordian égyptien-québécoise. Quand elle m'a donné le sac, elle m'a dit de ne pas regarder l'intérieur jusqu'à ce que j'ai été prêt pour mon café de matin. D'accord, after I poured my coffee this morning I reached into the bag et pulled out un DVD. Il a été intitulé : *"Awakening Your Light Body."* D'accord, okay. Un signe de l'univers ?

Je suis resté à la maison ce matin jusqu'à environ 11h, alors je suis allé au IGA acheter le lait. In the parking lot I ran into Dave Brown. Dave et Sophie sont devenus un couple cet été. J'ai dit Dave au sujet de Sophie me donnant le mot, "épanouissement," pour rechercher dans un dictionnaire, and I told him what I had found as definitions. Dave is extremely literate, en anglais et français. He told me that if he had to translate, "épanouissement," in a word or two, he would say: *"unfolding,* or *awakening."*

Aprés je suis allé dans l'IGA I ran into Francois Desjardins in the organic dairy department. He was so absorbed avec looking at a milk label that he did not make eye contact with me when we exchanged ca va's. Il a dit quelque chose au sujet l'IGA having such good prices for their soy milk. Alors, soudainement, il m'a tourné, avec un expression trés sérieux sur son visage, et a dit, "Mario, I know you are a healer and you are here for 2012. You must be seeing more...*unfolding.*"

I told Francois that Dave Brown had been talking to me just a few minutes before about, *"unfolding."* Francois replied, "That is synchronicity. The universe is telling you something, Mario. You only have to pay attention, carefully. Things will add up."

Je lui ai dit : "Things have been adding up aujourd'hui."

Oui, adding up. Et what it adds up to is: Je sens que je suis un chemin allumé ici, dans Stafford.

19 Novembre 2010
East End Bay, NY

"The American Way of Life"

Cher journal intime...Je suis dans un New York state of mind aujourd'hui. Which is to say: Yak-yak-yak, yak-yak-yak. Oui. Mais oui. Yak-yak-yak, yak-yak-yak. Billy Joel *Cadillac*...yak-yak, yak.

I have been away from Stafford, et on Long Island, for the past three weeks. C'est fou, ici ! And it is getting to me. In Stafford, I experience the raising of my consciousness. Ici, on Long Island, I experience the rising of my blood pressure.

Instead of climbing Mont Stafford every day, presque tous les jours je dois monter et descendre Bald Hill avec ma voiture. Instead of having les énergies de Mont Stafford resonate within me, habituellement my energies are bled from my being as I drive my car over Bald Hill.

Bald Hill, in Farmingville, New York, is the sister mountain to Mont Stafford, de Québec. I am affected so differently by these mountains parce que they are as different as two sisters can be, who were raised in two different countries with two different families. They are as different, and more, than the famous sisters Madame Montréal et Madame Manhattan.

Mont Stafford resides more than un heure à l'est de Montréal, par voiture, sans circulation et driving fast. Ironiquement, in typical traffic, this is about the same amount of time it takes to drive east from Manhattan to Bald Hill.

Mont Stafford is not the highest mountain in the region of the Eastern Townships, but it is thought of (at least by Staffordians) as the spiritual summit of Québec. Bald Hill is thought of (at least by local Tea Party Patriots) as a sacred mountain, aussi. En fait, Bald Hill is the most sacred of mountains in this region of The Empire State, because of the Vietnam Veterans War Memorial that stands at its summit, on the island in the middle of the roadway.

Locals also consider Bald Hill to be the highest geographic point on Long Island, an island which is about 100 miles, ou environ 160 kilometres long, et 20-something miles, ou peut-être 24 km wide. (Actually, the official records show that there are two other hills on Long Island that are higher than Bald Hill. And there are also several garbage dumps on Long Island that rise higher than Bald Hill, but their existence is ignored in the official records, of course. Inconvenient truths…C'est vrai, non ? Vérités d'Inconvienent. Au sujet de : Réchauffement de la planète. Ordures. Le Vietnam. It is all related, aussi. Non ?)

I wonder if people on Long Island protested when the road was built over Bald Hill. I doubt it very much. This points to a difference in values between the cultures east of Montreal and east of New York City. It would be enormously sacrilegious in the secular culture of Québec to build a road up and over Mont Stafford.

Thousands of cars drive up and over Bald Hill every day. The traffic is often heavy, and once it starts moving, it moves fast. Riverhead Raceway fast. Everyone is racing to work, or racing home, or racing to go shopping, or racing just to keep pace with everyone else, parce que life has become one big race to these people.

The speed limit, which is 55 miles per hour, means zilch, zippo, nada. Laws, rules, courtesy, mean nothing. Some drivers drive as if they are in a chase scene in a movie. Others drive as if they are driving a make-believe car, as part of a violent video game. It is capital letter "K" Krazy. C'est fou.

Et I am not talking about road rage. That is another matter. Very few of these people are giving the finger to each other as they cut each other off, or get cut off. Très peu. This is all the New Normal. Everyone is sipping on their 7-11 coffees, or their Starbuck's coffees, or the coffee they made at home if they had the extra five minutes to make it, and they are talking on their cell phones, or text-messaging, or putting on makeup, or trying to wake up, while they are racing. Encore, I am not talking about road rage on Bald Hill. This is all about what is called: "The American Way of Life."

29 décembre 2010

"Masonic Synchronicity"

J'ai fait une méditation courte ce matin, avant l'aube. Une méditation New York Minute. Although I did not plan to do so, I finished my meditation by asking the universe : *"Pourquoi est-ce que je suis ici, dans Stafford ?"*

Environ une demi-heure plus tard, l'univers a répondu sous la forme de pensée : *"Why not, Mario-Jacques? Pourquoi pas ? Egrek pas ?"* J'aime un univers avec un sens de l'humour.

Environ une autre demi-heure plud tard, l'univers a répondu avec une autre pensée : *"For healing. You are here for healing."*

I thought to myself: To heal others? To heal myself? Tous les deux ?

En tout cas, j'ai senti energized.

I was going to take a long walk ce matin, une longue méditation de marche. J'ai besoin une longue méditation de marche. Still coming down from New York. Toutefois, j'ai dû faire la lessive, et lave des planchers, et set mousetraps, et I ran out of time for the walk.

I had an appointment à 13h pour rencontrer avec mon ami Eliot Mason au Café Dumont, et I did not want to be en retard. Until today, it had been two years since I had seen Eliot. Which was at his wedding party, which was in a clearing in the woods, on Mount Echo. C'était une grande fête.

Eliot et son épouse Éve sont les écologistes vrais. Professionnels écologistes. High I.Q. people. Dédié au changement social. Sauveurs du monde. A part of la Génération d'Espoir.

149

Eliot est ponctuel retentive anal, donc je ne voulais pas être en retard. Toutefois, je ne pourrais pas trouver un endroit pour me garer ma voiture. Je n'ai jamais vu tant de personnes en ville. Skieurs. As it turned out, we both pulled into le stationnement près du gazebo, derrière le Café Monet, en même temps, exactement à 13h.

Pendant que je marchais vers lui, Eliot a dit, "It looks like there are more Montreal people here than in Bromont. The parking lot at the IGA is full. There isn't a single space. And I noticed that there were two empty grocery carts that were left in the parking lot. It wasn't Stafford people who did that, eh Mario?"

J'ai répondu : "Bien sûr not." I wanted to respond to Eliot in French, not franglais, mais that was what came out of my mouth. I couldn't remember fast enough that "pas" is the way to say, "not."

Eliot est mince et barely 5 feet tall. I was too enthusiastic when we hugged ca va's, and he cried out, "Prudent ! Careful!" J'ai pensé que je l'ai blessé, mais j'ai découvert qu'il avait peur que je pourrais avoir ridé la couverture du livre qu'il portait. Comme j'ai dit, il est rétentif anal.

Quand nous sommes arrivés au Café Dumont nous avons trouvé que chaque table, chaque chaise, a été utilisé. Je n'ai pas vu un visage que j'ai connu. Je presque senti comme j'étais à Starbucks, qui sont des versions de deuxième classe des Dumonts. Un autre exemple de ce qu'est précieux sur Québec.

We were chanceux, we waited for only a minute before we got une table pour deux, contre le mur arrière. Eliot est un *mensch.* As soon as we sat down, il s'est levé pour obtenir un café pour chacun de nous.

Il a apporté le café dans ma nouvelle tasse préférée, avec les mots, « Vive le Québec. » Quand j'ai mentionné ceci à lui, dit-il, "Ah, *synchronicity!* We see what we want to see, and you have to admit Mario-Jacques, you have a penchant for seeing synchronicity. However, I think it would be best if we talk about synchronicity later. I have to be at Cowansville Hospital in an hour and a half, to give blood. Therefore I am going to have lunch and I think I am going to try the *vegetarien chili*. I am told the *vegetarien chili* is quite good at Café Dumont."

J'ai dit: "Sounds good."

Elliot a continué, "We have just enough time for me to catch you up on my life, then for you to catch me up on your life. Then I want to show you this book I brought along, *The Ethical Imagination,* by Margaret Somerville. And my brother Michael might join us, but he will probably only be able to stay for a minute."

J'ai dit, "Sounds good, and it will be great to see Michael."

Michael est incroyable. Un autre sauveur du monde. Mais oui, et Michael is another member of la Génération d'Espoir. He finished his master's at McGill environ il ya un an. Maintenant he has a very responsible position, working for a non-profit, in Ghana. Michael a 26 ans. Trois ans plus jeune, et six pouces plus grand que son frère Eliot.

Eliot et moi had une discussion profonde, couvrant a large range des sujets, du politique à l'ésotérique et métaphysique. Michael est venu pour dire bonjour, mais il est resté pendant juste une minute. Si tout va bien, we will get together before he returns to Ghana, le neuvième de janvier, où il travaille pour un but non lucratif.

J'ai fini mon *vegetarien chili* avant Eliot ai fini le sien, parce que Eliot a fait la majeure partie de parler. Which was good. I enjoyed listening to Eliot as much as I enjoyed eating the chili, parce qu'il est tellement éloquent, et intelligent, et j'apprends de sa perspective.

Eliot parlait au sujet du livre qu'il est tellement enthousiaste au sujet, *The Ethical Imagination,* when he suddenly interrupted himself, to ask me if I had seen Francois Desjardins lately. J'ai été très étonné qu'Eliot would ask me au sujet de Francois, parce que je pense que la seule fois que j'ai jamais mentionné Francois à Eliot était il y a trois ans, dans l'été de 2007. J'ai dit à Eliot: "You remember the story about my conversation with Francois? How is it that you can remember his *name*? That is what some might call, *'random,'* Eliot."

En l'été de 2007, pendant un dîner j'ai eu avec Francois Desjardins à la Cascade, il m'avait demandé si j'étais venu à Stafford en raison de, *"2012,"* d'être un guérisseur, peut-être. At the time, je n'ai su rien des diverses paradigmes au sujet de 2012. At some point during the summer of 2007 I told Eliot about my discussion with Francois about healing, and about 2012. Jusqu'à aujourd'hui, j'ai oublié que j'avais partagé ceci avec Eliot. Yet, this was significant enough to Eliot that he remembered l'histoire et the name, "Francois Desjardins."

Eliot a dit, "For some reason, I have been thinking about Francois Desjardins the last few days." Eliot paused, and looked at my face to see if I was looking at him like he was a little fou, je pense. Alors, il a continué, "The issue of consensual reality, and people like Francois Desjardins, interests me. So, maybe because I knew I was going to have lunch with you today Mario-Jacques, was the reason why Francois Desjardins has come to mind." Envoyait-il quelque chose dehors à l'univers ? C'était une question que je ne pas lui demandé.

While Eliot was telling me that his thoughts had been turning to Francois Desjardins, I thought, peut-être, coincidentally once again, that I heard the voice of Francois, speaking en français. Au début, j'ai pensé que c'était juste mon imagination, mais quand j'ai écouté plus soigneusement, ca ressemblait Francois Desjardins à parlait à la table derrière moi !

Le Café Dumont a été rempli de touristes. Chaque table, chaque chaise. Je ne vois pas Francois Desjardins très souvent. La dernière fois j'ai vu lui était il y a des mois, à l'IGA. Mais ceci a ressemblé à de Francois tellement que j'ai dit à Eliot, dans un chuchotement, "Brace yourself Eliot, I think I hear his voice. I think Francois Desjardins is sitting at the table behind me."

Le visage de Eliot était enceinte, pas avec un grand signification, mais avec l'incertitude. I thought to myself : Could it possibly be that Francois Desjardins is, by coincidence, sitting at the table behind us? Une coïncidence significative ?

I turned and took a very quick look at the person who I thought was Francois. Nope. Mistaken identity. Ca n'était pas lui. Mais similaire. La voix de cet homme était la même comme la voix de Francois.

J'ai dit à Eliot, "Wow, that would have been one heck of a coincidence, eh? That he would have been the *one* Staffordian to come here for dejeuner, after you said you were thinking about him?"

Eliot a juste dit, evenly, "Well, he is not sitting behind you."

The thing is, the thing is, the thing is…après we left our table et went to the counter to pay, I looked back and saw that it was, *mais oui(!)*, Francois Desjardins qui s'était reposé derrière moi. He had

had his back to me, and I had looked only at the man who was facing me, because I thought *his* voice was the voice I heard. I am not good at localizing voices, et peut-être I was thrown off parce que Francois parlaient en français...Mais, it was Francois Desjardins, after all. I did not say it out loud, but I thought to myself: *Holy shit, ho-leee synchronicity!*

Comme nous tournions à partir la comptoir à quitter le café, j'ai dit à Eliot, "That *was* Francois I heard! He is the *other* guy at the table, wearing the white toque."

Eliot did not show any reaction, until a few minutes après, quand dit-il avec un grand sourire : "Synchronicity strikes again." Mais, ses pensées ont pu avoir été concentrées sur son prochain arrêt – donner le sang à l'hôpital de Cowansville.

Seulement plus tard il s'est produit à moi que j'ai demandé à l'univers ce matin, "Pourquoi est-ce que je suis ici, dans Stafford ?" Et j'ai perçu la réponse pour être au sujet de guérison. Bien sûr, it was Francois Desjardins who first suggested to me that perhaps the reason I was in Stafford was for healing. This was his intuitive sense.

Je ne sais pas dans quelle degré cet événement synchronistique a résonné avec Eliot. Nous avons dit que nous devons courriel bientôt.

10 janvier 2011

"Gathering au Café Dumont pour la Nouvelle Terre"

Je me suis réveillé avant l'aube aujourd'hui. After going to sleep at eight-thirty last night, after a long Zen Walk. Plus précisément : après une longue Raquette Zen, hier après-midi. Quand j'ai ouvert les rideaux devant mon bureau, j'ai regardé la noirceur dehors. I stared out at le noir. C'était un noir avec bienveillance. Ici, à Stafford, souvent il y a une énergie bienveillante dans le noir qu'est palpable. Souvent entre chien et loup. Avant l'aube, quelque fois. D'autres temps. Ce matin, I could not look deep into the darkness, but I had a sense that a special day was foretold là.

I turned on mon ordinateur et j'ai pris un chocolat chaud – *Tim Hortons toujours frais riche et delicieux*, tandis que j'ai lu mes nouveaux courriels. J'ai trouvé cinq courriels réfs : "Gathering." These emails were all from men I know on Long Island who were trying to organize une réunion, a gathering, at a restaurant.

Pendant le matin j'ai regardé la neige tomber, tumbling, flottant, à la terre. J'ai été captivé par la nature du vol des flocons de neige. Magie blanche. Encore, j'ai eu un sens qu'un jour spécial était prédit là.

Plus tard le matin, après le noir et le blanc, le ying et le yang, j'ai trouvé la carte de visite de Val Dufour dans la poche du pantalon que je n'avais pas porté depuis l'année dernière. La carte montre seulement le numéro de téléphone et le courriel adresse pour Val. Et une silhouette du Mont Pinacle. Val is a channeler. Je n'ai pas vu Val dans un long temps. J'ai mis la carte dans ma poche, pour me rappeler de le voir.

À midi, je suis allé au Café Dumont. As soon as I walked into the café, who do I see? Val Dufour. Bien sûr, Val Dufour. Synchronicité ! He was sitting at the counter in the center of the café. I sat down on the stool next to him, and then I asked him to reach into my shirt pocket and take out what was there.

Quand il a regardé la carte de visite, il a dit, stoïquement, avec une voix tranquille : "Why am I not surprised?"

J'ai répondu : "Why am I not surprised that you are not surprised, Val?"

Encore, stoïquement, avec un sourire subtile, speaking presque slooo-mo slow, il a dit : "You put it out to the Universe that you wanted to see me. I felt the call. I did not know who was calling me, but I knew I had to be here, à midi, at noon. I also knew that this was the seat I should sit in. I did not know why. Now, I think it was meant for me to sit here so that I would see your handsome face Mario-Jacques, as soon as you entered le café."

J'ai répondu, "Merci mon ami guapo. I happened to find your card this morning in the pocket of these pants, which I have not worn, peut-être, since last winter. I put the card in my shirt pocket to remind me to ask for you, because I wanted to see you. I figured you were in Montréal, ou Cuba."

Val a dit, "I was not going to come into la ville today, but I felt the call to come here. It must have been your call, Mario-

Jacques. The Universe called you with my calling card, and then you called me." He handed his card back to me, and added, "Pour toi, for another time." Puis, he took a sip from his coffee, cradled the cup with both his hands, and smiled at me. Ce qui a signifié, j'ai pensé : « Nous attendons. » Val est demi Abenaki. Il sait attendre. Neither of us spoke.

Un moment plus tard, j'ai senti une tape sur mon épaule. C'était Gaston Briere. Il était juste arrivé dans Stafford de Montréal. Tandis que Gaston was hanging up his coat and pouring un café for himself, Val a dit, "We are *gathering*, Mario-Jacques. This is the word, no? This is the word that describes what is happening now. We are *gathering*. Does this resonate with you, Mario-Jacques?"

Puis, what flashed to my mind was remembering that la première chose que j'ai vue sur mes courriels ce matin étaient cinq messages au sujet un : "gathering." J'ai dit, "Val, this resonates with me. This morning I received five courriels that were titled: 'gathering.'"

Val smiled. I put my arms across my chest and raised a finger to my lips. J'ai tapé mes doigts sur mes lèvres plusieurs fois, puis j'ai souri à Val.

Apparemment, the universe, as channeled through Val Dufour, was telling me that I was to be part of a meaningful gathering au Café Dumont aujourd'hui. Et maintenant, voici Gaston, à l'improviste, de Montréal, à notre rassemblement au comptoir au centre du café. Surprise. Surprise, surprise, surprise. Et synchronicité.

Après exchanging ca va's, Gaston a dit, "What are you saying here about, 'gathering?' Doucement, sans gravité dans sa voix, Gaston a ajouté, "It was meant for me to gather here with you, I think. I arrived earlier from Montréal than I expected. Pas circulation on the 10."

Gaston et Val ont commencé à parler entre eux en français. J'ai compris quelques mots, mais I did not get the gist of what they were saying. Je suis allé obtenir du café pour Gaston et moi-même. Quand je suis retourné ils ont commencé à parler en anglais. Gaston disait Val au sujet des peintures d'inukshuk qu'il avait faites. Il a dit qu'il avait vendu la plupart de ses peintures d'inukshuk dans les galeries à Manitoba. Gaston also told Val that he wanted to paint fewer inukshuks this year, and hardly any in 2012, no matter how much money he was making on these paintings. Avec un sourire dans sa visage, Val a demandé à Gaston, "Why do you paint? *Pourquoi* ?"

Gaston a répondu, "I *must* paint. It is like eating. It is a different kind of nourriture."

Val a dit, "I understand. Now tell me Gaston, why do you paint the inukshuk?"

Je suis sûr Gaston n'aimait pas obtenir cette question avec son café mais il ne le pas montre dans son visage. Je sais Gaston, et pour Gaston it was too early in the morning for philosophical questions, mais he is a patient person. Gaston a répondu en français. Il a dit quelque chose au sujet : "iconique."

J'ai écouté eux parler en français, mais j'ai seulement compris quelques mots. I did not comprehend enough to hear complete thoughts. Ils ont fait une pause de parler et Gaston a dit, "Mario-Jacques, are you able to understand what we are saying? Some of it?"

J'ai dit, très lentement : "Je comprends quelques mots, ici et là. Vous parlez trop rapide pour moi. Mais, j'ai pensé que tu a dit quelque chose au sujet le inukshuk est, 'iconique,' non ?"

Regardless of how lentement I spoke, they were impressed , too impressed, that I was able to respond to the question in my halting, and very slightly Brooklyn-accented français. Donc, ils sont commencé à parler en français encore. Et encore, je n'ai pas su qu'ils disaient. Toutefois, I interjected after a while : "L'inukshuk est iconique comme la croix, non ?"

Val souri et il a demandé à tous les deux nous : "Do you think the inukshuk is the symbol for *The New Earth*?"

Gaston a répondu, "For the people who are buying my paintings, it is. '"

J'ai ajouté, "It is a symbol of different things, to different people, but I can see where it is becoming a significant symbol for New Earth People."

Gaston a dit, "I am not sure what you mean by, 'New Earth People,' Mario-Jacques."

I looked to Val et j'ai demandé, "What does it mean to *you* when I say, 'New Earth People?'"

Val a répondu, "To me, when you say, 'New Earth People,' you are talking about the people who are gathering, as we are, to create a new Earth."

Gaston a dit, "I did not read about this in *Science* ou *Le Devoir.*" Puis, Gaston a commencé à parler français, trop rapide pour moi, et à la même temps j'ai entendu quelqu'un chanter dans un chuchotement, juste derrière ma tête. J'ai entendu : *"Om-Na-Ma-Shiva...Om-Na-Ma-Shiva."* C'était Monique Kassem, la seule Staffordian Québécoise-Éygyptien que je sais.

J'ai dit, "Aaah, je sais cette voix. You have such a lovely singing voice, Monique. Si belle ! C'est incroyable that you would sing that mantra into my ear, maintenant. I was playing my *Om Namaha Shivaya* CD beaucoup, while I was driving dans le circulation de New York. I feel quite a connection with that mantra. I have experienced synchronicity avec *Om Namaha Shivaya,* aussi."

En réponse à mes mots et à mon visage de sourire, Monique a ri et elle a dit, "Bien sûr. Of course you experience synchronicity! You experience synchronicity with so *many* things! Do you know the people, they call you, 'Monsieur Synchronicité ?'"

J'ai répondu, "Pas problème. I could be called worse things."

Tandis que Gaston et Val conversaient en français, Monique moved closer to me and said, "Mario, I can barely contain my energy. I do not know, je ne sais pas...I do not know how to express this in English. I cannot find the word...I do not think the English have a word for this..." Alors ses yeux se sont ouverts au loin, elle a ri, et elle a dit, "Um, there was a certain, *'resonation.'* Is there such a word? Probably not, but you know what I mean, non ? Something was touched inside me just a few minutes ago, when you said that you experienced synchronicity avec *Om Namaha Shivaya,* while you were driving your car. I was driving here just now from Cowansville, and on the radio in my car, before le stationnment, I was hearing *Om Namaha Shivaya.* I did not think to chant les mots until I stood beside you, here...and I am here to meet my friend, *Shiva!"*

I just nodded my head, as I was still processing what she said, et j'ai dit, "Aaah, ha. Et Shiva? Does he live in Stafford?"

Monique a dit, "Mais oui. But Shiva is a *she.* She lives in Stafford...in different places...and at the same time. She is not a citizen of Stafford; She is a citizen of the planet. Do not ask me to

157

explain what this means now. She will have to explain it to you."
Encore, grand sourire, les yeux grands ouverts.

Environ dix minutes plus tard, Shiva joined us. Plus précisément, elle s'est présentée nous. I heard soul man Curtis Mayfield singing, *"...she was a gypsy woman..."* when I laid eyes on her. Shiva was draped in scarves, from head to foot, and especially of head. Elle a eu cinq ou six écharpes, toutes les différentes couleurs, enroulées autour de sa tête. Certaines des écharpes tombent vers le bas à sa taille. She has très très long kinky curly brown afro hair, which she lets grow wild, except for some sections she has cut – like a pioneer woman who cuts out clearings in the woods, to make life easier. Some of the scarves were tied into each other, and each knot was tied in a different artistic way. She wore small ribbons of different colours that were tied into three or four braids of hair. She wears no makeup, mais Shiva is a work of art. Elle est entre trente-deux et quarante-cinq ans, je ne sais pas. Bohémienne Sauvage.

Shiva asked for and received a beverage which consisted of rien excepté l'eau chaude. I told her that I thought le propriétaire, Jean-Paul, who is a shrewd homme d'affaires, might get an idea about putting, *"Rien Excepté l'Eau Chaude,"* on the menu. Il pourrait charger la même comme *le thé vert,* s'il utilisait seulement les eaux sacrées de Mont Stafford.

Shiva a semblé être étonné que je savais sur les eaux sacrées de Mont Stafford, even though it is not such a secret that some Staffordians seek the water to derive the mountain energies it contains. She quizzed me, to see if I was talking about the same sacred water that she was thinking about. Elle a dit : "Where would la propriétaire obtain the water?"

J'ai répondu, "The easiest way would be from the spigot, the source, that is on the other side of the road, derrière l'IGA."

The talk about the water, and the magnetic resonance of Shiva, brought Val et Gaston dans notre conversation. Gaston a dit, "The water behind the IGA was shut off for months, because they found impurities."

Val a dit, "Oui, but the people complain. They want the water. No one gets sick from the water. They are energized when they drink the water."

Shiva a dit, "People will continue to drink the water, even if they remove the …how do you say it in English…the, '*spi-goat*?' People will go to the waterfalls and the rivers to get the water if the town closes the water près de l'IGA."

Shiva had brought her own tea with her, et je l'ai observée mettre un sac dans l'eau chaude. The little round tea bag had no markings on it. Il a regardé à moi comme le thé vert de Mystère(!) que Paddy O'Brien m'a donné il y a quelques mois, pour employer pour son thé quand il visite chez moi. Toutefois, avant que je pourrais poser à Shiva au sujet le thé, Monique a dit, "Shiva and I have talked about this. The water here is important, because this is a gathering place for The New Earth."

This sparked the conversation, bien sûr. Malheureusement pour moi, la conversation était en français. J'ai compris juste un peu. Monique, Shiva et Val ont eu beaucoup pour dire, et Gaston écouté et dit peu. Je me suis assis entre Gaston et Shiva, et deux d'entre eux m'a donné de petites traductions, de temps en temps.

Quand j'ai dit, 'à la prochaine,' à Shiva, ca n'était pas facile de l'embrasser sur les deux joues. J'ai touché les deux le côté de mon visage à ses cheveux. J'ai senti la Nouvelle Terre dans ses cheveux.

Après the kisses goodbye, she turned her head toward me, so that only I could hear her. Presque dans un chuchotement, mais avec l'excitation, elle a dit à moi, "I am a *Sovran* person. Do you know what that means, Mario-Jacques?"

Je secouais ma tête, 'non,' et elle a continué. "I am no longer a citizen of Canada. I am not a citizen of any nation, but of the universe. I am a Sovran. I can tell you about this at some other time, but for now I want you to know that Sovran people are talking about Stafford. I know people from far away – some in Vancouver – who are saying that Stafford is going to be the cradle of The New Earth. I do not know why, but now I know that the reason why I came here today was to sit with you and to say these things to you." Puis, elle a tourné sa tête vers les autres et a parlé plus fort, ainsi ils pourraient l'entendre. "We want the word to go out. We are gathering."

Mes yeux sont allés à Val, et ses yeux sont allés à moi. Val a dit, "Mais oui, Mario-Jacques. This is clear. *Gathering, gathering, gathering.* We are gathering for The New Earth."

J'ai demandé Val, "Comment dit-on : *'Gathering for The New Earth,'* en français?"

Val a dit : "Rassemblement pour la Nouvelle Terre."

J'ai dit, "Merci, Val. Okay, mes amies. À la prochaine." Et j'ai sorti.

À suivre.

13 janvier 2011

"Les Inukshuks et les Croix"

Je suis allé à la Galerie Bleu vers midi, après j'ai écrit tout le matin. Gaston était là. Il peignait. Marcel Charbonneau était là aussi. Marcel était le vendeur aujourd'hui. Demain Gaston est le vendeur et Marcel peindra. This is what they do. Gaston, Marcel, et Lynette Caron take turns dans la galerie, ce qu'est aussi un atelier. On most days one of the painters are there alone, mais on some days two stay in the gallery, and one paints. Quand je les observe tandis qu'ils peignent, il stimule quelquefois et c'est très détend quelquefois.

La première chose Gaston m'a dit était, "Hey, Mario-Jacques, what is going on in your country? The crazy tea party people are killing liberals in the supermarkets!"

J'ai répondu, "Je sais. Pas surpris. Hate radio and hate television have plenty of sponsors. Do you know that the congresswoman who was shot in la tête declared to Sarah Palin last year that her rhetoric was encouraging violence among Americans?"

Gaston et Marcel knew more details about this dark and historic day than I did. Mais oui, ils en savaient plus que moi sur les nouvelles aux États-Unis. Ce n'est pas une surprise, parce qu'ils ont des Canadiens, Québécois, et je suis Américain. (Plus précis : Un Amériquébécois, pure laine.)

Gaston a dit, "We can come back to the subject of the Barbie from Alaska plus tard. We have some breaking news maintenant. My associate here, Marcel Charbonneau, is on quite a hot streak, Mario-Jacques. Yes he is. He sold two paintings this morning."

Je me suis tourné vers Marcel et j'ai dit : "Félicitations, Monsieur !"

Marcel peint des paysages. He uses colours of the earth, and violet, a lot. Le jaune qu'il emploie est spécial. Il emploie un jaune qu'est comme le jaune de Van Gogh. C'est comme le jaune de quelques régions de l'Inde. Quelques artistes en Inde emploient l'urine des vaches pour créer une peinture jaune. Marcel told me about this, and that Van Gogh used the urine of cows to create his yellow. Mais oui. C'est un jaune qu'est unique en l'Inde, et peut-être, à Van Gogh. Marcel m'a dit que il emploie aussi un jaune unique, et seulement quelques personnes savent ceci. Marcel told me that the secret ingredient in his paintings is moose urine. Oui, urine original. Je ne suis pas certain que c'est vrai. Mais peut-être.

En tout cas, tandis que Gaston, Marcel et moi sipped our café au lait, nous sont commencé un discussion au sujet what they were painting. Gaston was formulating an idea for his next inukshuk and sketching with a pencil on a small pad. He said that he wants to paint an inukshuk that would be titled: *La Nouvelle Croix.*

Marcel a dit à Gaston, "In a way, you have been painting a series with this theme: 'La Nouvelle Croix.'"

Gaston a dit, "C'est vrai, c'est vrai. But this time I want to paint this idea in a way that will be…*plus explicite.*"

Marcel a dit, "What do you mean? Are you going to paint Jesus on the inukshuk?"

Gaston n'a dit rien, mais ses yeux se sont ouverts au loin. Il a commencé esquisser, et il a dit, "No, not Jesus on the inukshuk, I do not think so. But you give me other ideas…"

D'accord, we shall see what we shall see from Gaston. I expect quelque chose formidable, bien sûr.

Je remarque tant de croix sur les routes du Québec, qui y ont été placés il ya plusieurs années. Et maintenant, les inukshuks trouvent une place. Quelle sera la spiritualité du 21ème siècle ?

Coram, NY
18 février 2011

"What is Starbucks good for?"

Dear Diary…Today, at one o'clock in the afternoon, I went to a Starbucks located in Everywhere, U.S.A. More specifically, I went to a Starbucks in Coram, New York – which is smack in the middle of Long Island, I would guess about 50 miles to the east of New York City.

The view from the front window or la terrassee of Café Dumont – environ 8 hours away from Coram, in the Eastern Townships of Québec – is far more pleasing than the view from the windows of this Starbucks on Long Island. My table and chair next to the front window of Starbucks faced Middle Country Road – which runs down the middle of Long Island but is no longer a, "country road," but a two-lane-in-each-direction highway, that should be renamed: "McDonaldized American Road."

The sound of the music that was playing in this Starbucks only partially masked the sound of the cars and trucks and very large Wal-Mart tractor-trailers whizzing by at high speeds. This Starbucks is about 20 feet from the roadway, which adds an element of danger to sitting by the window, which I had to block out of my mind while I sat there. From where I sat I could look across the road to yet another five-store shopping center that was being built. Something else not to dwell upon.

I did not see a single person who entered this café sit down and converse with another person. This was a café that was filled with strangers, which was not the case today at Café Dumont in the Eastern Townships, je suis certain. Encore, pour moi, quite a different experience sitting ici, in this Starbucks, compared to being in le Café Dumont dans Stafford, Québec.

There is a sidewalk in front of this Starbucks, but it is extremely rare that anyone would actually walk on this sidewalk, in this particular part of the roadway. It is dangerous to walk along the road here. Every single person in this Starbucks came in a car and parked in one of the spaces that run around the building. No one leaves this Starbucks and *walks* to their next destination. Everyone will drive or be a passenger in a car.

A lot of these people – me among them today – come in alone, and sit alone. In fact, I checked and most of the tables were filled by people sitting alone. There were far fewer tables where two people were sitting. There is about as much socializing in this Starbucks as there is among drivers on the Long Island Expressway, or on Middle Country Road. One person to a table, sometimes two, just as there is usually one person to a car, and less often two people in a car, on the Long Island Expressway. At one point I saw that there were 23 people sitting alone at 23 little tables, and there were four more little tables with two people at them. I decided to count how many of the cars driving by had more than one person in them. They were going by too fast for me to get an accurate count, but most of the cars had only a driver, no passengers.

En tout cas, I found this Starbucks to be a good place for me to grade test papers.

5 mars 2011
McDonaldized America, NY

"Stop & Shop, Arrêt SVP"

Ce matin, après attending a meeting at the college, I went to a Stop & Shop near the school to do a little grocery shopping. Maintenant, since I have the consciousness of an amériquébécois, l'expérience de grocery shopping ici seems un peu weird, et un peu oppressif.

There were hundreds of spaces in the parking lot in front of the store and more than half of them were filled. There were no parking spaces close to the store, not even for the handicapped. All of the spaces were either occupied by a car, or by a discarded shopping cart. The corrals, where people are supposed to return their carts after they use them, were all empty or close to empty. Bien sûr, the parking spaces on both sides of one of the corrals were occupied by shopping carts, because people were not willing to exert the energy to push these carts five or ten feet farther. This is a good example of the leave-the-problem-for-the-next-guy mentality that is so prevalent ici.

A lot of cars and trucks in this parking lot had, *"Support our troops,"* bumper stickers on them. Je ne sais pas what the tabernac, *"Support our troops,"* means, exactly. Toutefois, I can see that a lot of these people are living by the credo that is *not* displayed on bumper stickers: *"Leave the problem for the next guy."* Mais oui, that goes for so many things, from shopping carts to the national debt to global warming.

Fortunately, I was playing my *Om Namaha Shivaya* CD while I was trying to find a parking space, donc I was in a semi-meditative state, somewhat shielded from the bad karma. I found a parking space at the far end of the parking lot, next to a 20-foot high pile of black-gray suburban parking lot snow. There were two shopping carts, tipped over on their sides, on the top of the snow pile. More than likely, the teenagers who went to the trouble of dragging these carts up to the top of this twenty-foot high snow mound are the children of people who are in the habit of leaving their shopping carts in the parking spaces here.

When I got to the entrance of the store I saw four soldiers standing there, dressed in green camouflage uniforms. They were military veterans, peut-être in their forties, peut-être Iraqnam vets, asking for donations for their vets organization. I gave one of them, a black man who struck me as being rather obsequious, a dollar. I had an empty 7-11 coffee container in my hand, and I moved to put it in the garbage pail that was beside us, but the pail was overflowing with trash, as per usual. Before I realized what he was doing, the obsequious soldier said, "allow me, sir," and gently wrested the container from my hand and stuffed it, with some effort, through the hinged lid of the garbage pail.

I said something about the pail overflowing and he commented that it's the same way at the Wal-Mart up the road, but they have more garbage pails there. I thanked him for putting his hand in the garbage for me, and he thanked me for, "helping to keep America great." Talk about overdoing it, I thought he was going to salute me. Aaah, he seemed like a nice enough guy. And if he went to Iraq, he put his life and limb on the line. Toutefois…the road to hell is paved with good intentions, and the big corporations get the no-bid contracts to do the paving, non ?

At the entrance to this Stop & Shop there are two doors. People can only enter through the big doors on one side and they can only exit through the small doors on the other side. The first entry door swings in, automatically, and customers must then walk another 20 feet to go through another door, before they can actually get inside the store. On both sides of the walkway between the two doors there are open cases, large cardboard boxes, of junk food. Shoppers must pass through a gauntlet of Drake's Devil Dogs, Chips Ahoy cookies, Ritz crackers, and an obscene amount of Utz potato chips, which are piled at least eight feet high on both sides of the walkway. Stop & Shop knows that people who enter this store while they are hungry will be tempted to pick up some of this crap, as the first things they will put into their shopping carts. Mais oui, these corporations use every opportunity and every inch of space – to grab you as you take your first step into their domains – to try to sell you something, anything. Ici, they are urging customers to pick up items for their shopping carts before the customers even have shopping carts.

Once I got inside, I had to try out three shopping carts before I could find one that had wheels that rolled smoothly. The shopping carts at Stop & Shop are at least two times as large as the carts I am used to using at the IGA in Stafford. When I use the Stop & Shop cart I can an put almost everything I need to buy in the flip-down compartment that is designed to function as a child's seat. By American standards, my way of grocery shopping is not representative of normal consumption, it's the equivalent of going to a McDonald's and ordering only a hamburger and a Coke – the "unhappy meal," without the french fries.

The child seats in the carts at this Stop & Shop have red nylon seat belts attached. On the seat belts it says: *"Please fasten child securely. Do not leave child unattended."* Good idea being expressed, but it was hard for me to read the words because the seat belts are so worn, and they are so filthy that they probably contain more germs than the customer toilets in this store. The thought occurred to me that I might see babies riding in these shopping carts with their tiny bare hands wrapped around these seat belts. Actually, pas peut-être, I knew I could count on it. Plus comme half the people who shop in this store vote republican if they vote at all, and more than half the people who shop in this store do not believe in global warming, and more than half the people who shop in this store believe that fussing about germs is something that only liberals and homosexuals do. Something like that. If their eyes can't see it, it doesn't exist.

En tout cas, I see The American Way, ou plus précis, The Corporate Way, embodied in this shopping cart. A red sign on the

165

back of the cart says: "*A Warning: Your child can fall out of cart and suffer a serious head injury.*" In a better world, a less litigious world, such a sign would also read: "*...and do not let your babies put their fingers in their mouths while they sit in this cart. Not even to eat tabernac Chips Ahoy cookies.*"

The reason why the shopping carts in this store are so run down is because they have a lot of mileage on them. After all, the store has 24(!) long aisles. Pourquoi ? For the same reason this country has only two major political parties: People seem to think it is the right number. Et peut-être they do not stop to think pourquoi pas about alternatives.

Encore, en tout cas, I wanted to go to the vegetable department, but that was at the far end of the store, to my left, so first I had to navigate my shopping cart past the garden furniture that this grocery store was now in the business of selling, and was on display next to where I picked up my cart. Once I got past the garden furniture I found that I still could not go left, because this aisle ran in front of the checkout counters, and that way was blocked with an overflow of people waiting to check out. Almost a grid-lock traffic jam. There are a lot of checkout counters in this store but almost all of them were closed. Bien sûr, all of the self-serve checkouts were open. They have it figured out so that just about any time you shop you are going to have to wait on line to check out. Je pense they purposely close checkout counters to keep the lines long, so that people will be forced to use the self-serve checkouts. Consumers need to be conditioned to serve themselves. This is also The Corporate Way, eh? Utilize every means possible to eliminate workers, maximize profits.

En tout cas, I felt like I was driving in traffic in New Jersey, and I had to go right before I could go left. I pushed my cart past the pharmacy department, which looks like a store in and of itself. Judging from the people I saw waiting on line there, it looks like this pharmacy specializes in medications for the obese. I cut down the aisle next to the pharmacy, which was a frozen food aisle. Mon Dieu, this aisle looked like a frozen pizza store, in and of itself. More than any other way, this is where America shows how much it values diversity: In frozen pizza. Jeeeeezus! I paused while I was walking, to look at all the varieties of frozen pizza displayed in one refrigerator case after another. And I looked back over my shoulder at all the obese people waiting on line for their medications at the pharmacy department, conveniently located at the beginning of the aisle. Mon Dieu !

Bien sûr, for many Long Islanders, for many Americans, walking in a supermarket is their main form of exercise in any given week. Bien sûr, on Long Island, which is a car culture, it is safer to hike across 24 aisles of a Stop & Shop than to try to walk on the roadsides.

In addition to having to listen to horrible grocery store background music, and announcements made at high volume from loudspeakers mounted in the ceiling throughout the store, shoppers and store workers must endure barrages of commercials for products that are sold in the store. *"Shoppers, buy three Mrs. Paul's fish fillets and get one free on your next visit...Shoppers, we have a special offer for you today: Blah, blah, blah, blah..."*

When the Board of Directors of Stop & Shop has a meeting, they should have to listen to the same blaring announcements during their meeting that their customers have to listen to while they are shopping. *"Deli kiosk order 21 ready for pickup at your convenience, thank you; Deli kiosk order 21 ready for pick-up at your convenience, thank you...Deli kiosk order 22 ready for pickup at your convenience, thank you; Deli kiosk order 22 ready for pickup at your convenience, thank you...Dave, 413; Dave, 413...Store manager to the deli department; Store manager to the deli department...Can Boar's Head move your truck, please?; Can Boar's Head move your truck, please?...Pharmacy, telephone call on 130; Pharmacy, telephone call on 130...Maintenance with a mop to aisle 3; Maintenance with a mop to aisle 3...Joe, when you get a chance, to the cereal aisle, by the Post section; Joe, when you get a chance, to the cereal aisle, by the Post section...Deli kiosk order 23 ready for pickup at your convenience, thank you; Deli kiosk order 23 ready for pickup at your convenience, thank you...Shoppers, buy three Italiano fish fillet frozen pizzas and get ten percent off your medications on your next visit to our pharmacy department; Shoppers, buy three Italiano fish fillet frozen pizzas, or a Very Happy Meal in the deli department, and get..."*

This was one of those days when I just wanted to buy the minimum and get in and out of the store as fast as possible. I bought some overpriced organic fruits and vegetables, a carton of eggs, and at the checkout I bought a package of Twizzlers, on impulse.

As I was walking away from the checkout counter I was approached by a young man and a young woman who were smiling broadly and were so well-dressed that I thought they were Jehovah Witnesses or perhaps young Mormons on a crusade. It turned out that they worked for Citizen's Bank, which actually has a branch office located in this store, strategically located next to the deposit bottle return. They asked me if I might want to open an account at the bank today. Joking, I asked them if I could apply for a mortgage before I brought my groceries to my car, and they said I could.

Some people would say that this is what makes America great. You can apply for a mortgage where you can buy lawn furniture, and get your prescription for medication filled, and buy frozen pizza. C'est incroyable, non ?

27 mars 2011

« The Oil Sacrée d'Abremelin »

Yesterday night je suis allé voir Merlin The Magician et Gwen Beckett à leur ferme. I had not seen either one of them depuis janvier. Alors, we had some catching up to do.

As I was turning into their driveway, at that time that some Québécois et tous Amériquébécois call *entre chien et loup*, I was startled by the sight of someone on a motorcycle, a dirt bike, come flying through the snow, from around the back of the house. The rear tire of the bike was kicking up snow, peut-être three meters in the air. The bike was headed toward me at first, but then it skidded to a stop and made a 90 degree turn, to face the greenhouse, to my right. The rider revved up the engine until it was screeeeeeeeeeeeeeeming so loud that I could not hear the French language CD that I was playing dans ma voiture. La moto a coupé à travers l'avant de la grange et accelerated fast enough to startle me, comme lui a été tiré d'un canon.

168

J'ai pensé que la moto allait s'écraser dans la serre, mais il a descendu une sentier étroit dans la neige, qu'était entre la serre et la grange, et il ai disparu dans la nuit.

Je me suis demandé qui pourrait être l'Evil Knevil ? J'ai pensé ce pourrait être John, le fils de Merlin et de Gwen, mais je me suis rappelé que Gwen m'a indiqué plus tôt l'après-midi que John était au Lake Placid, rencontre avec un entraîneur de gymnastique de Budapest qui veut que John construise un trempoline pour lui. Alors, je n'ai eu aucune idée qui le cavalier sur la moto était.

When I got out of my car I heard the motorcycle going through the snowfield, and then go into the forest, or down the road. When Merlin let me in the house, and I was taking off my Kamiks, j'ai dit à Merlin : « Qui est l'Evil Kneivel ?! »

Merlin a fait une pause avant la réponse. He had just come out of his library, where he was working on translating some ancient Sumerian writings. He had a large leather-bound book in his hands. Il avait traduit ce texte sumérien pour un professeur at Bristol University, in England. Il pensait encore en sumérien. My question seemed to snap him out of it. Il a dit, *"Qu'est l'Evil Kneivel ?* Ah, yes indeed, my lad. That was the good wife Gwen you saw taking a jump over the greenhouse. I expressed to her my concerns about choosing to ascend on snow and descend over glass, however to no avail. She is expert, but she is taking quite a risk by making that jump, especially without someone looking on, in case something goes wrong. But when I voiced my concerns earlier this evening, she looked at me like I was asking her to direct her passions at calligraphy, instead of motorcycling."

J'ai dit, "Quoi ! I just saw someone on a motorcycle go flying across the front of the barn and past the greenhouse. I didn't see anyone jumping *over* the greenhouse!"

Merlin a dit, "Oh, good. Then she took my advice. That's interesting."

J'ai dit, "Vous plaisantez ! Tu blague ! You mean to tell me that that was *Gwen* I saw rocketing across the driveway on that motorcycle?! And she was going to jump over the *roof of the greenhouse* until you convinced her not to do it?!"

Merlin a dit, "Come, come, Mario-Jacques. There are things in this world far more difficult to believe, are there not?" Then he launched into a discussion about what he has unearthed in the past

169

couple of weeks from the Sumerian writings he has been translating. The writings describe a visit from ancient astronauts. Il a parlé presque non-stop, pour la demi-heure suivante, au sujet des astronautes antiques dans Sumer – segueing now and then to related discussion au sujet ancient Mayans, ancient Hindus, Atlantis, Plato. Si je disais dix mots en cette demi-heure, j'ai dit beaucoup. Mais, j'étais intéressé à écouter, I was tuned in.

When Gwen came back from motorcycling, environ une heure après que je sois arrivé à la ferme, la conversation s'est tournée vers ce que Gwen appelle, « *Zen adventures in motorcycling.* "

Les trois de nous ont eu un repas léger : *Pinot grigio* avec tuna fish et olive sandwiches. Ca semble simple, mais c'était un repas gastronome, parce que Gwen had baked le pain de blé entier, les olives were home-grown from Merlie's greenhouse, et le *pinot grigio* était vintage, retrieved from Merlin et Gwen's wine cellar. Merlin rarely drinks anything with alcoholic content, mais yesterday night he indulged.

En fait, Merlin eu deux verres de vin, et ceci a pu l'avoir mis dans une humeur qui était plus euphorique que la normale pour lui. Gwen est parti après diner, parce que elle était cat-sitting pour un ami, et Merlie m'a persuadé d'avoir avec lui deux ou trois scoops de crème glacée de *Chagnon*(!), dans la pièce arrière de la bibliothèque, où nous nous asseyons rarement ensemble. Je ne sais pas si j'étais plus ivre par le *pinot grigio* ou par le parfum des orchidées blanches qu'étaient dans des pots, environ une douzaine, sur une des tables dans la bibliothèque. En tout cas, I was happy that Merlin suggested that we go into the library.

Tandis que Merlie was being the good host, putting the Chagnon vanille dans bols, je suis allé à la bibliothèque. En plus des livres sur les étagères, j'ai compté quatre vingt sept mortiers et pilons. Merlin told me that he has used every single one of these 87 mortars and pestles at least once. I looked at the collection of books in this room. No paperbacks, just hardcover, many in leather. Merlin The Magician is not a paperback man, unless we are talking about manuscripts in papyrus. Mais oui, je pense il lit le sumérien mieux que je lis des français. I sure hope so.

A book titled *The Complete Enochian Dictionary, a dictionary of the angelic language,* caught my eye. J'ai pris ce livre de l'étagère comme Merlin entrait dans la bibliothèque, avec notre crème glacée. Quand il a vu quoi je l'avais choisi, par hasard, il a commenté, "Ah, good choice, my lad. A synchronistic choice, je croix. As our good friend Paddy O'Brien is so fond of saying: *When the reader is ready, the book will come.*' It appears to me that perhaps you have found what you are ready to learn about."

Je n'ai pas ouvert le livre jusqu'à ce que nous nous soyons assis à la table pour manger notre crème glacée. J'étais très prudent d'où j'ai placé le livre, et d'où j'ai placé la crème glacée, parce que je n'ai pas voulu mettre une tache sur le livre. Merlin a noté que ceci et il a dit, "Do not fret, lad. The contents of that book is valuable, but the pages themselves, are not. In fact, a few Jackson Pollock drips of Chagnon vanilla ice cream would likely enhance the aesthetic character of the book."

J'ai scanné la table des matières et j'ai lu quelques paragraphes du livre, tandis que je mangeais ma crème glacée doucement. En attendant, Merlin était exceptionnellement tranquille, mangeant sa crème glacée et me regardant, regardant le livre. Ni l'un ni l'autre de nous n'ont semblé vouloir rompre le silence, jusqu'à je sois venu à un passage dans le livre qui dit : « *The sacred magic of Abra-Melon, the magician.* »

J'ai dit à Merlin, "What's this? *The sacred magic of Abra-Melon?*"

Merlin a dit, "Aaah, yes, Mario-Jacques. Those are precisely the words – *'What's this?'* – that I have been waiting for you to utter…and, of course, I should not be surprised that it is once again, coming from you, a rather synchronistic utterance. You see, it is only in the most recent past, within the last month, that I have returned to studying the sacred magic of Abra-Melon, and a certain eleventh century manuscript…This is precisely what I wanted to speak to you about. I repeat, this is *precisely* what I wanted to speak to you about. I put it out to the Universe that I wanted to speak to you about Abra-Melon, and apparently the Universe put that book in your hands, along with the Chagnon ice cream." Merlin a ri de sa blague, mais je pourrais voir qu'il était tout à fait sérieux en même temps. Et il a été enchanté éprouver ce synchronicity avec moi.

Merlin a dit, « Mario-Jacques, I want to talk to you about the art and science of using little known natural energies to cause changes in consciousness – and from there, externalization. In other words my lad, I am going to give you a recipe that is, I dare say, even better than the recipe for Chagnon vanilla ice cream!"

Bien sûr, I was all ears.

Il a dit, "You will recall, in the Book of Exodus, there are references to holy anointing oils, made by none other than Moses, himself. In fact, when they found the dead sea scrolls in 1947 – the year of Roswell and the year of the death of Aleister Crowley, I must add, parenthetically – they discovered vessels that contained holy anointing oil that was probably made by none other than Moses, himself."

Merlin a fait une pause, to allow me to react. J'ai dit, "Go ahead, Merlie. I am taking this in with my Chagnon vanilla ice cream, and enjoying."

He continued. "The ingredients in this anointing oil are not so *exotique*. Galangol root, cassia, cinnamon, myrrh – which is an hallucinogenic that three kings gave to Jesus at his birth, I must add, parenthetically – and there is…what did I leave out? Oh yes, mais oui, the olive oil! Variations of the formula have been used for thousands of years. The olive oil turns from green to silver during the early stages of the process that I carry out, to make *Essence of Galangol Root.*"

Merlin a expliqué qu'il a dû travailler dans son laboratoire pendant trois ans, avant qu'il ait pu perfectionner sa manière de faire *l'huile sacrée d'Abramelin*. Il a dit, "I must use my ceramic mortar and pestle, because I heat the mixture to create my base product, which is about six thimbles of oil. I distill my extract through the condensing system a hundred and one times. And I *do* mean one hundred and *one* times. The color of the oil goes from silver to black. The black oil is what I use to anoint the forehead."

J'ai dit, "What do you mean? Have you used the essence to anoint someone?"

Merlin a dit, "I have anointed only two people: Myself, and Robert. I still have my lab notes for the 1,361 times – and I do mean 1,361 times, *precisely* – that I anointed myself with *variations*, while I was learning to make the essence that was powerful enough for my satisfaction. I anointed my dear friend Robert with the perfected oil."

Sa tonalité de voix, the gravity in his voice, was noticeable, heavy. Merlin continued, as I urged him with my silence, my focused attention. "When I make my Abramelin oil Mario-Jacques I must carry out an extremely time-consuming and exhausting process. Aside from meeting the needs of my body – eating, drinking, sleeping, et cetera, I must devote all of my remaining energy to the process. It takes about three weeks, and it feels like running a marathon for three weeks – or enduring the labor of giving birth for a long, long time. I say this without trepidation, even though I have never run a marathon for three weeks, nor have I ever actually experienced what it is like to be in labor for a long, long, time...but I have delivered three babies...I digress! *Tu comprends, mon ami ?*"

J'ai dit, "Oui, oui. Mais oui."

Merlin a continué, "I have taught the process to others, and there is always the possibility, a good possibility, that I can obtain *Essence of Galangol Root* from one of my students, if need be. The Abramelin oil that is circulating through regular commercial networks, at least in North America, is a very mild version of the oil I make. What I make, Mario-Jacques – and I urge you to make note of this – has been known to *stop death in its tracks*. I repeat, my Abramelin oil has been known to *stop death in its tracks*."

Merlin a fait une pause encore, to let his words sink in, et pour rallumer sa pipe. I did not want to interrupt his train of thought, which I suspected was a very long train of thought. Après he took a puff from his pipe, Merlin a continué, "I went to the hospital to see Robert, who was a dear friend of mine from the time we were ten-years-old. It did not look like he would make it through the night. The doctors gave no odds on Robert making it through another day. His sister, Suzanne, was convinced that he had just a few hours left. He was due to get his ticket punched. No doubt about it, Mario-Jacques. I said to Suzanne, 'I will be back in the hospital in two hours. In the meantime, talk to him. Out loud. Talk to him until I get back. Even if he passes before I get back. Just keep talking.'"

"I was living in Clarenceville at the time...Ever been through Clarenceville, Mario-Jacques? I have a Clarenceville tale to tell. Well, once again, I digress...that is another story, for another time...Back to *this* story: I raced on the 10 to Clarenceville, left my truck running while I ran into my laboratory and got my vial of Abramelin oil, then raced on the 10 back to Montreal, and in two hours to the minute, almost to the second, I was standing shoulder-to-shoulder with Suzanne again, at the bedside of my dying friend, Robert. I said to Suzanne, 'Good girl, Suzanne. You have kept him alive for two hours, now let's see if I can keep him alive a little longer.' I did not make any promises to her. The only thing I said was: 'This is magick oil. Magick with a, *'k.'* We can only hope, I cannot promise.' Then I anointed Robert. There are a massive amount of chi lines at the temples. I made a cross within a circle, at the third eye...They said he might not make it through the night...however, shortly after the light of the sun broke through the clouds Robert opened his eyes, as if he was awaking from a rather long nap. He started to gesticulate, to communicate that he was hungry. His mouth, his tongue, his throat, were too dry to permit him to speak aloud, or he would have said – indeed, he would have shouted: *'Please get me some food!'* He had not eaten in three days, not through the mouth. Some might be inclined to call it a, *'miraculous recovery.'* The Epilogue: Robert lived for another fifteen years."

J'ai écrit des notes, tandis que j'étais dans la bibliothèque de Merlin, au sujet de la façon dont il fait *l'huile sacrée d'Abramelin*, et maintenant que je regarde les notes, je vois qu'elles sont insuffisantes. Toutefois Merlin m'a indiqué qu'il écrit un livre pour des alchimistes, et la formule est dans le livre.

4 août 2011

« La liberté est plus qu'une marque de yogourt »

Enfin, enfin, enfin, enfin. Enfin ! Finalement, j'ai vu La Femme de la Montagne encore.

Hier soir, après une souper léger, j'ai fait un randonnée sur la montagne, sur les sentiers, pour la première fois en deux semaines. Ma jambe gauche encore blessé, mais seulement un peu. I knew my leg would only hurt a little when I was on the descent, and I was anxious to hike Mount Stafford again.

Quand j'ai garé ma voiture au stationnement proche des sentiers, il était de trente degrés. (Sur le thermostat de ma voiture, my american car, it read 88 degrees. Presque 30.)

J'"était prêt. I wore shorts. J'ai eu une bouteille d'eau – l'eau sacrée, de la source derrière l'IGA. Et j'ai porté sur mon poignet gauche, « Super Band, » un insectifuge que j'ai acheté au nouveau magasin du dollar à Richford. I also wore a yellow shirt, which I read on-line would help to deter flying insects. I was mainly concerned about black flies, which I believe are related to piranhas. One evolved out of the other, je suis certain.

J'ai marché très lentement, parce que j'ai voulu être prudent en raison de ma jambe. J'ai marché pendant environ vingt minutes, et ensuite je me suis arrêté sur un pont.

D'habitude, je reste à ce pont pendant une minute, quelquefois pendant quelques minutes, et ensuite je continue ma randonnée sur le sentier. Yesterday night I stayed at the bridge for a minute, and then I decided to walk off the path, and follow the flow of the water. C'est bon, to go with the flow.

J'ai pu descendre la rivière en marchant sur des gros rochers, mais après environ dix minutes il est devenu très difficile de continuer plus loin, parce que l'eau était très profonde et il n'y avait pas beaucoup de gros rochers que je pouvais marcher sur. I had to go in the water up to my knees for a while. Ca faisait du bien de marcher dans l'eau. Et j'ai continué dans l'eau parce qu'il était impossible de marcher sur la terre à côté de la rivière, en raison de la densité des arbres.

Et ensuite, il y avait un grand arbre qu'était tombé dans la rivière. Ca n'était pas facile pour moi de passer au-dessus de l'arbre. I almost fell head first into the water, et j'ai crié : « Oh, shit ! »

J'ai pensé que j'avais alarmé d'un animal, peut-être une grande animal, dans la rivière. I heard what sounded like an awfully big splash in the river just ahead of me, around a turn. J'ai hésité à continuer. I did not want to move. J'"ai écouté. Rien. Alors j'ai continué, soigneusement, sur les roches. Malheuresement, l'eau est devenue très profonde et il n'y avait pas de roches pour moi de marcher. J'ai dû choisir entre aller dans l'eau, ou de retour.

I took off my shoes and socks, put them in mon sac à dos, et j'ai continué. I stepped on big rocks that were underwater, so it did not hurt my feet. J'avais besoin d'etre très prudent afin que je ne glisse pas. Je regardais vers le bas, looking into the water, quand j'ai entendu une femme, a woman with a famliar voice, qu'a dit : « Mario-Jacques, it is you! »

I looked et j'ai vu une femme debout sur une roche, au milieu de l'eau, en face de moi. C'était Femme de la Montagne ! Oui, Femme de la Montagne !

Bien sûr, she looked like the archetypical Mountain Woman that she is. At first glance, it looked like she was naked and that she had camouflaged her body with mountain colours. El'était vetûe d'un bikini noir. En fait, elle portait ses sous-vêtements.

Elle a dit, « I am happy to see that it is you, Mario-Jacques. When I heard you coming, I thought you were a touriste who is lost."

I had to think before I spoke, but I managed to spit out in French, "Toutefois, c'est moi, un étranger dans paradis."

Elle a dit, "Hey, *bravo* Mario-Jacques ! Your French, it improves so much ! » Alors elle a continué à parler en français et je n'ai pas compris ce qu'elle disait.

J'ai dit, « Tu parles trop vite pour moi. »

Elle a dit, « Okeh, we speak the English."

J'ai dit, « Non, s'il vous plait. Converse avec moi dans un mélange de français et d'anglais. »

Ensuite, elle a dit, « Enlever les vêtements, this way you can swim!"

Je n'ai savais pas que, "*enlever,* » veut dire, « take off », jusqu'à ce qu'elle faisait des gestes avec ses mains. Ensuite I figured it out that she was telling me to take off my clothes and swim.

J'ai hésité, et elle a dit, "Allons-y, allons-y. Go, go, go." She grabbed at my shirt and started to pull it off.

J'ai dit, « D'accord, d'accord, I will skinny dip with you. Peut-être ! Mais, I keep my underwear on. The water, est froid."

Elle a dit, "Quoi ? This I do not understand, Mario-Jacques. Your under-wear is not going to make you feel warm. And the water is warm. I was going to take off my sous-vêtements and then I heard you making the sound comme le touriste. »

J'ai dit, "What do you mean? How did I sound like un touriste ?"

Elle a dit, « You sound more like a touriste than a bear, when you were climbing over the tree. »

J'ai dit, "D'accord, je comprends. You should hear me snore. I snore plus comme un ours que comme un touriste."

Tous les deux nous gardé sur nos sous-vêtements. We both wore sous-vêtements noir. Noir avec des nuances de synchronicité.

La dernière fois j'ai vu Femme de la Montagne sur les sentiers était l'été dernier. Je suis allé dans l'eau just for short dips, parce que c'était froid. C'était agréable de s'asseoir sur une roche, in the warm air, after dips. Ce jour nous avons médité ensemble et Femme de la Montagne a demandé à l'univers ce qu'elle pourrait faire pour cela. Alors, après la méditation, elle m'a dit, "Ask the universe why you are here, Mario-Jacques." Je me souviens que she was the third person to tell me to do that, in those words, on this day.

Wading in the water with La Femme de la Montagne felt like a baptism of sorts, for me. Un baptême, mais sans cérémonie. Nous nous sommes assis ensemble, sur une dalle de roche dans l'eau. C'était bon, juste pour être. C'était bon d'être ensemble dans cet espace.

Nous nous sommes assis sur la roche avec nos pieds dans l'eau, sur un gros morceau de quartz. Femme de la Montagne m'a dit qu'elle aime faire ce. Elle médite tandis que son pieds sont sur le quartz.

I meditated alongside her. As Paddy would say, I « watched » my breath. Et je suis resté dans le moment présent. Je me suis observé. J'ai observé Femme de la Montagne. J'ai observé ce qui se déroulait.

S'il fait très chaud et elle va descend de la montagne pour aller en ville, ou ailleurs, Femme de la Montagne vient quelquefois à cet endroit. C'est privé et caché. Elle peut entrer dans l'eau sans ses vêtements. Pour Femme de la Montagne, être nu est naturel. As I soon found out, she has no inhibitions about being naked. For Femme de la Montagne, being unclothed is natural, much more than it is sexual. Which is not to say that what is sexual is not natural.

Nous avons médité peut-être six fois, avec nos pieds dans l'eau sur le morceau de quartz. Six mini-méditations. Entre une minute et cinq minutes chaque fois.

Normalement, quand je vois Femme de la Montagne, elle apparaît comme un caribou dans la brume, et elle disparaît comme un caribou dans la brume. Before yesterday, I had spoken with

Femme de la Montagne peut-être five or six times at length, je pense. Elle me fascine. Et je me sens aussi confortable avec elle comme je me sens avec Mont Stafford. Son énergie, son être, résonne en moi, de la même manière que la montagne de quartz que je vis sur résonne en moi.

Nous avons parlé entre les méditations. The talk was good, although we did not talk too much. We talked about l'epinette, mais c'était plus metaphysical et spirituel que au sujet l'epinette. J'ai parlé en français et anglais, mais pour le plupart en anglais, bien sûr. Elle a parlé en anglais, très peu en français. Quelquefois she would use an Abenaki word, parce que she is part Abenaki. El'est un mélange de québécoise, francaise, les anglais, Abenaki, Inuit, Cajun, et ché pas.

Every once in a while we would smell each other. C'était amusant et sérieux. Elle a senti mon épaule et elle a dit que je sentait comme un Abénaquis. J'ai senti son épaule et j'ai dit qu'elle a senti comme l'eau de montagne et l'epinette. Quand elle a senti mes cheveux, elle a dit, "You smell like l'Abénaquis et, et, et...New York shampoo."

Je lui ai demandé : « I smell like *New York shampoo* ? What is, 'New York shampoo' » ? J'ai pensé que peut-être New York shampoo était une marque.

Elle a répondu, « Je ne sais pas. New York shampoo is New York shampoo. I never smelled the hair of anyone from New York before. Your hair smells like un mélange de chemique et vanille. »

Aaah, I realized that the shampoo I have been using has vanilla in it. J'ai dit, "J'aime la vanille. Il ya probablement de vanille dans mon savon. »

Je lui ai dit que ses cheveux sentent comme l'air, les arbres, la terre. Her hair smells like the mountain. J'aime ca, cette odeur. J'aime ca.

Quand nous étions prêts à partir, après environ quarante-cinq minutes, elle m'à dit, « Before we leave this rock, listen to the music of the universe with me. »

Nous avons écouté, quelquefois regardant l'un l'autre et nous avons souri, comme les gens font quand ils écouter de la bonne musique.

J'estime que nous avons écouté pendant près de quatre minutes. Alors, j'ai dit : « That was, peut-être, the best version of *four minutes thirty-three seconds* I ever heard. » Je suis certaine que Femme de la Montagne did not know I was referring to the John Cage composition of silence : « *4'33''*. » Toutefois, elle a compris l'essence de ce que j'ai dit.

Quand nous avons fait un pas sur le terrain, Femme de la Montagne est allée vers la droite dans les arbres et je suis allé vers la gauche, to pee and to get dressed. Quand je suis retourné sur les arbres, el'était complètement nue, and she was casually wringing out her sous-vêtements. Pour être honnête, j'ai pensé qu'elle faisait une invitation sexuelle. This occurred to me at the instant before Femme de la Montagne crouched down and tore a leaf from a fern plant, which she used to blow her nose – which is generally not the sort of thing humans do as an erotic gesture. Ou, am I wrong about this? En tout cas…puis, elle prit une robe de son sac à dos et elle a glissé sur, au-dessus de sa tête.

Cette expérience avec Femme de la Montagne senti unique et naturel, à la même temps. What else is there to feel about being with a naked woman who blows her nose with a fern leaf ? Je lui ai dit : « Tu es plus naturelle, et plus écologique…comme *Liberté Yogourt* ». Mots drôles, non ? Where my humor came from, je ne sais pas.

Elle a répondu : « You are funny, Mario-Jacques. There is the wisdom in your spirit, and this is why I want to tell you why I am going to the town…You mention *Yogourt Liberté* …It reminds me what this man Pierre Falardeau says once : *"La liberté is more than the brand of the yogourt."* This is why I go to Stafford, to Café Dumont, to speak with others, about Sovran Nations. I am Sovran. This is the only way to protect my liberty. To be Sovran."

J'ai dit, "You must know Shiva." Bien sûr, I was thinking of Shiva Duschene, my Sovran Staffordian friend. Je ne pensais pas à la déité hindoue.

La Femme de la Montagne a répondu, "Yes, I know Shiva. She is my friend. And I know that Shiva has a third eye."

Encore, je ne savais pas si elle parlait de la Staffordian ou de la déité. Toutefois, avant que je pourrais dire toute autre chose, Femme de la Montagne m'a embrassé sur les deux joues, tournées, et a disparu comme un caribou dans la brume. Mais oui, she did a Van Morrison into the mist.

21 août 2011

"Hercolubus vient"

J'étais sur mon chemin à neuf le matin pour aller à l'exposition d'antiquités dans Ka-nowlton quand il a commencé à pleuvoir, alors j'ai fait un détour au Café Dumont. I thought I would have a bowl of le Café Dumont not-*yet*-world-famous homemade *muesli et yogourt,* and if the rain stopped I would go to Ka-nowlton later in the morning.

Le dimanche pluie a soustraite les touristes de la rue Principal et le café, mais je retrouvé ma table préférée, sur le mur arrière. J'allais m'asseoir quand Shiva Duschene est entrée dans le café. I think the last empty chair in the café was at my table, and I waved Shiva over, to offer her the seat.

Elle probablement avoir utilisé dix écharpes colorées différentes dans ses cheveux, qui sont devenus plus crépus par l'humidité. Elle portait son ordinateur portable avec une courroie d'épaule, attachés avec le même pêle-mêle des noeuds qu'elle a employés dans ses cheveux. Je dois dire, Shiva peut faire un rastafari ressemblerait un épiscopalien. She is a 21st century gypsy québécoise. Were we most anywhere else but Stafford, many eyes would have turned toward Shiva as she made her way over to me.

Je voulais parler à Shiva au sujet des nations de Sovran. Nos chemins se sont croisé plusieurs fois cet été, et Shiva m'avait expliqué, morceau par morceau, au sujet d'être un Sovran, et ce qui se passe avec le mouvement. Je suis allé au site web de Sovran Embassies pour apprendre plus. Le site web a une vidéo qui présente des personnes à l'idée d'être un Sovran : Une chair et un sang être qui n'est pas un citoyen d'aucun pays. La vidéo et le site web sont présentés en français, anglais, l'espagnol et l'italien. Seven other languages will be, "coming soon," the website says.

Après que nous ayons installé nos ordinateurs portables et arrangé dans nos chaises, j'ai dit à Shiva : "I am so happy to see you! I have wanted to talk with you, especially since Femme de la Montagne told me that she is also a Sovran. But she does not go to any meetings. I met her on the mountain a couple of weeks ago, on the day she was going down to meet with you."

Elle semblait qu'elle ne voulait pas parler au sujet ce. Shiva a dit seulement, "Yes, I know. Do you want the coffee?" J'ai eu l'impression que peut-être, pour quelque raison, elle n'a pas voulu pour parler de Femme de la Montagne, ou au sujet de la réunion qu'elle a eu avec elle, qu'était au Café Dumont, en fait.

Nous nous sommes levés pour aller chercher nos cafés et j'ai dit, "Wow, c'est interresante. I did not know that you and Femme de la Montagne knew each other, until she told me." Shiva a répondu avec un sourire, mais un sourire impénétrable, et elle n'a dit rien.

Shiva et Femme sont deux femme uniques, one-of-a-kind women, et elles sont mystérieux dans leurs manières. Je ne peux pas déterminer leurs âges. My guess is that they are at least in their middle thirties, mais peut-être in their middle forties, ou plus vieux? Je ne sais pas.

Ché pas si Shiva a un enfant. Don't know if Shiva has a mate or a love-interest. Je sais seulement qu'elle a habité dans Stafford, el'est sorti de la ville pendant quelques années, et el'ai renvoyé cet hiver. Elle enseigne le yoga à la gym, elle guérit par le toucher, et elle est, a channeler.

Bien sûr, Femme de la Montagne lives alone on Mount Stafford for most of the year, in a hidden cave, in a hidden part of the forest. Elle m'a dit que sa caverne est sur la propriété privée, et elle vit là avec la permission du propriétaire, une femme riche. Chez Femme est proche à les Sentiers de l'Estrie, et pas loin des sentiers où je la rencontre quelquefois, peut-être deux fois par année. As far as I know, she spends the winters in an apartment or a house in Stafford, with her grown daughter, je pense.

En tout cas, quand nous sommes revenus à notre table avec notre café, j'ai dit à Shiva, "This summer is coming to an end and this is the first time we are sitting down to have a coffee together."

Shiva m'a dit qu'elle a été très occupée cet été, parce qu'elle a pris un travail, caring for a fourteen-year-old autistic girl, six jours par semaine. Elle m'a dit que c'était la première fois elle jamais a eu des expériences avec un enfant autiste, mais she feels like she has been called to do this work.

J'ai dit à elle, "I would not be surprised if you were working miracles with this child."

Shiva a souri et a dit : "Mais oui, there have been miracles with her. There are miracles every day, Mario-Jacques." Puis Shiva a souri à moi, et elle a abaissé l'écran de son ordinateur portable et l'écran de mon ordinateur portable. Elle a dit, "I do not want these screens to interfere with the energy we exchange."

J'ai regardé dans ses yeux souriants et elle a regardé dans le mien, et puis elle a dit, "Okeh, now we are connected. Do you want to see the webcam I watch, from the Ant-arc-tica?"

J'ai répondu, "Mais oui," bien sûr.

Elle a soulevé vers le haut l'écran de mon ordinateur et puis l'écran de son ordinateur. Sur son ordinateur elle est allée au site web pour le Neumayer Research   Center en Antarctica, et alors elle m'a envoyé le lien. De cette façon je pourrais voir sur mon ordinateur ce que elle à regardé. Elle m'a dit qu'elle va à ce site web tous les jours, pour regarder le webcam.

Aussi, she told me that she is following the position of Hercolubus, a planet which I never heard of before. Elle m'a dit que cette planète est six fois la taille de Jupiter, et qu'elle orbite près de la Terre chaque 3600 ans.

Elle a dit, "Mario-Jacques, I have known since the day of my 25 birthday that this planet was coming. The information did not come to me from anything I read, it just came to me. It was channeled. I did not know the name of the planet at first, but I knew that a large planet was coming."

J'ai demandé Shiva si elle entendait une voix lui parlant au sujet de cette planète, et elle a dit qu'elle n'a pas fait. Elle n'a entendu aucune voix, mais un jour elle a juste su que cette planète venait, et elle a su qu'elle changerait la vie comme nous le savons, que elle changerait l'humanité.

Elle a dit, avec sa voix douce, "Hercolubus will orbit close to the Earth next month. Circle September 26 on your calendar. It is going to be very frightening to people around the world, because we will experience a planet shift. There will be earthquakes, great storms, floods, and the Internet will not be working very well on September 26." Elle a fermé doucement la couverture de son ordinateur, pour doucement souligner ses mots.

Elle a atteint à travers la table, a mis sa main sur le mien, et a dit, "Do not worry, Mario-Jacques. You will be alright, and your

182

loved ones will be alright, after September 26. It is going to be better."

J'ai dit, « How sure are you about September 26 ? »

Elle a dit, « I am as sure about this as I am sure about a weather report that shows the approach of un ouragan, a hurricane. Something could happen to change it, but we can see it is coming this way. »

Son attention est allée à un petit garçon qui s'asseyait avec ses parents à la table à côté de nous. Elle a commencé à parler au petit garçon et à ses parents en français. Je pourrais voir qu'ils ont été charmés par ce qu'elle disait, mais j'ai compris seulement quelques mots. J'ai pensé qu'elle disait quelque chose au sujet de l'aura du petit garçon.

Elle est devenue tranquille quand nous avons commencé à manger, et alors elle a dit, "The aura around that little boy is beautiful, and your aura is beautiful too, Mario-Jacques." Her sincerity was palpable. I felt it in the hair of my forearms, as if she had reached across the table again and touched me.

J'ai dit juste, "Merci, merci beaucoup," et j'ai souri.

During breakfast she talked to me about the early part of her life, and told me how she came to realize that not everyone saw auras. Elle était six ans, et elle jouait avec le sable avec deux amies. Elle lui a dit des amis qu'il a semblé drôle à elle que la lumière autour de leurs bras et jambes, et visages, ne pourrait pas être vue très bien, parce qu'ils ont eu la poussière de sable partout eux-mêmes. Les filles ne savaient pas quoi Shiva parlait au sujet et c'était bouleversant à elle. Elle a pensé que chacun a vu la lumière qu'elle a vue, émanant de la peau humaine. Cette nuit, en larmes, elle a dit sa mère au sujet de quoi s'est produit quand elle jouait avec ses amis. Sa mère l'a rassurée, et lui a dit que pouvoir voir des auras est un cadeau que seulement quelques personnes ont.

I digested my food, and what Shiva was telling me, one spoonful at a time. Tandis que nous mangions le déjeuner, elle m'a dit au sujet de ses expériences quand elle était jeune, de la beauté d'être psychique et des difficultés.

Elle m'a dit au sujet de l'étude de dame âgée qui était une psychique, alors que Shiva était un adolescent et une vie à Montréal. Shiva told me that this woman helped her to understand that the information that comes to psychics has to be interpreted, and psychics must be aware of their biases, as human beings.

Shiva m'a indiqué qu'elle n'a jamais employé ses capacités psychiques de gagner l'argent. Elle parle au sujet de ses capacités psychiques seulement aux amis qu'elle peut faire confiance. I felt honored that Shiva shared this with me, as her friend, and I told her I was honored.

La pensée d'une planète énorme approchant la terre est menaçante, mais derrière cette pensée il y avait quelque chose plus essentielle, et très belle, que Shiva a communiqué à moi. Elle a dit, "We must all make peace. I am thanking everything now. That is what I have been doing all morning, Mario-Jacques. This is what I have been doing for the last two days, and I will continue to do this. I thank the mountain, I thank the trees, the flowers, the people, the birds…I thank this coffee cup. I am thanking the Universe for this life."

Elle parlait certainement de son coeur à mon coeur. Elle a dit à moi, "Mario-Jacques, I speak to you because you listen, and I know you hear me, I can see it in your face." Et alors, elle a dit : "What I am telling you is the most important thing in your life…"

Je me suis penché en avant pour entendre son meilleur, et elle s'est penchée vers moi, et a dit, "What Hercolobus does to the planet Earth or does *not* do to planet Earth, in the physical, is not important. What is important is that people are awakened by this event. They have to realize that we are much more than flesh-and-blood bodies. We are spiritual beings having a human experience. On this planet people believe there is only existence in the bodily dimension, the Third Dimension. That is an illusion. All of this around us is an illusion. The reality is that we can exist in the Fourth Dimension, where we communicate from the heart, as you and I are doing now. The reality is, we are energy. In essence, we are light. That is what we will remember when we are in the Fifth Dimension."

Shiva a fait une pause après ces mots, et j'ai dit, "This is too much for me to process, at least on an intellectual level."

Shiva a dit, "I understand, Mario-Jacques. Remember that September 26 is only another stage in the evolution of human consciousness. Everything will be accomplished by December 21, 2012. But you do not need to try to understand all this on an intellectual level…All you need to do is live in the eternal now. And meditate."

Mon attention a été attrapé par le petit garçon s'asseyant à la table à côté de nous, qui me regardait très attentivement, avec un petit sourire sur ses lèvres. J'ai renvoyé son regard fixe, avec un petit sourire par moi-même, et considered the wider environment in which we sat: À une table dans le Café Dumont, sur rue Principal, dans Stafford, in the Eastern Townships of Québec, on planet Earth, JOE 2KP. Je me suis promis que je voudrais méditer, et ensuite je suis resté dans le moment présent.

6 octobre 2011

"À la gauche à Wall Street"

Ce matin, at three o'clock in the morning, I was driving on the Long Island Expressway, on my way ici for a five-night stay. Ninety-nine out of a hundred times, when I am driving to Stafford I do not listen to the radio, I listen to my French language lesson CDs. Toutefois last night, ou ce matin, I decided to put on the radio, and I tuned it to WCBS 880, the all-news station that is dedicated to New Yorkers who live much of their lives traveling in their cars through asphalt jungle. I was about to make a right turn off the expressway to head toward the Throg's Neck Bridge, when I heard an eight second report about the people who had taken over Zuccotti Park, near Wall Street, to protest the rich taking over the government of the United States.

WCBS 880 is one of the most listened to radio stations in the United States of America. Millions of Americans get their news of the world by listening to the eight second news reports on 880. Bien sûr, the people of the United States who are drinking and driving – that is, drinking enormous amounts of coffee and alcohol and spending a good part of their lives in their cars – get their news from sound bites. Sip of coffee, bite from a burger, sound bite on the radio. The listening audience of CBS 880 – and other stations like CBS – are big consumers of gasoline, empty calories, and shallow

185

thoughts. Donc, why did I decide to turn on the radio to CBS? Ché pas, mais I gave in to the urge, as if I was starving and happened to be driving past a tabernouche McDonald's. Et when I heard the eight second story about the occupation of Wall Street by protesters, I turned left, instead of right. Bien sûr, the occupation story was not new, but when I was reminded of what was going on, I decided to go downtown.

I went through the Midtown Tunnel and then drove down to Greenwich Village, where I parked at an all-night garage that I am used to using, on Tenth Street. Then I took a cab to Zuccotti Park. The cab driver was a Haitian, and we spoke français pour le plupart with each other. Une phrase à le temps. I told him that I call myself an, "amériquébécois," parce que my time and my mind is split between New York and Québec. By coincidence(!), he told me that he visits family en Montréal every summer, and that he is a friend of the guys in Tap-Tap, my favorite Haitian band, and my favorite dance band, that plays dans Stafford, quelquefois.

We had quite a conversation during the cab ride – about Haiti, Québec, the U.S.A, and places in the heart.

He told me that he hoped he would see me later in the day, because his wife was going to give him warm food to bring to the occupiers. C'est incroyable, non ? When I got out of the cab, we wished each other santé et bonne chance, and he thanked me profusely for going to Zuccotti Park. It was as if he was thanking me for traveling to Haiti, to rebuild the homes of the earthquake victims. He said to me that he thought the protests near Wall Street were very important for the poor people of Haiti, because the rich are the cause of the suffering of the Haitian people, not god.

I continued to talk to him through the car window, even after I got out of the cab. Then he had to go, because the driver in the car behind him, a Wall Street-typish man in a big black car, started blowing his horn. The cab driver shouted to me, "I will see you on December 21, 2012," and he waved good-bye and drove off. We had not talked about 2012 at all up to that point, so I was quite taken back by this. I wanted to shout, *"Quoi ?!"* toutefois he was already driving away. Maintenant, je suis trés fatigué, journal intime. Je suis arrivé à Stafford à 20h, il y a trois heures. I cannot write more now. I am going to sleep.

East End Bay
17 octobre 2011

"The secret occupation of Times Square"

Il y a deux jours, samedi, I took the 9:40 train from Ronkonkoma into the city. This was the second consecutive weekend that I was going to be participating in the protests in New York City, and I was hoping to see signs that the #Occupy Wall Street movement was going to continue to grow in numbers. When I arrived at the train station, it looked like it was packed with people who were going to the demonstration at Zuccotti Park. J'ai pensé, *"Wow, wow, wow! Could this be? America is finally waking up? Mon dieu, peut-être le revolution commence.* » Bien sûr, j'ai su que la foule des personnes pourrait aller voir un concert de rock.

Après I parked ma voiture et je suis allé dans la gare, j'ai vu que tout monde était là parce que de, *"ComicCon."* Yeah, mais oui, the train station was packed because hordes of young people – mostly in their late teens and early twenties – were on their way to the city, to the Javits Center, for the tabernouche comic book convention. The words on everyone's lips were, *"Comic Con! Comic Con! Comic Con!"* and not : *"Wall Street! Wall Street! Wall Street!"* A lot of these kids were dressed up to look like outlandish, other-worldly, comic book characters. It did not look like a train on the way to the revolution.

Je suis arrivé au Zuccotti Park environ 11h30m. There were a couple of thousand people in and around the small park, *talkin' 'bout a revolution*. I could almost hear Tracy Chapman singing a soundtrack for what I was seeing. Along the perimeter of the park hundreds of protesters marched with signs in their hands, or stood along the wall of the park with their signs in front of them, as tourists and curious people walked by and took pictures. Pour quelques des piétons, la scene était un autre roadside attraction, comme le trou dans le sol qu'était le World Trade Center.

I walked in and around the park for about half an hour, carrying in front of my chest the, *"Je Me Souviens,* Democracy! *"* sign that Gaston had painted for me in Stafford. Then I stood for more than an hour at a position near one of the entrances to the park, talking with a university student from Montréal, from Concordia College. He was waving a large Canadian flag, mounted on a wooden pole. We stood on top of a granite wall, about six feet above the sidewalk. It got warmer later in the day, mais à midi c'etait un peu froid, so I was glad that I was wearing a sweat shirt. But this kid was standing on the cold granite in his bare feet, waving the Canadian flag. Looked at through squinted eyes, he looked like he was storming the Bastille. I probably looked more like I was holding a protest sign than anything else.

J'ai parlé en français un peu à mon nouveau ami du Québec, et il m'a dit que la seule raison il agitait un drapeau canadien était parce qu'il n'a pas pu trouver un drapeau du Québec à acheter dans la ville de New York. Considering the fact that I was carrying my, *"Je Me Souviens,* Democracy! *"* sign, it would have been more synergistic if he was waving a Québec flag, mais le drapeau canadien était, encore une fois, le substitut.

I experienced some synchronicity avec this flag-waving québécois. He told me that he really liked the graphics of my sign. I explained to him que mon ami, un artiste named Gaston Briere, had painted the sign for me. He told me that he had heard of Gaston, that he had seen a painting that Gaston did of an inukshuk, at an art show en Trois Rivieres, l'été derniére ! When he told me this, I almost lost my balance on the wall. Je veux dire, j'ai été surpris. What are the odds? At that point, people were chanting near us, so I could only shout : "Wow, c'est *synchronistique !"* I do not think he understood what I meant, ou peut-être he did not hear me.

I stayed in the park all day, standing at different places, walking with my sign, playing the drums at the drum-in – that is, plus exactement, playing plastic container at the drum-in, et chatting with people, taking pictures of signs, taking notes. Je ne sais pas si c'était le travail d'art, ou le message, mais throughout the day, peut-être fifty times, peut-être plus comme cent fois, je ne sais pas, people took pictures of my, *"Je Me Souviens,* Democracy! *"* sign, or of me holding the sign. Je suppose *"Je Me Souviens Democracy!"* is a phrase of the #Occupy Movement maintenant, au moins en esprit.

I spoke with a lot of people who were from Québec, and even more people who were from France, who questioned me about the franglais wording of my sign. I found myself repeating : "Je suis un amériquébécois. J'habite ici et j'habite au Québec. And I was born in Brooklyn." Alors, we might get into a rap.

For those who did not know, I explained that, *"Je Me Souviens,"* is written on every license plate in Québec, et j'ai dit que, *"Je Me Souviens, Democracy!"* is the motto of *amériquébécois* who are part of the Occupy movement. Bien sûr, je suis encore le seule personne que je connais qui s'appele un "amériquébécois," mais ce n'est pas le point.

At four-thirty in the afternoon, a guy in his twenties who was wearing a San Francisco Giants baseball cap stood up on a milk carton and yelled out: "MIKE CHECK!...MIKE CHECK!... MIKE CHECK!" It is rare for, "mike check" – which is short for, "microphone check" – to be called out three consecutive times. The standard is to yell, "MIKE CHECK," once, or maybe twice, to get the attention of other people, and for everyone who hears the words to repeat in a shout: "MIKE CHECK!...MIKE CHECK!" Donc, there was a sense of urgency in *this* mike check.

I walked closer to the speaker and I repeated his words, shouting along with about fifty other people: "WE ARE GOING TO TIMES SQUARE!; WE ARE GOING TO TIMES SQUARE!" Then another group of at least fifty people repeated our shout: "WE ARE GOING TO TIMES SQUARE!; WE ARE GOING TO TIMES SQUARE!" Then, the speaker shouted: "WE WILL MEET IN FRONT OF THE ARMY RECRUITING STATION AT 6PM," which we repeated. Then he gave brief instructions, a few words at a time, about taking the subway to Times Square.

There were hundreds of uniformed police in the area of Zuccotti Park, within a radius of a few blocks. As soon as the police heard the words shouted, *"WE ARE GOING TO TIMES SQUARE,"* you could see them moving around, communicating with each other, like ants whose nest was disturbed. Less than five minutes after the guy with the San Francisco Giants hat announced that everyone was going to gather in Times Square, it became obvious that many of the police were carrying out a new command. Many of the police cars, and vans, and motorcycles that were surrounding the park, put on their flashing lights and drove off. Pas doute, they were headed to Times Square.

At five-thirty I followed the guy with the Giants hat, and about fifty other people, to the subway. When we left, Zuccotti Park was still crowded with people, so I was doubting whether there would be many people gathering to protest in Times Square.

Everyone in our group got into one car of the subway train. Whenever the train stopped at a station to pick up new passengers, we chanted: "We...are...the 99%! We...   are...the 99%!" and we sang out, "Occ-u-py Waaaaall Street! Occ-u-py Waaaaall Street...then paused for a measure and repeated: Occ-u-py Waaaaall Street! Occ-u-py Waaaaall Street!" The train was a local, so there were a lot of stops before we got to 42nd Street. C'était drôle. It was funny to watch the reactions of the people who entered the subway car at each station. They thought they would be on a Sunday afternoon humdrum subway ride, but instead, they found themselves on a subway train going to a revolution.

We came out of the subway about three blocks from Times Square. It was a beautiful warm evening, and the streets were packed with people. The fifty of us in our group were the only people I saw who were carrying protest signs instead of shopping bags. J'ai vu aussi plus de policiers dans un endroit comme j'ai jamais vu dans ma vie. The President of the United States does not get as many police for protection, si vous voyez ce que je veux dire. I worry about the president, mais that is another story.

As our group walked down 42nd Street to Times Square, police continued to pour into the streets. The flashing lights, the police sirens, cops on horses, police buses, the motorcycle cops who stormed through the streets at high speeds, created an atmosphere which was frightening to some of the tourists and shoppers – not to mention protesters, such as moi-même. I was mindful that there is such a thing as a police riot.

When we got to Times Square (to the very place where multitudes around the world watch on their television and computer screens the countdown of the last ten seconds of each year, as they watch the ball drop on New Year's Eve) I was surprised to see that an enormous crowd had gathered in the middle of the streets, to protest. My guesstimate is that there were peut-être 1500 protesters there, and je ne sais pas how many thousands of shoppers and tourists.

Mon dieu ! This was *big*. When Times Square is occupied by protesters it likely means a hell of a lot more than an American flag flying upside down in a small city park. This was not a protest against a war, and it was not a demonstration for peace, it was a manifestation of a mass of people who are seeking to change The Dollar Sign $ystem. Donc, I should not have been surprised to see the militaristic presence of the New York City police force. This was a protest that was taking place in Times Square(!), where time itself begins and ends in the western world. And time is money. Le temps est de l'argent, le temps est de l'argent, le temps est de l'argent.

When I walked inside the police barricades, onto the street with the other protesters, I felt liberated. But I also felt like I might be walking into a trap. The barricades blocked cars from entering the street, and there were only a few openings in the barricades for protesters to get on or off the street. The protesters were enclosed and contained within the barricades. La situation était volatil. I was careful to stand in places where I thought I could avoid being stampeded. I tried to watch the police more carefully than they were watching me, but they had more eyes in more heads, and there were surveillance cameras all over Times Square – which is the way it is now. Mais oui, the surveillance cameras put in place in the name of protecting people from Osama Bin Laden and Al-Qaeda terrorists, were now turned toward American citizens who were exercising their constitutional rights. And none of the protesters were Tea Party Americans.

In the year of their lord 2011, the Tea Party people in the states march to protect the rich, not the 99%. The people who were members of the Tea Party in 1776 would be more shocked to see this phenomenon than to see the phenomenon of the lights of Times Square, si vous voyez ce que je veux dire. Mais oui, history is being repeated ici, avec this latest uprising against the rich, the elite – even if the new members of the Tea Party have become loyalists instead of patriots. Nous avons besoin moins loyalistes, et plus patriotes, non?

I began taking pictures with the camera I was carrying in my pocket, and when the battery went dead I switched over to taking pictures with my cell phone. As I was taking a picture of the police helicopter hovering in the sky, I got a phone call from Grace Terranova, who is now a graduate student at the University of Colorado, in Boulder. I tried to speak with her, and I thought I heard her say, "wut's up?" but the crowd noise made it very difficult to hear her. While we were trying to talk to each other, I was looking at the helicopter in the sky above Times Square, in a perfect position to record my presence. I held my cell phone up and walked in a small circle, to share with Grace the sounds at that moment. I held the phone at arms length in front of me and raised my voice to say: "THIS IS WHAT A REVOLUTION SOUNDS LIKE." I was not sure how loud I was speaking, because of the crowd noise, and since I could not hear anything coming out of the phone, I told Gracie that I would call her back by the next day, and I told her to watch the news later on in the night.

At that point in time, I thought that every major news station would be providing live coverage of the Occupation of Times Square. Bien sûr, I found out later on that I was quite wrong about that.

We remained in the streets of Times Square for a couple of hours. There was a lot of chanting. *"We...are... the 99%...Occ-u-py Waaaaall Street. Occ-u-py Waaaaall Street. ...End the Fed! End the Fed!...We are fed up! We are fed up!...What does dem-ocracy look like? This is what dem-ocracy looks like! What does dem-ocracy sound like? This is what dem-ocracy sounds like!"*

Within circles as small as a dozen people, and as large as hundreds of people, protesters took turns improvising short speeches. Anyone who wanted to speak was given the opportunity. All who spoke were listened to with respect, and it did not matter how eloquent anyone was, or even how well anyone could express themselves in rudimentary English. There were one or two speakers who spoke English worse than I speak French. Peut-être. In the group I was in, one person spoke mainly in Spanish. I heard a woman of about thirty-years-old speak in a language that I did not recognize at all. But she spoke from her heart, that was clear. She spoke two or three phrases, and she was applauded.

Because the police would not allow anyone to use microphones, protesters had to amplify each others words via the "mike check" method. In the larger groupings of people, the words were echoed twice. As I listened, it occurred to me that this is the way the story of democracy is being rewritten: By the people, one sentence at a time. Slow process, bien sûr.

I took a turn to speak, and I was the next-to-the-last person to speak in the circle of people I stood with. The guy who spoke before me gave a fairly long speech, which he had written out in advance. He spoke for close to five minutes, which was an exceptionally long time to speak, because everyone I heard speak spoke for no more than a minute or two. He used the word, "revolution," a lot – which I am sure earned him a place within a few police and other government agencies anti-terrorist video files. I have no doubt that my image and words were recorded by Big Brother also. Encore, there are surveillance cameras all over Times Square. Yeah, mais oui, there are a lot of people in the United States who think that hanging a surveillance camera on a building is as patriotic as flying an American flag. *Ta-ber-nac.*

I kept my speech short, simple, and fairly light. I shouted quèkchose like: *"They say we are not intelligent...but three years ago they ran Sarah Palin for Vice-President of the United States...She said she could see Russia from her backyard. Can Sarah Palin see Times Square now?...There are thousands of people here who have more sense than Sarah Palin...They also say that they do not know what we stand for...They know too well what we stand for...We must continue to stand together."* Those were not my exact words, but I said something close to that. Chè pas if I got so much applause, mais je pense I got more laughs from my words than the other speakers.

The vast majority of the thousands of tourists and shoppers continued shopping and touring. But some tourists and some shoppers stopped, looked, and listened carefully. The police did their best to get these people back to being tourists, back to being good Americans, back to shopping. The police kept repeating to the people on the sidewalks: "Move along folks, move along folks." This reminded me of President Bush telling Americans on the night of September 11, 2001 that the best way to react to the terrorist attack on the Twin Towers was to go shopping. At least he did not say that the best way to react to the terrorist attack on the Twin Towers was to go shopping at Wal-Mart or buy a happy meal at McDonald's, as per the lead of George W. Bush.

The 10-17-11 Occupation of Times Square ended at around eight-thirty, about three hours after it had begun. Protesters returned without incident to Zuccotti Park, or gathered for another demonstration in Washington Square Park, or returned home, as I did.

After I left Times Square, as I was walking back to the subway station, a guy walked up next to me and told me that he had heard me speak up at the demonstration, and he just wanted to tell me that he thought I should not pick on Sarah Palin, because she has nothing to do with the protests. This guy had followed me for at least three blocks, and for more than ten minutes, before he approached me. Presque a case of stalking. There was something about him that put me on guard, physically. I stopped walking, to respond to him, but I was careful about how close I stood to him, and how I stood on my feet. I listened to him speak, without interrupting him. Then I told him in 25 words or less why I thought Sarah Palin was a tool used by the 1% to manipulate the 99%. And then I said, "ciao," because I did not want to get any more involved with this person. Bad karma. Peut-être he was an undercover agent for The Secret Tea Party Patriots, if there is such an organization.

When I got home I turned on the television to see how the Occupation of Times Square was being reported. I found that it was not being reported at all, or no longer being reported, or the news programs were giving the story the eight-second treatment. Mon dieu! C'était difficile à croire. This was a major Occupation of Times Square, such that the word, "Occupation," justifies a capital letter. 1500 protestors, and easily twice that number of armed police in uniform or plain clothes. But the media was dampening the story, almost keeping it secret.

The main thing is, I did not go to sleep feeling like I was fighting a lost cause, but rather, like the battle had just begun. Mais oui, la bataille était seulement juste commencer.

East End Bay
23 octobre 2011

"Common Sense II"

194

I was at Zuccotti Park again yesterday, participating in the #Occupy Wall Street demonstrations. I printed some of my thoughts on a hand-out which I titled : *Common Sense II.* I used just one page and wrote about 500 words. Below are some excerpts, dear Diary.

I wrote: "Consider the spectacle of the October 17 republican presidential candidate debate, televised by CNN. The republican candidates displayed a remarkable inability to wait for their own turns to speak. They behaved as if they were children, young children, with bad manners and poor impulse control.

When it came to offering solutions for complex and serious world problems, they did not respond like young children, but like spoiled and rebellious adolescents. The republican candidates bickered with each other, and offered overly-simple solutions, ridiculous solutions, and violent solutions. Consider what Herman Cain called for at the Mexican border: A wall with electrified barb-wire, with a moat in front of it filled with alligators, and a sign above the wall that warns people they will be killed if they take a step over the border. How much common sense does Cain have? Does he expect rational people to believe that this is just a very bad joke on his part?"

I also wrote: "Newt Gingrich, the wannabe Intellectual-in-Chief of the Republican Party, says that we 99%ers represent, 'hostility to classic America.' Why? Because we keep calling for a government of the people, for the people – instead of a government of the rich, for the rich?"

28 octobre 2011

« J'ai connections, man ! »

Je suis revenu à Stafford hier. Arrivé ici vers midi.

Je suis allé à la banque dans l'après-midi, et j'ai eu une conversation, quite a conversation, avec un des caissières à la banque, Rachele. Elle est si gentille. Toutes les caissières à la banque sont très gentilles. Il n'y avait personne se tenant sur la ligne derrière moi, donc nous pourrions parler sans être hâté, tandis que nous faisions les transactions. J'ai dit à Rachele au sujet des expériences que j'ai eu pendant les dernières semaines aux manifestations Wall Street. I told her about carrying my sign, « *Je Me Souviens, Democracy*!" everywhere, et tout monde taking a picture of the sign and of this guy holding the sign, le seul amériquébécois at the Wall Street protests.

J'ai parlé à Rachele au sujet d'être avec plus de 1500 des manifestants dans le Times Square, il y a deux semaines. She was surprised when I told her that very few people in the United States were aware of the protesting at Times Square, even though it may have been an historic event. My sense is that it was the first of what will be more and larger protest demonstrations at Times Square, if change does not come at a fast enough pace. Nous sommes dans l'âge de Matrix, prés de l'âge de Gaia, et le taux de changement accélère. Tout le monde doit affronter Choc Futur.

Anyway, there I was, à une banque dans Québec, conversais au sujet de l'avarice des financiers. J'ai pensé que le dollar américain et le dollar canadien echangeaient au pair, mais j'ai reçu moins que quatre-vingt-seize cents pour chaque dollar américain. Semble comme les honoraires de banque augmentent de ce côté de la frontière aussi. Hmmm.

Tandis que je marchais sur rue Principale, après que j'ai quitté la banque, j'ai vu Kenny, Pub Cantina Kenny. Il a vu le macaron sur mon chandail, "*Occupy Wall Street*," et he dragged me into le Cafe Dumont, to talk about le mouvement. Il m'a dit qu'il allait être un symbole de protestation de Wall Street, Guy Fawkes, (also known as, "Anonymous") for the Halloween party à Pub Cantina ce week-end. I gave Kenny my protest button, to wear with his costume. I was wearing the button with the intention of giving it to Kenny if I saw him. Synchronistic.

Guy Fawkes, ou "Anonyme," est maintenant the quintessential protest figure of the Occupy Wall Street movement. À l'entrée au Zuccotti Park à New York il y a une statue d'un homme, qui porte le masque de Guy Fawkes, le masque mis sur lui par des manifestants. Last week I put my, *"Je Me Souviens*, Democracy!"

sign in front of the statue and took a picture of it. I have to give a copy of that photo to Kenny.

Après le café avec Kenny, je me suis arrêté à la Tête de l'Ordinateur, pour dire bonjour à Susan Wright, et pour voir si Paddy pourrait parler, gabbing, avec Susan. Paddy n'était pas là, mais Susan m'a dit que lui et Annick étaient retournés de Manitoba. Elle m'a dit que Paddy ne pourrait pas attendre pour me voir, de dire à m'environ quelques expériences synchronistic qu'Annick a eu tandis qu'ils étaient dans Manitoba, tous connectés à inukshuks. Bien sûr, par force d'habitude, j'ai parlé avec Susan, autant que je pourrais, en français. She has almost given up on asking me why I speak to her in French so often. Elle est Madame Anglophone, mais she has such a good heart. Elle est un Staffordian.

I had a postcard for Susan to put on the wall with the other post cards she has from around the world. I was going to give her a Wall Street postcard, or an Empire State Building postcard, but instead I gave her a postcard that had a picture of a Long Island roadside attraction: the Flanders Duck. The Flanders Duck is a small building that was made in the 1920's, in the shape of a duck. She taped my Flanders Duck postcard on the wall between a Macchu Picchu postcard and a Stonehenge postcard.

Susan told me that she and Paddy were starting another poker game tonight at St. Brendan, and I was invited to come. But I told her that I heard about a new movie that I wanted to see (*French Immersion*) and if it was playing in Cowansville I was going to see it.

Quand j'ai quitté Susan Computer, j'ai dit à elle : « À plus ! »

Susan m'à dit, « Cheers ! Hope you experience some good synchronicity this week-end in Stafford. »

Tandis que je conduisais ma voiture hors du parking j'ai vu une affiche sur le gazebo, avec un schéma d'un grand canard là-dessus. Puisque le lac Brome est célèbre pour des canards, et le lac n'est pas très loin d'ici, je n'ai pas estimé que c'était une expérience synchronistique.

When I got home I was stuffing my coat in the closet, which caused something to fall off the shelf. It was a Long Island Ducks baseball hat. J'ai oublié que c'était là.

Synchronicity était dans l'aire, toutefois j'ai eu aller aux toilettes. I brought the latest edition of *le Tour* avec moi. I saw that on the front page of *le Tour* was the headline: *"Sérendipité/Serendipity."* Hmmm.

I did not go to see *French Immersion* hier soir, parce que j'était tellement fatigué. I fell asleep early, feeling connected. Ce matin, je me sens connecté à Mont Stafford, je me sens connecté aux énergies.

East End Bay
7 novembre 2011

« *Plus Common Sense* »

Yesterday I returned to Zuccotti Park for the #Occupy Wall Street demonstrations. I handed out a couple of hundred copies of my newest issue of *Common Sense II.*

Here is what I wrote in the opening paragraphs...

"God is not an American, and Jesus is not a republican opposed to universal health care. Sensible people know this.

A democracy is a government of the people, by the people, for the people. A democracy is not a government of the rich, by the rich, for the rich. Sensible people know this.

In the U.S.A the richest 1% are getting richer, and the other 99% are getting poorer. The reason why the richest are still getting richer is not because the invisible hand of God has been shedding his grace on them. The richest 1% are getting richer because they live in a society which has a government of the rich, by the rich, for the rich. Sensible people know this.

The richest 400 Americans now own more than the least wealthy 150 million Americans. We have an economic system in which 400 people have accumulated more wealth than half the population of the country. There is *no* rational justification for inequity of this magnitude. This is a *perversity.*"

My last words were: "*Je me souviens democracy!* **America's greatest need is to start a democracy. Isn't this just common sense?** "

Stony Brook University Hospital, Stony Brook, NY
27 décembre 2011

« Christmas Day at Stony Brook University Hospital »

Dear Diary...I thought I would be in Stafford aujourd'hui, toutefois je suis à New York, à Stony Brook University Hospital. On Christmas Eve grandma fell and broke her leg. Almost everyone in the family who lives nearby is sick with something contagious, so I have been spending a lot of time with grandma at the hospital. I have to postpone going to Stafford until grandma is discharged from the hospital and begins proper rehabilitation treatment.

I followed the ambulance to the hospital at 1h on Christmas day, and I was in the hospital until vers one o'clock in the afternoon. I will not remember the Christmas morning of 2011 as one of my happiest Christmas mornings. I will remember it as a Christmas morning with an intensely bittersweet taste. I say this because the nurses, the doctors, and everyone else who was working at the hospital radiated such loving kindness. Everyone I encountered gave so much love and care to my grandmother, to me, and to each other. It was disturbing, to see grandma in pain. But the loving kindness that seemed to exude from everyone sustained me. I felt like I had somehow become a very minor character in a very bitter, and somehow also sweet Christmas story.

1 janvier 2012

« 2012 Commence »

Il y a deux ou trois minutes j'ai lu un courriel de Grace Terranova, le premier courriel envoyé à moi cette année. Gracie a

199

écrit : « Salut Professor, Bonne Année, Happy New Year. It is going to be a 2012 year. Sourire » !

Mais oui, je crois que Gracie a raison.

...Ken Grudman m'a dit hier que lui avait reçu une nombre des courriels des gens qui retournent pour encore habiter dans Stafford, et les gens qui sont déplacent à Stafford pour la première fois, parce qu'ils veulent être ici pour le 21 décembre 2012.

C'est clair que 2012 commence.

11 janvier 2012

« Woody Allen à venir à Stafford ? »

Hier j'ai vu Paddy après ski à chez Susan Computer. Quand je suis arrivé à la boutique, Paddy envoyait un courriel à un Staffordian, Arthur Bookman, qu'est hivernage à un ashram en Inde.

Arthur est né à Brooklyn ! Il habite à New York City, et Boston, et Stafford, et l'Inde. He has a few bucks. Je pense qu'il est d'une famille riche. Chè pas s'il parle français. Il a enseigné la physique à New York University et s'est retiré il y a environ vingt ans pour poursuivre des intérêts spirituel-ésotériques. J'ai rencontré Arthur une fois, et je devine qu'il est environ soixante-quinze ans. Il ressemble beaucoup à Woody Allen, et il connaît Woody Allen ! Ils a habitent dans le même voisinage et ils sont allés au même lycée à Brooklyn : Midwood High School. Arthur m'a dit qu'il voit Woody tous les cinq ou dix ans dans les endroits aléatoires à New York City. Arthur m'a dit qu'ils bavarder toujours pour cinq minutes, au sujet de la physique de quantum, et phénoménologie, et la mort, et sandwiches grillés de fromage de Kropp's Restaurant sur Flatbush Avenue, et ensuite ils disent, « ciao » !

Arthur flipped out quand je lui ai dit que j'ai mangé chez Kropp's beaucoup de fois.

C'est drôle, n'est pas ? Arthur m'a dit que plusieurs fois il a invité Woody Allen à visiter Stafford ! Je ne serais pas étonné si soudainement Woody Allen est apparu ici dans Stafford d'un jour. Je ne serais pas tellement étonné si Woody Allen venait ici au même jour comme Ram Dass, et Scotty Bowman, et Leonard Cohen, et Yoko Ono. Peut-être ils seront tous à Stafford le 21 décembre 2012.

12 janvier 2012

« Pourquoi cet amériquébécois s'est inscrit au MQF »

Hier je suis devenu un membre du Mouvement Québec Français. Ça n'a pas été facile pour moi de le faire. Parce que le formulaire de demande était totalement écrit en français. À moins que je me trompe, le site web de MQF est entièrement écrit en français. Pas étonnant. S'il y avait un lien vers une traduction en anglais, je ne le vois pas. Je ne sais pas, mais je suppose qu'il n'y a pas beaucoup d'anglophones comme moi qui veulent devenir membres du Mouvement Québec Francais. Mais, bien sûr, if you are an anglophone of Québec who is not motivated to communicate in French as often as you can, then you might as well go to the nearest Wal-Mart, where you might register yourself as an American Republican, and buy a gun at the same time.

Je me suis inscrit au MQF parce que je crois que le Québec est une grande nation, une nation progressive, peut-être sur le seuil de devenir une nation qui mènera les nations qu'étaient les chefs du 20ème siècle.

Les nations qu'étaient des chefs au 20ème siècle ne sont pas adaptées pour mener le Québec maintenant.

17 février 2012

« Planet Yoga »

Chère Journal Intime...Je suis arrivé dans Stafford environ 10h30m, après j'ai quitté Long Island environ 3h. Il n'y avait aucun circulation et Interstate 91 au Vermont était sec. Il n'y avait aucune neige sur la route que va au-dessus de Jay Peak. C'était la première fois que je n'ai pas vu la neige sur rue Principal en février. Je n'ai vu aucune neige jusqu'à ce que j'ai conduit vers le haut de Mont Stafford près de chez moi. Global warming is making it easier to drive. This could be a slogan of Republicans in the United States. Mais oui. « Support Republicans to support global warming. You will have longer summers! » Je sais, sick joke. Like the Republican party.

Ce soir je suis allé à une lecture de poésie à l'église Big Pink. Les poèmes étaient un mélange de français et anglais, mais surtout l'anglais.

There were six poets. I recognized all of their faces but I do not know any of them personally. Je ne sais rien au sujet de la poésie, mais pour moi c'était poésie des beaux-arts. Beaux-arts ! Beaux, beux, Bo...Jackson...Pollack art. Bon, diversifiée, expérimentale. I enjoyed it so much.

The poetry was thoughtful, sometimes humorous. Spiritual. I noticed that there were many references au sujet du yoga. Mais également au sujet de la méditation. Et également au sujet d'être dans le moment présent, about being in The Now. Également au sujet de l'espace entre, the bardo, et également au sujet de l'évolution consciente. C'était également au sujet du 21 décembre deux mille douze. Three different poets referred to: « New Age Eve. »

L'église a été bondée. Je pense que pour beaucoup des personnes qu'étaient dans l'église, le yoga est une partie importante de leurs vies. Le yoga est une partie significative de la culture de Stafford.

J'ai vu Dave Brown après le lecture et je pense que, he nailed it. Il a dit : « In Quebec – at least in Montreal and the townships – yoga is almost the, « new hockey. » It's a hell of a lot bigger than rugby, eh? »

Je pense que c'est vrai. Je pense que yoga est un partie de la Nouvelle Spiritualité du Québec. My sense is that this phenomenon is driven more by women than by men. Bien sûr, my sense is that it is women, more than men, who are driving change for the better in Québec.

I see connections between the New Spirituality and yoga, and the poetry of Québec, and the night sky of Québec. Quand je suis dans Québec je regarde le ciel plus souvent de quand je suis à Long Island. La différence est remarquable. Ici, le ciel est clair. The night sky is spectacular in Québec. When I am standing in Québec and I look at the sky I feel like I am looking from Spaceship Earth at the universe. Je pense que I had to grow up and come to Québec to realize that all of us on this planet are astronauts, in orbit. Peut-être mon réflexion sur ces choses est parce que Dave Brown a dit a moi hier soir que je dois voir un film intitulé : « *Planet Yoga.* »

Le 1 avril 2012

« *JEU est plus que fun* »

Cher Journal...À ma quête pour parler français, il y a beaucoup de kilomètres que demeurent. Je pense, it is more probable that I will walk to Vancouver from Stafford before I will ever become literate ou conversationnel en français. Je ne pense pas randonée à Vancouver est dans mon avenir. The idea of *flying* to Vancouver from Stafford makes me feel très fatigué.

En tout cas, ce matin je suis allé à une réunion de JEU (Jardin d'Echange Universel) au Café Dumont. Seulement quelques membres étaient là, parce que c'était samedi et la plupart des membres ont été occupées avec d'autres choses. Ils ont pensé si la réunion était le plus tôt possible que tout le monde viendrait. Mais seulement les personnes qui sont les plus énergiques et qu'étaient libres étaient là.

Lieve était là. Cleo, qu'est maintenant le coordonnateur du groupe, était là. Monique Kassem était là. J'étais étonné de la voir. (Je n'ai pensé pas qu'elle aurait un intérêt dans JEU.) Un nouveau Staffordian, Luc, était là. Et moi-même.

Tout le monde a parlé français quand la réunion a commencé au café. J'ai écouté soigneusement et j'ai compris les matières de la conversation. Parfois mon cerveau pouvait traduire des expressions entières, mais c'était rare. When Lieve et Cleo began to talk about bookkeeping it became quite boring.

Mais j'étais content d'être dans le Café Dumont ce samedi matin. Every month a different Stafford artist places their art on the walls of the café. I enjoyed looking at the art, from where I sat. While I was doing this it occurred to me that if I was on Long Island on this Saturday morning I probably would have gotten coffee from a 7-11, where every month, instead of rotating works of art, they change the glossy posters on the walls – which advertise the 7-11 fat crap and 7-11's so-called « collectible » plastic cups. Which is a major rip-off of people who actually believe they are making an *investment*(!) by buying these cups. Yeah, and republicans will bring peace and posterity to America by letting the richest of the rich rule the country. I'll tell him as soon as he gets in. Mais, that is un autre histoire.

Cleo a invité Carnie Jack de s'asseoir à la table avec nous, et dix minutes plus tard il est devenu membre de JEU. Carnie va devenir bientôt riche avec des points de JEU. Il est un plombier, un charpentier, un électricien, un peintre, un maçon et je ne sais pas combien d'autres choses. Alors, I hope he will spend some points by letting me drive him dans ma voiture to the Hart Centre, à Cowansville. J'ai besoin des points. I have no points yet! Aucun!

La réunion a fini dans une heure. Ils ont décidé de ne pas parler de beaucoup de choses, parce qu'il n'y avait pas assez de membres présent. Je ne sais pas, mais j'espère qu'il n'y avait pas les agents secrets du RCMP au café. Using JEU points might be seen as more of a threat to the powers-that-be in Québec than using Canadian Tire money.

Bien sûr, quand nous parlons de JEU, nous ne parlons pas de l'argent ou même argent de jeu, nous parlons des points. The members of JEU who I know do not even like to use les mots, « play money » ou, « argent de jeu, » parce que, peut-être, en raison des implications légales, je ne sais pas.

Je pense que JEU fait partie d'un réseau qui s'appelle, en anglais : « LETS, » ou : « Local Employment Trading System ». C'est au sujet l'argent de temps qu'est libre de l'usure. This usury-free time currency has become a universal means of exchange. Les gens emploient ce système dans les communautés dans beaucoup endroits. Ce système est employé à Montréal, à Toronto, à New York City, à Ithaca, Burlington, Boulder et dans des petites villes de l'Estrie, ici dans Québec.

Au cours de la réunion, j'ai entendu Luc dit, à plusieurs reprises : « Éliminer les banques ! Éliminer les banques ! » Cleo et Luc étaient des partenaires, il y a années, quand ils ont habité NDG. Selon Cleo, Luc est tellement le rebelle. Il ne veut pas reformer les banques, il veut voir le système bancaire effondrer. Je voudrais converser avec Luc, toutefois je ne sais pas to what extent he is bilingue. He looks like a good guy and he is tellement intéressant à moi. I have not encountered too many québécois radical blacksmiths in my life. Aussi, Cleo m'a indiqué que Luc is thinking about relinquishing his citizenship in Canada, and perhaps he will become a Sov-ran. Il avait parlé à Shiva au sujet de devenir un Sov-ran.

I hope JEU points will become more popular than McDonald's coupons, not to mention Argent Pneu Canadien. J'ai parlé brièvement avec Monique après la réunion et elle m'a dit qu'elle aime JEU parce que JEU est un défi pour le système, mais elle croit aussi que JEU est pas nécessaire parce que tout va changer beaucoup après le 21 décembre 2012. I wanted to hear more about 2012 mais Monique m'a dit que elle n'avait pas plus temps pour parler.

Le 30 juin 2012, samedi
Stafford, QC

« The Universe explained sur les notes de réfrigérateur »

Après dejeuner hier, tandis que je faisais la lessive, je me sentais un grand besoin soudainement de méditer. C'était un événement. It seems that I never find the time to meditate unless I am doing my zen walk meditation, and I only do that on a regular basis quand je suis à Stafford.

Je me suis assis sur l'un de mes tapis de prière afghan, et j'ai médité pendant cinq minutes. C'était a power meditation. Après ma méditation de puissance, I stepped outside. J'ai resté dans la moment presente, feeling the soft warm breezes, smelling the air with my eyes closed, paying attention to my breathing... J'était dans : The Flow. Il y a rien que j'ai dois faire.

205

Aaaaaaaaaaaaaaaaaaaah. My body had returned to Stafford days ago, et maintenant mon ésprit a rétourné Stafford.

Instead of a potato chip, j'ai décidé de lire une page d'un livre, comme une sorte de collation intellectuelle. I scanned a shelf and a lovely book caught my eye : After the Ecstacy, the Laundry. Je pensais à moi-même : Mais-oui, je sens en ecstacy maintenant, mais je dois finis la lessive. Pour moi, à cette moment, c'était synchronistique. I was in a goof place.

I opened the book to a random page, et j'ai vu que j'avais écrit en haut de la page : « Everyday Nirvana. » Ces mots résonnaient avec moi, comme le quartz de cristaux de Mont Stafford.

I put the book back on the shelf and removed the one à côté d'elle : *A Path with Heart,* un livre par le même écrivain, Jack Kornfield. Encore, j'ai ouvert le livre à une page au hazard. I read a paragraph. C'était au sujet la synchronicité.

J'ai décidé que I would go outside and sit in the sun, and continue to read from *A Path with Heart.* J'ai besoin de, a bookmarker, et sur mon bureau je trouvait une carte 3 x 5, une annonce d'une concert à Bromont par Jean-Bruno Gagnon, intitulé : « *Musicdream, Manifester la paix du coeur.* » Encore. Un autre moment synchronistique.

I put the card on the cutting board on my kitchen counter, to remind me to find out more about le concert, and I looked on my desk for something else to use as a bookmark. J'ai trouvé un petit morseau de papier où j'ai écrit : « Jane Hirshfield...Pay attention, everything is connected, everything changes. » C'était une note que j'ai écrit à moi-même, il y a quelques semaines, au sujet un citation, that Paddy O'Brien had given to me.

Then my house phone rang, with perfect timing to be the exclamation point for the note. Bien sûr, continuait la synchronicité, c'était, who else? Oui, Paddy O'Brien. Il a dit quelque chose comme : « Hey Mario-Jacques, I see you're back and Susan Computer just told me all about you banging pots on rue Principal, because you're trying to start a revolution here in Québec since you don't have much hope for the states, and she is telling me they are calling you « Casserole Man » and you probably been called worse things, eh? Well like I said, you should be paying attention when you put your key into the lock. Have you been remembering to do that? And have you been practicing your tai-chi? There are 108 movements you know, and you're still learning the first two – okay, I take that back, maybe you're learning the first five or six. And I know what you're going to say – that your attention gets distracted in that New York rat race. Yeah okay, but I hope you been playing *om namaha shivaya* and watching your breath on the Long Island Expressway... »

J'interrompis, avec une voix douce : « Yo, Paddy...are you going to give me a chance to talk ? »

Il a dit, « No, I don't think so, Mario-Jacques, I got to get going now but I just want to tell you that Susan and I agree you are going to get yourself arrested on rue Principal, or poo-tit Saint Catherine Street, and you are going to be like that Julian guy, what's his name? Giuliani? You know who I mean, eh? The *leaks* guy. The *Wikileaks* guy! That's something, eh? Looks like the *Wikileaks* guy is going to spend the rest of his life in an embassy building in England – in a building that belongs to *which* country? El Salvador? No, the embassy belongs to Mexico, right? The Mexican drug cartel has an embassy in England and that's where the *Wikileaks* guy is, right? You see, you think Paddy doesn't know what's going on in the world, but he does! I learn it all from Bill Maher on my satellite dish. »

J'ai dit, « Yeah, but the man you're talking about is not Rudy Giuliani, the former Mayor of New York... »

Paddy a continué sans se laisser décourager. « It doesn't matter. What's-his-name is holed up in the embassy of the Mexican drug cartel – which is better than where you are going to be – because Susan Computer and I figure you'll need to find sanctuary in Mansonville, in The Reilly House. »

Je pourrais dire seulement, « Très drôle, Monsieur. I'm sure you know that means, 'very funny'. »

Mais Paddy juste continué, « But they've got good *Croque Monsieur* at The Reilly House, even if you don't like their Italian dishes, eh? Of course, they make *Croque Monsieur* without the meat for me at Reilly House. Anyway, I'm staying away from people in honor of Canada Day so I don't know when I'll see you, but you'll be here until September, eh? I'm on my way to Triple Falls. Meditating this afternoon. Okay, Mario-Jacques. Namasté. »

It was hard to get a word in edgewise, parce que Paddy was so energized. At the end of the conversation, j'ai dit seulement : «Namasté.»

I wanted to ask Paddy how he did at the casino. I guess he didn't win, et j'espère qu'il n'a pas perdu beaucoup. Aussi, j'ai voulu parler à Paddy au sujet le citation : « Prêter attention, tout est connecté, tout change. »

I spent the rest of the afternoon juste staying in the afternoon, enjoying moments as they happened. To say it in a way that Paddy would understand, my self was not taken away very often by a drunken monkey to other places.

Après souper, je suis allé à la ville. I was wondering what rue Principal would be like, on this Canada Day weekend. Et j'ai dit à Gaston que je serais venu le voir à la galerie.

Je ne pouvais pas garer ma voiture près de la gazebo, comme je le fais d'ordinaire. Les espaces de stationnement étaient consomme par les gens vélo qui, had swarmed, dans des proportions biblique – oui, comme les locustes – à la ville.

J'ai vu Ken assis sur la terrase du Pub Cantina, alors j'ai arrêté pour voir comment Ken ca va. Il a parlé à moi au sujet DNA et l'univers de l'intérieur, qu'existe dedans de chaque personne. C'était le taoisme et la physique, comme distillée par un propriétaire de pub de Stafford.

Ken was not speaking from his head, his brain, his ego, so much as from son coeur. He is mourning so many people. Il est évident qu'il porte beaucoup de poids. Porter une âme morte est plus difficile que portant d'un corps vivant.

Je me suis assis avec Ken pendant environ une demi-heure, et ensuite il avait besoin de travailler, parce que les touristes brulé rouge par le soleil – avec les voitures rouges, et avec les vélos rouges, et avec l'argent rouge-canadienne – étaient soif.

Ken parle souvent de son utopie : un monde sans drapeaux. Alors I wanted to ask him about his feelings related to the Maple Leaf being waved by so many people this week. We never got to that. We will have that conversation bientôt, je pense. Je vais avoir besoin de parler bleu avec lui. A propos d'un nouveau drapeau bleu, pour le Nouveau Québec.

Je suis allé pour voir Gaston sans un autre arrêt pour bavarder et sans dire bonjour à n'importe qui sur le chemin. Rue

Principal était sans les Staffordians, pour le plupart. Il y avait seulement Staffordians qui travaillaient. Il y avait beaucoup de touristes dans le ville à partir de Montréal.

C'est incroyable que Gaston a décidé d'ouvrir une nouvelle galerie il y a un mois, et maintenant, déjà, c'est ouvert. La nouvelle galerie est entre deux restaurants populaire – Le Cheval Bleu et Chez Pastafazzoli – et proche d'une nouvelle boutique de cadeaux. Maintenant plus des gens verront son travail. Aussi, l'art de Gaston sera le seule art affichée à la galerie tout les temps. Il y aura aussi artistes invités. Will the secret that is Stafford be discovered, because the outside world will be coming to see the art of Gaston Briere ?

Gaston a un atelier dans la galerie. Quand j'ai entré, il peignait. He was giving the finishing touches to a painting. Before the paint was dry, I told Gaston that I wanted to buy the painting. Je sais, it sounds farfelu, ou pastafazzoli, très impulsif, mais this is the way it usually is for me when I buy a painting.

Le titre qu'il a donné à la peinture était : « *La Luminosité.* » Dans cette peinture la lumière du soleil est un coup de projecteur sur une chaise rouge vacant à côté d'une fenêtre ouverte, attendant quelqu'un revenir. Il y a une peinture dedans la peinture, qu'est quelque chose que Gaston fait beaucoup dans son travail. Sur le mur derrière la chaise rouge est une peinture d'une femme rousse debout dans un champ ouvert, regardant au loin, peut-être attendant quelqu'un revenir. In the painting a gentle breeze tosses the curtain that is next to the red chair, and it seems that this same gentle breeze is also tossing the hair of the woman in the painting-within-the-painting. Quand j'ai remarqué cela, je me souvenais ce que j'avais écrit sur un morseau de papier que je mets dans ma poche de chemise : « Prêter attention, tout est connecté, tout change. » I took the note from my pocket and read it out loud.

Gaston était préoccupé. Il a été absorbée par la peinture sur son chevalet. Il ne pouvait pas se concentrer suffisamment sur mon français amériquébécois, filtré d'un accent de Brooklyn/Long Island. Il a dit, « *Quoi ?* What is it that you are saying, Monsieur Mario-Jacques ? You want me to pay attention to *what* ? »

J'ai répondu, « I am having a *synchronistic* day ! The universe has been telling me : *'Pay attention, everything is connected, everything changes ;* And to: *'Follow a path with heart.'* Peut-être I am going to write about this synchronicity, dans mon journal intime. » Je devine que je vais courriel à Gaston cette entrée de journal, après je fin d'écrire.

Encore, Gaston était preoccupé avec ses pensées – il a dit qulque chose au sujet une opthamologiste, et il avait besoin d'aller à l'IGA. Mes derniers mots à Gaston ont été : « À demain, mon ami. À suivre. »

Les derniers mots de Gaston ont été : « À demain, mon ami. Maintenant... *Je vais Iiii-GA !* » He said, *« Je vais Iiii-GA ! »* like the character in *Frankenstein* movies: Igor. Which told me that he was a little stressed about quékchose, but still in good spirits.

I stepped outside the door of the gallery as Shiva Duschene was walking into the parking lot, from behind le Cheval Bleu, where the railroad tracks are. Trains pass two times every 24 hours, je pense. Shiva est l'un des beaucoup des Staffordians qui je connais qui préfèrent marcher sur la voie ferée, au lieu de rue Principal.. I did not ask her if she had been walking on the railroad tracks, toutefois je suis certain qu'elle a fait.

Nous avons embrasée sur les joues, et puis Shiva tenaient ses mains devant son coeur, et a dit, « Namasté. » C'était plus qu'un, « bonjour. » This was not a mundane, « I bow to you » greeting, either. I felt like I was, pour le moment, dans l'espace entre. The devine light in Shiva was honoring the devine light in me. Mais oui. La beauté de Shiva résonné en moi.

My eyes were drawn to her abundant lion hair, almost as spectacular as a fireworks show to celebrate St-Jean-Baptiste – grandes explosions de cheveux blancs et cheveux bleu Québec, attachés avec brins de rubans bleus, pas deux le même. Gypsy de Cantons de l'Est. Elle portait une robe longue blanc avec des boutons sur le devant, et pour le plupart ouverts. Peut-être she was not wearing a bra, but I did not notice, par le tissu leger.

I put my hands together, et j'ai répondu, « Namasté ». Et ensuite j'ai parlé en français. Fran-çais té-lé-graph-ique.

Elle a dit, « Mario-Jacques, your French is getting better! I see this by the way you pronounce, "Namasté. »

J'ai ri. Et j'ai dit, « Tu es drôle ! Encore, je parle français comme un gringo. »

In halting franglais, elle a dit, « C'est Mario-Jacques qu'est drôle, always funny. You touch my heart. » Ensuite she reached out et doucement elle a touché ma poitrine sur mon coeur. Shiva guérit par le toucher. Je le crois. I had on my shirt a square made from red tape. Elle a dit : « I see you wear le carré rouge on your heart. »

J'ai dit, « Mais oui. I support les étudiants, les manifestations, le mouvement. C'est très, très, très importante. J'ai marché deux fois à Montréal et trois fois ici, à Stafford, avec les casseroles. »

Elle a dit, « Bravo, Mario-Jacques. You are un allié, an *ally* for the students. *L'Allié Amériquébécois !* »

J'ai dit, « C'est vrai. C'est mon...*destin*...être, 'l'Allié Amériquébécois'...Did I say that correctly, Shiva ? Comment dit-on, *'destiny'* en français ? »

Elle a dit, « You say : 'destin' »

J'aime le nom de, « l'Allié Amériquébécois » mieux que le nom : « Casserole Man. » Mais les deux sont bonnes.

J'ai dit à Shiva, « Je pense que, the meaning of le carré rouge that I wear on my chest will evolve, expand. »

Shiva understood. Elle a dit, « Yes, I am sure it will evolve and expand. It is part of the evolution of consciousness. It is part of the awakening, Mario-Jacques. It is happening around the world. We are moving to the unity. »

J'ai dit, « Je comprends, je comprends. C'est deux mille douze. The students that I saw marching à Montrèal for le Carré Rouge *know* they are changing the world. When they march, it is not an *angry* protest ; They are *celebrating* en avance de great changes, parce qu'ils sont si confiant, je pense. Québéc, and the world, should be so proud of these students. In a certain way, they are all the offspring of René Levesque, non ? »

Shiva a répondu, « Mais oui, Mario-Jacques. I think what you say is true. The students touch your heart, and they touch my heart. How do I say this, en anglais ? ...Their hearts are in *resonation* with your heart and my heart, non ? Is this a word : *'resonation ?'* »

J'ai dit, « Je ne pense pas. Toutefois, je comprends. »

I could see that this was the beginning of a longer conversation, which I always enjoy with Shiva, so I offered to buy un verre de vin, or a cold beverage for her, ou café, à Chez Pastafazoolie.

Elle a dit qu'elle aurait un thé. We went inside and sat at the counter, and within a few minutes all four of the waitresses came over to say, 'bonjour,' et, 'ca va bien ?' to Shiva, et moi-même. J'ai appris plus tard que Shiva a fait de guèrison par le toucher pour toutes les femmes qui travaillent à Chez Pastafazoolie.

Shiva commandé *le thé vert indien* et j'ai commandé mon préféré : *la même chose*. Marie Chantal a apporté le thé pour nous, comme si...je ne sais pas...the best way I can put it is : the way she served the tea was as if the devine light in Marie Chantal was honoring the devine light in us. She brought each of us a small green metal teapot, and various dishes, utensils and cloth napkins. The way she placed everything on the counter, in front of us, seemed presque comme une cérémonie. Elle a placé les objets doucement, précisément. Quand elle finit plaçant tout, elle tenaient ses mains devant son coeur, et a dit : « Namasté. »

Elle nous ont parlé pour le plupart en français et elle m'a regardé pour le plupart quand she sprinkled in some English. J'ai compris seulement un peu. Toutefois, le langue quelquefois est quatre-vingt pour cent du langue du corps. J'ai compris assez pour voir que Marie Chantal est : a mensch and a bodhisattva. She was treating Shiva like someone who deserves to be named after a deity...bien que Shiva l'hindou était un dieu, pas une déesse. Shiva et Marie Chantal bavardé pour une minute au sujet le thé. My best guess is that they were talking about where the tea is grown, and the properties of the tea, and when are the best times to drink it. Je pense qu'ils dit quelque chose au sujet l'utilisation de l'eau sacrée derrière l'IGA, mais je ne suis pas certain.

I was going to ask about using the water behind the IGA for the tea, but my thoughts soon went elsewhere, as Marie Chantal went to serve others, et Shiva m'a demandé au sujet encore le carré rouge que je portais sur mon coeur. Tandis que nous avons bu notre première tasse de thé, nous avons parlé de la grève des étudiants, et des manifestations, et Occupy Wall Street.

Pendant un pause pour notre deuxieme tasses de thé, I pointed to her hair, et j'ai dit a Shiva, « J'aime ca ! I like your hair. Québec bleu et Québec blanc. Les mêmes coleurs comme le drapeau du Québec. »

Shiva responded avec quékchose en français and when she saw that I was not understanding, she switched encore to anglais pour moi. Parlant très lentement, elle a dit, « Mario-Jacques, probably I am so much blue and white, probably you see this, because the Blue Kachina comes. Have you noticed the moon?

Have you noticed it is not where it should be? The Inuit are talking much about this. The Abenaki here also are talking about this. If every day you pay attention to what is nature – if you pay attention to the earth, to the sky – you will look carefully at the moon and the stars every night, and you will notice that the position of the moon, dans le ceil, has changed. And do you know what les gens hopi are saying? They say Kachina is arriving. It is arriving today. Aujourd'hui. This fulfills the prophecy...I did not send you the e-mail about this, hier? »

J'ai dit, « I have not received your courriels in a long time, Shiva. More than a month. »

Elle a dit, « Aaah, okeh Mario-Jacques. I will email a link to you about the Blue Kachina Star. This is happening Mario-Jacques, and you need to know about it. The axis of the earth is tilting. The planet will soon be standing on its head. The old world is coming to an end. There will be a great shaking up until the twenty one décembre, deux mille douze. *This* world, all this illusion, is coming to an end. La dualité est terminée. Oh yes, the world of duality, of illusion, is over. Now we move to the unity. Nous allons à la quatrième dimension. You understand enough of my French and what I mean, I know. »

Je pense que she saw worry on my forehead. Elle ajouté, « You will be safe, Mario-Jacques. Your family will be safe. Because all that matters is the vibration of the heart. » Elle s'est tourné vers moi, et avec sa main droit, elle a touché mon avant-bras. Et encore mon coeur.

Encore, parler au coeur. J'ai dit, « C'est incroyable, Shiva. Tous le journée, all day, tout monde has been talking to me au sujet le coeur, speaking from the heart. Et tout monde has been talking to me au sujet moving from the third dimension to the fourth dimension, the dimension of the heart. C'est incroyable ! C'cst... très, très, très incroyable ! »

Marie Chantal a retournée pendant que je disait, « ...très, très, très incroyable. » We could see that she was holding a question in her folded hands. Nous avons utilisé notre langage du corps d'inviter Marie Chantal de poser sa question.

Elle a dit, « Puis-je vous demander, ce qu'est, 'très, très, très incroyable ?' »

J'ai répondu, « La vie... et Shiva. »

213

Shiva répondu, « And all of us. And today everyone has been talking to Mario-Jacques about the fourth dimension, the dimension of the heart. It is all connected. »

J'ai regardé Marie Chantal pendant que j'ai dit, « Encore ! Encore j'entends : 'Everything is *connected* !' »   J'ai continué, « What I was going to say after I said : 'C'est très, très, très incroyable,' was : This morning I was searching on my desk for a bookmarker to use in a book titled, *A Path with Heart*.   I found a small piece of paper on which I had written, weeks ago : 'Pay attention, everything is connected, everything changes'...Tout la journée, the universe has been speaking to me, repeating these words to me. »

Marie Chantal a dit, « Je vois. Put that note on your refrigerator, Mario-Jacques! »

Après une pause momentanée, j'ai dit : « What has not been repeated to me so much today is the thought that: Everything changes. »

Shiva corrigé moi, poliment. « But at the same time Mario-Jacques, it is *all* about change. Mais oui, everything changes when we leave the third dimension and rise to the fourth dimension, the dimension of the heart. »

Dans la réalité de notre monde mondain, c'était temps pour nous d'aller. Chez Pastafazoolie était prêt à fermer.

Comme j'ai dit, je voulais acheter le thé pour Shiva. Toutefois, quand je suis allé a payer la facture, j'ai trouvé qu'il était payé par Marie Chantal. Elle a dit, « I have payed le facture for Shiva, because she stopped a bus for me and my friend, because she was trying to help us. » Je n'ai pas demandé Marie Chantal me dire plus de cette histoire. Un autre fois, quand elle ne pas occupé.

Comme nous marchions dans le stationnement, Shiva m'a dit, « This has been a day of the heart for you, Mario-Jacques. For me, it has been un autre journée de l'abondance. »

Ensuite, Elle a pris un pas près de moi, et elle a dit, « Not too long ago, I had no money to buy food, and I had only a very small piece of baguette, small like my thumb. During my meditation I asked the universe what I should do. When I opened my eyes after my méditation, there was un oiseau on the ground, à côte de moi. L'oiseau is my power animal...I gave the bread to the bird, bien sûr. Since then, I have had l'abondance in so many ways... Food comes to me, Mario-Jacques. In the last two weeks, I spend less than twenty dollars to buy food. I do what I can do for people, and they give me food...quelquefois le thé. »

Encore, la lumière sacrèe de Shiva touché ma lumière sacrèe. J'ai dit a Shiva, « C'est appropriate, c'est parfait, that your name is Shiva, parce que Shiva est le Dieu de la pureté. »

La réponse de Shiva était, « Merci, Mario-Jacques. Of course, we are all the gods and the goddesses. »

Ensuite nous avons dit, « à la prochaine, » et a embraséesur les   joues.

Après je suis rentré, j'ai écrit une note et l'attaché à un clip magnetique. Comme le suggerait de Marie Chantal, j'ai mis la note sur mon réfrigérateur : « Prêter attention, tout est connecté, tout change. »

Le 1 juillet 2012, dimanche
Stafford, Qc

« White Hat Patriote »

Hier je suis allé au Marché du Samedi, comme c'est mon habitude. Après déjeuner aux tables de pique-nique, je suis allé parler à Pierre, mon bon ami qui vend des choses merveilleuses au marché. Toujours, I look forward to seeing Pierre when I go to the Saturday Market. He is a gentleman and a scholar, si vous voyez ce que je veux dire. We have interesting talks. Mais oui.

J'ai acheté sept tapis de Pierre au cours des dernières quelques années. Mais c'est plus que le tapis qu'il vend. Il vend également des livres, et l'art et les antiquités. Pour moi, ces tables sont récouvertes de morseaux de chocolat. Pour moi, standing with Pierre is better than standing in a chocolate shop or a chocolate museum. When I listen to him speak, I feel like I am eating delicious chocolates and it is good for me, très santé ! Sans faute, ses pensées sont bonnes pour mon âme. This communication we have, entre un québécois pur laine et un amériquébécois sicilienne, est fantastique.

Hier encore, I was wearing a red square of duct tape, mon carré rouge, on my shirt. We said bonjour with hugs, et Pierre a dit, « I see you wear le carré rouge on your heart. You remind me I must cut red cloth for myself. » Pour un moment il a cherché des mots en anglais, et il a ajouté: « This crisis will be an important happening in the history of Québec. »

J'ai dit, « Mais oui. C'est historique.   Je pense que les étudiants sont patriotes. »

Pierre me parle au sujet l'histoire du Québec, et la politique d'aujourd'hui au Québec et les états. Il me parle au sujet le carré rouge et les manifestations, la Révolution Tranquille, les plains d'Abraham, Réne Levesque, et Che Guevara, et Geronimo, et Jackie Robinson, et Abraham Lincoln, et speaking white.

Pierre n'est pas juste un homme à le Marché du Samedi qui vend des tapis de prière de l'Afghanistan, et qui porte un chapeau blanc de Cuba au-dessus ses cheveux longs blanc. Pierre is the archetypical Man in The White Hat, and le Sage, à la même temps.

Il était un professeur de la littérature à l'Université du Québec à Chicoutimi. Il a commencé à enseigner là en 1969, dont il se souvient comme un millésime pour les raisins de la colère.   He retired some years ago from teaching at the university. Maintenant, une ou deux fois par ans, il parle en public à une université, ou un CÉGEP, ou une bibilothèque.   Je suis chanceux parce que j'entends les courtes conferences de Pierre au Marché du Samedi. Qui sait, peut-être bientôt he will be on *YouTube* for the world.

En tout cas, hier Pierre m'a donné un cadeau, a gift of a CD : un film d'un autre Pierre, Pierre Falardeau, intitulé : « *15 février 1839.* » Yesterday night, I watched the film.

Tandis que j'ai regardé le film, je me sentais comme histoire m'a été racontée par Maurice Richard et Pierre Falardeau. Je veux dire cela comme un compliment à les deux hommes. And it was as if my friend – The Wise Man in The White Hat – was sitting next to me while I watched the film, whispering to me : « You see, this is what it was like. »

La partie de cette amériquébécois qu'est québécois est devenue plus de québécois après j'ai regardé ce film, peut-être parce que de l'ébullition de mon sang. Je pense que mon sang sicilien est le même type de sang comme un vrai québécois.

Je me demande comment l'histoire du Québec est enseignée au Québec, particulièrement dans les écoles. The history of Québec is still being written, et je suis sûr que la version française ne semble pas le même comme la version anglaise. Mais, we have not yet begun to fight, non?

Stafford, QC
Le 2 juillet 2012, lundi

« Canada Day dans l'Estrie »

Hier soir je suis allé à ma première fête du Canada Day. I felt honored to be invited to this party, as it has been one of the big events of the year for a group of family and friends who have been gathering together every July 1st since 1976. J'ai parlé à les gens à la fête qui m'a dit que leurs famille a commencé à célébrer la fête du Canada dans les cantons de l'Est d'avant Canada existait. Apparemment, the roots of this celebration can be traced back to *17(!)76*.

La fête était à une ferme de Frelighsburg, ou what used to be an active farm à Frelighsburg. Maintenant, the farm family remains à la ferme sans cultures, avec some farm animals – including two bisons, a cow and her calf, who are new additions to the farm.

J'ai été invité à la fête par Josh Taylor, who is one of the members of the Taylor clan, the owners of the farm. Josh est âgé d'environ quarante ans. Il est le plus jeune membre de la famille. His father, Seth Taylor, is ninety-seven years old and he looks like he is eighty years old. Je me demande si Seth utilise l'eau sacrée derrière l'IGA. Hmm, peut-être il boit le thé qu'est la même du thé que Paddy O'Brien boit. Mais oui, there must be something in the water.

I had been to this farm once before. En fait, je suis arrivé à la ferme il y a quelque années avec Paddy O'Brien et un couple de ses amis, old-timers. Seth Taylor allowed us to come on his property and follow paths that begin within his land et conduire à des sites mystérieuses sur le Mont Pinacle.

La fête n'était pas à la maison de ferme mais dans une vaste clairière dans les bois. I had to drive my car through the woods on a

217

path that was not much wider than my car. Je ne sais pas comment Seth et sa famille conduisent leurs camions sur cette sentier. Toutefois, once I drove through this safari adventure, I came to a clearing of grass, where there were about twenty vehicles parked, half of them small trucks or family vehicles.

Ma voiture était la seule voiture avec plaques de New York, mais il y avait deux camionnettes avec plaques de Vermont, et quand j'ai vu une Mercedes avec plaques de New Jersey, j'ai dit, « Oh, shit » out loud. Ce n'était pas une jugement à l'avance sur le propriétaire de la voiture, mais une réaction involontaire de ma parte...parce que...I am used to getting cut off by people who drive Mercedes avec New Jersey plates. Bien sûr, if the owners of this car were invited to this party, I thought to myself, they were probablement courteous drivers and nice people, who happen to like living in New Jersey and driving a Mercedes, for some reason. Then again, I thought to myself, who knows ? These people could have been republicans who had not yet slapped a Romney bumper sticker on their car. Ensuite encore, I thought to myself, who knows ? Qui sais, qui sais, qui sais ? I recalled that I had met a lesbian couple at the Abercorn Bakery this winter who had a second home in Abercorn, right on rue Scenic, and they lived ten months out of the year somewhere in Jersey, and they were democrats, and Zen Buddhists, even though they had a Mercedes. An old Mercedes. Et my dear uncle Mario drives a Mercedes. En tout cas, je dois admettre, je dois admettre chère journal intime, en raison de mes préjugés, je ne voulais pas de converser avec quelqu'un à la fête du Canada Day qu'était du Jersey, et conduie un Mercedes.

J'ai marché à travers une deuxième clairière, où il y a peut-être dix plus de camions et voitures garées, avec peut-être trois plaques de Vermont et le reste avec des plaques du Québec. Puis finalement, je suis arrivé à un troisième clairière, devant d'une grange très grande et très vieux. It was like walking for a long time and finally coming to a mountain lake. I knew it would be there, but it was still a bit of a surprise to see this huge barn, tucked away as it is, in the woods.

I found out later that a count was made, et il y avait plus de 80 personnes là, at one time. My guess is that plus de 100 personnes came et left the party at different times. Tout le monde était bavardant tranquillement, debout, ou assise sur le pliage des chaises

218

ou des bancs de pique-nique ou des couvertures qu'ils avaient apporté avec eux.

Il y avait nouveau-nés et les personnes qu'étaient vivants avant la première guerre mondiale. Tout le monde était dans un arc, orienté vers un tas de bois – environ six mètres de haut et quatre mètres de larges – qui deviendra un feu de joie plus tard, vers entre chien et loup.

A large maple leaf flag, le drapeau du Canada, was hanging high on the barn, flanked by two smaller American flags. J'ai demandé moi-même : Pourquoi deux drapeaux américains ? Et aucun drapeau du Québec ?

When Josh invited me to la fête I asked him what I could bring, et il a dit : « bring some fireworks from the IGA. »

À l'après-midi, avant que je suis allé à la fête, *je vais IiiiGA...*et j'ai acheté quelque feux d'artifice. J'ai acheté des feux d'artifice qu'affiche les couleurs bleus et blancs du Québec. J'aime les couleurs du drapeau au Québec. Mais, comme j'ai dit, il n'y avait aucun drapeaux du Québec à cette fête de Canada Day. I felt honored to be a guest at this party and I did not want to offend. I would not wave a Maple Leaf in the city of Québec à la fête de la Saint-Jean Baptiste. Non, that would be a red flag I would not want to wave.

On the back of a farm truck there was a feast of homemade food. No *eggplaint parmagiana,* or *scotchia,* but food for farm families to eat. C'est parfait pour moi. There is an old amériquébécois proverbe that I believe is true : « *In order to know a people, one must not only smell their breath, on doit manger leurs nourriture.* » Donc j'ai mangé. C'était bonne. Smorgasbord townshipper/québécoise, et pour le plupart townshipper. Delicieux.

I did not see Josh until I noticed that he was way the hell up on the roof of the barn with a video camera. When he waved to me I cringed, parce que I was afraid he was going to lose his balance on the roof, and tumble down to an undignified Albert Cumus death on Canada Day. I waved at Josh, and he shouted out that he was going to come down and say hello in a couple of minutes, donc j'ai marché autour pendant quelque minutes pour voir s'il y avait quelqu'un là que je connaissais.

J'ai vu trois personnes différentes qui je connais, de Stafford. Deux anglophones et un québécois. C'était la première fois qu'un d'eux était venu à ce fête.

When Josh came down from the roof he introduced me to a few of his friends and family. Super nice people. Mais oui, gens très, très, très sympa. J'ai conversé avec un couple qu'ont une ferme à Farnham. Very cool people. Farm people who live in the townships and in the world. We talked about farming, Barack Obama and Johnny Holliday. Tout est connecté.

J'ai aussi parlé avec un homme qu'est un architecte de Montréal et qui vit à Frelighsburg. Il m'a dit qu'il a été professeur à New York University dans les années 1990, and he commuted entre Frelighsburg et Greenwhich Village chaque semaine ! He used to use the same parking garage that I like to use, on West 10th Street. I told him that I identify so strongly avec les gens du Québec that I have become an amériquébécois. I did not ask him, but it is obvious that he never became a quebecer-american. Il ne savait pas qu'est un *egg cream*. C'est un épreuve de vérité, un vrai litmus test. A quebecer-american who does not know what an egg cream is, est comme un amériquébécois qui ne sait pas ce que *poutine* est.

When I returned to the truck to fill up a plate with pieces of United Empire Loyalist homemade pies (which were quite good) I met up with Trisha Landry, lovely lady and improvisational dancer extraordinaire. Trisha va danser à Stafford en août, à l'Esprit du Village. I cannot wait to see her dance encore. Elle est incroyable. Elle est *plus* d'incroyable, elle est innnnnnnnnnnncroyable. She puts her body into positions that I have never seen before, and with exquisite control. When she is fully *in* her dance – when she is capital "O" One with her dance – her spirit flows through her body.

Trisha and I ate desserts as if we were insatiably faim. She talked to me about what it is like for her when she goes into a meditative state while she is dancing. Elle a dit que lorsequ'elle danse et el'est In The Flow, el'est dans un état de méditation profonde. Quelquefois she is channeling l'univers, elle dit.

Trisha m'a parlé de la connexion entre la spiritualité et la création d'art. Yesterday I was reading a book called *The Artists Way, a spiritual path to higher creativity*. J'ai écouté attentivement à Trisha. Ses mots étaient les mêmes mots que j'ai lu dans le livre.

Quand j'ai mentionné cela à elle, elle m'a dit qu'elle avait lu le livre et c'est un livre spécial pour elle.

Notre conversation s'est terminée lorsque notre attention est allé à l'éclairage de la feu de joie. Trisha went off to toast marshmallows. Entre autres choses, elle est une cinquante-plus ans enfant.

Leah Turner, who is la petite amie de Josh, came to me with a cold beer. La bière était un Rickards. Je ne suis pas un buveur de bière, mais I never heard of this beer. Jamais. Probablement this shows my ignorance about beer. Peut-être Rickards is the Budweiser (or the Dos Equis?) of United English Loyalists? Chè pas. En tout cas, c'était bon.

This was a serious bonfire. Un feu de joie très, très, très sérieux. One of the guys lit it avec quelque sorte de dispositif, a device that looked like a homemade flame thrower. I cannot imagine what they do with this thing when they are not using it to light the fire on Canada Day. If you tried to cross the border with this thing, the Vermont National Guard would be called to active duty. No joke.

Le feu était si grand et si chaud qu'il n'était pas possible se tenir debout dans trois mètres d'elle. Les gens – tout les femmes, en fait – utilisées longues branches d'arbres pour faire griller des guimauves. In some cases it took two people to hold a very large and long tree branch, to keep it steady enough, to toast a marshmallow. I wonder if they have marshmallow holders in *The Guinness Book of World Records.*

Aussitôt que le ciel était assez sombre, ils sont décidé de commencer le spectacle d'feux d'artifice. I have seen serious world class fireworks shows in the states. On Long Island there is the Grucci brothers, who manufacture fireworks for spectacular shows held around the world. Their shows are *too* awesome for my taste – like too much sauce on the pasta.

Les feux d'artifice à cette fête de jour du Canada ne pas alarme mes sens. Les images et les sons n'étaient pas un affichage avec violence. Un autre exemple de la facon dont la culture Est de Montréal est différente de la culture East of New York City. Un autre exemple de comment le Canada est différente des États. Canada is not about shocking and awing, eh ?

Je me sentais comme j'étais avec les américains à cette fête. I did not feel like I was with urban New Yorkers, but I felt like I was with Americans. Bien sûr, I *was* with Americans. C'est encore l'Amérique au nord du 49e parallèle. C'est ne pas America, Inc. – mais, à certains facons, c'est l'Amérique, ltd.

Stafford, Qc
Le 9 juillet 2012, dimanche

« Never doubt citizens réflechis et déterminés »

Je garde une casserole et un bâton de tambour dans ma voiture – et aussi mon signe : *« Je Me Souviens* Democracy! *»* De cette facon, je suis prêt pour En Casserole. Malheureusement, aucune manifestations à Stafford pendant les trois dernières semaines. Les hommes, les femmes et les enfants qui marchent a rencontré le comportement odieux, le comportement laid, de certaines personnes qui vivent à Stafford, mais ne sont pas vraiment Staffordians. I have not participated in les manifestations for the past couple of weeks. Mais I am told that le carré rouge people were being cursed at, threatened, and told to, « get a job, » by a few people who actually live in Stafford, people who get their daily bread in the same places as their neighbors who wear the little red square above their hearts. This is sad. C'est très, très, très triste. It is sad that the little red square is a big red flag in the eyes of some.

Je pense que having a manifestation un fois par semaine à Stafford would be fantastique. Maintenant, pour le plupart, les manifestations sont en dormance au Québec. My understanding is that the big marches in Montréal et Québec are set for le 22e of every month. I believe that the biggest marches are yet to come, even if they are a few years away. Mais oui, comment dit-on, « You ain't seen nada yet, » en français ?

En tout cas, cet après-midi je conduisais à la rue Principale en Stafford sur mon chemin de Bromont, quand j'ai vu un groupe de Staffordians qui je connais d'En Casserole. C'était fantastique ! Je pouvais voir immédiatement que c'était un genre de manifestation.

Instead of driving to Bromont, I turned my car into the gazebo parking lot. Le manifestation était entre deux bâtiments à rue Principale – à l'espace entre l'immobilier et la boutique Partout Libre. Il y avait environ dix personnes du Carré Rouge là, tous les Staffordians je pense, and everyone was standing derrière le trottoir, so that they were not blocking pedestrians in any way. Comme polite ici comme les manifestants à Zuccotti Park, à Wall Street.

These Staffordians were doing street theatre, le genre que j'appelle, « guerilla theatre. » Il y avait un grand chiffon rouge sur le terre, couper pour être un carré. Four women were reposed in fetal positions on the four corners of the fabric, as if they were asleep. Patrick White jouait la mandoline. Un autre homme, a man I did not know, who was peut-être twenty-three or twenty-five years old, was reading out loud from a script that he held in his hands. Il a parlé en français, donc je n'ai compris pas très bien. Toutefois, I understood le sentiment. Charles Lussier, the anthropologist, était là, avec two of his children, et he was making a video of this demonstration, for the Internet. Il y avait un homme who was dressed as a clown. Je pouvais voir immédiatement que ce clown était une personne sérieuse, mais c'est un autre histoire. I recognized almost all of the faces there, and I had seen some of them vendredi soir at the birthday party that I went to on Mount Echo.

Les piétons qui marchent sur cette section du trottoir étaient touristes du dimanche. Most of them did not pause to watch the street theatre, mais a few did. J'ai regardé avec trois ou quatre autre personnes, alors que les femmes qui dorment sur le carré rouge, réveillés, un à la fois. Each of the women spoke short soliloquies, en français, bien sûr. I understood few of the words, bien sûr.

Pour moi, c'était comme ils étaient parlons au sujet what they had been dreaming, et then they began to talk to each other, but I did not understand the conversation. En tout cas, to me this theatre was a good way to declare, en public, that, that, that...*a Great Awakening is occurring, and it is a good thing, so if you want to step off the sidewalk (and get off your ass) and join us: Bienvenue.*

J'ai regardé très attentivement, et j'ai écouté très attentivement. Encore, pour le plupart, les touristes et the townspeople who walked by, or drove by, did not care to pay much attention. In this way, they were acting similar to many of the pedestrians I saw at the Occupy Wall Street demonstration in Times

Square, in September. Seules quelques personnes s'est arrêté, ou faites une pause, pendant leurs voyages à Stafford. Mais j'étais captivé par ce drame. Most American middle class would dismiss these people as harmless oddballs, spending a beautiful Sunday afternoon in a very odd way. But I could see that these women and these men were very socially-conscious, and committed heart and soul to acting for social change. Oui, avec leurs cœurs et leurs âmes. This is what I felt in the energy they transmitted. C'était très puissant et très jolie. What they radiated was *quèkchose*. Mon dieu, the smoke from their fire got in my eyes, and actually brought tears. It was a peak experience, une expérience de pointe rapide pour moi, si vous voyez ce que je veux dire.

Après the performance, which also included the singing of songs by Woody Guthrie, and Bob Dylan, the group began walking to another spot, à la parc derrière l'Ultramar, faire guerilla theatre encore, une fois de plus. Je suis allé avec eux, et le long du chemin Patrick White me présenta à des personnes qui je ne connaissais pas. Toutes les bodhisattvas, menschen, people of a higher class than taber billionaires.

J'étais presque le seul publique pour le deuxième spectacle. Très peu de gens utilisaient le trottoir là. Some of the cars that drove past us slowed up, and some people who realized that it was un Carré Rouge demonstration shouted out or gave a thumbs-up to show they approved.

Il y a un nombre égal de francophones et anglophones qui vivent à Stafford, mais I did not hear any words of approval in English. Pas un mot de l'approbation en anglais. Pas une seule ! En tout cas, c'est une autre histoire.

Après le deuxième spectacle, j'étais invité pour aller avec tout le monde, pour parteger le dîner. I was invited by the clown – his name is Richard Doucet – who spoke to me en anglais, avec un accent français. J'étais honoré d'être invité, et j'ai accepté.

Chez Richard est à rue Southern, just over the railroad tracks, près de La Cascade. Richard et trois ou quatre personnes qu'ont participé à la manifestation vivent dans des appartements dans cette grande maison. Le dîner était un pique-nique. Tout le monde sat on le carré rouge chiffon ou autour le carré rouge. We ate Ignazio Silone bread, wine, cheese, fruits et raw vegetables. There was also a bag of Tostitios sur le chiffon carré rouge. Ce que était plus

224

incongru, les Tostitos ou moi – l'anglophone de l'États ? Mais, comprenez-moi bien, je me sentais accueilli dans le cercle d'amis. Mais oui, I could not have felt more welcomed by tout monde.

Je suppose qu'il y avait une quinzaine de personnes là, y compris trois petits garçons et une fille de bébé. I could not tell who the parents of the children were, because presque everyone was taking care of the children as if they were their own children. Telles beaux enfants. Angélique.

Je pense que tout le monde avait bons sentiments au sujet le théâtre de rue. Quelquefois, to awaken people it may be necessary to bang on pots. Quelquefois c'est nécessaire pour réveiller les gens doucement. Today they sought to awaken people in a gentle way, without arousing a violent reaction. Ca fait partie de la transition vers l'âge de Gaia.

Tout le monde est resté pendant environ une heure. La dernière partie de l'histoire est peut-être la meilleure partie de l'histoire...

Richard, le clown, m'a demandé de rester après que tout le monde a quitté, parce qu'il voulait me parler. I was happy to accept this invitation, parce que je sentais un lien avec Richard. Après tout le monde a quitté, we sat outside, at a table next to the door of his apartment, which is on the ground floor and in the rear of the house. Il m'a demandé en anglais se il devrait se exprimer en français ou en anglais. J'ai dit, « Speak with me avec un mélange de français et anglais, mais pour le plupart en anglais. Mon français est très, très, très mauvais. Je suis désolé, j'essaie converser en français, toutefois c'est très difficile pour moi. »

Richard a dit, « This is not a problem. I can speak to you in English. I will speak to you with short phrases. But I will speak to you about the large ideas, about les paradigmes. » His pronounciation of the words in English was good, but I could tell that he was not in the habit of speaking en anglais.

Richard eu mon attention, mais lorsque les mots suivantes sont sortis de sa bouche je suis presque tombé hors de ma chaise. Il a dit, « I have a belief, since meeting you today, that the most important thing for me to talk to you about is synchronicity. »

Plutôt que de tomber de ma chaise, qu'était un tabouret haut, je me suis levé. J'ai dit, « *Quoi ?* Synchronicity? C'est incroyable ! I have friends who call me, 'Monsieur Sychronicité.' Do you know about me from my friends in Stafford ? »

Il a dit, « No, I did not know anything about you, Mario-Jacques. I do not think I met you before today, unless we passed each other by the poste, or at Café Dumont, or the IGA. »

Je ne crois pas que j'ai jamais vu Richard, avant ce jour. Probablement I would remember, parce que Richard is someone I would notice because of his striking head of red hair et Québec bleu eyes.

En tout cas, j'étais très, très, très intéressé à entendre ce que Richard voulait me dire. If I tried to convey in writing, in this diary, what he said to me, it would probably take me several days to do this. Et je ne serais pas capable de rendre justice à la profondity de ses pensées, et l'éloquence simple de ses mots.

Il s'est référé à la célèbre citation de Margaret Mead : « Never doubt that a small group of thoughtful commited citizens can change the world. Indeed, it is the only thing that ever has. »

En réponse, j'ai dit à Richard que la citation de Margaret Mead est un favori de moi, et que j'avais lu ces mots à le dernier jour ou deux. Après que je suis allé à la maison, j'ai réalisé que ces mots sont sur un signet que j'utilise.

J'ai dit à Richard : « Toutes les armées du monde ne sont pas fortes comme un idée dont temps est ici, maintenant. » Je pouvais voir dans son expression qu'il ne me comprenait pas. J'ai ajouté, « Tu ne comprends pas ? It must be my Brooklyn accent. » Ensuite, j'ai essaié encore, en franglais : « Toutes les armées...all the armies in the world...ne sont pas fortes...are not as strong...comme un idée whose time has arrived. »

Bien sûr, Richard savait cette citation de Victor Hugo. Il m'a dit, en réponse, « Yes, Mario-Jacques. The words of Victor Hugo are true. We know about this power from the stories of Victor Hugo, and we know about this power from the story of Jesus Christ. He lived in a town that was smaller than Stafford. »

Nous avons marqué une pause après que Richard a parlé ces mots. Nous tous les deux mettre un petit morceau de pain dans notre bouches et prit une petite gorgée de nos vins, comme si nous étions improvisation un rituel. We were in communion, bien sûr.

Comme j'ai dit, Richard a une abondance de cheveux roux. Encore, c'était peigné au côté, comme un clown de cirque. His blue clown's nose, attached to an elastic band, was pulled down around his neck, with the mala he wore. Je pouvais voir qu'il ne était pas un vrai clown. Richard est plus serieux que Pagliacci. Richard a dit, « There is much I want to talk to you about Mario-Jacques. But for today I only want to say a few things to you, and I want to give you something to read. »

Il a parlé à moi pendant quelques minutes, pas plus de cinq minutes, au sujet la Grande Charte de 1215 et the need for a new Magna Carta. Ensuite il m'a donné un pamphlet de 30 pages intitulée : « *La Grande Charte 2012...Penser, agir, vivre autrement en démocratie au Québec.* »

I asked Richard to translate « agir » et « vivre autrement » for me. Ensuite, j'ai ouvert le pamphlet à une page au hasard. C'était toute en français, mais I recognised the words of Gandhi, even en français : « *Nous devons être le changement que nous voulons voir dans le monde.* » Encore, synchonicité. While I was sitting with Richard, the words of Victor Hugo, Margaret Mead and Gandhi were quoted. I have two bookmarkers in books on my night table. One shows the same Margaret Mead quote and the other shows the same Gandhi quote, both en anglais. Elles sont les seules citations sur les signets. Et le citation d'Hugo ? It is framed in my guest room.

Je pense que Richard was right when he said he had a strong sense that he needed to talk to me about synchronicity.

When it was time for good-bye et à la prochaine, we hugged et a dit : « Namasté.»

For now, I can only say, « to be continued, » et je pense que il y a beaucoup à être continué avec Richard et les gens du carré rouge.

Encore, à suivre.

Stafford, Qc
Le 4 août 2012, samedi

« *Parlez Bleu* »

Comme j'écris ceci, c'est samedi matin. Il y a environ une demi-heure, j'étais lu un histoire, in the on-line version of *The*

Montreal Gazette. Le gros titre de l'histoire était : « *Parti Québécois leader Pauline Marois says 'non' to English-language election debate.* »

Mon question est : Is it not possible, *pas possible*, pour les francophones et les anglophones, to be in the same room at the same time, and speak as equals? Mais oui, la même salle à la même temps, et parler dans une manière c'est égal ?

What can francophones et anglophones faire ensemble ? *This* should be la question la plus importante in la politique du Québéc. La réponse ne peut pas être simplement: commettre le génocide culturel.

Pour parler on equal terms, d'égal à égal, est possible. Non ?

Je pense que c'est necessaire pour les anglophones de *parlez bleu*, parlez français. Peut-être this is what Pauline Marois a besoin à dire aux anglophones. The anglophones are not going to vote for her anyway. Mais so many of the francophones et le bilingue doivent se réveiller et de sentir les fleurs. C'est 35 ans après le Loi 101, et c'est necessaire d'avoir le debat en anglais ? The English language is being protected very well by Law 101, isn't it?

Stafford, Qc
Le 8 août 2012

« La calme avant la tempête »

This summer it has been très, très, très tranquille à Stafford. Je pense que c'est la calme avant la tempête.

Quand l'été a commencé, En Casserole – les manifestations du carré rouge – étaient fortes. Mais maintenant, les manifestations dans Stafford sont dormantes. Toutefois, les manifestations sont dormantes presque partout du Québec. Ici à Stafford, le groupe du carré rouge will be doing théâtre de rue, je pense.

Aussi, je pense que les élections au Québec sont le centre d'attention maintenant. J'aimerais que le Parti Québécois à gagner, bien sûr, mais qui sait ? I can see that les anglophones will vote for Charest, even though they do not really want him. I have heard Anglophones say they think he is the lesser of evils. Fear of separation, les Anglophones sont dans un relationship symbiotique avec leur leaders. En tout cas, anything can happen dans les prochaines semaines.

There is a candidate for Parti Québécois who lives over in Sutton, named Richard Leclerc. Si j'organise Parti Québécois Américain, we could endorse him. Je doute que the endorsement de PQA will aide beaucoup Monsieur Leclerc, mais qui sait ?

Les politiques sont très, très, très importantes. Nous avons besoin de nouveaux systèmes des politiques...et de nouveaux systèmes sociaux, et nouveaux systèmes spritules. Nous avons besoin de nouveaux systemes, ou : we dead. We need the world to be turned upside down.

Mais oui, je crois que : toutes les armèes du monde ne sont pas aussi fortes que l'idée dont l'heure est arrivée. Maintenant, il y a beaucoup d'idées dont l'heure est arrivée. Ici, à Stafford, au centre de l'univers, Staffordians are changing the world. Comment ? If you ask a Staffordian how, she would answer : "By meditating."

Et maintenant, je vais méditer.

Stafford, Qc
Le 9 août 2012

« Nous avons besoin de plus anglophones séparatistes »

Cet après-midi, I stopped at Tête de l'Ordinateur, a.k.a Susan Computer. There was an Anglophone woman there, named Linda, qu'était, *ranting*, au sujet les élections. She is worried that Parti Québécois is going to win a majority September 4, and that will mean that there will be un autre référendum, et peut-être que le Québec se sépare, before she can move to New Brunswick, ou Acapulco. Je pense Linda has made a religion out of being an anglophone. I did not say this to her, but I said, « Yo Linda, you and

Susan are *tellement* anglophone. You more anglophone than an apostrophe, girl! »

Elle a répondu, « Thank you for the compliment. I *am* an anglophone, you know. And can you tell me, Mister A-mer-eeee-québécois... talking about apostrophes...why is it that Tim Hortons is not allowed to use an apostrophe, but McDonalds can ? Tim Hortons should paint apostrophes on all their signs tomorrow, and take it to the Supreme Court in Ottawa. »

J'ai dit, « I don't think McDonalds should be permitted to use an apostrophe in Québec, either. »

Susan jumped in et elle a dit, « What have you got against this punctuation? I suppose you want Paddy O'Brien to take the apostrophe out of his name, too? »

J'ai dit, « No, Paddy O'Brien is a human being. He has the right to his name. Tabernouche McDonalds ! You know what Susan, from now on, whenever I write, « McDonalds » I'm going to write it without the apostrophe. *Sans* apostrophe ! Another way for me to be the change I want to see in the world. »

Elle a dit, « If Parti Québécois had their way, McDonalds would have to take the apostrophe off their name in Québec, or they would be nationalized. »

I did not know if she was kidding. It's difficult for me to know sometimes when Susan is being serious or joking. Mais j'ai dit, « C'est une bonne idée, c'est une bonne idée ! J'aime ca ! Nationalize McDonalds if they don't take the apostrophe out of their name in Québec. And make them pay an additional tax for all the garbage they generate. Vingt-deux pour cent of all the trash on all the roads in Québec consists of tabernouche McDonalds wrappers. Forgive me, if I exaggerate un peu, mais pas trops, en substance. »

Susan a dit, « You're making me hungry talking about McDonalds, and I haven't had lunch yet. »

Puis, nous avons parlé au sujet les élections. Susan m'a dit que maintenant Coalition Avenir Québec, CAQ, will have un site Web en anglais. J'ai dit, « This is coincidental. Chè pas if I would call it, 'synchronistic,' mais peut-être. I went to the Parti Québécois website the other day, and I could not find a way to translate to anglais, without going through a lengthy process. I think PQ should reach out to anglophones more. »

Susan a répondu, « Keep dreaming, Mario-Jacques. PQ is not going to reach out to anglophones, and anglophones don't want them to reach out. You might find a couple of anglophone artists in Stafford who would vote for PQ, but that's all you're going to find. »

J'ai dit, « If I could vote, I would vote PQ. En fait, I am thinking about organizing PQA, Parti Québécois Américain, and then PQA would endorse candidates in Québec. » I was joking about organizing such a party, mais I wanted to make a point.

She did not comment au sujet PQA, toutefois Susan m'a dit qu'elle a pensé que je pouvais voter. J'ai dit à elle, « Quoi ? Quoi, quoi, quoi, quoi ? Tu pense que, I should be able to vote in Québec, even though I am not a citizen? I can't believe how many people who live in Québec have said this to me ! Why should I be able to vote in Québec ? I don't hold dual citizenship. »

Elle a dit, « You own property here, you are a homeowner. If I was a homeowner in Guatemala, I would want to be able to vote there, because I would be investing my hard-earned money there. » Je ne sais pas, peut-être Susan plaisantait ?

J'ai dit, « You know, two years ago in the states the Supreme Court ruled that the corporations could donate as many billions of dollars as they wanted to political campaigns. Google, "Citizens United," Susan. The Supreme Court ruled that corporations have the inalienable right to free speech, as if they are human beings. Good one, eh ? I don't think corporations are human. I don't think corporations are human when they are *conceived*, I don't think corporations are human in the *fetal stage*, and I don't think corporations are human after they are *born* – if we can use the word "born" to refer to the date on which a corporation gets certified by the state. My point is, the United States Supreme Court is allowing *money* to rule – and if you give people the right to vote simply because they own property in a country, it is just another way to allow money to rule. »

Susan a dit, « Money is always going to rule, Mario. It has been that way since the beginning of time, and it will be that way until the end of time. »

Bien sûr, Susan Computer's middle name est : Cynique. C'est la seule chose de Susan qu'est français.

Susan says she is moving out of Québec even if PQ does not win a majority on September 4. If she moves, this would be a loss for Québec, and for Stafford. Susan est cool. Le cœur d'un vrai Staffordian bat en elle. Je pense que peut-être Susan deviendra un séparatiste. Peut-être. Peut-être quand le ciel est plus bleu.

Stafford, Qc
Le 22 août 2012

« Une bonne journée, I meet Gabriel Nadeau-Dubois »

Cet aprè-midi je suis allé à Montréal pour participer à la manifestation du Carré Rouge. J'ai pensé que la manifestation was going to be ce soir. Mais I found out at the last minute, vers 12h, que la manifestation would be à Montréal à 14h.

Trois ou quatre femmes qui participents toujours dans les manifestations En Casseroles à Stafford were going à Montréal pour le manifestation du Carré Rouge. Mais, I could not go with them, parce que I did not find out that they were meeting at l'IGA à 12h, jusqu'a 11h45m. I had to take a shower, jump dans ma voiture, get on the 10, and shoot into Montréal, avant de 14h.

Cosette Lafreniere m'a dit que le groupe de Stafford would be at the parc proche de la station métro de Victoria, au coin de rue Peel, vers 14h. Je ne sais pas comment, mais I got to le parc vers 14h30m. There were thousands of people there, pour le plupart les étudiantes de l'université, mais aussi les autres, comme moi-même.

Bien sûr, j'ai eu mon pancarte, « *Je Me Souviens* Democracy! » I wore my carré rouge made from red duct tape on my t-shirt. And under le carré rouge I wore mon bouton, qui dit : « Occupy this moment. » Which I bought in New York City when I marched there a few months ago, for the May Day demonstration.

I have carried my sign, « *Je Me Souviens* Democracy! » au moins six fois à New York City, for the Occupy Wall Street demonstrations là, et a few times in Stafford sur rue Principal, for the En Casserole demonstrations, et à Montréal deux ou trois fois, pour les manifestations du Carré Rouge. This sign is holding up. C'est un bon signe, in more ways than one.

Tandis que j'ai cherché pour mes amis Staffordians, j'ai rencontré Gabriel Nadeau-Dubois ! Oui, I met Gabriel Nadeau-Dubois, par hasard. Je ne sais pas how it came to be que mon chemin a traversé le chemin de Gabriel, au même l'instant précisément, but it happened.

I have enormous respect for what Gabriel Nadeau-Dubois has done as one of the three leaders of the student strike and the Carré Rouge demonstrations. I have read in feature stories and in newspaper columns that many people in Québec believe that Gabriel Nadeau-Dubois is on his way to becoming le Premier ministre du Québec, in the years to come. C'est incroyable, that this is projected by so many people at this time, considering that Gabriel Nadeau-Dubois is quite young – très, très jeune – environ 22 ou 23 ans, je pense. C'est facile pour moi d'imaginer Gabriel comme le Premier ministre, toutefois à présent c'est même plus facile pour moi d'imaginer la jeune militante Martine Desjardins comme le leader d'un nouveau pays. Because it is women who will lead us to a better future, if there is to be a better future. En tout cas…

The parc was packed, mais j'ai trouvé une place on the grass qu'était ouvert. I practically bumped into Gabriel, who was standing next to an older man, who was sitting on the grass. J'ai reconnu son visage, mais j'ai dit : « Excusez-moi. Leo ? » Bien sûr, Leo Bureau-Blouin est au autre chef étudiant. It was like meeting John Lennon on the street and saying, « Mick Jagger ? » Ou peut-être c'était comme j'ai rencontré Fidel Castro dans la rue et j'ai dit : « Che ? » Yikes.

The thing is, I was thinking about becoming un bénévole, peut-être volunteer pour un journée, for Leo Bureau-Blouin, who is running for an office in a riding not far de Montréal. J'espérais que je pourrais rencontrer Leo, et inviter Leo à Long Island, to speak at Suffolk County Community College. Donc, Leo Bureau-Blouin was on my mind quand j'ai vu Gabriel Nadeau-Dubois, je suppose. En tout cas, j'ai parlé avec Gabriel pour environ trois minutes et puis quelqu'un est venu avec une caméra de télévision et Gabriel shook my hand and said he had to go. Ensuite, a small crowd gathered around Gabriel as he was being interviewed.

C'était très, très, très chaud. Cuba dans Québec. Après le printemps d'érable, c'est un peu de Cuba qu'est venu au Québec pour l'été, in more ways than one.

Lorsque tout le monde a commencé à marcher, je debout sur un mur, avec ma signe au-dessus de ma tête. Environ vingt minutes plus tard, mes amis de Stafford m'a vu, donc I jumped down from the wall to march with them. We should have carried a banner that read : « Carré Rouge Stafford. » Je me demande combien de villes du Québec étaient représentées lors de la manifestation. Les étudiants sont de Montréal, et du Québec, la ville et la pronvince. La jeunesse du Québec, particulièrement la jeunesse francophone du Québec, étaient unis.

Nous marchions derrière un grand groupe de personnes, des centaines, qu'ont porté la bannière de Québec Solidaire, et devant un petit contingent des professeurs du CÉGEP Édouard-Montpetit. Tandis que we walked, the five of us from Stafford conversed a lot with the people marching for Québec Solidaire and with the professors from Édouard-Montpetit. Nouveaux amis, coming to Stafford soon. Je pense que certains deviendront Staffordians. Je ne sais pas pourquoi je dis cela, mais je pense.

For a short time, moins de deux minutes, we also walked with two young women who were topless, save for small pieces of strategically-placed red duct tape on their breasts. Nous démontrons notre engagement de différentes manières, non ? Je n'ai voit pas personne reluquer ces femmes. Leur declaration était plus des politiques que sexuelle. Bien sûr, le sexuelle est des politiques également.

Nous avons marché pour pendant deux heures. Cette marche n'avaient pas l'energie énorme des autres marches du 22e jour du mai, mais c'était une démonstration que les gens seront prêts à retourner dans la rue, si un bien meilleur gouvernement n'est pas créé par les élections le 4 septembre. Je pense que the world is changing before my eyes.

As Paddy O'Brien likes to remind me : Pay attention, everything is connected, everything changes.

À suivre.

Stafford, Qc
Le 23 août 2012

« Une lettre to an anglophone newspaper »

Hier soir, avant de je suis allé bon dodo, j'ai décidé d'écrire une lettre à l'éditeur d'un journal anglophone. Je ne sais pas qui anglophone newspaper I might send this to, mais voici la lettre que j'espère sera publié :

"Dear Editor,
I live about half the time in the states and half the time in the townships. As I see it, as an amériquébécois, the coming elections in Québec will affect the future of the world. And Québec will change the world for the better if Québec votes to make itself as different as possible from the country in which I am a citizen : USA Incorporated.

In a world in which the richest 1% are getting richer, and the other 99% are getting poorer, Québec can create a new kind of nation – one which is not of the rich, by the rich, for the rich. Unlike Québec, the rest of Canada is lost in a 20th century American dream turned nightmare – adopting the fantasy that filthy rich people and their soul-less corporations will create a better world.
Mario-Jacques
Stafford, Qc."

Stafford, Qc
Le 24 août 2012
« Une lettre à un journal francophone »

J'ai décidé d'envoyer une autre lettre d'éditeur. Cette fois ma lettre est en français. I wanted my french to be correct, donc j'ai demandé Monique Marois à traduire ma lettre de l'anglais à français.
Voici la lettre :
« Je pense que le Québec changera le monde pour le mieux s'il vote de façon à se démarquer le plus possible du pays dont je suis citoyen, les États-Unis Incorporés. C'est mon espoir que le Québec forme bientôt une nouvelle sorte de gouvernement : un

gouvernement du peuple, par le peuple, pour le peuple. Au lieu de suivre le modèle d'une pseudo démocratie dans États-Unis, où les 400 personnes les plus riches ont accumulé des fortunes que sont supérieur à celle des 150 millions les plus pauvres gens, le Québec peut créer un modèle que les Américains pourront suivre. »

    Sais pas où I will send this. Peut-être *Le Guide* ? Peut-être *Le Voix de l'Est* ? Peut-être *Le Devoir* ?!

    À suivre.

Stafford, Qc
Le 22 septembre 2012, vendredi

« Chit »

    Aujourd'hui j'ai reçu un courriel de Eliot Mason. He is going to start publishing a literary magazine in the townships this fall, et il y a environ un mois, he asked me if I might be interested in contributing a piece. Je l'ai dit que je voudrais écrire quelque chose, mais j'aimerais écrire en français, si possible. Bien sûr, j'écris français comme un gringo, mais je pense que je peux écrire quelque chose en français si j'écris phrases simples, et si je les garder courte.

    Eliot a dit que le journal aura des contributions en français et en anglais, mais pour le plupart en français, parce que la plupart des lecteurs sera francophones. Eniway, il a dit que je pourrais écrire quelque chose en français, si la grammaire est presque correcte, et si je voudrais écrire quelque chose dans le futur en anglais.

    J'ai dit: "Okeh." I told Eliot que peut-être I will write quekchose for the literary magazine in the future. Mais oui, toutefois, "in AMERICAN(!) English – the language of Mark Twain, Kerouac and Shakespeare." Eliot appreciated my attempt to be humorous, je pense.

    Eliot a dit que, he would need to edit mon français. I am a little concerned about how much he would edit what I write, alors j'ai dit que I would give him quelque chose that would need very little editing, probablement. Clean up la grammaire, if he wants to do so. Et j'ai dit que he does not have to print what I give him and I would understand.

The deadline for the piece will be le 10 octobre. 650 mots. Et il a dit que je devrais écrire quelque chose sur exubérance. Fiction ou pas fiction. Je suis exubérante à écrire à propos d'exhubérance. I sent une autre courriel to Eliot this afternoon, to tell him that I would send him quelque chose sur l'exhubérance avant le 10 novembre.

Quand il était entre chien et loup, je suis allé l'IGA, acheter le lait et les œufs. Dans le stationnement d'IGA, j'ai rencontré un de mes amis en Casserole, Jean-Carol. La dernière fois que j'ai vu Jean-Carol était à la manifestation à Montréal, le 22 août. Jean-Carol parle pour le plupart en français. J'ai essaié de parler en français à Jean-Carol, mais I could not find the words in French to communicate adequately with him. Tant pis pour nous, moi en particulier.

J'ai essayé de parler en français sur les politiques des États, mais il n'était pas bon. Nous avons conversé un peu, mais je n'était pas sûr si Jean-Carol a compris ce que je disais au sujet de Romney, et quoi Romney a dit au sujet de « 47%. » Ensuite, voila Eliot Mason ! This was quite a coincidence, parce que Eliot does not come to Stafford very often. Il est très, très, très rare pour Eliot aller à l'IGA à Stafford. C'était ma chance. Eliot est parfaitement bilingue. Donc, Eliot did translations, and as it turned out, Jean-Carol knew all about the 47% issue and Romney being caught by a hidden camera, but I guess mon français est encore si mauvais que he did not understand what I was saying. Chit.

East End Bay, NY
Le 4 octobre 2012, jeudi

« Obama/Romney débâcle débat »

Yesterday night was a bad night. Barack Obama and Mitt Romney debated. Romney was at his best, Barack at his worst. Romney clearly won the debate. Only a sociopath or a grand master of deceit can lie and reverse his positions as Romney did last night, without blinking an eye, non ? Why Barack was not up to the challenge of exposing the lies, je ne sais pas. Peut-être he was stunned by the magnitude of Romney's willingness to be unethical.

Today, the unthinkable – that Mitt Romney will succeed Barack Obama as President of the United States – is far more possible than it was yesterday. Mais oui, yesterday night was a nightmare, un vrai cauchemar. J'ai besoin de méditer.

East End Bay, NY
Le 8 octobre 2012, lundi

« Dial 800 for Free Miracle Spring Water »

Yesterday night I got up from bed environ 2h parce que I was not sleeping. I went to the couch and turned on the television, which is my sleeping pill of choice when I am in the states, on Long Island. I turned off the lights, closed my eyes, and kept the volume low on the TV, so that I could barely hear it. Seemed like most of the 181 stations were playing info-mercials so I just used la télécommande to pick one at random. It turned out to be an infomercial by some kind of kooky minister selling: "Free Miracle Spring Water." Even with the volume set extremely low on the TV, I could not help but open my eyes to watch this lunatic minister, a man who immediately struck me, by what he was saying and how he was saying it, as someone just as patently dishonest and as spiritually bankrupt as Mitt Romney. With a straight face and sometimes with a pasted-on Romney smile, this old white man with black ink hair was telling story after story about people who have called the 800 number flashing on the screen to get: "Free Miracle Spring Water."

Mais oui, all you have to do is call an 800 number and God will step into your life. Call the 800 number and God will cure your cancer, your diabetes, your heart disease, your paralysis, your poverty. There seemed to be testimonials for everything but cures for mental illness and religious fanaticism.

This was not a cheap infomercial, but a rather elaborate production, showing testimonials from people all over North America. Including people who claim to have used this Free Miracle Spring Water as directed – by splashing it on their foreheads, or doorways, or check books – and then experiencing miracle cures, or

238

having great sums of money bestowed upon them. Encore, all they had to do was call the 800 number.

I actually watched this crap for about a half-hour. Trickle-down-from-God-within-the-trickle-down-from-the-rich-free-enterprise-system Free Miracle Spring Water. I just hope that the people who are calling this 800 number are not a substantial part of the population in this country who are still undecided about voting for Barack or Romney.

I finally changed the station, and the next channel was playing an infomercial for: "Free No Evil Oil." The minister in this infomercial looked straight into the camera, with a sociopathic straight face, and said something like: "God just told me that great miracles will come to the next 288 people who call the 800 number for Free No Evil Water."

Why is it that people can advertise on television that they have holy water which will cure cancer, diabetes, paralysis? If they did not say it was *holy water* – if they said it was just *water,* unadulterated H2O, it would be illegal to make such a claim. This is how Freedom of Religion has been transformed in the United States of America, Incorporated.

East End Bay, NY
Le 13 octobre 2012, samedi

« *Calendrier Maya, Fiscal Year* »

Déjà, le 13 octobre deux mille douze. How many more days is it from now until December 21, 2012? Je ne pense pas que je suis prêt a compter les jours. Pas encore.

The Mayan calendar, si c'est correct, sur le 21 décembre deux mille douze the world as we know it will come to an end. Ce que cela signifie, exactement, je ne sais pas. Peut-être inukshuks seront érigées où il ya des croix.

Aujourd'hui the sun still shines. The 99-cent stores and Walmart and all the corporate stores have been selling their Christmas crap since September, if not earlier. They do not believe the Mayan calendar is correct. For them, the Mayan calendar can go « F » itself. As they see it, there is only one calendar that matters:

The Holy Sacred Corporate Calendar Of The Fiscal Year. For those who worship The Almighty Dollar, only The Holy Sacred Corporate Calendar Of The Fiscal Year marks the dates when prophecy is manifested or not.

Je sais qu'il ya quelque chose comme de vingt jours jusqu'au 6 novembre, Election Day. Anything, good or bad, can happen between now and then. Maybe, peut-être, there are enough people out there who will decide not to vote to make the rich richer. En même temps, there are also people out there, sans aucun doute, who believe they would be serving their God to assassinate Barack Obama.

Mardi soir sera le deuxième débat entre Barack et Shit Romney. The debate will occur not far from where I sit at this moment – which is a drive of perhaps an hour by car, in normal, horrible, Long Island traffic to Hofstra University. Je ne sais pas qui va gagner le débat, whatever "winning" means, mais je suis certain Barack va continuer à suivre un chemin du coeur. Barack will stand for moving forward, and Romney will stand for whatever he thinks he needs to stand for to win the election.

Maintenant, je suis essayer de rester dans le présent. Dans le moment présent, le soleil brille.

Stafford, Qc
Le 27 octobre 2012, samedi

« Exubérance en pause, Hurricane Sandy à venir »

Je suis à Stafford pour quelques jours. C'est une bonne chose, parce que j'ai besoin distance de les États-Unis. They are talking about Hurricane Sandy hitting Long Island – actually, the East Coast – on Monday or Tuesday, so I am going to have to drive back tomorrow, probablement. Lundi, je sera dans la tempête. J'espère que le temps de cette semaine ne pas un prélude à la semaine prochaine, à l'élection. Le karma n'est pas bon.

Eniway, au moins j'ai commencé à écrire pour Eliot sur « l'exubérance. » Voici ce que j'ai écrit, so far…

« L'Exx-uuu-bérance Amériquébécois »
Par Mario-Jacques

If there is anything I have exuberance about, it is le Québec, particulièrement la région des Appalaches, dans l'Estrie. Il ya énergie dans l'air des montagnes qui résonne en moi.

I am fortunate to have lived as I have lived, as a citizen of the United States, and now I am fortunate to live almost half the time in Québec. Maintenant, je m'appele un amériquébécois, and it is with exuberance that I call myself an amériquébécois.

I speak French with a Brooklyn accent et je parle français comme un gringo, souvent avec un mélange de français et d'anglais. Les francophones sont très patient avec moi. Quand je parle français aux anglophones, ils demandent quelquefois : « Why are you speaking French to me ? » Je réponds : « Je dois pratiquer mon français. C'est important. » Sometimes, when I say this, my anglophone friends look at me like I am trying to sell them the Brooklyn Bridge *and* le pont Champlain. Toutefois, mon exubérance d'essayer de parler le français n'est pas diminuée.

I have never been questioned by the language police as to why I speak or write as I do. Toutefois, si les autorités me demandent pourquoi je parle et j'écrire comme je le fais, je dirai simplement : « Parce que je suis un amériquébecois, et quoi je me sens pour le Québec est exx-uuu-bérance ! »

East End Bay, Long Island, NY
Le 2 novembre 2012, vendredi

"Hurricane Sandy a small taste of war"

The reality is still setting in, as to the enormity of the devastation caused by this storm. Hurricane Sandy has passed, but what remains to be faced are bigger challenges, that will not pass as fast as Sandy did. People are staying remarkably calm in certain ways, but the level of stress is increasing, and there are signs of real stress and panic   developing. There is not much food in the

241

supermarkets, among the markets that are open. Most everything is shut. Most people do not have electricity. I can write this only because I have some battery power left in my laptop. Some hospitals had to evacuate their patients to other hospitals. It is bad here on the East End of Long Island, but it is far worse in New York City and in New Jersey. Let me be the first of many, or perhaps the only, to draw a comparison between what is happening now and 9-11, in terms of Americans getting a small, a *miniscule taste*, of what it is like to be in a war zone where people suffer and must go without, albeit on a far greater scale. I have never been in the hell of a war zone, but this tastes like nothing I have ever tasted before.

Last night people waited on lines for six hours and more, to buy gas, which is being rationed in some places. Most white people would not wait this long to vote, eh? And today it is much more difficult to get gas than yesterday. At a gas station that I went to at 10:30 this morning, people were waiting in a line that was a half-mile long...and people kept getting on that line, even though the line was not moving...and without knowing when gas would be for sale. I spoke to some of the people on line after I parked my car behind them and while I was walking toward the gas station, to find out when they might be selling gas. I had to walk half-way to the gas station before I talked to someone on line who told me that workers at the gas station said they were expecting a delivery in another one to four hours. Wow, they expect white people to wait to buy gas as if they were black and latino people waiting to vote! This is the system of the 1%.

I went back to my car and drove home. I have an eighth of a tank left. Peut-être I will wait jusqu'a 3h ou 4h, et ensuite I will see if gas is available later.

East End Bay, NY
Le 3 novembre 2012, samedi

« *A small taste of poverty ici, et l'univers protège Stafford* »

Hier soir je suis allé pour le gaz après minuit et je ne pouvais pas trouver une station qu'était ouvert. Even after midnight, there were lines of cars a half-mile long at gas stations that had no gas. I went to Stop & Shop to buy needed groceries, and they were closed. Normalement, this store is open 24/7. How many babies do not have their formula or milk to drink? How many people are desperate for food, in what is supposed to be the land of plenty?

In Hoboken, New Jersey – the birthplace of Saint Frank Sinatra – there are still 20,000 people who are stranded in their houses and apartments, due to the floodwaters. Many have no electricity, no plumbing, no heat, little or no water to drink, and they have had little or no food for days.

The official death toll from this storm is already close to 100 people, but the final count is going to be higher, I am sure. Meanwhile, up until last night they were planning on going ahead with the New York City Marathon. C'est incroyable. Enfin, ils l'ont annulé.

This storm has also given many middle-class people a small taste of poverty, a *miniscule taste*, for the first time in their lives.

…Meanwhile, mes amis de Stafford have been sending me les courriels, de se demander comment ça va. Encore, les Staffordians me donner de l'énergie. I was concerned about how the storm may have affected Stafford. Shiva told me dans un courriel que l'univers protégé Stafford. Aussi, j'ai recu un courriel de Medicine Woman, et elle a dit : "What we talked about a few years ago is now coming to pass. If you do not feel safe there, come to Stafford now. You will be safe here le 21 décembre."

East End Bay, NY
Le 10 novembre 2012, samedi

« *Election Day fini, maintenant le 21 décembre 2012* »

It has been four days since Barack Obama was re-elected. Four days since the planet tilted on its axis in a way that was measurable. Même avant les élections, la réalité semble différente. Le changement de la réalité a commencé avec Hurricane Sandy, la semaine dernière. Mais oui, first it was Hurricane Sandy, but the culmination was on Election Day, or the night of the election, proche de minuit New York time, when Barack Obama was declared the winner, le Président encore.

Aujourd'hui, j'ai recu des courriels de Shiva et Monique Kassem. They were having breakfast ensemble at le Café Dumont and both of them sent short emails to me, which they wrote en anglais, even though les deux sont francophones.

Shiva a écrit : « Bonjour Mario-Jacques ! Ça va ? I am with Monique at Dumont. We talk about the Universe sent Sandy for acceleration of le changement. It was good that people were brought together by this, non? Knowing we are not alone helps us to remember who we are. Be grounded in your body. Be présent. Namasté, Shiva. »

Monique a écrit : « Allô Mario-Jacques. Ça va ? Ça va. Félicitations ! Obama is four more years the president of the world ! One voice, one people, one earth. Namasté, Monique. »

Now that the election is over, my thoughts are turning to December 21, 2012. I returned their emails, and I wrote en français, avec l'aide du traducteur Google. In my emails, I asked both of them the same question : « Il y aura un rassemblement de quelque sorte dans Stafford le 21 décembre 2012 ? »

Je ne suis pas certain ce que Shiva et Monique croire. Peut-être they believe 2012 marks a turning point, or peut-être they believe it is the end and only those who move to another dimension will be saved.

We shall see what we shall see.

East End Bay, NY
Le 22 novembre 2012, Thanksgiving Day

« *Thanksgiving Day : Merci de donner ?* »

Audjourd'hui est « Thanksgiving Day » aux États-Unis. As far as I am concerned, U.S.A Inc. is a nation that honors selling more than giving, alors maintenant Thanksgiving est Le Jour – mais oui, THE DAY, Le Jour avec lettres capitales – que debut le shopping de Noel. Ce soir, à 20h, Walmart will be open for business. Macy's will be open at 21h. These are the two largest department stores in U.S.A Inc., and in North America. Many of the large corporate stores will be open tonight. More than at any other time in the history of Thanksgiving in the states, Thanksgiving Day 2012 is about working and shopping, not giving.

*Work and shop, work and shop, work and shop. Gotta shop, gotta shop, gotta shop; Gotta buy new, gotta buy new, gotta buy new; No more old, no more old; Stand on line, pay the price; Stand on line, pay the price; No more money, no more money, no more money...Credit card, credit card, credit card...*It's a bad jam.

Mais oui. Leave your family to work or shop at Walmart or Macy's, or some other corporate store, on the most important American family holiday. Shop at Macy's or Walmart on the most important American family holiday, so that you can buy their crap in the name of celebrating the most religious of holidays in this so-called Christian nation.

In the parking lots of these great American stores there will be many thousands of cars with bumper stickers that say : « *Keep Christ in Christmas.* » Je pense que if you can go to war in the name of Christ, there is no problem in going shopping in the name of Christ. Mais oui, pay attention, everything is connected.

Stafford, Qc
Le 21 décembre 2012, vendredi

« Bon Vendredi »

C'est ici. Le moment présent. Aujourd'hui est le jour que tout le monde a été d'attente. La fin du monde. And even though the world is coming to an end today, it feels like an ordinary day.

C'est avant l'aube. Pendant que j'écris ce, je regarde par la fenêtre. Je regarde vers les montagnes au-delà de la vallée. Je vois beaucoup de lumières éparpilleés sur les montagnes. Ce que je vois

245

ressemble les feux de camp, des gens intelligents préhistoriques. J'aime cette vue.

Dans le centre de la chaîne de montagnes, comme je le vois de ma fenêtre, les lumières rouges de la tour relai cyberespace flash sur et en dehors. Le tour de relais se tient si haut au-dessus des arbres les plus hauts sur les plus hautes montagnes. Il n'est plus les églises qui se tiennent le plus haut au Québec, ce sont les tours de communication.

Stafford, Qc
Le 22 décembre 2012, samedi

« Sur l'Avènement Atlas Shrugged »

Il est maintenant. Le toujours présent présent. Selon la réalité consensuelle, selon le calendrier grégorien, c'est un moment dans le 22 décembre 2012.

As I write these words, it is before dawn, on the dawning day of The New World.

C'est avant l'aube, et c'est seulement quelques heures avant l'Avènement. L'avènement de la Nouvelle Terre. Will new calendars – next year, or in years to come – note the 22nd of December as the day of Advent?

Hier soir, un monde a terminé et un autre monde est venu à l'existence. Et, comme Shiva m'a dit hier soir : « This new existence is lighter. » Maintenant, dans le moment présent, je me sens plus léger. Je me sens comme Atlas a haussé les épaules. Mais oui, Atlas has shrugged.

Si des milliers de gens s'étaient rassemblées à Stafford, et ont convergé sur le Mont Stafford hier soir, je n'aurais pas été surpris. Mais la naissance de la Nouvelle Terre a été célébré tranquillement, dans de petits rassemblements tout au long de Stafford.

Je ne savais pas où je serais hier soir, mais je savais que je voulais être ici, à Stafford. Merlin et Gwen m'invita à leur ferme, à participer dans une cérémonie Abenaki/Druide, mené par Medicine Woman. Since it was Medicine Woman who had prophesized to me four years ago that I was destined to be here on December 21, 2012, I felt drawn to accepting the invitation from Merlin and Gwen. En même temps, je voulais être avec Shiva et Monique Kassem, et d'autres Staffordians. Mais j'ai eu très peu communication avec mes amis Staffordian pendant que j'étais à New York pour les dernières quelques semaines. Je savais que Diana Stuart allais faire un spectacle spécial à Knowlton, et le spectacle était sur 2012, mais je ne voulais pas de passer la nuit dans l'audience d'un théâtre.

Je suis allé au Café Dumont à l'après-midi et j'ai eu un bol de soupe. J'ai pensé que je pourrais voir Shiva là, ou Monique là, ou des autres Staffordians pourraient me dire au sujet un rassemblement. Aucun bon. Seulement touristes.

Rue principal a été rempli de touristes de Montréal, pour le plupart des skieurs. Il ne ressemblait pas d'un monde qui touchait à sa fin en seulement quelques heures. Il ne ressemblait pas ces gens étaient prêts à tourner la dernière page sur leurs calendriers Maya. Selon la réalité consensuelle, c'était un autre vendredi soir dans une petite ville dans les Cantons de l'Est du Québec. Bien sûr, je savais mieux.

Dans l'après-midi j'ai rentré chez moi et j'ai fait une petite sieste. Je voulais avoir un maximum d'énergie en cette nuit. Également, je n'ai pas senti que j'ai dû faire quelque chose. J'ai seulement avais besoin d'être. Mon intuition me dit que je serais au bon endroit, au bon moment, en cette nuit. Á la même temps, I reminded myself several times during the afternoon to maintain my thoughts in the present moments.

Après j'ai mangé le souper, je suis allé à Knowlton. Je savais que c'était un acte incongru en cette nuit, mais c'est ce que j'ai observé moi-même faire. Si j'avais été appelée à Wal-Mart à Cowansville pour une raison quelconque, au lieu de Ka-nowlton, je serais sentie moins à l'aise avec ce que j'ai choisi de le faire, je pense.

Alors, je suis allé à Knowlton, et je suis resté au spectacle pendant une heure. Le spectacle n'était pas ce que je m'attendais, même si Diana était bonne, comme toujours.

En tout cas, j'ai décidé d'aller chez Merlin et Gwen. J'ai pensé que je pouvais arriver à la ferme avant 22h. Et, l'heure de 22 était significative pour moi. J'ai estimé que le Solstice d'hiver allait commencer autour de ce temps, au Québec. Et, le commencement de ce Solstice d'hiver était de marquer l'espace entre – l'espace entre inhaler et exhaler, l'espace entre un monde et l'autre, l'espace entre 2012 et l'Âge de Gaia.

J'ai décidé d'utiliser un raccourci, en passant à travers la rue Mont Echo. Bien sûr, je suis devenu perdu. Et j'ai dû utiliser mon GPS. Ensuite, mon GPS était hors de gamme d'un satellite, alors j'ai dû conduire par intuition, par les étoiles. Mont Echo in Québec is a long way from the Long Island Expressway.

La route est devenue un chemin de terre. Et ensuite un chemin de terre cahoteux. Et ensuite un chemin de terre *très* cahoteux. Il n'y avait pas de maisons. Aucun inukshuks. J'ai décidé d'arrêter et retourner. Maintenant c'était certain que j'allais arriver en retard chez Merlin et Gwen, probablement pas avant 22h.

C'était difficile pour moi de tourner autour de ma voiture, parce que la route était tellement étroite. J'ai fait les virages très lentement, parce que je n'ai voulais pas tomber dans un fossé. Pendant que je faisais la dernière virage, j'ai regardé dans la forêt, où les lumières de ma voiture a brillé, et j'ai vu quelqu'un marcher derrière un arbre, et dans l'obscurité. Je ne pouvais pas dire si c'était un homme ou une femme, mais il était un adulte avec un grand sac à dos noir.

Cette personne n'ai semble pas être la Femme de la Montagne – le corps était trop vague – mais pour quelque raison mes pensées sont allés vers la Femme de la Montagne, presque immédiatement.

Pour quelque raison, cette personne marchait dans la forêt cette nuit. Peut-être elle était recherche d'un inukshuk pour guider son chemin. Femme de la Montagne construit les inukshuks, pour la guider dans les montagnes.

Il n'y avait pas de maisons sur cette route pour au moins d'un kilomètre. Je me suis arrêté ici pour regarder vers la forêt, puis j'ai conduit ma voiture l'avant de nouveau, très lentement. Environ dix mètres d'où j'ai vu la personne aller dans les bois, j'ai vu à la bord de la forêt, a ma gauche, un inukshuk, que se tenait pres d'un mètre de haut. Je n'ai pas le voir quand je conduisais dans l'autre sens. De nouveau, mes pensées sont allés à la Femme de la Montagne. Inexplicablement, peut-être inexplicablement, j'ai eu ce sentiment qu'el'était proche.

Cinq minutes plus tard, mon GPS a fonctionné de nouveau. Et, après une autre éternité, j'étais sur la rue Principale à Stafford. Alléluia. Alléluia, alléluia. Un millier de alléluias Leonard Cohen. *Finalement, enfin,* sur rue Principale, Stafford. C'était un voyage. Et, une partie de mon Odyssée.

Alors, j'ai vu, debout sur le coin, quelqu'un qu'avait un grand sac à dos, un grand sac à dos noir. This looked like the same person, avec la même sac à dos qui j'ai vu près de Mont Echo. La personne se tourna vers moi, et j'ai vu que c'était la Femme de la Montagne ! Oui. Et c'etait une synchronicité accueilli.

Nos yeux se rencontrèrent, et we just stared at each other for I don't know how long. I felt like un chevreuil was looking into my eyes. Just at the time that un chevreuil would have darted away, la Femme de la Montagne recognized my car, avec the New York plates, and then she recognized me. Elle jeta le sac à dos sur le siège arrière et elle grimpa dans la voiture.

 Quand elle a fermé la porte de la voiture, j'ai senti la forêt d'hiver. Après we exchanged les ça vas et les petits baisers, j'ai dit, « Femme, you smell like *Wintergreen* chewing gum ! C'est si bon de voir toi, et sentir toi, encore. »

Elle a répondu en français...and in halting anglais : « Mario-Jacques, ton français s'amélioré ! Bravo ! But I do not know this chewing gum. This is something good, to smell like this chewing gum américain ? »

J'ai dit, « I think it is not always so good to smell like Wintergreen chewing gum, mais maintenant, c'est qekchose bon. » Soudainement, je me suis souvenu que j'ai eu un paquet de Wintergreen chewing gum dans la console de ma voiture. J'ai ouvert la console et en tira le paquet. J'ai dit à la Femme de la Montagne : « Voila ! »

Elle a répondu, « I do not like the chewing gum. I chew the leaves de la forêt, quelque fois d'ippinette. C'est le vrai winter green. It is better for la santé, better for the health than the chewing gum. Mais, this is good, très bon. We have la synchronicité and tonight is to be for much of la synchronicité, Mario Jacques. » Elle a continué a dire qu'elle était sur son chemin vers chez Bruno Thibodeau, de faire partie de quelque chose qu'elle a appellé, « l'Evolution Solstice d'Hiver. »

C'était très, très, très frappant à moi, que le mot «evolution» a été utilisé de marquer cette nuit, cette nuit du Solstice d'hiver. Parce que pendant des années j'ai pensé de la nuit du 21 décembre 2012 comme la nuit où d'une conscience collective qui serait centrée sur la création d'un niveau supérieur de conscience. On pourrait dire que, comme un peut-êtreist, je suis venu à croire que les êtres humains sur cette nuit serait consciemment s'engager dans la co-création de leur évolution, peut-être.

Maintenant, voila. *Voi...la.* Sur la nuit du 21 décembre 2012, à quelques minutes avant du Solstice d'hiver, et approchons des dernières heures avant le calendrier Maya se terminera...et voici la Femme de la Montagne, assis sur le siège avant de ma voiture, avec icycles dégoulinant de son nez, me demandant d'aller avec elle de faire partie d'un, « Evolution Solstice d'Hiver. »

Bien sûr, j'ai dit à la Femme de la Montagne : « Allonz-y ! »

Bruno habite juste après la voie ferrée, où la rue Principale et rue Southern intersecter. Nous sommes arrivés là en moins de deux minutes. Tandis que nous conduisions là, je demandé à Femme de la Montagne si elle pouvait me dire ce que allait se passer ce soir.

Elle a répondu : « Mario-Jacques, I am sure you know that tonight we remember who we are. » C'est tout ce qu'elle a dit. Ces paroles me revinrent plus fort qu'un écho d'une montagne. En fait, j'ai dit ce à la Femme, comme nous sorti de la voiture, chez Bruno. She gave me a funny look. It made me wonder, for the moment, if it was her that I saw walking into the woods near Mont Echo. I did not get a chance to ask her about that. Not even later in the night.

J'étais allé chez Bruno un nombreux de fois. C'est un bon endroit de rassemblement pour Staffordians. Il ya toujours un bon feu dans cette maison. Il ya toujours de la musique. Il ya toujours de la nourriture. Toujours des enfants. Toujours gens que je connais, et toujours des gens que je vais rencontrer pour la première fois. Je savais que ce soir serait comme nuits passées, mais je m'attendais également à ce qu'allait être différent. Je n'ai pas oublie que c'était la nuit du 21 décembre 2012... Finalement, le 21 décembre 2012...

Nous avons marché à l'intérieur de la maison sans frapper. Nous avons enlevé nos bottes et les mettre sur le plancher, à côté de environ vingt paires de bottes qu'étaient de toutes tailles – début de la taille de bébé. Nous avons jeté nos manteaux sur un tas qui s'est déversé partir d'une table au plancher.

La Femme de la Montagne smiled at me, avec le sourire d'une mère ou a momma bear, qu'est écouter sa famille profiter d'une célébration. La plupart du temps, la Femme de la Montagne habite seule, sans autres humains. Dans son sourire, je pouvais voir qu'elle est tellement comme tout le monde, mais peut-être plus pur...peut-être plus organique.

Sous son manteau, elle portait des couches de vêtements isolés. Elle tourna le dos à moi et les autres chambres, et enlevé ses vêtements jusqu'à elle était nu dessus de la taille, l'exception du collier qu'elle portait, un morceau de quartz sur un brin de cuir. El'était pieds nus, et elle portait une jupe gitane longue. Elle transpirait abondamment. Son odeur, le parfum de son corps non lavé, mélangé avec le parfum des montagnes, le parfum de la forêt, et la terre, et remplissait la pièce. Ce n'était pas un parfum que l'on trouve dans de petites bouteilles au Centre Eaton ou chez Macy's. Ce n'était pas un parfum qui serait utilisé par les femmes avec des lévres rouges. Mais pour moi, à ce moment-là, son parfum a été intoxicante. Étrangement intoxicante. Comme clair de lune. Pas clair de lune Claude Debussy. Non, son parfum était intoxicant comme clair de lune *cajun* – Allegheny moonshine, un alcool puissant fait maison.

Son parfum était distincte pendant secondes, pas en minutes, et puis mélangé avec les senteurs de la combustion du bois, et des bougies allumées, et arômes de cuisine. Au fond, j'ai senti son énergie et de l'énergie dans la pièce mélangeant ensemble.

Femme de la Montagne était sur le point de tirer sa chemise dessus sa tête quand deux petites filles courut dans la pièce et jeta leurs bras autour de ses jambes. Elle tourna, leva les enfants dans ses bras, et les embrassa contre ses seins nus, qui les filles ont commencé à jouer avec, et qu'a causé Femme à rire hystériquement, qu'a causé les filles à rire hystériquement, et les encouragés à chatouiller ses seins, son cou, son visage, la facon dont petites filles faire.

Une jeune femme, qu'était la mère d'une des filles, entra dans la pièce, et elle enroula ses bras autour du trois d'entre eux, puis joint les filles en chatouillant Femme de la Montagne. Ils étaient tous bavardage en français, puis ils ont commencé à bavarder dans une langue que je n'avais jamais entendu parler avant. J'ai pensé que peut-être ils parlaient joual, mais j'ai appris plus tard dans la nuit que ce n'était pas le cas. Ils parlaient un mélange de français et Abénaquis.

Il n'était pas jusqu'à ce que Femme de mis les enfants en bas, tandis qu'elle mettait sur sa chemise, que la jeune femme tourné autour et m'a vu debout dans la pièce. Elle a souri et m'a parlé en français. J'ai compris seulement les mots : « Je m'appelle Charlotte. » Aprés cela, peut-être elle a parlé de la cuisson du pain, ou la philosophie de Nietzsche, je ne sais pas quoi.

J'ai répondu : « Bonjour. Enchanté. Je m'appelle Mario-Jacques. Pardonnez-moi, mon français est mauvais. Je suis un amériquébécois. »

Charlotte a dit, « Aaah, okeh. You are Mario-Jacques, l'amériquébécois. My tante, she tells me about you. »

Femme de la Montagne interjected, « Mario-Jacques, I tell Charlotte you are this crazy man amériquébécois who marches with le carré rouge à Montréal, and you find me quelquefois près de sentiers. »

Charlotte a dit, « Mario-Jacques, probablement you are the only person who knows how to find my tante in the mountains. My mother, she is not able to do this very good. »

J'ai répondu, « Je suis chanceux. C'est pas souvent, rare, que je trouve votre tante. Mais, c'est incroyable aussi, quelquefois. Votre tante et moi, we have la *synchronicité*. Mais oui, la *synchronicité* ! »

Je dois dire que j'ai été surpris, parce qu'il est pas souvent, rare, que je peux m'exprime complètement en français, en conversation, pendant trois ou quatre phrases consécutives. Bien sûr, cela a causé Charlotte à surestimer mes capacités à comprendre le français quand je l'entends parlé dans la conversation. Elle a commencé à me parler en français. Très rapidement. Je sais qu'elle a parlé de synchronicité, mais c'était difficile pour moi d'entendre les pensées complètes. Toutefois, j'ai compris ses paroles quand elle a dit : « Aujourd'hui est le jour de la synchronicité. Et ce soir c'est la nuit de la synchronicité. »

Ses mots résonnaient avec moi. Fortement. Viscéralement. J'ai dit : « C'est vrai. » Mais c'était tout ce que j'ai dit, parce que notre attention est allé aux petites filles, qu'avaient commencé leur jeu de nouveau. Presque au même temps, Bruno est venu dans la pièce et il rejoint le jeu de chatouillement jusqu'à ce qu'il tourné et m'a vu. Il a dit – d'une voix tranquille, tranquille mais clairement excité, « Mario-Jacques, Mario-Jacques, Mario-Jacques ! Je suis très, très, très...happy to see you ! » Puis il marché jusqu'à moi et nous avons mis nos bras autour de l'autre. Coeur à coeur.

La Femme de la Montagne et Charlotte et les filles sont allés à la cuisine. Je me suis assis sur le banc près de la porte d'éntrée avec Bruno et nous avons parlé. Bruno aime à parler de l'écriture de Ken Wilber et le Dalai Lama. Et il parle aussi à moi a propos le dossier akashique, et la méditation. Sa connaissance de ces choses est très bon. Il a un noble profession comme charpentier, et il peindre les maisons, et il enseigne le yoga à la gym. Mais je ne sais pas, peut-être he missed his calling.

Notre conversation s'est terminée lorsque nous avons entendu le battement des tambours dans le salon. If there was going to be a tam-tam, I wanted to play a drum !

Quand nous sommes passés par la cuisine pour aller à le salon, j'ai vu qu'il y avait six ou huit les femmes là-bas. De six mois à quatre-vingts ans. Je connaissais seulement une des femmes : la belle Vénus. Elle lavait la vaisselle – parce que Vénus est belle à l'intérieur *et* l'extérieur. Quand elle m'a vu, elle m'a donné son sourire. Nous avons embrassé sur les deux joues, à travers la pièce.

Tout le monde was working, and everyone was nibbling, sipping, laughing. Si un opéra a été faite au sujet Stafford, ce que j'étais témoin dans la cuisine ferait une bonne scène. Les mouvements de ces femmes Gaia me semblait comme un chorégraphie complexe, et ils a chanté à l'autre, ou chanté à eux-mêmes. Ils ne étaient pas conscients du fait qu'ils chantaient. C'était un belle opéra. Les québécoises.

Mon goût pour la musique est plus primitif que l'opéra, et un tam-tam allait commencé dans le salon et je voulais être l'un des percussionistes. Je suis retourné à le salon et j'ai trouvé qu'il y avait environ douze ou quinze personnes là, et ils étaient tous des femmes et des enfants, à l'exception de moi-même, Bruno, et trois autres hommes. Il n'y avait pas beaucoup de places libres dans la pièce pour s'asseoir ou se tenir debout, mais la pièce n'était pas bondée. C'était intime. Les gens étaient assis sur deux divans, un banc, sur un escalier, et sur le plancher, où une nappe a été couvert avec des bols de nourriture.

J'ai tout de suite vu trois ou quatre Staffordians que je connaissais bien, mais il y avait seulement un ou deux autres personnes dont les visages étaient familiers pour moi. Encore une fois, c'était surtout les femmes et les enfants. J'ai aussi remarqué que sur les divans tout monde était allongé sur l'autre, aussi détendu comme des chats dorer au soleil.

J'étais presque *startled*...il a été si *frappante* a moi(!), de voir que Francois Desjardins était là. Aussitôt que je l'ai vu, j'ai pensé au fait que c'était Francois qui m'avait demandé, à l'automne 2007, si j'avais été appelé à Stafford, if I had been called to Stafford to heal or to be healed. I remember, very clearly, the moment that he asked me that question. Et, je me souviens qu'il a également dit ce soir-là que les gens se rassemblaient à Stafford parce qu'ils attendaient pour le 21 décembre 2012...Alors, voilà : à la Solstice, le 21 décembre 2012...Et voilà Francois...Voilà la synchronicité.

Although I was fulfilling a destiny prophesized by Francois, I said nothing to him about this. I do not know if he remembers the evening that we had dinner together at la Cascade, five years ago, and he introduced me to the idea that many people, scattered around the world, were expecting December 21, 2012 to be a day that would determine the fate of humankind.

Francois et une femme d'environ 20 ans, et une petite fille d'environ trois ans, étaient assis sur le plancher autour la nappe recouverte de bols de nourriture, et ils mangeaient. Francois m'a invité à manger, avant que les bols ont été effacés de la nappe. J'ai mangé un peu. Nourriture de confort. Nouvelle Terre nourriture de confort – qui n'est pas lourd dans la bouche ou dans l'estomac. Un mélange de la nourriture du Québec, de l'Inde, du Tibet, et les pays latino-américains. Mais oui, you are what you eat. C'est la nourriture du Nouveau-Québec. From the farm to the table, in this way the food of the past is becoming the food of the New Earth.

Robert Richard, qu'est quelqu'un que j'ai assis à côté de pendant les trois dernières fois que j'ai participé à un tam-tam à Stafford, est venu avec son tambour. Bien sûr, nous nous sommes assis à côté de l'autre, sur un banc. J'ai dit à Robert : « Encore une fois ! C'est synchronicité ! Encore une fois ensemble, avec les tambours. »

Robert a d'environ 35 ans. Il était un ministre anglican. Maintenant, il est dans l'entreprise de crème glacée. La façon dont il explique ce changement: « One day I decided to be cool. » Robert est bilingue, mais sa langue maternalle est le français. Il me parlait dans un mélange du français et en anglais, parce que Robert sait que mon français est si limité – même si elle s'est beaucoup améliorée depuis que je l'ai vu, pendant l'été.

J'ai dit à Robert : « Do you think that they will ever have cette nourriture dans le menu au Café Dumont ? »

Robert a dit : « Mario-Jacques, I do not know what will exist after this night. »

Mon Dieu ! Comment peut-on répondre à une telle déclaration? Je me tournai   pour regarder Robert et j'ai vu que ses yeux étaient fermés. Il m'a semblé qu'il méditait. J'ai regardé autour du salon et j'ai vu d'autres avec les yeux fermés, qui semblait méditer.

Soudainement, c'était plus calme dans la pièce. Quelques personnes parlaient à une à l'autre, mais tout monde parlait à voix basse.

J'ai pris mon assiette vide à la cuisine, où Vénus a insisté sur les prendre de mes mains, de se laver. Tout le monde dans la cuisine était encore bavardait, chatting avec beaucoup d'animation – ils me semblait comme ils faisaient une sorte de danse gitane. À mes yeux, c'était un ballet gitan. Mais oui, je ne regardais pas les femmes et les petites filles dans une cuisine, je regardais un ballet gitan. L'opéra qu'était dans la cuisine était maintenant un ballet gitan !

Pour ces québécoises, la vie quotidienne est un art. Their bodies glided past each others. They kept passing things to each other. Glasses, dishes, candles, scarves. Quand ils touchaient, ils ont touché doucement. J'étais la seule personne dans leur audience, et c'était un ballet qu'était digne de grand théâtres à Paris, ou à Montréal, ou à New York. La Première au Stanstead Opera House, et alors Paris, Montréal, New York.

Quand je suis revenu à le salon, j'ai vu que Robert n'etait pas encore dans un état de méditation et qu'il était maintenant chevauchants son tambour et il était prêt pour le tam-tam de commencer. Il me sourit, et il me fit signe de le rejoindre.

I sat at the end of the bench, Robert sat to my right, and a man whom I did not know sat to the right of Robert. This man, an older man with long gray hair tied back in a pony tail, was holding what looked like a very high-quality mandolin. J'ai pensé à moi-même : « *D'accord. Pourquoi pas bring a mandolin to a tam-tam ?* »

J'ai regardé comme plus de bougies ont été allumées et de l'encens a été brûle, cérémonieusement. Et alors, Bruno et Francois ont porté un grand tambour dans la pièce, et ils mis le tambour sur le plancher, au centre de la pièce.

Bientôt, tout le monde était dans le salon. Tout le monde était assis, sur les meubles ou sur des couvertures sur le plancher. Les lumières étaient éteints dans les autres pièces, et seulement des bougies allumées le salon. C'était comme si tout le monde était assis autour d'un feu de camp, avec la même lueur chaleureuse dans les yeux et les visages.

Au lieu d'un feu de camp, les yeux de cette bande Nouvelle Terre était tournés vers le grand tambour. C'est un tambour qui pourrait être dans un musée national. Bruno m'a parlé de ce tambour une fois avant, mais c'était la première fois que je l'ai vu. Il a une circonférence d'environ un mètre. Le tambour est au moins deux cents ans, et peut-être trois cents ou quatre cents ans. C'est un tambour Abénaquis. Le tambour est considéré par la tribu des Abénaquis comme un objet qui contient et transmet puissante énergie spirituelle. C'est toujours traitée sérieusement, et n'a jamais joué avec nonchalance, n'a jamais joué pour juste l'amusement ou de divertissement, je pense.

J'ai regardé Bruno met deux coussins sur le plancher à côté du grand tambour, et puis tendis un maillet à chacune des deux filles qu'ont couru embrasser Femme de la Montagne quand nous sommes entrés dans la maison. Les coussins étaient pour le deux petites filles à s'asseoir. Le tambour a été faite par les ancêtres de Bruno et les deux petites filles.

Bruno a chuchoté quelque chose dans les oreilles des deux filles. The three of them closed their eyes, comme si dans la méditation. C'était apparemment un signal à tout le monde pour mettre en pause – pour apporter un silence momentané à la pièce.

Bruno a battu le tambour une fois avec sa main droite et puis une fois avec sa main gauche, avec ses mains nues. Chaque de les petites filles batte le tambour une fois, avec leurs maillets. Cela semblait etre un rituel qu'ils avaient pratiqué.

Bientôt, tout le monde est impliqué – en battant sur un tambour, ou de secouer un hochet, ou se balancant au rythme. Soon, the tam-tam transported everyone, including the children, into varying degrees of meditation. I kept my eyes closed, surtout, and my drumming became part of my meditation. The ear in my mind heard, for a short time, the mantra *om mani padme hum* and then I became absorbed in listening to the mantra spoken by the drums.

Je devenais comme un automate. Dans le temps, I only needed to observe my hands beating my drum, I did not need to direct them. I closed my eyes and the drumbeats directed me in and out of la méditation.

Mon sens de temps a été perdu. J'ai continué à observer mes mains battre mon tambour pendant j'ai regardé les petites filles passe les maillets à certaines des femmes et des hommes. J'ai regardé tandis que chaque membre du clan battre le tambour, cérémonieusement. Presque toujours ce n'était pas une personne, mais deux personnes, qui battaient le tambour, et le mainten le même rythme, avec des variations sur un thème.

Si je ne savais pas Staffordians mieux, j'aurais pensé que je regardais un rituel au lieu d'un écoulement naturel vers l'unité en toutes choses.

Mes mains, et ma conscience, ont été emportés dans le flot d'énergie dans la chambre. Mais oui, my hands moved as if they had a will of their own, and the me who is called « Mario-Jacques » did not compel his hands to move, but merely witnessed their movements. Aucun effort nécessaire.

Je ne sais pas combien de temps il était que j'était dans un joli écoulement avec les battements de tambour et les autres battements de coeur, quand j'ai entendu quelqu'un commence à chanter, puis s'arrête. J'ai écouté, comme quelqu'un écoute parfois quand la pluie commence tomber.

Les gouttes de chansons restés seulement gouttes et n'a pas rempli l'air.

I saw that a woman – une femme de quarante-quelque chose – was making these vocalizations. Her head was resting on the back of the couch and her eyes were closed, but I recognized her as someone whom I have seen working as un bénévole at the theatre, *l'Esprit du Village.* Je me souviens que la première fois que je l'ai vue à *l'Esprit,* je pensais qu'elle était la Femme de la Montagne. Leurs cheveux est similaire – longs, frisés-crépus, sauvage, brun et gris. She must be related to Femme de la Montagne. Je n'ai pas appris son nom. Je pense d'elle maintenant comme : « la Femme Transcendant. »

This woman, la Femme Transcendant, began to wail – at first very softly, and then a bit louder. It was as if she was in a reverie, calling out in her sleep. C'était comme si elle chantait une chanson autochtone, peut-être une chanson Abénaquis, ou une chanson Inuite. À la même temps, son appel a été primordiale. Universel, pas d'une langue particulière. J'ai continué à me frapper la tambour, mais j'ai ralenti mon rythme, comme si j'étais ralentir de ma marche sur un chemin forestier tandis que j'ai donné attention au son d'un autre être humain à proximité.

Bientôt, elle gémit à nouveau. Pas si fort que d'être un appel à l'aide. Elle prononcait quelque chose qu'elle ne voulait pas prononcer. It was an adieu.

Puis, ses appels s'arrêté pendant un certain temps. Assez longtemps pour moi de me poser la question : Est-ce qu'elle va crier à nouveau, ou elle a cessé de crier ?

Puis, c'était comme si elle avait entendu ma question, et elle a décidé qu'elle devrait répondre à ma question. Elle a continué à murmurer quelque chose chaque minute ou deux, et puis plus souvent. Peut-être qu'elle murmurait des mots, je ne sais pas, mais ce n'est pas d'une grande importance. Ce qu'elle murmura communiqué plus que s'elle utilisait la langue française, ou la langue anglaise ou la langue des Abénaquis. Mais oui, elle a communiquée à moi, et à tout le monde.

Tous les nous étaient capables d'entendre ses prononcements, ses marmonne, parce que les tambours n'ont pas été pilonné fort, mais avec une passion douce, avec les mains lentes. J'étais immergé dans le karma kollective, j'ai été immergé dans le tam-tam. Et puis elle murmura de nouveau. Et de nouveau, de nouveau, un peu plus fort à chaque fois. Ils étaient des cris d'espoir.

Cries..........of..........hope... Même les gens emprisonnées dans une tour de Babel peut entendre des cris d'espoir, s'ils écoutent. Dans cette chanson qui pourrait être entendu une fois et seulement une fois, elle a exprimé ce que des écrivains comme Sartre et Thoreau exprimés en beaucoup de mots, et en beaucoup de pages, au sujet désespoir tranquille, et au sujet transcendance.

Il n'a pas d'importance ce que l'horloge a déclaré que le heure était. Quand le cri de la Femme Transcendant est devenu un cri d'espoir, c'était le moment où l'Age de Gaia a commencé, je pense...Oui, when the cry of the Transcendent Woman became a cry of hope, that is the moment when the Age of Gaia began.

L'Age de Gaia a commencé, et le tam-tam est devenu une célébration de l'espoir et de la transcendance. Je me sentais plus léger. The lightness was palpable.

Le tam-tam terminé après environ trente minutes, et plus de bougies ont été allumées, jusqu'à ce que la pièce était aussi calme et crystallin que la forêt du Mont Stafford sur une nuit d'hiver étoilerempli. Les yeux du clan sont encore concentrés sur le feu de camp – le grand tambour – mais alors Lynette Gagnon s'assit sur un coussin, à côté du grand tambour, et tous les yeux sont allés à elle, y compris le mien.

Lynette était pieds nus, comme la plupart des femmes du clan, et contrairement aux autres femmes – qui portait de longues robes multicolores, ou simplement des jeans – elle portait une robe de gaze blanche à ses chevilles. La jolie Lynette ressemblait comme plus que l'Impératrice de Crème glacée, comme elle ressemblait à une prêtresse.

Cérémonieusement, Lynette placé un certain nombre de tibétains laiton bols de différentes tailles sur le petit tapis en face d'elle. Elle a enroulé ses jambes dans une position méditative, et elle a parlé à tout le monde. En français, bien sûr. Elle parlait doucement, et dit seulement quelque mots, que je ne comprenais pas. Mais j'ai compris qu'elle menait tout le monde dans une méditation de groupe.

J'ai gardé les yeux fermés pendant que je recevais les sons qu'ont émané des bols de laiton, quand Lynette frotté les bols. La modulation était sur une fréquence qu'était vraiment spirituel, entendu par les oreilles du soi supérieur à l'intérieur de chaque de nous. Alors, comme j'ai recu ces sons, j'ai recu la Communion. J'étais dans la Communion, dans l'Unité, avec les autres. C'était un sens d'unité rare dans mes expériences. C'était a peak experience.

Bientôt, les sons émanant du laiton bols arrêté, ce qui m'a amené et tout le monde de faire attention à ce silence. Oui, pay.............attention.

C'était l'essence de ma méditation, prêter attention au moment présent.

Juste d'être dans cet espace, à ce époque – et de me permettre *d'être juste* dans cet espace, à ce époque – non seulement a libéré mon âme, mais touché souvenirs d'expériences similaires dans mon passé, à partir du moment où les clans d'animaux humains d'abord a commencé à s'asseoir autour de feux de camp, tard dans la nuit. À un certain niveau, au fond de mon inconscient collectif, il y avait le souvenir d'avoir été dans une caverne dans ce qu'on appelle aujourd'hui : « France. »

Vive la France. Vive les êtres humains. Vive le Québec, vive le Québec, vive... le Nouveau-Quebec. Oui, vive le Nouveau-Québec et vive la Nouvelle Terre. These thoughts were not articulated in as many words in my mind, but these thoughts resonated there, and in my total being – *si vous voyez ce que je veux dire.* Oui, endorphines coulaient dans mon corps, mais ma conscience de la réalité n'a pas été influencés par le vin, ou la marijuana, ou l'ayahuasca.

Un courant chaud de l'énergie coulé dans cette pièce, et chaque bûche dans le feu, chaque femme, chaque homme et enfant contribué à l'écoulement du courant, sa force, son goût. J'ai eu une prise de conscience que ce qu'était résonner en moi était synchrone avec ce qu'était résonner dans les autres qui partagé le feu de camp et les énergies dans cet espace. Unité.

Then there was, de nouveau, le silence du Mont Stafford on a star-filled winter night. Nous avons écouté le silence. Sons occasionnels n'étaient pas plus fort qu'une bouffée de neige tombant d'une branche d'arbre. Nous sommes restés dans le silence pendant longtemps.

C'était comment un monde fini – not with a bang, or a whimper – mais avec le silence.

Sans cérémonie, un très long moment de silence pour la mort d'un monde.

Et entre un souffle et le prochain souffle, un nouveau monde, que certains appellent déja, « La Nouvelle Terre,» a commencé.

Oui, au début, il y avait pas de mots. Seulement le silence.

Ecoutez pour voir, ecoutez pour voir. I listened to the silence to see. Dans le silence, j'ai vu que nous étions tous au centre de l'univers.

Chez Bruno est situé au point le plus bas de l'espace triangulaire à Stafford où les Abénaquis il y a longtemps découvert le puissant vortex d'énergie qu'émane de la terre et les eaux, remplies de quartz. Un beaucoup grand nombre des Abénaquis et des Staffordians sont venus ici au cours des années, « pour guérir, et pour être guéris. » En cette nuit du 21 décembre 2012, l'appele, « pour guérir, et pour être guéri, » n'était jamais plus fort. Sans paroles prononcées à haute voix, dans le silence de nos méditations, nous avons partagé la compréhension que nous répondu au même appel en cette nuit.

Mais oui, in the silence of our meditations, we listened to see, and we saw that we had gathered to heal, and be healed.

Pendant que j'écris ceci, je suis rappelé, synchronistically – par un coup d'oeil à le marqueur de livre qu'est scotché sur la porte de mon réfrigérateur dit – les mots de Margaret Mead, qui, traduit de l'anglais au français, disent : « *On ne devrait pas douter que le monde peut être changé par un petit groupe de gens...en effet, c'est le seule facon dont elle change.* »

En cette nuit du 21 décembre 2012, il n'était pas seulement la petite bande de gens qui s'étaient rassemblés chez Bruno qu'avaient été appelé pour guérir, pour être guéri. En cette nuit, les Staffordians rassemblés en petits groupes partout la ville de Stafford. Dans des appartements rue Principale, dans des chalets et des condos sur la montagne, et en manoirs qu'avaient inukshuks à leurs entrées, pas de lions, les Staffordians sont rassemblés pour répondre pour le même appel.

Si, en cette nuit du 21 décembre 2012, des milliers de personnes s'étaient rassemblées ici dans une masse sur le Mont Stafford, il aurait été un événement qui a été remarqué par de nombreux gens – de nombreux gens qui ne sont pas Staffordians, de nombreux gens incapables de comprendre ce qui se passait. La police serait là, et les premiers répondants. Lumière de bougie est bon pour la méditation, mais lumières rouges clignotants ne sont pas bonnes.

En cette nuit du 21 décembre 2012, ceux qui se sont rassemblés à Stafford savaient qu'ils faisaient partie de quelque chose de beaucoup plus grand qu'un rassemblement d'un certain nombre de gens sur une montagne.

Pendant ma méditation, je me sentais connectée non seulement aux Staffordians chez Bruno, mais à tous les Staffordians qu'avait rassemblés ce soir autour des feux de camp autres. Je me sentais connectée aussi aux Staffordians qu'avaient répondu à un appel à méditer *seul* à cette nuit.

Everything is connected. Tout est connecté. Combien de fois ai-je entendu Paddy O'Brien me dire : « Everything is connected ? » Combien de fois ai-je lire la note sur mon réfrigérateur qui dit : « *Tout est connecté ?* » En cette nuit, je suis venu à comprendre ces paroles plus pleinement que jamais.

En cette nuit du 21 décembre 2012 nous Staffordians ont été connectés aux gens partout le monde, et nous avons senti la connexion, si seulement pour le moment du temps qui s'écoule entre un inspiration et une expiration. Je dois mentionner, Shiva est venu chez Bruno, avec d'autres, juste avant mon départ. Ses premiers mots à moi : « Mario-Jacques, in the space of time between one inhale and one exhale, a New Earth is created. »

Within a quantum moment of time, a quantum leap was made in the evolution of humankind, as a new sphere of human consciousness emerged. Dans le temps, ce sera peut-être appelé : la noosphère.

C'est comment la Nouvelle Terre était né...

Bien sûr, ce sont les femmes qu'ont donné naissance à la Nouvelle Terre. Et maintenant c'est, enfin, leur âge : L'Âge de Gaia. Bien sûr, c'était surtout les femmes que je me suis assis autour du feu de camp dans la nuit du 21 décembre 2012. J'étais avec des femmes qui continueront à propager et nourrir leur espèce, *Homo bonhomie*.

La Nouvelle Terre n'a pas été crée avec un Big Bang. Ce n'est pas le chemin des femmes. The New Earth was created as silently as a wave of thought travels.

Pendant que je conduisais chez moi, j'ai vu qu'un nouveau inukshuk a été construit sur le chemin Pin, au tournant du chemin après le cimetière. Déjà, dans le nouvel âge, les inukshuks sont debout où il y avait des croix, ou les panneaux de Coca-Cola.

Maintenant, everything changes. *Tout change*. Mais oui. It is more than a paradigm shift that is occuring. The Hercolubus prophecy that the planet would be turned upside down has come to pass. Ce qu'a été fermement enracinée hier ne sera plus nourri par la Nouvelle Terre.

La lumière et l'énergie du soleil ne seront plus sentir de la même facon. Partir de maintenant, il sera bien entendu que le Soleil n'est pas un Dieu bienveillant d'être adoré comme les peuples primitifs ont adoré d'autres étoiles, et les rois, et le plus riche des riches.

Sur la Nouvelle Terre les religions qui servent ce qu'est le plus impie ne seront plus prospérer. Pendant que j'écris ces mots, je vois de ma fenêtre que le ciel a été ouvert, et ce n'est pas le signe du dollar que je vois là-bas. Mais, I see : le *Québec bleu*.

Le Nouveau-Québec va prospérer dans l'âge de Gaia. Vive le Nouveau-Québec, vive le Nouveau-Québec, vive le Nouveau-Québec. Aussi longtemps que les drapeaux volent, laissez le drapeau du Nouveau-Québec voler le plus haut sur Mont Stafford, et à Montréal, et Longueuil, et Rimouski. Dans la Nouvelle Terre, vive le drapeau du Nouveau-Québec...tandis que on rêvons du monde sans les drapeux.

Pour ceux qui gardent les yeux fermés, et les oreilles couvert, la Révolution tranquille au Québec semble avoir disparu dans le vent – mais the echos from The Quiet Revolution will be louder than a shot heard around the world.

Pendant que j'écris ces mots, je vois que je viens à la dernière page du mon livre, mon journal. Il semble que mon entrée pour le 22 décembre 2012 sera la dernière entrée dans ce livre. Bien sûr. Destinée réalisé. Synchronistically.

Alors, what shall I do with this diary? J'ai entendu l'appel à chronique des événements contenus dans ce journal. Et maintenant ?

Peut-être je vais attacher un ruban autour de ce livre et le stocker dans une boîte pour mes descendants, ou un raton laveur. Peut-être je vais bientôt permettre aux yeux des autres à regarder ces pages. Mais il y a encore tel un grand nombre de Néandertaliens et d'Homo sapiens sur la planète qui ne acceptera jamais cette. Ils préfèrent encore vivre comme les gorilles nus, et ils sont très dangereux pour l'Homo bonhomie. Si ce livre tombe entre les mains de Néandertaliens ou peut-être de Homo sapiens, la plupart vont réagir comme des chiens regarder la télévision, mais ne voyant pas. D'autres ne vont pas aimer l'odeur du livre, tout comme ils n'aiment pas l'odeur d'Homo bonhomie.

Si je passe ce livre entre les mains de Staffordians, ou Homo bonhomie qui vivent ailleurs dans les Cantons de l'Est, ou qui vivent ailleurs au Québec, ou qui vivent ailleurs sur la Nouvelle Terre, peut-être leurs esprits seront nourris par ce qu'ils lisent. Peut-être mes amis Staffordians passeront cette chronique aux autres, et dire : « C'est la facon dont el'était avant l'Âge de Gaia. Vive la Gaia ! » ... ou : « This is the way it was just before The Age of Gaia. Vive la Gaia! »

Oui. Mais oui. Vive la Gaia ! Vive la Gaia, vive l'Homo bonhomie, vive le Nouveau-Québec. Et vive Stafford et les Staffordians. Les pèlerins Homo bonhomie vont continuer à venir à Stafford, mais ils ne seront pas guéris simplement par en touchant leurs mains sur la roche de quartz en face de l'hôtel de ville, ou en buvant de l'eau sacrée qui coule du bec derrière l'IGA, à moins que

264

leurs pensées, leurs paroles, et leurs sentiments se connectent avec l'univers.

Ce qu'est maintenant appelé Stafford – ou, par les Abénaquis, « la montagne de l'énergie de quartz, » va continueront à résonner avec certains pèlerins. Et certains touristes va se rendre compte qu'ils sont vraiment pèlerins après qu'ils éprouvent assez de résonance, et assez de synchronicité, à Stafford. Même après Stafford est appelé par un autre nom, ce sera un endroit de guérison, mais il y aura des changements. *Tout change.*

Those who are not true allies of humanity will continue to seek to pave Shangri-la, and put up parking lots for fast food. Pour les Wal-Martiens, pour les étrangers de terres étranges qui sont les propriétaires d'énorme grand magasins, Stafford est juste un autre morceau de terre sacrée à ajouter à leur empire commercial. Bien sûr, si les Wal-Martiens essayer de venir à Stafford, ils va auront allés trop loin. Les Wal-Martiens va rencontrer les québécoises et les québécois qui croient que le drapeau du Nouveau-Québec doit voler plus élevé au Nouveau-Québec que le drapeau de Wal-Mart.

Bien sûr, nombreux des Staffordians vont et viennent. Certains continueront à se déplacer à Frelighsburg, ou de Saint-Armand, ou Montréal. Ou Tadoussac. Ou Bangkok ou Brooklyn. Et, Homo bonhomie continuera à se rassembler dans les bandes et les tribus où ils peuvent vivre en paix, où les Néandertaliens et Homo sapiens ne pas faire leurs batailles.

C'est une bonne chose que la belle province du Québec est demeurée hors de la vue et de l'esprit de presque tous les êtres humains qui peuplent la planète hors du Canada. Mais maintenant, cela change, et ce sera aussi une bonne chose.

C'est une bonne chose que Stafford est encore un Shangri-la secret. Mais comment peut Stafford continuera d'être un Shangri-la secret ?

Peut-être, je devrais utiliser d'enlèvement d'encre où j'ai écrit « Stafford » dans mon journal et utiliser un nom fictif pour la ville ? Je devrais peut-être changer les noms réels des Staffordians à des noms fictifs ? Peut-être.

Homo sapiens de l'ancien monde qui pourrait peut-être lire mon journal comme il est, sans changements, vont penser que c'est un oeuvre de fiction, un roman, mais peut-être avec des personnages qui sont de vrai personnes d'une vrai ville dans les Cantons de l'Est du Québec. Bien sûr, les Staffordians seraient mieux connaître. Et, si ce journal est ait jamais lu par Homo bonhomie qui habitent ailleurs sur la Nouvelle Terre, qui ne sait rien de Stafford, peut-être rien du Québec, je suis sûr qu'ils auront le sentiment que ce qu'ils lisent est beaucoup plus vraie que le vérité biblique, et que j'écris de vrai personnes d'une vrai ville dans les Cantons de l'Est du Québec.

NOTATION

To learn where John-Jean will be speaking in public (at book stores, libraries, campuses, coffee shops) or to arrange to have him speak before your group about the writing of *Synchronicity Bleue*, or Parlez Bleu, or the Age of Gaia as it is manifesting today, or the Québec independence movement from the perspective of an Amériquébécois, visit synchronicitybleu.com. John-Jean is especially interested in helping people to raise money for good causes.

Synchronicity Bleue can be ordered from Amazon.com.

Pour savoir où John-Jean va parler en public (aux universités, les librairies, les bibliothèques, les cafés) ou pour prendre des dispositions pour John-Jean à parler à votre groupe au sujet : les idées contenues dans *Synchronicity Bleue*, Parlez Bleu, l'Age de Gaia et le mouvement de l'indépendance du Québec de la perspective d'un Amériquébecois, aller à : synchronicitybleu.com. Il est particulièrement intéressé à aider les gens à lever des fonds pour les besoins de la communauté et le progrès social.

Pour acheter une copie de *Synchronicity Bleue* aller à : synchronicitybleu.com ou Amazon.com.

www.ingramcontent.com/pod-product-compliance
Lightning Source LLC
Chambersburg PA
CBHW070336260626
47160CB00003B/1060